THE
AWAKENING
AND
SELECTED STORIES

THE
AWAKENING
AND
SELECTED STORIES

KATE CHOPIN

EDITED WITH AN INTRODUCTION BY
NINA BAYM

THE MODERN LIBRARY
NEW YORK

1993 Modern Library Edition

Copyright © 1981 by Random House, Inc.

Published in the United States by Random House, Inc., New York,
and simultaneously in Canada by Random House of Canada Limited, Toronto.

Modern Library and colophon are registered trademarks
of Random House, Inc.

Jacket portrait courtesy of the Missouri Historical Society

LIBRARY OF CONGRESS CATALOGING-IN-PUBLICATION DATA
Chopin, Kate, 1851–1904.
The awakening and selected stories/Kate Chopin; edited and with
an introduction by Nina Baym.
p.   cm.
Includes bibliographical references.
ISBN 0-679-42469-5
I. Baym, Nina. II. Title.
PS1294.C63A6   1993
813'.4—dc20   92-51067

Modern Library website address: www.modernlibrary.com

Printed in the United States of America on acid-free paper

6   8   9   7   5

CONTENTS

INTRODUCTION

Kate Chopin (1851-1904) did not begin to write until she was thirty-six years old. Up to that time, her life gave no hint of either literary talent or literary ambition. Yet after the publication of her first stories in 1889, she enjoyed ten years of a productive, serious, and fairly successful career. Her first novel, *At Fault* (1890), had difficulty finding a publisher, so she brought it out at her own expense and sent review copies to important journals. Her short stories—close to a hundred of them—were published for the most part in prestigious national magazines. They gave her a solid reputation as a gifted "local color" writer—that is, an author specializing in the depiction of a particular region of the country and its inhabitants. From these many stories, she culled two well-reviewed collections: *Bayou Folk* in 1894 and *A Night in Acadie* in 1897. *The Awakening*, now her best-known work, appeared in 1899.

Critics of Chopin's own day disapproved of the sexual frankness of *The Awakening* and were especially disturbed by the narrator's neutrality toward the unconventional behavior of Edna Pontellier, the heroine. All reviews of the novel were unfavorable. Soon after this setback, a planned third collection of short stories was rejected by a publisher, and Kate Chopin essentially ceased to write. In poor health, she died some five years after *The Awakening* appeared. She was only fifty-three.

Her work quickly went out of print. Her name was virtually forgotten until the early 1960s. At that time, a few scholars rediscovered the stature of *The Awakening* and worked to revive her reputation. The women's movement in the late 1960s gave added impetus to this revival, for *The Awakening* tells a searching story of marital dissatisfaction, from a woman's point of view. Having rediscovered *The Awakening*, readers are now going back to Chopin's regional fiction also, and they are finding much of cultural and artistic interest in it. As a work of art, *The Awakening* draws importantly on the local color skills and narrative attitudes developed earlier in her stories.

She was born Kate O'Flaherty in St. Louis—then (1851) a small city of 75,000. Originally settled by the French, St. Louis at midcentury was a turbulent blend of frontier and commercial town with pockets of traditional, kin-oriented, French Catholic society remaining. Her father, Thomas, had emigrated from Ireland in 1825 as a youth of twenty; he became a prosperous merchant. Her mother, Eliza Faris, belonged to the old French culture, with relatives dispersed along the Mississippi and in New Orleans. The atmosphere in the O'Flaherty home was heavily French, and there were visits back and forth, to and from New Orleans kin. The French quality became even more intense after Kate's father was killed in a train wreck when she was only four. Living in the house then were Kate's widowed mother, her widowed maternal grandmother, and her widowed maternal great-grandmother. This was a somber yet loving and close-knit community of women with memories stretching far back into the eighteenth century.

Kate began school in 1860 and continued as a day

student at the St. Louis Academy of the Sacred Heart until she was seventeen. Her education, according to the going standards for women, was a good one. Of course, it was measurably inferior to the standard education for men. The Sacred Heart Academy provided religious instruction that did not appear to touch Chopin very deeply—at least, there are few religious attitudes to be discerned in her writing, although she certainly portrays the piety and devotion of the Louisiana culture in her fiction. From the first, Chopin was an avid independent reader, and since she was fluent in both English and French, she covered a very large field of literature on her own.

A studious and somewhat reserved young woman, she missed her reading and longed for solitude after graduation. But she participated fully in the social whirl that was expected in her social class, and for two years her life was a conventional round of outings and parties. Apparently, she accepted conventional expectations without question. As was expected, she fell in love—with a distantly related Louisiana cousin, Oscar Chopin—and married just two years after her graduation, when she was nineteen.

Oscar was several years older than his bride and in the process of establishing himself as a cotton broker in New Orleans. His family was settled in and around Natchitoches (pronounced *Nackitosh*) Parish, in the western part of the state, and Oscar owned land there as well. But Oscar was striking out for himself, and he and his young wife entered with enthusiasm into the rich social and cultural life of the United States' most colorful city. Chopin carried out her duties as wife, hostess, and mother of a quickly increasing family, with gusto and ability. She had five children, all of whom survived. Frequently, she went back to St. Louis to visit her mother, to whom she remained very close. Some of her children were born in St. Louis. The biographical record of these years is very sketchy, but what there is suggests that she was very happy in her marriage; or at least that she had no questions about her life.

In 1879, after having suffered business reverses, Oscar decided to move with his family back to Natchitoches Parish. They lived in the tiny town of Cloutierville for four years. Oscar managed the land he owned, and ran a general store. It seems that here, too, Kate was happy. But in 1883 Oscar was stricken in a epidemic of what was then called swamp fever (and to this day is undiagnosed) and died very suddenly. The twelve-year idyll had come to a shocking close. For a short time Kate Chopin tried to carry on Oscar's business and land dealings, but she then decided to return to St. Louis. With her children, she moved back into her girlhood home. Although she changed houses several times in the subsequent years, St. Louis was to be home for the rest of her life.

Two years after Oscar's death, Kate's mother died. This second blow, coming so soon after the first, left her profoundly unsettled and depressed. She had lost the two people she most loved and on whom she most depended. With five children to raise, she was forced to be independent—not merely financially, but emotionally as well. Finances were not the major problem, for she had inheritances. But the loneliness and responsibility were immense. It seems that at this critical low point in her life, a good friend suggested writing as a form of therapy—not self-expressive writing, but professional writing. Although Chopin had written little more than some adolescent journals and numerous letters, she seized on the suggestion very seriously. Her output—two novels and close to a hundred stories, as well as some poetry and essays— testifies to her commitment, as does the energy with which she sought publication and notice.

Even while devoting herself to a literary career, Chopin maintained a full schedule of social and family activities. She seems to have devoted no more than two mornings a week to writing, and many of her friends in St. Louis (those who did not read the national magazines in which she was publishing) were unaware that she was an author. The rest of the time was spent with her family and in social activities— including a weekly reception that was considered to be one of the more fashionable and intellectual gatherings in St. Louis.

It is tempting to see this behavior as a kind of "double life," in which a woman secretly pursues a career in a society that is not prepared to accept women as professionals. This doubleness could be seen as a holding back on Chopin's part, a failure of full commitment; or perhaps it could be seen as the inevitably destructive influence of social convention on women. But when all is said and done, it is hard to see the production of two novels and almost a hundred stories as "holding back." It is also tempting to blame the short-sighted critics for destroying her career by condemning *The Awakening*. Yet if we do so, we are indulging in a familiar myth of the misunderstood artist without having the necessary biographical information to apply it in Kate Chopin's case.

The really crucial point for Kate Chopin's life as an artist is the late beginning. It is clear that without a series of terrible tragedies, which forced her to an emotional low point, Chopin would not have become a writer at all. Thus although her writing has little of the autobiographical about it, it represents in the most important sense her constructive response to misfortune, her way of taking control of her life and her emotions.

But Chopin could not have done this had there not been, by 1890, a long tradition in America of professional female authorship. The most active and popular writer in the nation's infancy had been a woman— Susannah Rowson—who produced six of the thirty-eight original works of fiction that appeared in this country before 1800. One of these, *Charlotte*, had been reprinted more than eighty times by the middle of the nineteenth century—and this in a country that could scarcely support a publishing industry.

By the middle of the nineteenth century, woman authors had become so numerous that Nathaniel Hawthorne, writing to his publisher, described them as a "damn'd mob of scribbling women." They started by writing for the "ladies' magazines," a new type of publication that had sprung up in the early nineteenth century for the instruction and amusement of an ever-larger literate population. They addressed themselves solely to women readers, fashioning story after story of heroines successfully overcoming adversity and proving their worth in situations in which they start out with little respect or appreciation. These fictions dominated the commercial market for fiction before the Civil War, and authorship became one of the very first professions available to women in America. There is no way to explain this phenomenal success except to suppose that most readers in America were women.

Along with their depiction of heroines successfully coping with varieties of adversity, the professional woman writers of the pre-Civil War generation deliberately tried to record the manners and traditions of the various societies in which their heroines lived. Their aim here was partly to achieve variety—for the plot line of these novels was very much a formula. But they were also interested in history. They felt that they had a share in the experiment of the new, democratic nation; they knew that the country was changing rapidly, and they wanted to preserve what they saw. Consequently, one finds an early form of literary realism in their meticulous depiction of settings and social customs.

It is possible that this type of realism was particularly attractive to women writers because some of the larger themes were closed to them, owing to more limited education and more limited mobility for women than men. Whatever the explanation, there is a very strong correlation between women's writing and regional writing, evident in the earliest American fiction and continuing down to our own day in such modern women authors as Flannery O'Connor, Eudora Welty, and Carson McCullers—all of whom are closely identified with the South.

When woman authors of the second generation—that is, the generation after the Civil War—transcended their forerunners' popular writing and produced truly major fiction, they did so in a manner clearly derived from the earlier woman writers and clearly rooted in regional realism. One thinks of Sarah Orne Jewett, Mary Wilkins Freeman, Rebecca Harding Davis, Constance Fenimore Woolson, Mary Noailles Murfree, Ellen Glasgow, Willa Cather; all of these writers grew from the soil of the regional tradition. Naturally enough, then, when Chopin began to write, she too turned to regionalism.

Local color writing had its most vigorous flowering after the Civil War. Ironically, the genre became increasingly popular because the pace of change in America became so rapid that the regions—on which local color writing depended—were threatened as autonomous, vital centers. Local color writing was thus fueled by anxiety over the loss of the familiar, nostalgia for ways that were passing, and protest against the supplanting of the regions by a new mass urban society. A number of interrelated trends that had gathered momentum throughout the century were enormously accelerated after the Civil War. They operated to transform the nation from a collection of widely dispersed, relatively autonomous rural communities, adapted to their particular landscape and climate, to a thoroughly interdependent network of urban industrial centers. Reality in late nineteenth-century America lay in the big city; but the American imagination proposed two myths of protest. One, the men's myth, focused on the frontier, on open spaces and unlimited opportunities. The second, the women's myth, turned back to the stable regions, where the human life cycle remained rooted in landscape and in the deep connections of kin and neighbors.

The changes of which we are speaking affected both the cities and the rural areas. Kate Chopin's St. Louis, for example, had only 1,000 or so inhabitants when it became part of the United States through the Louisiana Purchase. At the time she was born, the population was 75,000; and by the time she returned in the late 1880s, it had grown to 451,000. The St. Louis of 1890 was five times the size of the city of

Chopin's girlhood. Where did all these people come from? There was, to be sure, a climbing birth rate. But people also were coming in from the farms and outlying communities. Some came eagerly and willingly, attracted by the opportunities for work and by the social variety of a city as opposed to the sameness of a country existence. But others were forced off their farms by crop failures, mortgage foreclosures, and other rural disasters. About every twenty years in America there was a business depression, and each depression led inevitably to a new influx of rural people into the cities. There is a real sense in which one can think of these people as refugees.

Then, people were coming from abroad. Irish—like Kate Chopin's father—and Germans came before the Civil War; after, they were joined by Danes, Swedes, Poles, Italians, all with different traditions and languages. Many of these immigrants tried to live on the land, but some failed; many others settled in the cities by choice. Thus by the end of the nineteenth century, America was an urban nation. And its cities bore little resemblance to the cluster of large towns along the Eastern seaboard that had been its urban centers one hundred years earlier. These older cities found themselves unable to deal with large new groups of aliens. Traditional city governance had to give way to bureaucracy. The cultural systems of both the immigrants and the rural dwellers were shattered or submerged in the new environment. Fortunes were made in such urban developments as gasworks, waterworks, streetcar lines.

The end result of all this change—although in fact change showed no sign of coming to an end—was cities that seemed merely impersonal masses of people, with no ties other than a common pursuit of security or material success. In the same city lived immensely rich people and horribly poor people, people climbing up the social ladder and people tumbling down it, and a mass at the bottom that made the longtime city dweller both frightened and ashamed. It is little wonder that local color writing seemed appealing, with its evocation of a simpler, more stately kind of life.

But the vogue of regional literature was not accompanied by a flight to the land. On the contrary, Rural areas were becoming ever more depopulated. Those left on the land saw their way of life left behind—the way they had thought of as the particularly American way—the way of the small farmer who owns his land and is free. Regions had been settled, had prospered, and had been left to decay within the memory of living individuals. Historical processes seemed grotesquely accelerated; there was a sense of loss, and of fear. Regional writing could thus be one thing to the city reader and something entirely different to the regional writer herself, a member of the culture whose passing she was recording.

The regions were being destroyed, it seemed to many, by large and powerful forces that single individuals could neither understand nor control; hence the literature that was based on the regions was, to a great extent, a literature confirming—or attempting to confirm—the centrality and force of the individual character. Few aspects of the late nineteenth century seemed so perfectly to symbolize the new times as did the railroad, a symbol of the enormous physical forces that were changing the nation, as well as of the new speed at which change was taking place.

Railroads and the railroad industry were for the

later nineteenth century what the automobile has been for us: the underpinning of the national way of life and a major occupation in their own right. Among many crucial effects was that of bringing the far-flung sections of the country together and permitting—even demanding—rapid communication among them. In 1893, Kate Chopin could go to New York from St. Louis in thirty-two hours; the earlier stage coach (which could cover forty miles a day in summer, twenty-five in winter) had required twenty-four to thirty-eight days for the same journey! Such a remarkable change clearly threatened the special characteristics of regions that had developed in relative isolation. It brought a huge influx of standardized, city-made goods, into the small towns, driving out the local artisans in the process; it also brought tourists. Regional writing can be perceived, in a sense, as a tourism of the imagination. But the actual tourist alters the region he visits, whereas the tourist of the imagination has recourse to an unspoiled region that is preserved forever. This desire for preservation in the imagination, when preservation in fact is impossible, certainly underlies much regional writing. Kate Chopin's country characters go on foot, occasionally on horseback, and only for very special occasions— which the reader should be alert for—by train.

Although the industrializing and urbanizing of the South lagged behind that of other regions of the country, the region's defeat in the Civil War made the local color emotions especially intense here. To many Southerners, their region had represented a land-based social system, an economy of self-sufficient country estates, a way of life based on tradition and history and respectful of individual variety. Looking ahead, nostalgic Southerners saw that the end was not in sight—change itself was perhaps to become the essence of the American life experience. The closing of the frontier has been taken by many historians as the crucial event of the 1890s, the event that changed America's vision of itself. But in the 1890s it was not closings but openings—perpetual openings—that seemed distressing to Americans.

Thus the regional writers after the Civil War, whether writing about Maine or Tennessee or Louisiana, were looking backward rather than forward; there was an elegaic tone to their writing even at its most lively and energetic. They set their declining regions over against contemporary urban America or an America of the near future wherein these regions would no longer exist except in the literature.

It will easily be seen that Kate Chopin had a special opportunity in her experiences in Louisiana and had special, personal motives that accorded well with the thrust of local color. If there was a national nostalgia for the passing of these regions, her nostalgia could also be deeply, intensely, private. Whatever difficulties she might have experienced in Louisiana, her life there had unfolded according to plan; nothing untoward, nothing unforeseen, and nothing uncontrollable had occurred. The jarring dislocations that she later experienced in her personal life put her Louisiana days behind her as permanently as the regions were disappearing from American life. Thus, one might say, she did not have to make her stories autobiographical for them to express her sense of a pastoral, protected, yet vulnerable beauty.

Although "Americans" came into the state, as into St. Louis, after the Louisiana Purchase, the French and Spanish character of the original settlement remained strikingly apparent even at the end of the nineteenth century. Visitors to New Orleans were continually impressed by its Continental character, even though only 17 percent of the population in 1890 was actually descended from French people. The Creole community retained a strong internal structure. (Creoles are descendants of French and Spanish settlers, and the designation is sometimes extended to include Afro-Americans who descended from the servants of the Creoles.) The Creoles were generally middle- or upper-class merchants or landowners, practicing Catholics, native speakers of their own dialect of French, and socially very close to one another and to the blacks who also spoke the dialect. In such Chopin stories as "La Belle Zoraïde" and "Ozème's Holiday" one finds examples of black-white relations.

Most of Chopin's characters are Creoles, but on occasion she writes about the Acadians (Cajuns), another French-speaking group that had resettled from Canada early in the eighteenth century. These tended to be lower-class people—fishermen, trappers, woodchoppers—yet closely related to the Creoles by their common linguistic and religious heritage. Cajuns figure in "Love on the Bon-Dieu" and "At Chênière Caminada" and are unforgettably depicted in Mme. Antoine and Tonie of *The Awakening*. This world-within-a-world of Creole whites, Creole blacks, and Cajuns constituted the subject matter of all the Louisiana local colorists, who included most notably, along with Kate Chopin, George Washington Cable (1844-1925) and Grace King (1851-1932).

Because they were Catholic, Continental, and

tropical—rather than Protestant, British, and temperate—these people offered certain unique opportunities to the regional chronicler: they represented not only a past that was quickly fading away, but a present that America had never chosen to embrace. Their lives could be presented as more pleasure-oriented, more easy-going, more gracious, and more sensuous than those of the mainstream Americans who would in all probability be reading about them. And while they were rural, they still had a European sophistication which might well be beyond that of the average American; where most local color characters were more primitive than the assumed reader, the Creole was in many ways more sophisticated. Observe, for example, the subtle interrelations in such stories as "Athénaïse" or "A Visit to Avoyelles," where the characters, although very rustic, are also capable of extremely subtle kinds of behavior. The natural surroundings were luxuriant and provided both a beautiful setting and a chance for the writer to stress sensuous attractiveness. Unlike the Spartan existence of the other rural regions, life in Louisiana included an appreciation of food, wine, furnishings, and enjoyment—one sees this as early as the box of bonbons in Chapter 3 of *The Awakening*. The pace of life was slow, and the mood of nature benign—except to a Northerner, who might find it too rich a diet.

As a group, Creoles were profoundly home-centered and socially exclusive; their religious and political views were quite conservative. The Ratignolles, in *The Awakening*, are representatives of the type, and so too are the chief characters in such stories as "A Matter of Prejudice" and "Regret." Within the security of their traditions and their relations, they tended to be open in thought and expression, physically demonstrative and playful in relationships. These freedoms testified to their lack of anxiety. There is abundant mental health in all Chopin's Creole and Cajun characters. Their lives offer a continuous contrast to the new, frenzied, anonymous, mass-produced America and to such other regions as New England with its rugged, stony, impoverished landscape and its stern, Spartan inhabitants.

Whoever the author, and regardless of region, all local color writing had certain formal qualities in common. The chief constraint was the certainty on the author's part that the people of the region would not be the readers, so that the literary work was a communication from writer to reader over the heads, so to speak, of the subject. Local color characters could never perceive themselves in local color terms, could never find the significance in their own lives that the writer found and communicated. Hence, in even the simplest kind of local color writing one will find differing angles of vision. In the best local color writing these differences are raised to the level of a theme. The writer—and the reader—becomes aware that meaning or significance is being attributed to the action in a willful manner. One perceives that different meanings or significances could be attributed, by different observers, to the same body of materials.

The simplest type of regional literature developed portraits of local character that were sharply set off from modern urban people. Sometimes an urban person was introduced to make the point more clear—as in "Athénaïse," for example, although "Athénaïse" is by no means a simple type of local color fiction. Some writers developed characters for their strange,

comical, picturesque, odd, or sensational qualities—
certainly many characters in Chopin's short stories
are exploited for cuteness. Certain authors carried
this approach so far as to create caricature rather than
character, although Chopin seldom falls into this trap.
Regions were seen as inhabited by simple, primitive,
happy types whose mode of existence was a continuous round of enjoyments, often of a sensual nature.
These types provided a voyeuristic thrill, or a pastoral
reproach, to more urban readers. (Treatments of this
sort persist in our own day in the stereotypical depiction of the "hillbilly.") But to do this to character
implies a fundamental lack of respect for the type,
of which Chopin is never guilty.

Other regional authors were more like historians,
assuming an air of objectivity and showing up character
in strength and weakness, but always with a clear
regional identity. Yet few could present a value-free
picture, and inevitably those qualities were stressed
that modern life seemed all too ready to discard—
such qualities as self-reliance, hardihood, independence, community, and a sense of kin. Behind all these
values lay the root objection of the regional writer to
the homogenization of American life. The loss of
individual character in a new mass style, the weakening
of areas of life in which the individual could control
his or her own destiny, were highlighted by showing
characters of strength and integrity. Writers presented
organic, living communities of people who accepted
their mutual obligations and understood their individual differences; and these were implicitly contrasted
with modern, bureaucratic, anonymous forms of
"community." A persistent theme or plot-motif in
Chopin's short stories is the interaction between a

person's sense of himself (or herself) and the recognized obligations to community. But in Chopin's world—or at least the world of her short stories—these two forces are not really in opposition to each other. Self is strengthened by membership in a group—in contrast to modern life, where self can only be weakened by joining the crowd.

Because the chief outlet for local color writing was the magazine, most local color writing took the form of short fiction. Its formal qualities developed as a blend, thus, of the inner pressures of the material and the outer realities of publishing. As it turned out, the short form was extremely appropriate for local color writing, whose main objective was to sketch a situation efficiently, indicate at least one strong character, and make a powerful, immediate impact.

When local color writers attempted to write longer works while remaining entirely within the genre, they had only limited success. It seems extremely difficult to create a plot of sufficient complexity and weight while retaining an exclusive local color focus. Invariably, the writer wishes to go further. Perhaps for this reason, local color writing is thought of as a minor trend in American literature. Nevertheless, many major American novels have been immeasurably strengthened by their strong local color elements. It is impossible to imagine *Huckleberry Finn*, for example, without local color. It is impossible to imagine *The Awakening* without local color.

Chopin's wide reading meant that when she began to write she could call on a variety of literary models and examples. She knew the major writers of local color fiction and greatly admired Sarah Orne Jewett (1849-1909) and Mary Wilkins Freeman (1852-1930).

Both of these writers specialized in the New England scene. Jewett's masterpiece, *The Country of the Pointed Firs*, was not to appear until 1896; but Chopin knew her earlier volumes of short stories, *Deephaven* (1877) and *A White Heron* (1886). Mary Wilkins Freeman had published two superb volumes of local color fiction at just the time Chopin turned professional. These were *A Humble Romance* in 1887 and *A New England Nun* in 1891.

But these chroniclers of the New England scene were not as influential on Kate Chopin's writing as some of the great contemporary French authors. Gustave Flaubert had published his masterly treatment of a dissatisfied wife, *Madame Bovary*, in 1857. This work has much in common with *The Awakening*. At the outset of her writing career, however, Chopin was much more immediately influenced by the stories of Guy de Maupassant. Maupassant had perfected a form of short story that featured a detached, slightly ironic, all-knowing yet reticent authorial voice. His character delineation was realistic, his presentation of details economical. And his plots usually had a pathetic or ironic twist at the end, sometimes delivered through a punch line or a telling bit of dialogue. Maupassant was not an explicit or graphic author in his treatment of physical detail, but he treated his characters with a frankness about their motives and a skepticism about their virtue. It was this frankness and skepticism that Victorian America thought of as typically "French." Thus Maupassant was an author who provided a good model for the treatment of "French" characters and the creation of "French" effects. Certainly, in her short stories, Chopin was striving for the sense of a French, rather than an American, culture.

Chopin's special achievement in local color was to utilize Maupassant's techniques for a society that was actually quite moral—although perhaps not by "American" standards—and to create a detached authorial voice that was, unlike Maupassant's, permeated with affection for its characters. Both "A Night in Acadie" and "Athénaïse" provide excellent examples of these accomplishments. Often, the Maupassant-like twist at the end consists of a revelation of moral depth where we had previously seen nothing but Creole charm (or Creole stubbornness). But equally often, the twist consists in the character's *denial* of the moral value of some clearly good or generous act just performed—as in "Ozème's Holiday" or "A Matter of Prejudice." Amusingly, the character's disavowal of high morality makes him or her more attractive to the reader. It seems that Chopin meant to endear her characters to the audience by stressing both their surface charm and their ultimate depth of feeling. She is fond of juxtaposing oddly related characters—old and young, servants and mistresses—in reversed roles, as a means of bringing out the depths of loyalty and affection that she perceives in these assorted types. Above all, her characters are able to blend passion and morality so that each intensifies the other; the traditional "Anglo" code tended to see passion always as the antagonist of moral virtue.

Chopin's Creoles and Cajuns also combine a highly developed self-dramatizing ability with a remarkable lack of self-consciousness. One might say that they are natural actors. Also, they seem to lack guilt and the tendency toward self-analysis that might make them brooding, inward, reflexive. Certainly characters like Athénaïse move from one moral position to its opposite without suffering guilt feelings over their inconsistency. They are more attuned to the natural flow of their own emotions; they are more trusting of themselves than the typical representative of the American moral code.

It would be an easy matter to claim that the purpose of Chopin's work is to hold this natural, vivid character up to American readers as a comment on their hyperdeveloped "modern" anxiety. However, Chopin leaves the reader to apply the character to his or her situation or not; hers is the attitude of a connoisseur, presenting the character as an object for appreciation.

Beyond the individual character is always the community of which he or she is a part. When compared to mainstream America, this community presents an alternative of variety and diversity because the characters are so colorful and individual. But within itself, the chief characteristic of the community is unanimity. It is almost as if the characters are only partly separated into individual selves; they all remain importantly attached to the larger group. In a sense, their truest self lies in their attachment to this group. Thus a personal defeat—as in "In Sabine"—is not really a setback to the individual. Gestures of loyalty and sacrifice build the group at the expense of the self. But these gestures do not lead to tragedy, for the character gets back more than he loses through his participation in that group. Thus in sum, the Chopin character contrasts both to modern mass society and to such alternatives to it as the lonely, stubborn selves of New England local color.

Chopin belongs to that group of local colorists whose work did not acknowledge late nineteenth-century change. Although Louisiana and New Orleans were altering along with the rest of the country, the strength of Creole traditions permitted Chopin to ignore such alteration. Her vision in a sense is truly "pastoral," in that there seem to be no traces of history or economics in her people's lives. One might say that in this ignoring of time, Chopin demonstrates a fierce resistance to its inroads; or one might say that she is deliberately evoking a timeless world as an alternative to the mutable world she knew all too well. The themes of time and timelessness occur in all literature, and in America are particularly associated with Southern writers. But for Chopin to admit that theme into her writing might have been to jeopardize the particular beauty of her world, where only character and community matter.

Most of Chopin's stories are very short—rarely more than 3,000 words, or eight or nine printed pages. She had to work very efficiently, and she relied on dialogue to do the double task of advancing the plot and developing the characters. As a secondary technique, she chronicled, from a removed vantage point, the thoughts and actions of one major character through whom the rest of the story is channeled—the "limited third-person point of view." In each story, it is possible to identify one character through whom most of the perceptions are funneled; sometimes this will be the main character, but not always.

Whoever the viewpoint character is, however, Chopin uses a different vocabulary and voice from that character's—one might say, her own voice—to articulate the perceptions; thus, we never mistake the viewpoint character for the narrator. In *The Awakening*, for example, the narrator very rarely departs from Edna's perceptions—there is a scene in which Mme. Ratignolle talks about Edna to Robert Lebrun, and another in which Léonce Pontellier talks to Dr. Mandelet. But these are about the only scenes that are not channeled through Edna. Yet we are always aware of some other voice telling the story; we always know that Edna is not the narrator. And we can see Chopin working on this separation of viewpoint and narrator throughout her short stories.

The stories also employ a minimal descriptive technique. They establish setting and background rapidly, avoiding set pieces of description. The larger scale and slower pace of the novel permitted Chopin to expand her descriptive and atmospheric writing. Thus it is that although one cannot fully describe *The Awakening* by calling it a piece of local color writing, this novel actually contains her fullest descriptions of place and evocations of atmosphere. And these aspects of the novel stay with the reader after the reading experience has ended.

One might say that the point of a story in local color writing is to bring out, in strong relief, some aspect of the culture being depicted—usually through character delineation. This purpose is usually not enough to sustain a long fiction, where more general plots are expected. The purpose of local color in a novel is more to make the story seem real and particular than to be an end in itself. One problem that local color writers have when they attempt longer fiction is to merge the local color aspect of their work with the more general story they are trying to tell. The story of Edna Pontellier could have been set anywhere in the world that allowed some freedoms to women without giving them complete freedom. That is to say, it could have been set *anywhere* in the world. But to be appreciated by readers, it had to be set *somewhere*, and this is how local color enters, and immeasurably strengthens, the novel.

In her early novel, *At Fault*, Chopin had not been successful in her fusion of general story and particular setting. Its heroine, Thérèse Lafirme (in French "the firm one"), is a young widow running a plantation in Natchitoches Parish. She permits a lumber company to establish a mill on her land and falls in love with its manager, David Hosmer. Hosmer loves her in return; but he is a divorced man, and his ex-wife, an alcoholic, is still living. When Thérèse finds out about this, she exerts her moral influence to persuade him to remarry this woman and thereby carry out the original marriage vow, "in sickness and health, till death do us part." But the wife continues her drinking, and there is misery all around until she perishes in a storm.

The chief characters and their problems are not grounded in the locale; longish set pieces of description ornament the action but do not contribute to it. A more serious flaw in the novel is its lack of congruence between the depiction of the heroine and the narrator's comments about her. Thérèse comes across as a well-meaning but rather insensitive and self-righteous woman. She is totally insensitive to the agony she causes by forcing Hosmer to cohabit with a woman he does not respect, and thus in an odd sense Thérèse seems to lack sexual morality. But the narrator has nothing but praise for her moral excellence. Such dissonance suggests that Chopin was not fully aware of the potentialities of her own material.

After the writing of *At Fault*, Chopin devoted herself exclusively to short fiction, and one can see the stories as exercises that led her to correct the defects of the novel. Her more detached, nonjudgmental narrator in the short fiction, for example, represents a solution to the problem of a narrator who is inadequate to the story.

Such a detached narrator functions in *The Awakening*; in this sense the second novel is the converse of the first. The earlier novel showed that codes of right and wrong are not easily translated into action; human beings are so much more complicated than their codes. *The Awakening* shows that actions are not easily classified by codes of right and wrong. Ironically, had Chopin included a judging narrator to find Edna "at fault," her difficulties with the reviewers might have been avoided. Certainly, according to a conventional moral code, Edna is "punished" at the novel's end. But the narrator never labeled the character as a "bad woman." And without that label, the meaning of Edna's suicide is not clear. But judging or even interpreting are not Chopin's purposes in *The Awakening*.

Kate Chopin originally intended to call her book *A Solitary Soul*, and in many respects the title finally used is cruder. It tends to make the reader look for a process that is more definite and positive than that which the heroine actually undergoes. The book begins with intimations of a romance between Edna and Robert Lebrun, son of the proprietor of the resort where Edna is spending the summer. It ends when that romance is decisively terminated by Robert. We recognize the underpinnings of a traditional triangle plot. A married woman falls in love with a man who is not her husband. Gradually, and only partly aware of what she is doing, she prepares to accept this man as her lover. She offers herself to him only to be rejected; she has grown beyond social conventions, but he has not.

The plot line is thickened by the introduction of a third man, Alcée Arobin, who provides a sensuous attraction that neither her husband nor her beloved gives Edna; for Robert is a romantic rather than a passionate love. Alcée is necessary to the plot, for without her affair with him Edna would not have realized the significance of sex in life and would not have been prepared to make a direct sexual approach to Robert. And it is just this sexual approach that drives Robert away, forces him to reject her in a decisive manner.

The plot is also complicated by Edna's two children and by the conflicting counsel offered to the confused heroine by two contrasting woman friends. Adele Ratignolle is the wife-mother, entirely engrossed in her family. Mlle. Reisz, the pianist, stands for the artist, entirely engrossed in her work. Neither of these roles, with their particular mixes of self-satisfactions and self-denials, is right for Edna. Each friend causes her to feel even more alone, more singular, in her dilemma. This is so even though both women are intelligent and devoted to Edna. Neither, however, is a woman that she can ever be. But who can she be? Who is she?

At the age of twenty-eight, Edna "wakes up," as it were, to a feeling that her life has been a dream thus far; but she does not know who she is or where she is in the real world. She is anxious to cast off all the trappings of what she feels to be her false self. But she does not know what her true self might be or how to go about finding it. Experiencing all of her life as imprisonment, she makes a wholly ambiguous gesture at the end; for her suicide may be seen equally as a transcendence of her prison or a giving in to it. From a moral point of view, her suicide may represent an act of defiance or an act of self-punishment—resistance or submission. Kate Chopin does not provide a single interpretation of Edna's story; she refuses to reduce it to one meaning.

Local color elements augment and emphasize this story in two specific ways. The lush climate and atmosphere of Louisiana, the heat and humidity and the luxurious idleness of Creole life, have an erotic and narcotic effect on Edna. So does the continuous display of fine things—silver, linen, furnishings, and above all, food—which define the Creole sense of the good life. Edna has been brought up in Kentucky by Calvinists, and this continuous sensuousness is difficult for her to deal with; she responds to her own senses as though they were alien to her, even though she is a very sensuous person. Where the Creole such as Mme. Ratignolle can easily incorporate the physical into her life, for Edna it always is a temptation to let go entirely.

Second, the profound intimacy of Creole society, the instinctive understanding each has of the others, sets Edna apart as an outsider, no matter how kindly the Creoles feel toward her and how accepting they are of her differences. Because the Creoles are so open, because they have so little sense of privacy, because they know each other intuitively, Edna's hidden inner life takes on a significance that it might not have had in a society where more people were like her. She thinks of that inner life as her "real self"; and yet that inner life has no means of finding expression in any kind of outward behavior. This contrast, incidentally, between an outsider and the insiders, is not to be found in any of Chopin's short fiction. It is a hint—but no more than that—that Chopin herself may not have been entirely comfortable in Oscar Chopin's world.

The particular delicacy of *The Awakening* consists in the manner in which Chopin shows the reader (long before Edna discovers it herself, although eventually she does so) that Robert is only a symbol or a substitute for the much vaguer and grander longings and desires that are actually propelling her. Hers is the immemorial romantic quest for beauty, happiness, fulfillment—ideals that nothing in life can actually satisfy. Like many romantics, Edna is unable to participate in many of the satisfactions that life offers to more realistic people—precisely *because* of the vastness of her ideals. Yet the ideals are progressively incarnated by her in limited human beings who, if attained, would disappoint her. Because the reader sees very early that Robert is such a limited being, the book becomes much more than yet another chronicle of middle-class boredom or frustrated erotic energies.

Chopin's attitude toward this romanticism is complex. Some critics have complained about the narration because it seems at times to share and at other times to reject Edna's own way of responding to and thinking about the world; they have gone so far as to accuse Chopin of confusion or lack of control. Yet much of *The Awakening*'s effect on a reader comes from the way in which the narration presents Edna's viewpoint sympathetically and still attains distance from it. The narrator, one might say, is a person who has had experiences like Edna's, understood them, and survived to tell the tale. Edna, who cannot reach this level of understanding, does not survive. The narrator encloses

Edna's perceptions in a sympathetic but larger perspective.

The issue of self and society is certainly bigger than a "woman's issue," and Chopin's greatest contribution to the woman question—as it was called in her own day—may well be her use of a female protagonist to represent a universal human dilemma. But it is impossible not to see specific women's questions in *The Awakening*. Certainly, in this work Chopin is more concerned with her heroine's life as a woman, and with how being a woman may be a constraint on a person's full humanity, than she is in any of her short fiction. In the short fiction, women function within their allotted roles with considerable gusto and satisfaction. Only a few stories—"A Respectable Woman," for example—suggest clashes between self and role. But in considering the ways in which *The Awakening* deals with questions specific to women, one needs to have a sense of how these questions were perceived in Chopin's own time.

By the end of the nineteenth century, feminist ideas had been actively circulating in the United States for more than fifty years. Feminists were dealing almost exclusively with public issues: legal equality for women, protection for working women, access to sources of political and economic power, education, the vote. Many reform movements of the time— settlement house movements, labor laws, temperance—had a woman's dimension to them. By the end of the century, too, middle-class women were joining clubs and volunteer organizations that were bringing them out of the home and giving their lives a public, activist dimension that was beyond their traditional preserves of family and hostessing.

By 1899 there had been progress toward women's emancipation and expanded opportunities of all sorts—property laws, divorce, education, freedom of expression, access to the professions. Some professions—teaching and authorship, for example—were open to women but on an unequal basis, since woman teachers were paid less than men, and woman authors were expected to write mostly for women. Other professions—such as medicine and journalism—were in the process of becoming open to women. Many others—such as politics and business—remained closed.

In 1899, when *The Awakening* appeared, the vast majority of women were—despite all the turbulence and the clear signs of change—either homebound in much less comfortable circumstances than Edna or working at low-status, badly paying jobs. It must be remembered that the percentage of population qualifying as middle-class was much smaller then; the average housewife was married to a poor man, and the working woman was generally not a professional. The 1890 census puts the female work force at 3.7 million, or some 23 percent of the female adult population. This seems a high figure; but the point is that the employed were not in "middle-class" jobs. Fully a third of the total—1.2 million—were in domestic service. Almost half a million were farm workers. There were 216,000 laundresses and 300,000 dressmakers (including factory hands). 246,000 women were schoolteachers, but mostly in the lower grades. Saleswomen and bookkeepers together accounted for only 86,000 women; and as we move up into the professional ranks, the numbers drop off to almost nothing—4,500 women physicians, 888 journalists, 208 lawyers.

Women in the home without servants had a much

more onerous life than the housewife of today. Many homes lacked running water, which meant that water had to be well-drawn; the iron stove was replacing the fireplace, but it still required to be stoked with wood. Store-bought clothes were becoming the norm, but women still baked their own bread. The processes of cooking and cleaning were thus not only time-consuming but physically laborious in a way that they are not today. Children, for those who lacked nurse-maids, were certainly a major preoccupation; families tended to be larger, and children's health much more precarious, than in our own times.

We can thus clearly see how untypical Edna's life was for her time. Surrounded by servants and untouched by any financial necessity, hers is rather an ideal than a woman's real life—at least from a feminist point of view. Yet of course there were elite women, and their lives were heavily circumscribed by role expectations. The elite woman's role demanded that she be devoted to home and children in spirit, even though no actual labor was demanded of her; and that she serve, so far as her husband was concerned, as the means by which he might display his wealth and social standing. These restrictions could clearly be intensely galling to a woman of energy and a sense of self, for they added up to a life of mandatory idleness and forced dependency. For many women of Edna's class, the way out of their confinement lay through voluntary activities, acts of charity and beneficence. But—let us admit it—Edna is a wholly self-absorbed character, and these outlets never figure as possibilities. Self-forgetfulness or self-transcendence does not lie within her personal capabilities. Thus within the frame of feminist thinking of the time, Edna's "case" does not really develop as a "woman's issue" story.

A contemporary reader may well be inclined to understand Edna's sexual emancipation as a feminist issue. But such a reading would be somewhat anachronistic. "Free love" spokespersons certainly existed in those times, but insofar as nineteenth-century women's righters considered the issue of sex, they were more likely to perceive sexual freedom as being freedom *from* sex rather than freedom *through* sex. What they wanted for women was the right to say no, rather than the right to say yes whenever and wherever they pleased. The reasons for this striking difference from our own culture are complex. Much of the difference derives from the relatively crude forms of birth control and the enormous risks of childbearing of those days—every act of sexual intercourse was, for a woman, a literally life-endangering act. As for the unmarried mother, she was a social outcast and had virtually no means of self-support; there was no welfare system except the local workhouse or poorhouse. As a matter of ideology, these Victorian and late Victorian feminists tended rather to downgrade the body and its passions than find life's essence there; they wanted women to develop their willpower and their intellect, not their capacity for pleasure.

If we understand this background, we will see that Chopin's treatment of Edna's sexual awakening, with its intensely private focus, is not particularly feminist either in its way of formulating the question or in its "answers" to it. Sexuality is portrayed with unusual frankness for the time and place, but that frankness does not derive from any conviction that more honest or open sexual behavior will lead to socially or personally desirable goals for women. Edna is really no better off as a result of her expanded sexual consciousness. Had she not committed suicide, Edna would probably have gone on to a series of sexual affairs; but this prospect is not enough for her, and it is not suggested as being enough by the author. No large-scale growth in psychological, intellectual, or spiritual freedom follows from Edna's sexual awakening. She is awakened to sex, but that awakening has no consequences. In fact, we are given to understand that like her financial "enthrallment" to her husband and her emotional "enthrallment" to Robert, Edna's sexual "enthrallment" to Alcée Arobin (or any other male) is finally another impediment to absolute freedom. The treatment of Edna's sexual nature and experience is thus eccentric both for its own time and for our time. It is too frank for an earlier age, and too traditional for a later one, in its insistence that sex is not the gateway to freedom.

Another eccentric element in the treatment of Edna's life from a woman's point of view is the problem of her children. By the novel's end Edna seems to have overcome every obstacle to her emancipation— her husband, lover, ideal—except her children. She cannot reject them. Earlier in the novel she told her friend Adele: "I would give up the unessential; I would give my money, I would give my life for my children; but I wouldn't give myself" (Chapter 16). Adele does not understand what Edna is saying here, nor does the reader at the time. But one important thought in Edna's mind when she walks into the sea is her inability to reconcile any possible independent existence with the lives of her children. They require a return to her husband and her previous style of life, which is no longer possible for her. "The children appeared before her like antagonists who had overcome her; who had overpowered and sought to drag her into the soul's slavery for the rest of her days. But she knew a way to elude them" (Chapter 39). Ironically, Edna ends not by giving her life *for* her children, as she had earlier said, but by giving her life in order not to give up her "self" through a return to "slavery."

Of course one cannot identify Edna's feelings with Chopin's, but it is difficult not to conclude from this carefully orchestrated motif that Chopin perceived the claims of children to be different from all others. Here, as in other ways, *The Awakening* is best characterized not so much as a feminist work but as an individual and indecisive meditation on feminist themes, resisting translation into ideology.

The Awakening also resists translation into autobiography. Kate Chopin clearly shared with her heroine that quality of tremendous reserve and an active inner life that is never expressed outwardly or perceived by others. In her many writings, that reserve is never breached; the author's inner life is never exposed to view. There are not many external points of correspondence between the author and her heroine. Chopin seems to have married for love, seems to have been happy with her husband, and was unequivocally a devoted mother. Unlike the motherless Edna, Chopin drew great strength from her own ties to her mother, not to mention to her grandmother and great-grandmother. She seems to have had no emotional entanglements with any man other than her husband; she never considered a second marriage. She had some traits in common with Adele; and others, again, in common with Mlle. Reisz.

It is fair to say that Chopin, like Edna, experienced a tremendous awakening in her own life. But it arose from different causes—the tragic and unexpected loss of those she loved and was supported by, the need to raise her children on her own. This awakening might have led her to the perception of the essential isolation of all human beings, even those in the most social surroundings. But it is clearly an awakening of a different order from that undergone by Edna. Chopin grew into independence and self-reliance because she had to. No doubt she had known deep depression and suicidal despair; yet she retained an orderly and proper outward existence and never struggled against the claims of her children. Above all, Edna Pontellier could never have imagined, or given textual life to, Kate Chopin.

Nina Baym
Urbana, Illinois
October 1980

A NOTE ON THE TEXTS

In all cases, the first publication in book form has served as the text for this edition. The stories "Love on the Bon-Dieu," "Beyond the Bayou," "A Visit to Avoyelles," "La Belle Zoraïde," and "In Sabine" are from *Bayou Folk* (Boston and New York: Houghton Mifflin), 1894. The stories "Ozème's Holiday," "A Matter of Prejudice," "At Chênière Caminada," "A Respectable Woman," "Regret," "Athénaïse," and "A Night in Acadie" are from *A Night in Acadie* (Chicago: Way and Williams), 1897. *The Awakening* is from the text published by Herbert S. Stone (Chicago and New York), 1899.

SELECTED READINGS

Addams, Jane. *Twenty Years at Hull-House.* New York: Macmillan, 1910. (Many reprints available)

Berthoff, Warner. *The Ferment of Realism: American Literature 1894–1919.* New York: Free Press, 1965.

Chopin, Kate. *The Complete Works of Kate Chopin.* Edited by Per Seyerstad. 2 vols. Baton Rouge: Louisiana State University Press, 1969.

Degler, Carl N. *At Odds: Women and the Family in America from the Revolution to the Present.* New York: Oxford University Press, 1980.

Gilbert, Sandra, and Susan Guber. *Sexchanges.* New Haven: Yale University Press, 1989.

Gilman, Charlotte Perkins. *Women and Economics.* New York: Harper & Row, 1966. (Originally published 1898)

Jewett, Sarah Orne. *The Country of the Pointed Firs.* New York: Anchor, 1956. (Originally published 1896)

Jones, Howard Mumford, and Ludwig, Richard M. *Guide to American Literature and Its Backgrounds Since 1890.* 4th ed. Cambridge: Harvard University Press, 1972.

King, Grace. *Memories of a Southern Woman of Letters.* New York: Macmillan, 1932.

Koloski, Bernard. *New Approaches to Teaching Kate Chopin's "The Awakening."* New York: Modern Language Association, 1988.

Lerner, Gerda. *The Female Experience: An American Documentary*. Indianapolis: Bobbs-Merrill, 1977.

Parker, Gail (ed.). *The Oven Birds: American Women on Womanhood*. New York: Anchor, 1972.

Pizer, Donald (ed.). *American Thought and Writing in the 1890s*. Boston: Houghton Mifflin (Riverside edition), 1972.

Putnam, Emily James. *The Lady: Studies of Certain Significant Phases of Her History*. Chicago: University of Chicago Press, 1969. (Originally published 1910)

Rankin, Daniel S. *Kate Chopin and Her Creole Stories*. Philadelphia: University of Pennsylvania Press, 1932.

Rubin, Louis D. (ed.). *A Bibliographical Guide to the Study of Southern Literature*. Baton Rouge: Louisiana State University Press, 1969.

Ryan, Mary P. *Womanhood in America: From Colonial Times to the Present*. New York: Franklin Watts. 1975.

Schlesinger, Arthur M. *The Rise of the City, 1878-1898*. New York: Macmillan, 1933.

Seyerstad, Per. *Kate Chopin: A Critical Biography*. Baton Rouge: Louisiana State University Press, 1969.

Simpson, Claude M. (ed.). *The Local Colorists: American Short Stories 1857-1900*. New York: Harper & Brothers, 1966.

Springer, Marlene. *Edith Wharton and Kate Chopin: A Reference Guide*. Boston: G. K. Hall, 1976.

Wilson, Edmund. *Patriotic Gore*. New York: Oxford University Press, 1962.

Ziff, Larzer. *The American 1890s: Life and Times of a Lost Generation*. New York: Viking, 1966.

DOCUMENTS

From *The Picayune's Creole Cook Book*

[*The New Orleans* Picayune *was one of the city's three leading newspapers in the latter part of the nineteenth century. It was the first Southern daily to be published by a woman, Eliza Poitevent Nicholson (1849-1896), who took over the paper upon the death of her husband in 1876. The* Picayune *employed several woman journalists, including Elizabeth M. Gilmer, who, under the pen name Dorothy Dix, became the nation's first and most popular writer of advice columns. The* Picayune's *cookbook appeared at the end of the century and then in a revised and enlarged second edition in 1901. Its recipes and commentary preserve the ideals and publicize the customs of Creole society.*]

Introduction

. . . Time was when the question of a Creole Cook Book would have been, as far as New Orleans is concerned, as useless an addition to our local literature as it is now a necessity, for the Creole negro cooks of nearly two hundred years ago, carefully instructed and directed by their white Creole mistresses, who received their inheritance of gastronomic lore from France, where the art of good cooking first had birth, faithfully transmitted their knowledge to their progeny, and these, quick to appreciate and understand,

and with a keen intelligence and zeal born of the desire to please, improvised and improved upon the products of the cuisine of Louisiana's mother country; then came the Spanish domination, with its influx of rich and stately dishes, brought over by the grand dames of Spain of a century and a half ago; after that came the gradual amalgamation of the two races on Louisiana soil, and with this was evolved a new school of cookery, partaking of the best elements of the French and Spanish cuisines, and yet peculiarly distinct from either, a system of cookery that has held its own through succeeding generations and which drew from even such a learned authority as Thackerary, that noted tribute to New Orleans, "the old Franco-Spanish city on the banks of the Mississippi, where, of all the cities in the world, you can eat the most and suffer the least, where claret is as good as at Bordeaux, and where a 'ragout' and a 'bouillabaisse' can be had, the like of which was never eaten in Marseilles or Paris."

But the civil war, with its vast upheavals of social conditions, wrought great changes in the household economy of New Orleans, as it did throughout the South; here, as elsewhere, she who had ruled as the mistress of yesterday became her own cook of to-day; in nine cases out of ten the younger darkies accepted their freedom with alacrity, but in many ancient families the older Creole "négresse," as they were called, were slow to leave the haunts of the old cuisine and the families of which they felt themselves an integral part. Many lingered on, and the young girls who grew up after that period had opportunities that will never again come to the Creole girls of New Orleans. For one of the most significant changes and one of the saddest, too, in this old city, is the passing of the faithful old negro cooks—the "mammies," who felt it a pride and honor, even in poverty, to cling to the fortunes of their former masters and mistresses, and out of the scant family allowance to be still able to prepare for the "ole Miss'" table a "ragout" from a piece of peck meat, or a "pot-au-poivre" from many mixtures that might grace the dining of a king.

But the "bandana and tignon" are fast disappearing from our kitchens. Soon will the last of the olden negro cooks of ante-bellum days have passed away and their places will not be supplied, for in New Orleans, as in other cities of the South, there is "a new colored woman" as well as a new white. The question of "a good cook" is now becoming a very vexing problem, and the only remedy for this state of things is for the ladies of the present day to do as their grandmothers did, acquaint themselves thoroughly with the art of cooking in all its important and minutest details, and learn how to properly apply them. To assist them in this, to preserve to future generations the many excellent and matchless recipes of our New Orleans cuisine, to gather these up from the lips of the old Creole negro cooks and the grand old housekeepers who still survive, ere they, too, pass away, and Creole cookery, with all its delightful combinations and possibilities, will have become a lost art, is, in a measure, the object of this book. . . .

Creole Home Dining

. . . No homes in the South suffered more through the loss of fortunes by the war than did the Creole homes of Louisiana. But the old social customs still remain, and many a hostess who years ago could invite her friends to a superb dining, which would have gladdened the heart of even the most fastidious old Creole gourmet, now finds herself reduced to perhaps even less than a dollar a day, and she has nobly accommodated herself to circumstances. And have her friends of former days fallen away? Not at all. For the Creoles hold good birth, good breeding and education higher than wealth. The poor little Creole seamstress over the way can still go into what is considered the best society, if her birth and education are good. . . .

Soirées

"Soirées" are pleasant forms of entertainments that have come down from earliest Creole days in Louisiana. While elaborate entertaining was also done, the Creole character being naturally gay and happy, and inheriting a French fondness for the dance, for music and song and social intercourse, the young folks had a way of giving weekly "Soirées" at which their parents served simple, light refreshments, such as the famous "Sirops" given in a preceding chapter, ices of various kinds, lemonades and Petits Fours, or small cakes, wafers and fruits. These refreshments were passed around by the old-time servants, decked in gay bandana tignon, guinea blue dress, and white apron, and kerchief pinned across the bosom. Later in the evening tea was served, and as the "Soirée" advanced to the wee hours, coffee, chocolate and consommé in cups.

Fathers took the greatest interest in the "Soirées" in their homes, and did the honors with distinguished courtesy, inviting the older gentlemen, who acted as escorts for their daughters, to take a glass of wine or champagne, but liquors were never offered to the young people, a custom that might well be adopted in our day generally. Ice Cream, Lemonade and Cakes, with a cup of Consommé or Café Noir, as the evening advanced, were considered sufficient refreshment.

Again, at these "Soirées" the simple "Eau Sucré" was served in the homes of families of most limited means. Lack of money has never debarred a Creole to the manor born from what is called the best society. These old-time "Soirées" still continue, though the "Eau Sucré" parties have passed away with changing conditions. . . .

Conclusion

The Creole women of Louisiana have long been the subject of song and story—their beauty, their accomplishments, their grace and dignity of character, united to singular vivacity and charm of temperament, no less than the difficulty that even the most aristocratic visitors to New Orleans encounter in receiving invitations to visit them in their homes, unless presented by some intimate mutual friend, who stands as sponsor for the stranger, have invested them with a romance and charm that attach to no other women in the United States. And these charming characteristics they will be found to have retained even when, as in many instances, they have been forced into rude stations of society and employments, by reason of the misfortunes that swept over their once princely and opulent homes. . . .

It is often said in New Orleans that no one dresses better and with more taste than the Creole women.

Even the woman of humble means will always appear neat and nice, well shod and well gloved, when she is seen on the street. . . .

The Creole mother eminently merits the term that was bestowed upon her long ago by a sweet Louisiana poet, and which has become a household word in the French Quarter, "Femme de l'Intérieure." These words indicate her life, that beautiful, interior, hidden home life, not given to solving the many vexing questions of woman suffrage and woman's rights, that agitate the minds of many of the sex in our day, for she is no aggressive competitor in the ranks and callings of men; she is indeed the "Femme de l'Intérieure," the queen of the hearth and home. She holds the home as woman's supreme sphere, her ideal realm, where Love is her throne, a throne reared in the hearts of her husband and children, and of which the attendant ministers are Purity, Truth and Fidelity. She is cultured, gracious, refined; as able to grace the parlor as she is capable of presiding in the kitchen; thoroughly conversant with all the leading topics of the day, with which she familiarizes herself, not that she may be regarded simply as a brilliant woman, not for the sake of argumentative discourse on public platforms, but for her own inner satisfaction and pleasure, and that she may be the fitting companion of her husband, the pleasing, intelligent confidant of her children, the wise and earnest director of their moral and intellectual aspirations and ambitions. And so her husband learns to look to his home during the weary working hours of the day as to a beacon star, for he knows that within bloom the fairest flowers of modest worth; the violet and the rose are there, the chrysanthemum and the lily, and those that bloom in

God's own garden shed not a sweeter fragrance than do these heavenly exotics around the hearth of the true Creole home. . . .

[Source: *The Picayune's Creole Cook Book*, 2nd ed. (New Orleans, 1901), pp. 5-6, 437-438, 440-441.]

Elizabeth Blackwell (1826-1910)

[*Elizabeth Blackwell was a pioneering woman physician. This letter, written in 1848, testifies to ideas that were in the air all during Kate Chopin's life.*]

. . . It is true, I look neither for praise nor blame in pursuing the path which I have chosen. With firm religious enthusiasm, no opinion of the world will move me. . . . My whole life is devoted unreservedly to the service of my sex. The study and practice of medicine is in my thought but one means to a great end, for which my very soul yearns with intensest passionate emotion, of which I have dreamed day and night, from my earliest childhood, for which I would offer up my life with triumphant thanksgiving, if martyrdom could secure that glorious end:—the true ennoblement of woman, the full harmonious development of her unknown nature, and the consequent redemption of the whole human race. "Earth waits for her queen." Every noble movement of the age, every prophecy of future glory, every throb of that great heart which is laboring throughout Christendom, call on woman with a voice of thunder, with the authority of a God, to listen to the mighty summons to awake from her guilty sleep, and rouse to glorious action to play her part in the great drama of the ages, and finish the work that man has begun.

Most fully do I respond to all the noble aspirations

that fill your letter. Women are feeble, narrow, frivolous at present: ignorant of their own capacities, and undeveloped in thought and feeling; and while they remain so, the great work of human regeneration must remain incomplete; humanity will continue to suffer, and cry in vain for deliverance, for woman has her work to do, and no one can accomplish it for her. She is bound to rise, to try her strength, to break her bonds;—not with noisy outcry, not with fighting or complaint; but with quiet strength, with gentle dignity, firmly, irresistibly, with a cool determination that never wavers, with a clear insight into her own capacities, let her do her duty, pursue her highest conviction of right, and firmly grasp whatever she is able to carry.

Much is said of the oppression woman suffers; man is reproached with being unjust, tyrannical, jealous. I do not so read human life. The exclusion and constraint woman suffers, is not the result of purposed injury or premeditated insult. It has arisen naturally, without violence, simply because woman has desired nothing more, has not felt the soul too large for the body. But when woman, with matured strength, with steady purpose, presents her lofty claim, all barriers will give way, and man will welcome, with a thrill of joy, the new birth of his sister spirit, the advent of his partner, his co-worker, in the great universe of being.

If the present arrangements of society will not admit of woman's free development, then society must be remodeled, and adapted to the great wants of all humanity. Our race is one, the interests of all are inseparably united, and harmonic freedom for the perfect growth of every human soul is the great want of our time. . . . I feel the responsibility of my position, and I shall endeavor, by wisdom of action, purity of motive, and unwavering steadiness of purpose, to justify the noble hope I have excited. To me the future is full of glorious promise, humanity is arousing to accomplish its grand destiny. . . .

[Source: Susan B. Anthony *et al.*, *History of Woman Suffrage*, 6 vols. (Indianapolis: Hollenbeck Press, 1881, 1902), 1: 90-92.]

Elizabeth Cady Stanton (1815-1902)

[*This address, arguing in favor of woman suffrage, was delivered to a Senate committee, on February 20, 1894. Subsequently it became known as the "Solitude of Self" speech. Stanton was one of the earliest, and most active, proponents of the woman suffrage amendment. She participated in the first women's rights convention at Seneca Falls, N.Y., in 1848 and spent a long life devoted largely to women's concerns.*]

The point I wish plainly to bring before you on this occasion is the individuality of each human soul—our Protestant idea, the right of individual conscience and judgment—our republican idea, individual citizenship. In discussing the rights of woman, we are to consider, first, what belongs to her as an individual, in a world of her own, the arbiter of her own destiny, an imaginary Robinson Crusoe with her woman Friday on a solitary island. Her rights under such circumstances are to use all her faculties for her own safety and happiness.

Secondly, if we consider her as a citizen, as a member of a great nation, she must have the same rights as all other members, according to the fundamental principles of our Government.

Thirdly, viewed as a woman, an equal factor in civilization, her rights and duties are still the same—individual happiness and development. . . . In discussing the sphere of man we do not decide his rights as an individual, as a citizen, as a man, by his duties as a father, a husband, a brother or a son, some of which he may never undertake. Moreover he would be better fitted for these very relations, and whatever special work he might choose to do to earn his bread, by the complete development of all his faculties as an individual. Just so with woman. The education which will fit her to discharge the duties in the largest sphere of human usefulness, will best fit her for whatever special work she may be compelled to do.

The isolation of every human soul and the necessity of self-dependence must give each individual the right to choose his own surroundings. The strongest reason for giving woman all the opportunities for higher education, for the full development of her faculties, her forces of mind and body; for giving her the most enlarged freedom of thought and action; a complete emancipation from all forms of bondage, of custom, dependence, superstition; from all the crippling influences of fear—is the solitude and personal responsibility of her own individual life. The strongest reason why we ask for woman a voice in the government under which she lives; in the religion she is asked to believe; equality in social life, where she is the chief factor; a place in the trades and professions, where she may earn her bread, is because of her birthright to self-sovereignty; because, as an individual, she must rely on herself. No matter how much women prefer to lean, to be protected and supported, nor how much men desire to have them do so, they must make the voyage of life alone, and for safety in an emergency they must know something of the laws of navigation. . . .

How the little courtesies of life on the surface of society, deemed so important from man towards woman, fade into utter insignificance in view of the deeper tragedies in which she must play her part alone, where no human aid is possible!

Nothing strengthens the judgment and quickens the conscience like individual responsibility. Nothing adds such dignity to character as the recognition of one's self-sovereignty; the right to an equal place, everywhere conceded—a place earned by personal merit, not an artificial attainment by inheritance, wealth, family and position. Conceding then that the responsibilities of life rest equally on man and woman, that their destiny is the same, they need the same preparation for time and eternity. The talk of sheltering women from the fierce storms of life is the sheerest mockery, for they beat on her from every point of the compass, just as they do on man, and with more fatal results, for he has been trained to protect himself, to resist, to conquer.

Whatever the theories may be of woman's dependence on man, in the supreme moments of her life he can not bear her burdens. . . . We see reason sufficient in the outer conditions of human beings for individual liberty and development, but when we consider the self-dependence of every human soul, we see the need of courage, judgment and the exercise of every faculty of mind and body, strengthened and developed by use, in woman as well as man. . . . We may have many friends, love, kindness, sympathy and charity to smooth our path-way in everyday life, but in the tragedies and triumphs of human experience each mortal stands alone.

But when all artificial trammels are removed, and women are recognized as individuals, responsible for their own environment, thoroughly educated for all positions in life they may be called to fill; with all the resources in themselves that liberal thought and broad culture can give; guided by their own conscience and judgments; trained to self-protection by a healthy development of the muscular system and skill in the use of weapons of defense, and stimulated to self-support by a knowledge of the business world and the pleasure that pecuniary independence must ever give; when women are trained in this way they will, in a measure, be fitted for those years of solitude that come to all, whether prepared or otherwise.

[Source: Anthony *et al.*, *History of Woman Suffrage*, 4: 189-91.]

Charlotte Perkins Gilman (1860-1935)

[*Charlotte Perkins Gilman was in her time the leading intellectual of the women's movement in the United States. She began her active career as writer and lecturer in the 1890s, and* Women and Economics, *published in 1898, is considered her most important work.*]

. . . When man began to feed and defend woman, she ceased proportionately to feed and defend herself. When he stood between her and her physical environment, she ceased proportionately to feel the influence of that environment and respond to it. When he became her immediate and all-important environment, she began proportionately to respond to this new influence, and to be modified accordingly. In a free state, speed was of as great advantage to the female as to the male, both in enabling her to catch prey and in preventing her from being caught by enemies; but, in her new condition, speed was a disadvantage. She was not allowed to do the catching, and it profited her to be caught by her new master. Free creatures, getting their own food and maintaining their own lives, develop an active capacity for attaining their ends. Parasitic creatures, whose living is obtained by the exertions of others, develop powers of absorption and of tenacity,—the powers by which they profit most. The human female was cut off from the direct action of natural selection, that mighty force which heretofore had acted on male and female alike with inexorable and beneficial effect, developing strength, developing skill, developing endurance, developing courage,—in a word, developing species. She now met the influence of natural selection acting indirectly through the male, and developing, of course, the faculties required to secure and obtain a hold on him. Needless to state that these faculties were those of sex-attraction, the one power that has made him cheerfully maintain, in what luxury he could, the being in whom he delighted. For many, many centuries she had no other hold, no other assurance of being fed. The young girl had a prospective value, and was maintained for what should follow; but the old woman, in more primitive times, had but a poor hold on life. She who could best please her lord was the favorite slave or favorite wife, and she obtained the best economic conditions.

With the growth of civilization, we have gradually crystallized into law the visible necessity for feeding the helpless female; and even old women are maintained by their male relatives with a comfortable assurance. But to this day—save, indeed, for the increasing army of women wage-earners, who are changing the face of the world by their steady advance toward economic independence—the personal profit of women bears but too close a relation to their power to win and hold the other sex. From the odalisque with the most bracelets to the débutante with the most bouquets, the relation still holds good, —women's economic profit comes through the power of sex-attraction.

When we confront this fact boldly and plainly in the open market of vice, we are sick with horror. When we see the same economic relation made permanent, established by law, sanctioned and sanctified by religion, covered with flowers and incense and all accumulated sentiment, we think it innocent, lovely, and right. The transient trade we think evil. The bargain for life we think good. But the biological effect remains the same. In both cases the female gets her food from the male by virtue of her sex-relationship to him. In both cases, perhaps even more in marriage because of its perfect acceptance of the situation, the female of genus homo, still living under natural law, is inexorably modified to sex in an increasing degree. . . .

To the young woman confronting life there is the same world beyond, there are the same human energies and human desires and ambition within. But all that she may wish to have, all that she may wish to do, must come through a single channel and a single choice. . . . All this human progress has been accomplished by men. Women have been left behind, outside, below, having no social relation whatever, merely the sex-relation, whereby they lived. Let us bear in mind that all the tender ties of family are ties of blood, of sex-relationship. A friend, a comrade, a partner,—this is a human relative. Father, mother, son, daughter, sister, brother, husband, wife,—these are sex-relatives. Blood is thicker than water, we say. True. But ties of blood are not those that ring the world with the succeeding waves of progressive religion, art, science, commerce, education, all that makes us human. Man is the human creature. Woman has been checked, starved, aborted in human growth; and the swelling forces of race-development have been driven back in each generation to work in her through sex-functions alone.

This is the way in which the sexuo-economic relation has operated in our species, checking race-development in half of us, and stimulating sex development in both.

[Source: Charlotte Perkins Gilman, *Women and Economics* (Boston: Small, Maynard, 1898), pp. 61-75, *passim*.]

FROM
Bayou Folk

LOVE ON THE BON-DIEU.

Upon the pleasant veranda of Père Antoine's cottage, that adjoined the church, a young girl had long been seated, awaiting his return. It was the eve of Easter Sunday, and since early afternoon the priest had been engaged in hearing the confessions of those who wished to make their Easters the following day. The girl did not seem impatient at his delay; on the contrary, it was very restful to her to lie back in the big chair she had found there, and peep through the thick curtain of vines at the people who occasionally passed along the village street.

She was slender, with a frailness that indicated lack of wholesome and plentiful nourishment. A pathetic, uneasy look was in her gray eyes, and even faintly stamped her features, which were fine and delicate. In lieu of a hat, a barège veil covered her light brown and abundant hair. She wore a coarse white cotton "josie," and a blue calico skirt that only half concealed her tattered shoes.

As she sat there, she held carefully in her lap a parcel of eggs securely fastened in a red bandana handkerchief.

Twice already a handsome, stalwart young man in quest of the priest had entered the yard, and penetrated to where she sat. At first they had exchanged the uncompromising "howdy" of strangers,

3

and nothing more. The second time, finding the priest still absent, he hesitated to go at once. Instead, he stood upon the step, and narrowing his brown eyes, gazed beyond the river, off towards the west, where a murky streak of mist was spreading across the sun.

"It look like mo' rain," he remarked, slowly and carelessly.

"We done had 'bout 'nough," she replied, in much the same tone.

"It's no chance to thin out the cotton," he went on.

"An' the Bon-Dieu," she resumed, "it's on'y to-day you can cross him on foot."

"You live yonda on the Bon-Dieu, *donc?*" he asked, looking at her for the first time since he had spoken.

"Yas, by Nid d'Hibout, m'sieur."

Instinctive courtesy held him from questioning her further. But he seated himself on the step, evidently determined to wait there for the priest. He said no more, but sat scanning critically the steps, the porch, and pillar beside him, from which he occasionally tore away little pieces of detached wood, where it was beginning to rot at its base.

A click at the side gate that communicated with the churchyard soon announced Père Antoine's return. He came hurriedly across the garden-path, between the tall, lusty rosebushes that lined either side of it, which were now fragrant with blossoms. His long, flapping cassock added something of height to his undersized, middle-aged figure, as did the skullcap which rested securely back on his head. He saw only the young man at first, who rose at his approach.

"Well, Azenor," he called cheerily in French, extending his hand. "How is this? I expected you all the week."

"Yes, monsieur; but I knew well what you wanted with me, and I was finishing the doors for Gros-Léon's new house;" saying which, he drew back, and indicated by a motion and look that some one was present who had a prior claim upon Père Antoine's attention.

"Ah, Lalie!" the priest exclaimed, when he had mounted to the porch, and saw her there behind the vines. "Have you been waiting here since you confessed? Surely an hour ago!"

"Yes, monsieur."

"You should rather have made some visits in the village, child."

"I am not acquainted with any one in the village," she returned.

The priest, as he spoke, had drawn a chair, and seated himself beside her, with his hands comfortably clasping his knees. He wanted to know how things were out on the bayou.

"And how is the grandmother?" he asked. "As cross and crabbed as ever? And with that"—he added reflectively—"good for ten years yet! I said only yesterday to Butrand—you know Butrand, he works on Le Blôt's Bon-Dieu place—'And that Madame Zidore: how is it with her, Butrand? I believe God has forgotten her here on earth.' 'It is n't that, your reverence,' said Butrand, 'but it's neither God nor the Devil that wants her!'" And Père Antoine laughed with a jovial frankness that took all sting of ill-nature from his very pointed remarks.

Lalie did not reply when he spoke of her grandmother; she only pressed her lips firmly together, and picked nervously at the red bandana.

"I have come to ask, Monsieur Antoine," she began, lower than she needed to speak—for Azenor had withdrawn at once to the far end of the porch—"to ask if you will give me a little scrap of paper—a piece of writing for Monsieur Chartrand at the store over there. I want new shoes and stockings for Easter, and I have brought eggs to trade for them. He says he is willing, yes, if he was sure I would bring more every week till the shoes are paid for."

With good-natured indifference, Père Antoine wrote the order that the girl desired. He was too familiar with distress to feel keenly for a girl who was able to buy Easter shoes and pay for them with eggs.

She went immediately away then, after shaking hands with the priest, and sending a quick glance of her pathetic eyes towards Azenor, who had turned when he heard her rise, and nodded when he caught the look. Through the vines he watched her cross the village street.

"How is it that you do not know Lalie, Azenor? You surely must have seen her pass your house often. It lies on her way to the Bon-Dieu."

"No, I don't know her; I have never seen her," the young man replied, as he seated himself—after the priest—and kept his eyes absently fixed on the store across the road, where he had seen her enter.

"She is the granddaughter of that Madame Izidore"—

"What! Ma'ame Zidore whom they drove off the island last winter?"

"Yes, yes. Well, you know, they say the old woman stole wood and things,—I don't know how true it is,—and destroyed people's property out of pure malice."

"And she lives now on the Bon-Dieu?"

"Yes, on Le Blôt's place, in a perfect wreck of a cabin. You see, she gets it for nothing; not a negro on the place but has refused to live in it."

"Surely, it can't be that old abandoned hovel near the swamp, that Michon occupied ages ago?"

"That is the one, the very one."

"And the girl lives there with that old wretch?" the young man marveled.

"Old wretch to be sure, Azenor. But what can you expect from a woman who never crosses the threshold of God's house—who even tried to hinder the child doing so as well? But I went to her. I said: 'See here, Madame Zidore,' —you know it's my way to handle such people without gloves,—'you may damn your soul if you choose,' I told her, 'that is a privilege which we all have; but none of us has a right to imperil the salvation of another. I want to see Lalie at mass hereafter on Sundays, or you will hear from me;' and I shook my stick under her nose. Since then the child has never missed a Sunday. But she is half starved, you can see that. You saw how shabby she is—how broken her shoes are? She is at Chartrand's now, trading for new ones with those eggs she brought, poor thing! There is no doubt of her being ill-treated. Butrand says he thinks Madame Zidore even beats the child. I don't know how true it is, for no power can make her utter a word against her grandmother."

Azenor, whose face was a kind and sensitive one, had paled with distress as the priest spoke; and now at these final words he quivered as though he felt the sting of a cruel blow upon his own flesh.

But no more was said of Lalie, for Père Antoine
drew the young man's attention to the carpenter-
work which he wished to intrust to him. When they
had talked the matter over in all its lengthy details,
Azenor mounted his horse and rode away.

A moment's gallop carried him outside the village.
Then came a half-mile strip along the river to cover.
Then the lane to enter, in which stood his dwelling
midway, upon a low, pleasant knoll.

As Azenor turned into the lane, he saw the figure
of Lalie far ahead of him. Somehow he had expected
to find her there, and he watched her again as he had
done through Père Antoine's vines. When she passed
his house, he wondered if she would turn to look at
it. But she did not. How could she know it was his?
Upon reaching it himself, he did not enter the yard,
but stood there motionless, his eyes always fastened
upon the girl's figure. He could not see, away off
there, how coarse her garments were. She seemed,
through the distance that divided them, as slim and
delicate as a flower-stalk. He stayed till she reached
the turn of the lane and disappeared into the woods.

.   .   .   .

Mass had not yet begun when Azenor tiptoed into
church on Easter morning. He did not take his place
with the congregation, but stood close to the holy-
water font, and watched the people who entered.

Almost every girl who passed him wore a white
mull, a dotted swiss, or a fresh-starched muslin at
least. They were bright with ribbons that hung from
their persons, and flowers that bedecked their hats.
Some carried fans and cambric handkerchiefs. Most

of them wore gloves, and were odorant of *poudre de riz* and nice toilet-waters; while all carried gay little baskets filled with Easter-eggs.

But there was one who came empty-handed, save for the worn prayer-book which she bore. It was Lalie, the veil upon her head, and wearing the blue print and cotton bodice which she had worn the day before.

He dipped his hand into the holy water when she came, and held it out to her, though he had not thought of doing this for the others. She touched his fingers with the tips of her own, making a slight inclination as she did so; and after a deep genuflection before the Blessed Sacrament, passed on to the side. He was not sure if she had known him. He knew she had not looked into his eyes, for he would have felt it.

He was angered against other young women who passed him, because of their flowers and ribbons, when she wore none. He himself did not care, but he feared she might, and watched her narrowly to see if she did.

But it was plain that Lalie did not care. Her face, as she seated herself, settled into the same restful lines it had worn yesterday, when she sat in Père Antoine's big chair. It seemed good to her to be there. Sometimes she looked up at the little colored panes through which the Easter sun was streaming; then at the flaming candles, like stars; or at the embowered figures of Joseph and Mary, flanking the central tabernacle which shrouded the risen Christ. Yet she liked just as well to watch the young girls in their spring freshness, or to sensuously inhale the mingled odor of flowers and incense that filled the temple.

Lalie was among the last to quit the church. When

she walked down the clean pathway that led from it to the road, she looked with pleased curiosity towards the groups of men and maidens who were gayly matching their Easter-eggs under the shade of the China-berry trees.

Azenor was among them, and when he saw her coming solitary down the path, he approached her and, with a smile, extended his hat, whose crown was quite lined with the pretty colored eggs.

"You mus' of forgot to bring aiggs," he said. "Take some o' mine."

"Non, merci," she replied, flushing and drawing back.

But he urged them anew upon her. Much pleased, then, she bent her pretty head over the hat, and was evidently puzzled to make a selection among so many that were beautiful.

He picked out one for her,—a pink one, dotted with white clover-leaves.

"Yere," he said, handing it to her, "I think this is the pretties'; an' it look' strong too. I'm sho' it will break all of the res'." And he playfully held out another, half-hidden in his fist, for her to try its strength upon. But she refused to. She would not risk the ruin of her pretty egg. Then she walked away, without once having noticed that the girls, whom Azenor had left, were looking curiously at her.

When he rejoined them, he was hardly prepared for their greeting; it startled him.

"How come you talk to that girl? She 's real canaille, her," was what one of them said to him.

"Who say' so? Who say she 's canaille? If it 's a man, I'll smash 'is head!" he exclaimed, livid. They all laughed merrily at this.

"An' if it's a lady, Azenor? W'at you goin' to do 'bout it?" asked another, quizzingly.

"T ain' no lady. No lady would say that 'bout a po' girl, w'at she don't even know."

He turned away, and emptying all his eggs into the hat of a little urchin who stood near, walked out of the churchyard. He did not stop to exchange another word with any one; neither with the men who stood all *endimanchés* before the stores, nor the women who were mounting upon horses and into vehicles, or walking in groups to their homes.

He took a short cut across the cotton-field that extended back of the town, and walking rapidly, soon reached his home. It was a pleasant house of few rooms and many windows, with fresh air blowing through from every side; his workshop was beside it. A broad strip of greensward, studded here and there with trees, sloped down to the road.

Azenor entered the kitchen, where an amiable old black woman was chopping onion and sage at a table.

"Tranquiline," he said abruptly, "they's a young girl goin' to pass yere afta a w'ile. She's got a blue dress an' w'ite josie on, an' a veil on her head. W'en you see her, I want you to go to the road an' make her res' there on the bench, an' ask her if she don't want a cup o' coffee. I saw her go to communion, me; so she did n't eat any breakfas'. Eve'ybody else f'om out o' town, that went to communion, got invited somew'ere another. It's enough to make a person sick to see such meanness."

"An' you want me ter go down to de gate, jis' so, an' ax 'er pineblank ef she wants some coffee?" asked the bewildered Tranquiline.

"I don't care if you ask her poin' blank o' not; but

you do like I say." Tranquiline was leaning over the gate when Lalie came along.

"Howdy," offered the woman.

"Howdy," the girl returned.

"Did you see a yalla calf wid black spots a t'arin' down de lane, missy?"

"Non; not yalla, an' not with black spot'. *Mais* I see one li'le w'ite calf tie by a rope, yonda 'roun' the ben'."

"Dat warn't hit. Dis heah one was yalla. I hope he done flung hisse'f down de bank an' broke his nake. Sarve 'im right! But whar you come f'om, chile? You look plum wo' out. Set down dah on dat bench, an' le' me fotch you a cup o' coffee."

Azenor had already in his eagerness arranged a tray, upon which was a smoking cup of *café au lait.* He had buttered and jellied generous slices of bread, and was searching wildly for something when Tranquiline reëntered.

"W'at become o' that half of chicken-pie, Tranquiline, that was yere in the *garde manger* yesterday?"

"W'at chicken-pie? W'at *garde manger?*" blustered the woman.

"Like we got mo' 'en one *garde manger* in the house, Tranquiline!"

"You jis' like ole Ma'ame Azenor use' to be, you is! You 'spec' chicken-pie gwine las' etarnal? W'en some'pin done sp'ilt, I flings it 'way. Dat's me—dat's Tranquiline!"

So Azenor resigned himself,—what else could he do?—and sent the tray, incomplete, as he fancied it, out to Lalie.

He trembled at thought of what he did; he, whose

nerves were usually as steady as some piece of steel mechanism.

Would it anger her if she suspected? Would it please her if she knew? Would she say this or that to Tranquiline? And would Tranquiline tell him truly what she said—how she looked?

As it was Sunday, Azenor did not work that afternoon. Instead, he took a book out under the trees, as he often did, and sat reading it, from the first sound of the Vesper bell, that came faintly across the fields, till the Angelus. All that time! He turned many a page, yet in the end did not know what he had read. With his pencil he had traced "Lalie" upon every margin, and was saying it softly to himself.

. . . .

Another Sunday Azenor saw Lalie at mass—and again. Once he walked with her and showed her the short cut across the cotton-field. She was very glad that day, and told him she was going to work—her grandmother said she might. She was going to hoe, up in the fields with Monsieur Le Blôt's hands. He entreated her not to; and when she asked his reason, he could not tell her, but turned and tore shyly and savagely at the elder-blossoms that grew along the fence.

Then they stopped where she was going to cross the fence from the field into the lane. He wanted to tell her that was his house which they could see not far away; but he did not dare to, since he had fed her there on the morning she was hungry.

"An' you say yo' gran'ma 's goin' to let you work? She keeps you f'om workin', *donc?*" He wanted to question her about her grandmother, and could think of no other way to begin.

"Po' ole grand'mère!" she answered. "I don' b'lieve she know mos' time w'at she 's doin'. Sometime she say' I aint no betta an' one nigga, an' she fo'ce me to work. Then she say she know I'm goin' be one canaille like maman, an' she make me set down still, like she would want to kill me if I would move. Her, she on'y want' to be out in the wood', day an' night, day an' night. She ain' got her right head, po' grand'mère. I know she ain't."

Lalie had spoken low and in jerks, as if every word gave her pain. Azenor could feel her distress as plainly as he saw it. He wanted to say something to her—to do something for her. But her mere presence paralyzed him into inactivity—except his pulses, that beat like hammers when he was with her. Such a poor, shabby little thing as she was, too!

"I'm goin' to wait yere nex' Sunday fo' you, Lalie," he said, when the fence was between them. And he thought he had said something very daring.

But the next Sunday she did not come. She was neither at the appointed place of meeting in the lane, nor was she at mass. Her absence—so unexpected—affected Azenor like a calamity. Late in the afternoon, when he could stand the trouble and bewilderment of it no longer, he went and leaned over Père Antoine's fence. The priest was picking the slugs from his roses on the other side.

"That young girl from the Bon-Dieu," said Azenor—"she was not at mass to-day. I suppose her grandmother has forgotten your warning."

"No," answered the priest. "The child is ill, I hear. Butrand tells me she has been ill for several days from overwork in the fields. I shall go out to-morrow to see about her. I would go to-day, if I could."

"The child is ill," was all Azenor heard or understood of Père Antoine's words. He turned and walked resolutely away, like one who determines suddenly upon action after meaningless hesitation.

He walked towards his home and past it, as if it were a spot that did not concern him. He went on down the lane and into the wood where he had seen Lalie disappear that day.

Here all was shadow, for the sun had dipped too low in the west to send a single ray through the dense foliage of the forest.

Now that he found himself on the way to Lalie's home, he strove to understand why he had not gone there before. He often visited other girls in the village and neighborhood,—why not have gone to her, as well? The answer lay too deep in his heart for him to be more than half-conscious of it. Fear had kept him,—dread to see her desolate life face to face. He did not know how he could bear it.

But now he was going to her at last. She was ill. He would stand upon that dismantled porch that he could just remember. Doubtless Ma'ame Zidore would come out to know his will, and he would tell her that Père Antoine had sent to inquire how Mamzelle Lalie was. No! Why drag in Père Antoine? He would simply stand boldly and say, "Ma'ame Zidore, I learn that Lalie is ill. I have come to know if it is true, and to see her, if I may."

When Azenor reached the cabin where Lalie dwelt, all sign of day had vanished. Dusk had fallen swiftly after the sunset. The moss that hung heavy from great live-oak branches was making fantastic silhouettes against the eastern sky that the big, round moon was beginning to light. Off in the swamp beyond the

bayou, hundreds of dismal voices were droning a
lullaby. Upon the hovel itself, a stillness like death
rested.

Oftener than once Azenor tapped upon the door,
which was closed as well as it could be, without
obtaining a reply. He finally approached one of the
small unglazed windows, in which coarse mosquito-
netting had been fastened, and looked into the room.

By the moonlight slanting in he could see Lalie
stretched upon a bed; but of Ma'ame Zidore there
was no sign. "Lalie!" he called softly. "Lalie!"
The girl slightly moved her head upon the pillow.
Then he boldly opened the door and entered.

Upon a wretched bed, over which was spread a
cover of patched calico, Lalie lay, her frail body only
half concealed by the single garment that was upon it.
One hand was plunged beneath her pillow; the other,
which was free, he touched. It was as hot as flame; so
was her head. He knelt sobbing upon the floor beside
her, and called her his love and his soul. He begged
her to speak a word to him, — to look at him. But she
only muttered disjointedly that the cotton was all
turning to ashes in the fields, and the blades of the
corn were in flames.

If he was choked with love and grief to see her so,
he was moved by anger as well; rage against himself,
against Père Antoine, against the people upon the
plantation and in the village, who had so abandoned a
helpless creature to misery and maybe death. Because
she had been silent—had not lifted her voice in
complaint—they believed she suffered no more
than she could bear.

But surely the people could not be utterly without
heart. There must be one somewhere with the spirit

of Christ. Père Antoine would tell him of such a one, and he would carry Lalie to her,—out of this atmosphere of death. He was in haste to be gone with her. He fancied every moment of delay was a fresh danger threatening her life.

He folded the rude bed-cover over Lalie's naked limbs, and lifted her in his arms. She made no resistance. She seemed only loath to withdraw her hand from beneath the pillow. When she did, he saw that she held lightly but firmly clasped in her encircling fingers the pretty Easter-egg he had given her! He uttered a low cry of exultation as the full significance of this came over him. If she had hung for hours upon his neck telling him that she loved him, he could not have known it more surely than by this sign. Azenor felt as if some mysterious bond had all at once drawn them heart to heart and made them one.

No need now to go from door to door begging admittance for her. She was his. She belonged to him. He knew now where her place was, whose roof must shelter her, and whose arms protect her.

So Azenor, with his loved one in his arms, walked through the forest, sure-footed as a panther. Once, as he walked, he could hear in the distance the weird chant which Ma'ame Zidore was crooning—to the moon, maybe—as she gathered her wood.

Once, where the water was trickling cool through rocks, he stopped to lave Lalie's hot cheeks and hands and forehead. He had not once touched his lips to her. But now, when a sudden great fear came upon him because she did not know him, instinctively he pressed his lips upon hers that were parched and burning. He held them there till hers were soft and pliant from the healthy moisture of his own.

Then she knew him. She did not tell him so, but her stiffened fingers relaxed their tense hold upon the Easter bauble. It fell to the ground as she twined her arm around his neck; and he understood.

.   .   .   .

"Stay close by her, Tranquiline," said Azenor, when he had laid Lalie upon his own couch at home. "I'm goin' for the doctor en' for Père Antoine. Not because she is goin' to die," he added hastily, seeing the awe that crept into the woman's face at mention of the priest. "She is goin' to live! Do you think I would let my wife die, Tranquiline?"

BEYOND THE BAYOU

The bayou curved like a crescent around the point of land on which La Folle's cabin stood. Between the stream and the hut lay a big abandoned field, where cattle were pastured when the bayou supplied them with water enough. Through the woods that spread back into unknown regions the woman had drawn an imaginary line, and past this circle she never stepped. This was the form of her only mania.

She was now a large, gaunt black woman, past thirty-five. Her real name was Jacqueline, but every one on the plantation called her La Folle, because in childhood she had been frightened literally "out of her senses," and had never wholly regained them.

It was when there had been skirmishing and sharpshooting all day in the woods. Evening was near when P'tit Maître, black with powder and crimson with blood, had staggered into the cabin of Jacqueline's mother, his pursuers close at his heels. The sight had stunned her childish reason.

She dwelt alone in her solitary cabin, for the rest of the quarters had long since been removed beyond her sight and knowledge. She had more physical strength than most men, and made her patch of cotton and corn and tobacco like the best of them. But of the world beyond the bayou she had long known nothing, save what her morbid fancy conceived.

People at Bellissime had grown used to her and her way, and they thought nothing of it. Even when "Old Mis'" died, they did not wonder that La Folle had not crossed the bayou, but had stood upon her side of it, wailing and lamenting.

P'tit Maître was now the owner of Bellissime. He was a middle-aged man, with a family of beautiful daughters about him, and a little son whom La Folle loved as if he had been her own. She called him Chéri, and so did every one else because she did.

None of the girls had ever been to her what Chéri was. They had each and all loved to be with her, and to listen to her wondrous stories of things that always happened "yonda, beyon' de bayou."

But none of them had stroked her black hand quite as Chéri did, nor rested their heads against her knee so confidingly, nor fallen asleep in her arms as he used to do. For Chéri hardly did such things now, since he had become the proud possessor of a gun, and had had his black curls cut off.

That summer—the summer Chéri gave La Folle two black curls tied with a knot of red ribbon—the water ran so low in the bayou that even the little children at Bellissime were able to cross it on foot, and the cattle were sent to pasture down by the river. La Folle was sorry when they were gone, for she loved these dumb companions well, and liked to feel that they were there, and to hear them browsing by night up to her own inclosure.

It was Saturday afternoon, when the fields were deserted. The men had flocked to a neighboring village to do their week's trading, and the women were occupied with household affairs,—La Folle as well as the others. It was then she mended and washed her handful of clothes, scoured her house, and did her baking.

In this last employment she never forgot Chéri. Today she had fashioned croquignoles of the most fantastic and alluring shapes for him. So when she saw the boy come trudging across the old field with his gleaming little new rifle on his shoulder, she called out gayly to him, "Chéri! Chéri!"

But Chéri did not need the summons, for he was coming straight to her. His pockets all bulged out with almonds and raisins and an orange that he had secured for her from the very fine dinner which had been given that day up at his father's house.

He was a sunny-faced youngster of ten. When he had emptied his pockets, La Folle patted his round red cheek, wiped his soiled hands on her apron, and smoothed his hair. Then she watched him as, with his cakes in his hand, he crossed her strip of cotton back of the cabin, and disappeared into the wood.

He had boasted of the things he was going to do with his gun out there.

"You think they got plenty deer in the wood, La Folle?" he had inquired, with the calculating air of an experienced hunter.

"*Non, non!*" the woman laughed. "Don't you look fo' no deer, Chéri. Dat's too big. But you bring La Folle one good fat squirrel fo' her dinner tomorrow, an' she goin' be satisfi'."

"One squirrel ain't a bite. I'll bring you mo' 'an one, La Folle," he had boasted pompously as he went away.

When the woman, an hour later, heard the report of the boy's rifle close to the wood's edge, she would

have thought nothing of it if a sharp cry of distress
had not followed the sound.

She withdrew her arms from the tub of suds in
which they had been plunged, dried them upon her
apron, and as quickly as her trembling limbs would
bear her, hurried to the spot whence the ominous
report had come.

It was as she feared. There she found Chéri
stretched upon the ground, with his rifle beside him.
He moaned piteously: —

"I'm dead, La Folle! I'm dead! I'm gone!"

"*Non, non!*" she exclaimed resolutely, as she knelt
beside him. "Put you' arm 'roun' La Folle's nake,
Chéri. Dat's nuttin'; dat goin' be nuttin'." She lifted
him in her powerful arms.

Chéri had carried his gun muzzle-downward. He
had stumbled—he did not know how. He only knew
that he had a ball lodged somewhere in his leg, and he
thought that his end was at hand. Now, with his head
upon the woman's shoulder, he moaned and wept
with pain and fright.

"Oh, La Folle! La Folle! it hurt so bad! I can' stan'
it, La Folle!"

"Don't cry, *mon bébé, mon bébé, mon Chéri!*"
the woman spoke soothingly as she covered the
ground with long strides. "La Folle goin' mine you;
Doctor Bonfils goin' come make *mon Chéri* well
agin."

She had reached the abandoned field. As she
crossed it with her precious burden, she looked
constantly and restlessly from side to side. A terrible
fear was upon her,—the fear of the world beyond the
bayou, the morbid and insane dread she had been
under since childhood.

When she was at the bayou's edge she stood there, and shouted for help as if a life depended upon it:—

"Oh, P'tit Maître! P'tit Maître! Venez donc! Au secours! Au secours!"

No voice responded. Chéri's hot tears were scalding her neck. She called for each and every one upon the place, and still no answer came.

She shouted, she wailed; but whether her voice remained unheard or unheeded, no reply came to her frenzied cries. And all the while Chéri moaned and wept and entreated to be taken home to his mother.

La Folle gave a last despairing look around her. Extreme terror was upon her. She clasped the child close against her breast, where he could feel her heart beat like a muffled hammer. Then shutting her eyes, she ran suddenly down the shallow bank of the bayou, and never stopped till she had climbed the opposite shore.

She stood there quivering an instant as she opened her eyes. Then she plunged into the footpath through the trees.

She spoke no more to Chéri, but muttered constantly, "Bon Dieu, ayez pitié La Folle! Bon Dieu, ayez pitié moi!"

Instinct seemed to guide her. When the pathway spread clear and smooth enough before her, she again closed her eyes tightly against the sight of that unknown and terrifying world.

A child, playing in some weeds, caught sight of her as she neared the quarters. The little one uttered a cry of dismay.

"La Folle!" she screamed, in her piercing treble. "La Folle done cross de bayer!"

Quickly the cry passed down the line of cabins.

"Yonda, La Folle done cross de bayou!"

Children, old men, old women, young ones with infants in their arms, flocked to doors and windows to see this awe-inspiring spectacle. Most of them shuddered with superstitious dread of what it might portend. "She totin' Chéri!" some of them shouted.

Some of the more daring gathered about her, and followed at her heels, only to fall back with new terror when she turned her distorted face upon them. Her eyes were bloodshot and the saliva had gathered in a white foam on her black lips.

Some one had run ahead of her to where P'tit Maître sat with his family and guests upon the gallery.

"P'tit Maître! La Folle done cross de bayou! Look her! Look her yonda totin' Chéri!" This startling intimation was the first which they had of the woman's approach.

She was now near at hand. She walked with long strides. Her eyes were fixed desperately before her, and she breathed heavily, as a tired ox.

At the foot of the stairway, which she could not have mounted, she laid the boy in his father's arms. Then the world that had looked red to La Folle suddenly turned black—like that day she had seen powder and blood.

She reeled for an instant. Before a sustaining arm could reach her, she fell heavily to the ground.

When La Folle regained consciousness, she was at home again, in her own cabin and upon her own bed. The moon rays, streaming in through the open door and windows, gave what light was needed to the old black mammy who stood at the table concocting a tisane of fragrant herbs. It was very late.

Others who had come, and found that the stupor

clung to her, had gone again. P'tit Maître had been there, and with him Doctor Bonfils, who said that La Folle might die.

But death had passed her by. The voice was very clear and steady with which she spoke to Tante Lizette, brewing her tisane there in a corner.

"Ef you will give me one good drink tisane, Tante Lizette, I b'lieve I'm goin' sleep, me."

And she did sleep; so soundly, so healthfully, that old Lizette without compunction stole softly away, to creep back through the moonlit fields to her own cabin in the new quarters.

The first touch of the cool gray morning awoke La Folle. She arose, calmly, as if no tempest had shaken and threatened her existence but yesterday.

She donned her new blue cottonade and white apron, for she remembered that this was Sunday. When she had made for herself a cup of strong black coffee, and drunk it with relish, she quitted the cabin and walked across the old familiar field to the bayou's edge again.

She did not stop there as she had always done before, but crossed with a long, steady stride as if she had done this all her life.

When she had made her way through the brush and scrub cottonwood trees that lined the opposite bank, she found herself upon the border of a field where the white, bursting cotton, with the dew upon it, gleamed for acres and acres like frosted silver in the early dawn.

La Folle drew a long, deep breath as she gazed across the country. She walked slowly and uncertainly, like one who hardly knows how, looking about her as she went.

The cabins, that yesterday had sent a clamor of voices to pursue her, were quiet now. No one was yet astir at Bellissime. Only the birds that darted here and there from hedges were awake, and singing their matins.

When La Folle came to the broad stretch of velvety lawn that surrounded the house, she moved slowly and with delight over the springy turf, that was delicious beneath her tread.

She stopped to find whence came those perfumes that were assailing her senses with memories from a time far gone.

There they were, stealing up to her from the thousand blue violets that peeped out from green, luxuriant beds. There they were, showering down from the big waxen bells of the magnolias far above her head, and from the jessamine clumps around her.

There were roses, too, without number. To right and left palms spread in broad and graceful curves. It all looked like enchantment beneath the sparkling sheen of dew.

When La Folle had slowly and cautiously mounted the many steps that led up to the veranda, she turned to look back at the perilous ascent she had made. Then she caught sight of the river, bending like a silver bow at the foot of Bellissime. Exultation possessed her soul.

La Folle rapped softly upon a door near at hand. Chéri's mother soon cautiously opened it. Quickly and cleverly she dissembled the astonishment she felt at seeing La Folle.

"Ah, La Folle! Is it you, so early?"

"*Oui*, madame. I come ax how my po' li'le Chéri to, 's mo'nin'."

"He is feeling easier, thank you, La Folle. Dr. Bonfils says it will be nothing serious. He's sleeping now. Will you come back when he awakes?"

"*Non*, madame. I'm goin' wait yair tell Chéri wake up." La Folle seated herself upon the topmost step of the veranda.

A look of wonder and deep content crept into her face as she watched for the first time the sun rise upon the new, the beautiful world beyond the bayou.

A VISIT TO AVOYELLES

Every one who came up from Avoyelles had the same story to tell of Mentine. *Cher Maître!* but she was changed. And there were babies, more than she could well manage; as good as four already. Jules was not kind except to himself. They seldom went to church, and never anywhere upon a visit. They lived as poorly as pine-woods people. Doudouce had heard the story often, the last time no later than that morning.

"Ho-a!" he shouted to his mule plumb in the middle of the cotton row. He had staggered along behind the plow since early morning, and of a sudden he felt he had had enough of it. He mounted the mule and rode away to the stable, leaving the plow with its polished blade thrust deep in the red Cane River soil. His head felt like a windmill with the recollections and sudden intentions that had crowded it and were whirling through his brain since he had heard the last story about Mentine.

He knew well enough Mentine would have married him seven years ago had not Jules Trodon come up from Avoyelles and captivated her with his handsome eyes and pleasant speech. Doudouce was resigned then, for he held Mentine's happiness above his own. But now she was suffering in a hopeless, common, exasperating way for the small comforts of life. People had told him so. And somehow, today, he could not stand the knowledge passively. He felt he must see those things they spoke of with his own eyes. He must strive to help her and her children if it were possible.

Doudouce could not sleep that night. He lay with wakeful eyes watching the moonlight creep across the bare floor of his room; listening to sounds that seemed unfamiliar and weird down among the rushes along the bayou. But towards morning he saw Mentine as he had seen her last in her white wedding gown and veil. She looked at him with appealing eyes and held out her arms for protection—for rescue, it seemed to him. That dream determined him. The following day Doudouce started for Avoyelles.

Jules Trodon's home lay a mile or two from Marksville. It consisted of three rooms strung in a row and opening upon a narrow gallery. The whole wore an aspect of poverty and dilapidation that summer day, towards noon, when Doudouce approached it. His presence outside the gate aroused the frantic barking of dogs that dashed down the steps as if to attack him. Two little brown barefooted children, a boy and girl, stood upon the gallery staring stupidly at him. "Call off you' dogs," he requested; but they only continued to stare.

"Down, Pluto! down, Achille!" cried the shrill voice of a woman who emerged from the house, holding upon her arm a delicate baby of a year or two. There was only an instant of unrecognition.

"*Mais* Doudouce, that ent you, *comment!* Well, if any one would tole me this mornin'! Git a chair, 'Tit Jules. That's Mista Doudouce, f'om 'way yonda Natchitoches w'ere yo' maman use' to live. *Mais*, you ent change'; you' lookin' well, Doudouce.''

He shook hands in a slow, undemonstrative way, and seated himself clumsily upon the hide-bottomed chair, laying his broadrimmed felt hat upon the floor beside him. He was very uncomfortable in the cloth Sunday coat which he wore.

"I had business that call' me to Marksville," he began, "an' I say to myse'f, '*Tiens*, you can't pass by without tell' 'em all howdy.' "

"*Par exemple!* w'at Jules would said to that! *Mais*, you' lookin' well; you ent change', Doudouce.''

"An' you' lookin' well, Mentine. Jis' the same Mentine.'' He regretted that he lacked talent to make the lie bolder.

She moved a little uneasily, and felt upon her shoulder for a pin with which to fasten the front of her old gown where it lacked a button. She had kept the baby in her lap. Doudouce was wondering miserably if he would have known her outside her home. He would have known her sweet, cheerful brown eyes, that were not changed; but her figure, that had looked so trim in the wedding gown, was sadly misshapen. She was brown, with skin like parchment, and piteously thin. There were lines, some deep as if old age had cut them, about the eyes and mouth.

"An' how you lef' 'em all, yonda?" she asked, in a high voice that had grown shrill from screaming at children and dogs.

"They all well. It 's mightly li'le sickness in the country this yea'. But they been lookin' fo' you up yonda, straight along, Mentine.''

"Don't talk, Doudouce, it's no chance; with that po' wo' out piece o' lan' w'at Jules got. He say, anotha yea' like that, he 's goin' sell out, him."

The children were clutching her on either side, their persistent gaze always fastened upon Doudouce. He tried without avail to make friends with them. Then Jules came home from the field, riding the mule with which he had worked, and which he fastened outside the gate.

"Yere 's Doudouce f'om Natchitoches, Jules," called out Mentine, "he stop' to tell us howdy, *en passant.*" The husband mounted to the gallery and the two men shook hands, Doudouce listlessly, as he had done with Mentine, Jules with some bluster and show of cordiality.

"Well, you' a lucky man, you," he exclaimed with his swagger air, "able to broad like that, *encore!* You couldn't do that if you had half a dozen mouth' to feed, *allez!*"

"Non, j'te garantis!" agreed Mentine, with a loud laugh. Doudouce winced, as he had done the instant before at Jules's heartless implication. This husband of Mentine surely had not changed during the seven years, except to grow broader, stronger, handsomer. But Doudouce did not tell him so.

After the midday dinner of boiled salt pork, corn bread and molasses, there was nothing for Doudouce but to take his leave when Jules did.

At the gate, the little boy was discovered in dangerous proximity to the mule's heels, and was properly screamed at and rebuked.

"I reckon he likes hosses," Doudouce remarked. "He take' afta you, Mentine. I got a li'le pony yonda home," he said, addressing the child, "w'at ent no use to me. I'm goin' sen' 'im down to you. He 's a good, tough li'le mustang. You jis' can let 'im eat grass an' feed 'im a han'ful o' co'n, once a w'ile. An' he 's gentle, yes. You an' yo' ma can ride 'im to church, Sundays. *Hein!* you want?"

"W'at you say, Jules?" demanded the father. "W'at you say?" echoed Mentine, who was balancing the baby across the gate. " 'Tit sauvage, va!"

Doudouce shook hands all around, even with the baby, and walked off in the opposite direction to Jules, who had mounted the mule. He was bewildered. He stumbled over the rough ground because of tears that were blinding him, and that he had held in check for the past hour.

He had loved Mentine long ago, when she was young and attractive, and he found that he loved her still. He had tried to put all disturbing thought of her away, on that wedding day, and he supposed he had succeeded. But he loved her now as he never had. Because she was no longer beautiful, he loved her. Because the delicate bloom of her existence had been rudely brushed away, because she was in a manner fallen, because she was Mentine, he loved her, fiercely, as a mother loves an afflicted child. He would have liked to thrust that man aside, and gather up her and her children, and hold them and keep them as long as life lasted.

After a moment or two Doudouce looked back at Mentine, standing at the gate with her baby. But her face was turned away from him. She was gazing after her husband, who went in the direction of the field.

LA BELLE ZORAÏDE

The summer night was hot and still; not a ripple of air swept over the marais. Yonder, across Bayou St. John, lights twinkled here and there in the darkness, and in the dark sky above a few stars were blinking. A lugger that had come out of the lake was moving with slow, lazy motion down the bayou. A man in the boat was singing a song.

The notes of the song came faintly to the ears of old Manna Loulou, herself as black as the night, who had gone out upon the gallery to open the shutters wide.

Something in the refrain reminded the woman of an old, half-forgotten Creole romance, and she began to sing it low to herself while she threw the shutters open:—

> "Lisett' to kité la plaine,
>   Mo perdi bonhair à moué;
>   Ziés à moué semblé fontaine,
>   Dépi mo pa miré toué."

And then this old song, a lover's lament for the loss of his mistress, floating into her memory, brought with it the story she would tell to Madame, who lay in her sumptuous mahogany bed, waiting to be fanned and put to sleep to the sound of one of Manna Loulou's stories. The old negress had already bathed

her mistress's pretty white feet and kissed them
lovingly, one, then the other. She had brushed her
mistress's beautiful hair, that was as soft and shining
as satin, and was the color of Madame's wedding-ring.
Now, when she reëntered the room, she moved softly
toward the bed, and seating herself there began gently
to fan Madame Delisle.

Manna Loulou was not always ready with her
story, for Madame would hear none but those which
were true. But tonight the story was all there in
Manna Loulou's head—the story of la belle
Zoraïde—and she told it to her mistress in the soft
Creole patois, whose music and charm no English
words can convey.

"La belle Zoraïde had eyes that were so dusky, so
beautiful, that any man who gazed too long into their
depths was sure to lose his head, and even his heart
sometimes. Her soft, smooth skin was the color of
café-au-lait. As for her elegant manners, her *svelte*
and graceful figure, they were the envy of half the
ladies who visited her mistress, Madame Delarivière.

"No wonder Zoraïde was as charming and as dainty
as the finest lady of la rue Royale: from a toddling
thing she had been brought up at her mistress's side;
her fingers had never done rougher work than sewing
a fine muslin seam; and she even had her own little
black servant to wait upon her. Madame, who was her
godmother as well as her mistress, would often
say to her:—

" 'Remember, Zoraïde, when you are ready to
marry, it must be in a way to do honor to your
bringing up. It will be at the Cathedral. Your wedding
gown, your corbeille, all will be of the best; I shall see
to that myself. You know, M'sieur Ambroise is ready

whenever you say the word, and his master is willing to do as much for him as I shall do for you. It is a union that will please me in every way.'

"M'sieur Ambroise was then the body servant of Doctor Langlé. La belle Zoraïde detested the little mulatto, with his shining whiskers like a white man's, and his small eyes, that were cruel and false as a snake's. She would cast down her own mischievous eyes, and say:

"'Ah, nénaine, I am so happy, so contented here at your side just as I am. I don't want to marry now; next year, perhaps, or the next.' And Madame would smile indulgently and remind Zoraïde that a woman's charms are not everlasting.

"But the truth of the matter was, Zoraïde had seen le beau Mézor dance the Bamboula in Congo Square. That was a sight to hold one rooted to the ground. Mézor was as straight as a cypress tree and as proud looking as a king. His body, bare to the waist, was like a column of ebony and it glistened like oil.

"Poor Zoraïde's heart grew sick in her bosom with love for le beau Mézor from the moment she saw the fierce gleam of his eye, lighted by the inspiring strains of the Bamboula, and beheld the stately movements of his splendid body swaying and quivering through the figures of the dance.

"But when she knew him later, and he came near her to speak with her, all the fierceness was gone out of his eyes, and she saw only kindness in them and heard only gentleness in his voice, for love had taken possession of him also, and Zoraïde was more distracted than ever. When Mézor was not dancing Bamboula in Congo Square, he was hoeing sugar-cane, barefooted and half naked, in his master's field outside of the city. Doctor Langlé was his master as well as M'sieur Ambroise's.

"One day, when Zoraïde kneeled before her mistress, drawing on Madame's silken stockings, that were of the finest, she said:

"'Nénaine, you have spoken to me often of marrying. Now, at last, I have chosen a husband, but it is not M'sieur Ambroise; it is le beau Mézor that I want and no other.' And Zoraïde hid her face in her hands when she said that, for she guessed, rightly enough, that her mistress would be very angry. And, indeed, Madame Delarivière was at first speechless with rage. When she finally spoke it was only to gasp out, exasperated:

"'That negro! that negro! Bon Dieu Seigneur, but this is too much!'

"'Am I white, nénaine?' pleaded Zoraïde.

"'You white! *Malheureuse!* You deserve to have the lash laid upon you like any other slave; you have proven yourself no better than the worst.'

"'I am not white,' persisted Zoraïde, respectfully and gently. 'Doctor Langlé gives me his slave to marry, but he would not give me his son. Then, since I am not white, let me have from out of my own race the one whom my heart has chosen.'

"However, you may well believe that Madame would not hear to that. Zoraïde was forbidden to speak to Mézor, and Mézor was cautioned against seeing Zoraïde again. But you know how the negroes are, Ma'zélle Titite," added Manna Loulou, smiling a little sadly. "There is no mistress, no master, no king nor priest who can hinder them from loving when they will. And these two found ways and means.

"When months had passed by, Zoraïde, who had

grown unlike herself—sober and preoccupied—said again to her mistress:—

" 'Nénaine, you would not let me have Mézor for my husband; but I have disobeyed you, I have sinned. Kill me if you wish, nénaine; forgive me if you will; but when I heard le beau Mézor say to me, "Zoraïde, mo l'aime toi," I could have died, but I could not have helped loving him.'

"This time Madame Delarivière was so actually pained, so wounded at hearing Zoraïde's confession, that there was no place left in her heart for anger. She could utter only confused reproaches. But she was a woman of action rather than of words, and she acted promptly. Her first step was to induce Doctor Langlé to sell Mézor. Doctor Langlé, who was a widower, had long wanted to marry Madame Delarivière, and he would willingly have walked on all fours at noon through the Place d'Armes if she wanted him to. Naturally he lost no time in disposing of le beau Mézor, who was sold away into Georgia, or the Carolinas, or one of those distant countries far away, where he would no longer hear his Creole tongue spoken, nor dance Calinda, nor hold la belle Zoraïde in his arms.

"The poor thing was heartbroken when Mézor was sent away from her, but she took comfort and hope in the thought of her baby that she would soon be able to clasp to her breast.

"La belle Zoraïde's sorrows had now begun in earnest. Not only sorrows but sufferings, and with the anguish of maternity came the shadow of death. But there is no agony that a mother will not forget when she holds her first-born to her heart, and presses her lips upon the baby flesh that is her own, yet far more precious than her own.

"So, instinctively, when Zoraïde came out of the awful shadow she gazed questioningly about her and felt with her trembling hands upon either side of her. 'Où li, mo piti a moin? where is my little one?' she asked imploringly. Madame who was there and the nurse who was there both told her in turn, 'To piti à toi, li mouri' ('Your little one is dead'), which was a wicked falsehood that must have caused the angels in heaven to weep. For the baby was living and well and strong. It had at once been removed from its mother's side, to be sent away to Madame's plantation, far up the coast. Zoraïde could only moan in reply, 'Li mouri, li mouri,' and she turned her face to the wall.

"Madame had hoped, in thus depriving Zoraïde of her child, to have her young waiting-maid again at her side free, happy, and beautiful as of old. But there was a more powerful will than Madame's at work—the will of the good God, who had already designed that Zoraïde should grieve with a sorrow that was never more to be lifted in this world. La belle Zoraïde was no more. In her stead was a sad-eyed woman who mourned night and day for her baby. 'Li mouri, li mouri,' she would sigh over and over again to those about her, and to herself when others grew weary of her complaint.

"Yet, in spite of all, M'sieur Ambroise was still in the notion to marry her. A sad wife or a merry one was all the same to him so long as that wife was Zoraïde. And she seemed to consent, or rather submit, to the approaching marriage as through nothing mattered any longer in this world.

"One day, a black servant entered a little noisily the room in which Zoraïde sat sewing. With a look of strange and vacuous happiness upon her face, Zoraïde arose hastily. 'Hush, hush,' she whispered, lifting a warning finger, 'my little one is asleep; you must not awaken her.'

"Upon the bed was a senseless bundle of rags shaped like an infant in swaddling clothes. Over this dummy the woman had drawn the mosquito bar, and she was sitting contentedly beside it. In short, from that day Zoraïde was demented. Night nor day did she lose sight of the doll that lay in her bed or in her arms.

"And now was Madame stung with sorrow and remorse at seeing this terrible affliction that had befallen her dear Zoraïde. Consulting with Doctor Langlé, they decided to bring back to the mother the real baby of flesh and blood that was now toddling about, and kicking its heels in the dust yonder upon the plantation.

"It was Madame herself who led the pretty, tiny little 'griffe' girl to her mother. Zoraïde was sitting upon a stone bench in the courtyard, listening to the soft splashing of the fountain, and watching the fitful shadows of the palm leaves upon the broad, white flagging.

"'Here,' said Madame, approaching, 'here, my poor dear Zoraïde, is your own little child. Keep her; she is yours. No one will ever take her from you again.'

"Zoraïde looked with sullen suspicion upon her mistress and the child before her. Reaching out a hand she thrust the little one mistrustfully away from her. With the other hand she clasped the rag bundle fiercely to her breast; for she suspected a plot to deprive her of it.

"Nor could she ever be induced to let her own child approach her; and finally the little one was sent back to the plantation, where she was never to know the love of mother or father.

"And now this is the end of Zoraïde's story. She was never known again as la belle Zoraïde, but ever after as Zoraïde la folle, whom no one ever wanted to marry—not even M'sieur Ambroise. She lived to be an old woman, whom some people pitied and others laughed at—always clasping her bundle of rags—her 'piti.'

"Are you asleep, Ma'zélle Titite?"

"No, I am not asleep; I was thinking. Ah, the poor little one, Man Loulou, the poor little one! better had she died!"

But this is the way Madame Delisle and Manna Loulou really talked to each other:

"Vou pré droumi, Ma'zélle Titite?"

"Non, pa pré droumi; mo yapré zongler. Ah, la pauv' piti, Man Loulou. La pauv' piti! Mieux li mouri!"

IN SABINE.

The sight of a human habitation, even if it was a rude log cabin with a mud chimney at one end, was a very gratifying one to Grégoire.

He had come out of Natchitoches parish, and had been riding a great part of the day through the big lonesome parish of Sabine. He was not following the regular Texas road, but, led by his erratic fancy, was pushing toward the Sabine River by circuitous paths through the rolling pine forests.

As he approached the cabin in the clearing, he discerned behind a palisade of pine saplings an old negro man chopping wood.

"Howdy, Uncle," called out the young fellow, reining his horse. The negro looked up in blank amazement at so unexpected an apparition, but he only answered: "How you do, suh," accompanying his speech by a series of polite nods.

"Who lives yere?"

"Hit's Mas' Bud Aiken w'at live' heah, suh."

"Well, if Mr. Bud Aiken c'n affo'd to hire a man to chop his wood, I reckon he won't grudge me a bite o' suppa an' a couple hours' res' on his gall'ry. W'at you say, ole man?"

"I say dit Mas' Bud Aiken don't hires me to chop 'ood. Ef I don't chop dis heah, his wife got it to do. Dat w'y I chops 'ood, suh. Go right 'long in, suh; you

41

g'ine fine Mas' Bud some'eres roun', ef he ain't drunk
an gone to bed."

Grégoire, glad to stretch his legs, dismounted, and
led his horse into the small inclosure which
surrounded the cabin. An unkempt, vicious-looking
little Texas pony stopped nibbling the stubble there
to look maliciously at him and his fine sleek horse, as
they passed by. Back of the hut, and running plumb
up against the pine wood, was a small, ragged
specimen of a cotton-field.

Grégoire was rather undersized, with a square,
well-knit figure, upon which his clothes sat well and
easily. His corduroy trousers were thrust into the legs
of his boots; he wore a blue flannel shirt; his coat was
thrown across the saddle. In his keen black eyes had
come a puzzled expression, and he tugged thought-
fully at the brown moustache that lightly shaded his
upper lip.

He was trying to recall when and under what
circumstances he had before heard the name of Bud
Aiken. But Bud Aiken himself saved Grégoire the
trouble of further speculation on the subject. He
appeared suddenly in the small doorway, which his
big body quite filled; and then Grégoire remembered.
This was the disreputable so-called "Texan" who a
year ago had run away with and married Baptiste
Choupic's pretty daughter, 'Tite Reine, yonder on
Bayou Pierre, in Natchitoches parish. A vivid picture
of the girl as he remembered her appeared to him: her
trim rounded figure; her piquant face with its saucy
black coquettish eyes; her little exacting, imperious
ways that had obtained for her the nickname of 'Tite
Reine, little queen. Grégoire had known her at the

'Cadian balls that he sometimes had the hardihood to
attend.

These pleasing recollections of 'Tite Reine lent a
warmth that might otherwise have been lacking to
Grégoire's manner, when he greeted her husband.

"I hope I fine you well, Mr. Aiken," he exclaimed
cordially, as he approached and extended his hand.

"You find me damn' porely, suh; but you've got
the better o' me, ef I may so say." He was a big
good-looking brute, with a straw-colored "horse-
shoe" moustache quite concealing his mouth, and a
several days' growth of stubble on his rugged face. He
was fond of reiterating that women's admiration had
wrecked his life, quite forgetting to mention the
early and sustained influence of "Pike's Magnolia"
and other brands, and wholly ignoring certain inborn
propensities capable of wrecking unaided any
ordinary existence. He had been lying down, and
looked frouzy and half asleep.

"Ef I may so say, you 've got the better o' me, Mr.
—er"—

"Santien, Grégoire Santien. I have the pleasure o'
knowin' the lady you married, suh; an' I think I met
you befo',— somew'ere o' 'nother," Grégoire added
vaguely.

"Oh," drawled Aiken, waking up, "one o' them
Red River Sanchuns!" and his face brightened at the
prospect before him of enjoying the society of one
of the Santien boys. "Mortimer!" he called in ringing
chest tones worthy of a commander at the head of his
troop. The negro had rested his axe and appeared
to be listening to their talk, though he was too far to
hear what they said.

"Mortimer, come along here an' take my frien' Mr.

Sanchun's hoss. Git a move thar, git a move!" Then
turning toward the entrance of the cabin he called
back through the open door: "Rain!" it was his way
of pronouncing 'Tite Reine's name. "Rain!" he cried
again peremptorily; and turning to Grégoire: "she 's
'tendin' to some or other housekeepin' truck." 'Tite
Reine was back in the yard feeding the solitary pig
which they owned, and which Aiken had mysterious-
ly driven up a few days before, saying he had bought
it at Many.

Grégoire could hear her calling out as she
approached: "I'm comin', Bud. Yere I come. W'at you
want, Bud?" breathlessly, as she appeared in the door
frame and looked out upon the narrow sloping gallery
where stood the two men. She seemed to Grégoire to
have changed a good deal. She was thinner, and her
eyes were larger, with an alert, uneasy look in them;
he fancied the startled expression came from seeing
him there unexpectedly. She wore cleanly homespun
garments, the same she had brought with her from
Bayou Pierre; but her shoes were in shreds. She
uttered only a low, smothered exclamation when she
saw Grégoire.

"Well, is that all you got to say to my frien' Mr.
Sanchun? That 's the way with them Cajuns," Aiken
offered apologetically to his guest; "ain't got sense
enough to know a white man when they see one."
Grégoire took her hand.

"I'm mighty glad to see you, 'Tite Reine," he said
from his heart. She had for some reason been unable
to speak; now she panted somewhat hysterically:—

"You mus' escuse me, Mista Grégoire. It's the truth
I did n' know you firs', stan'in' up there." A deep
flush had supplanted the former pallor of her face,

and her eyes shone with tears and ill-concealed excitement.

"I thought you all lived yonda in Grant," remarked Grégoire carelessly, making talk for the purpose of diverting Aiken's attention away from his wife's evident embarrassment, which he himself was at a loss to understand.

"Why, we did live a right smart while in Grant; but Grant ain't no parish to make a livin' in. Then I tried Winn and Caddo a spell; they was n't no better. But I tell you, suh, Sabine's a damn' sight worse than any of 'em. Why, a man can't git a drink o' whiskey here without going out of the parish fer it, or across into Texas. I'm fixin' to sell out an' try Vernon."

Bud Aiken's household belongings surely would not count for much in the contemplated "selling out." The one room that constituted his home was extremely bare of furnishing,—a cheap bed, a pine table, and a few chairs, that was all. On a rough shelf were some paper parcels representing the larder. The mud daubing had fallen out here and there from between the logs of the cabin; and into the largest of these apertures had been thrust pieces of ragged bagging and wisps of cotton. A tin basin outside on the gallery offered the only bathing facilities to be seen. Notwithstanding these drawbacks, Grégoire announced his intention of passing the night with Aiken.

"I'm jus' goin' to ask the privilege o' layin' down yere on yo' gall'ry to-night, Mr. Aiken. My hoss ain't in firs'-class trim; an' a night's res' ain't goin' to hurt him o' me either." He had begun by declaring his intention of pushing on across the Sabine, but an imploring look from 'Tite Reine's eyes had stayed the

words upon his lips. Never had he seen in a woman's
eyes a look of such heartbroken entreaty. He resolved on the instant to know the meaning of it
before setting foot on Texas soil. Grégoire had never
learned to steel his heart against a woman's eyes, no
matter what language they spoke.

An old patchwork quilt folded double and a moss
pillow which 'Tite Reine gave him out on the gallery
made a bed that was, after all, not too uncomfortable
for a young fellow of rugged habits.

Grégoire slept quite soundly after he laid down
upon his improvised bed at nine o'clock. He was
awakened toward the middle of the night by some
one gently shaking him. It was 'Tite Reine stooping
over him; he could see her plainly, for the moon was
shining. She had not removed the clothing she had
worn during the day; but her feet were bare and
looked wonderfully small and white. He arose on his
elbow, wide awake at once. "W'y, 'Tite Reine! w'at
the devil you mean? w'ere 's yo' husban'?"

"The house kin fall on 'im, 't en goin' wake up Bud
w'en he's sleepin'; he drink' too much." Now that she
had aroused Grégoire, she stood up, and sinking her
face in her bended arm like a child, began to cry
softly. In an instant he was on his feet.

"My God, 'Tite Reine! w'at 's the matta? you got
to tell me w'at 's the matta." He could no longer
recognize the imperious 'Tite Reine, whose will had
been the law in her father's household. He led her to
the edge of the low gallery and there they sat down.

Grégoire loved women. He liked their nearness,
their atmosphere; the tones of their voices and the
things they said; their ways of moving and turning
about; the brushing of their garments when they

passed him by pleased him. He was fleeing now from the pain that a woman had inflicted upon him. When any overpowering sorrow came to Grégoire he felt a singular longing to cross the Sabine River and lose himself in Texas. He had done this once before when his home, the old Santien place, had gone into the hands of creditors. The sight of 'Tite Reine's distress now moved him painfully.

"W'at is it, 'Tite Reine? tell me w'at it is," he kept asking her. She was attempting to dry her eyes on her coarse sleeve. He drew a handkerchief from his back pocket and dried them for her.

"They all well, yonda?" she asked, haltingly, "my popa? my moma? the chil'en?" Grégoire knew no more of the Baptiste Choupic family than the post beside him. Nevertheless he answered: "They all right well, 'Tite Reine, but they mighty lonesome of you."

"My popa, he got a putty good crop this yea'?"

"He made right smart o' cotton fo' Bayou Pierre."

"He done haul it to the relroad?"

"No, he ain't quite finish pickin'."

"I hope they all ent sole 'Putty Girl'?" she inquired solicitously.

"Well, I should say not! Yo' pa says they ain't anotha piece o' hossflesh in the pa'ish he' d want to swap fo' 'Putty Girl.'" She turned to him with vague but fleeting amazement,— "Putty Girl" was a cow!

The autumn night was heavy about them. The black forest seemed to have drawn nearer; its shadowy depths were filled with the gruesome noises that inhabit a southern forest at night time.

"Ain't you 'fraid sometimes yere, 'Tite Reine?" Grégoire asked, as he felt a light shiver run through him at the weirdness of the scene.

"No," she answered promptly, "I ent 'fred o' nothin' 'cep' Bud."

"Then he treats you mean? I thought so!"

"Mista Grégoire," drawing close to him and whispering in his face, "Bud's killin' me." He clasped her arm, holding her near him, while an expression of profound pity escaped him. "Nobody don' know, 'cep' Unc' Mort'mer," she went on. "I tell you, he beats me; my back an' arms —you ought to see— it's all blue. He would 'a' choke' me to death one day w'en he was drunk, if Unc' Mort'mer had n' make 'im lef go—with his axe ov' his head." Grégoire glanced back over his shoulder toward the room where the man lay sleeping. He was wondering if it would really be a criminal act to go then and there and shoot the top of Bud Aiken's head off. He himself would hardly have considered it a crime, but he was not sure of how others might regard the act.

"That's w'y I wake you up, to tell you," she continued. "Then sometime' he plague me mos' crazy; he tell me 't ent no preacher, it's a Texas drummer w'at marry him an' me; an' w'en I don' know w'at way to turn no mo', he say no, it's a Meth'dis' archbishop, an' keep on laughin' 'bout me, an' I don' know w'at the truth!"

Then again, she told how Bud had induced her to mount the vicious little mustang "Buckeye," knowing that the little brute would n't carry a woman; and how it had amused him to witness her distress and terror when she was thrown to the ground.

"If I would know how to read an' write, an' had some pencil an' paper, it's long 'go I would wrote to my popa. But it's no pos'-office, it's no relroad,— nothin' in Sabine. An' you know, Mista Grégoire, Bud

say he 's goin' carry me yonda to Vernon, an' fu'ther
off yet,—'way yonda, an' he 's goin' turn me loose.
Oh, don' leave me yere, Mista Grégoire! don' leave
me behine you!" she entreated, breaking once more
into sobs.

" 'Tite Reine," he answered, "do you think I 'm
such a low-down scound'el as to leave you yere with
that"— He finished the sentence mentally, not
to offend the ears of 'Tite Reine.

They talked on a good while after that. She would
not return to the room where her husband lay; the
nearness of a friend had already emboldened her to
inward revolt. Grégoire induced her to lie down and
rest upon the quilt that she had given to him for a bed.
She did so, and broken down by fatigue was soon fast
asleep.

He stayed seated on the edge of the gallery and
began to smoke cigarettes which he rolled himself of
périque tobacco. He might have gone in and shared
Bud Aiken's bed, but preferred to stay there near
'Tite Reine. He watched the two horses, tramping
slowly about the lot, cropping the dewy wet tufts of
grass.

Grégoire smoked on. He only stopped when the
moon sank down behind the pine-trees, and the long
deep shadow reached out and enveloped him. Then
he could no longer see and follow the filmy smoke
from his cigarette, and he threw it away. Sleep was
pressing heavily upon him. He stretched himself
full length upon the rough bare boards of the gallery
and slept until daybreak.

Bud Aiken's satisfaction was very genuine when he
learned that Grégoire proposed spending the day and
another night with him. He had already recognized in

the young creole a spirit not altogether uncongenial to his own.

'Tite Reine cooked breakfast for them. She made coffee; of course there was no milk to add to it, but there was sugar. From a meal bag that stood in the corner of the room she took a measure of meal, and with it made a pone of corn bread. She fried slices of salt pork. Then Bud sent her into the field to pick cotton with old Uncle Mortimer. The negro's cabin was the counterpart of their own, but stood quite a distance away hidden in the woods. He and Aiken worked the crop on shares.

Early in the day Bud produced a grimy pack of cards from behind a parcel of sugar on the shelf. Grégoire threw the cards into the fire and replaced them with a spic and span new "deck" that he took from his saddlebags. He also brought forth from the same receptacle a bottle of whiskey, which he presented to his host, saying that he himself had no further use for it, as he had "sworn off" since day before yesterday, when he had made a fool of himself in Cloutierville.

They sat at the pine table smoking and playing cards all the morning, only desisting when 'Tite Reine came to serve them with the gumbo-filé that she had come out of the field to cook at noon. She could afford to treat a guest to chicken gumbo, for she owned a half dozen chickens that Uncle Mortimer had presented to her at various times. There were only two spoons, and 'Tite Reine had to wait till the men had finished before eating her soup. She waited for Grégoire's spoon, though her husband was the first to get through. It was a very childish whim.

In the afternoon she picked cotton again; and the

men played cards, smoked, and Bud drank.

It was a very long time since Bud Aiken had enjoyed himself so well, and since he had encountered so sympathetic and appreciative a listener to the story of his eventful career. The story of 'Tite Reine's fall from the horse he told with much spirit, mimicking quite skillfully the way in which she had complained of never being permitted "to teck a li'le pleasure," whereupon he had kindly suggested horseback riding. Grégoire enjoyed the story amazingly, which encouraged Aiken to relate many more of a similar character. As the afternoon wore on, all formality of address between the two had disappeared: they were "Bud" and "Grégoire" to each other, and Grégoire had delighted Aiken's soul by promising to spend a week with him. 'Tite Reine was also touched by the spirit of recklessness in the air; it moved her to fry two chickens for supper. She fried them deliciously in bacon fat. After supper she again arranged Grégoire's bed out on the gallery.

The night fell calm and beautiful, with the delicious odor of the pines floating upon the air. But the three did not sit up to enjoy it. Before the stroke of nine, Aiken had already fallen upon his bed unconscious of everything about him in the heavy drunken sleep that would hold him fast through the night. It even clutched him more relentlessly than usual, thanks to Grégoire's free gift of whiskey.

The sun was high when he awoke. He lifted his voice and called imperiously for 'Tite Reine, wondering that the coffeepot was not on the hearth, and marveling still more that he did not hear her voice in quick response with its, "I 'm comin', Bud. Yere I come." He called again and again. Then he arose and

looked out through the back door to see if she were
picking cotton in the field, but she was not there. He
dragged himself to the front entrance. Grégoire's bed
was still on the gallery, but the young fellow was
nowhere to be seen.

Uncle Mortimer had come into the yard, not to
cut wood this time, but to pick up the axe which was
his own property, and lift it to his shoulder.

"Mortimer," called out Aiken, "whur 's my wife?"
at the same time advancing toward the negro.
Mortimer stood still, waiting for him. "Whur 's my
wife an' that Frenchman? Speak out, I say, before I
send you to h—l."

Uncle Mortimer never had feared Bud Aiken; and
with the trusty axe upon his shoulder, he felt a
double hardihood in the man's presence. The old
fellow passed the back of his black, knotty hand
unctuously over his lips, as though he relished in
advance the words that were about to pass them.
He spoke carefully and deliberately:

"Miss Reine," he said, "I reckon she mus' of done
struck Natchitoches pa'ish sometime to'ard de middle
o' de night, on dat 'ar swif' hoss o' Mr. Sanchun's."

Aiken uttered a terrific oath. "Saddle up Buckeye,"
he yelled, "before I count twenty, or I'll rip the black
hide off yer. Quick, thar! Thur ain't nothin' four-
footed top o' this earth that Buckeye can't run
down." Uncle Mortimer scratched his head dubiously,
as he answered:—

"Yas, Mas' Bud, but you see, Mr. Sanchun, he done
cross de Sabine befo' sun-up on Buckeye."

FROM
A Night in Acadie

OZÈME'S HOLIDAY

Ozème often wondered why there was not a special dispensation of providence to do away with the necessity of work. There seemed to him so much created for man's enjoyment in this world, and so little time and opportunity to profit by it. To sit and do nothing but breathe was a pleasure to Ozème; but to sit in the company of a few choice companions, including a sprinkling of ladies, was even a greater delight; and the joy which a day's hunting or fishing or picnicking afforded him is hardly to be described. Yet he was by no means indolent. He worked faithfully on the plantation the whole year long, in a sort of methodical way; but when the time came around for his annual week's holiday, there was no holding him back. It was often decidedly inconvenient for the planter that Ozème usually chose to take his holiday during some very busy season of the year.

He started out one morning in the beginning of October. He had borrowed Mr. Laballière's buckboard and Padue's old gray mare, and a harness from the negro Sévérin. He wore a light blue suit which had been sent all the way from St. Louis, and which had cost him ten dollars; he had paid almost as much again for his boots; and his hat was a broad-rimmed gray felt which he had no cause to be ashamed of. When Ozème went "broading," he dressed—well,

55

regardless of cost. His eyes were blue and mild; his hair was light, and he wore it rather long; he was clean shaven, and really did not look his thirty-five years.

Ozème had laid his plans weeks beforehand. He was going visiting along Cane River; the mere contemplation filled him with pleasure. He counted upon reaching Fédeaus' about noon, and he would stop and dine there. Perhaps they would ask him to stay all night. He really did not hold to staying all night, and was not decided to accept if they did ask him. There were only the two old people, and he rather fancied the notion of pushing on to Beltrans', where he would stay a night, or even two, if urged. He was quite sure that there would be something agreeable going on at Beltrans', with all those young people— perhaps a fish-fry, or possibly a ball!

Of course he would have to give a day to Tante Sophie and another to Cousine Victoire; but none to the St. Annes unless entreated—after St. Anne reproaching him last year with being a fainéant for broading at such a season! At Cloutierville, where he would linger as long as possible, he meant to turn and retrace his course, zigzagging back and forth across Cane River so as to take in the Duplans, the Velcours, and others that he could not at the moment recall. A week seemed to Ozème a very, very little while in which to crowd so much pleasure.

There were steam-gins at work; he could hear them whistling far and near. On both sides of the river the fields were white with cotton, and everybody in the world seemed busy but Ozème. This reflection did not distress or disturb him in the least; he pursued his way at peace with himself and his surroundings.

At Lamérie's cross-roads store, where he stopped to buy a cigar, he learned that there was no use heading for Fédeaus', as the two old people had gone to town for a lengthy visit, and the house was locked up. It was at Fédeaus' that Ozème had intended to dine.

He sat in the buckboard, given up to a moment or two of reflection. The result was that he turned away from the river, and entered the road that led between two fields back to the woods and into the heart of the country. He had determined upon taking a short cut to the Beltrans' plantation, and on the way he meant to keep an eye open for old Aunt Tildy's cabin, which he knew lay in some remote part of this cut-off. He remembered that Aunt Tildy could cook an excellent meal if she had the material at hand. He would induce her to fry him a chicken, drip a cup of coffee, and turn him out a pone of corn-bread, which he thought would be sumptuous enough fare for the occasion.

Aunt Tildy dwelt in the not unusual log cabin, of one room, with its chimney of mud and stone, and its shallow gallery formed by the jutting of the roof. In close proximity to the cabin was a small cotton-field, which from a long distance looked like a field of snow. The cotton was bursting and over-flowing foam-like from bolls on the drying stalk. On the lower branches it was hanging ragged and tattered, and much of it had already fallen to the ground. There were a few chinaberry-trees in the yard before the hut, and under one of them an ancient and rusty-looking mule was eating corn from a wood trough. Some common little Creole chickens were scratching about the mule's feet and snatching at the grains of corn that occasionally fell from the trough.

Aunt Tildy was hobbling across the yard when Ozème drew up before the gate. One hand was confined in a sling; in the other she carried a tin pan, which she let fall noisily to the ground when she recognized him. She was broad, black, and misshapen, with her body bent forward almost at an acute angle. She wore a blue cottonade of large plaids, and a bandana awkwardly twisted around her head.

"Good God A'mighty, man! Whar you come from?" was her startled exclamation at beholding him.

"F'om home, Aunt Tildy; w'ere else do you expec'?" replied Ozème, dismounting composedly.

He had not seen the old woman for several years—since she was cooking in town for the family with which he boarded at the time. She had washed and ironed for him, atrociously, it is true, but her intentions were beyond reproach if her washing was not. She had also been clumsily attentive to him during a spell of illness. He had paid her with an occasional bandana, a calico dress, or a checked apron, and they had always considered the account between themselves square, with no sentimental feeling of gratitude remaining on either side.

"I like to know," remarked Ozème, as he took the gray mare from the shafts, and led her up to the trough where the mule was—"I like to know w'at you mean by makin' a crop like that an' then lettin' it go to was'e? Who you reckon's goin' to pick that cotton? You think maybe the angels goin' to come down an' pick it fo' you, an' gin it an' press it, an' then give you ten cents a poun' fo' it, hein?"

"Ef de Lord don' pick it, I don' know who gwine pick it, Mista Ozème. I tell you, me an' Sandy we wuk dat crap day in an' day out; it's him done de mos' of it.''

"Sandy? That little—"

"He ain' dat li'le Sandy no mo' w'at you rec'lec's; he 'mos' a man, an' he wuk like a man now. He wuk mo' 'an fittin' fo' his strenk, an' now he layin' in dah sick—God A'mighty knows how sick. An' me wid a risin' twell I bleeged to walk de flo' o' nights, an' don' know ef I ain' gwine to lose de han' atter all.''

"W'y, in the name o' conscience, you don' hire somebody to pick?"

"Whar I got money to hire? An' you knows well as me ev'y chick an' chile is pickin' roun' on de plantations an' gittin' good pay.''

The whole outlook appeared to Ozème very depressing, and even menacing, to his personal comfort and peace of mind. He foresaw no prospect of dinner unless he should cook it himself. And there was that Sandy—he remembered well the little scamp of eight, always at his grandmother's heels when she was cooking or washing. Of course he would have to go in and look at the boy, and no doubt dive into his traveling-bag for quinine, without which he never traveled.

Sandy was indeed very ill, consumed with fever. He lay on a cot covered up with a faded patchwork quilt. His eyes were half closed, and he was muttering and rambling on about hoeing and bedding and cleaning and thinning out the cotton; he was hauling it to the gin, wrangling about weight and bagging and ties and the price offered per pound. That bale or two of cotton had not only sent Sandy to bed, but had pursued him there, holding him through his fevered dreams, and threatening to end him. Ozème

would never have known the black boy, he was so
tall, so thin, and seemingly so wasted, lying there in
bed.

"See yere, Aunt Tildy," said Ozème, after he had,
as was usual with him when in doubt, abandoned
himself to a little reflection; "between us—you an'
me—we got to manage to kill an' cook one o' those
chickens I see scratchin' out yonda, fo' I'm jus'
about starved. I reckon you ain't got any quinine in
the house? No; I didn't suppose an instant you had.
Well, I'm goin' to give Sandy a good dose o' quinine
to-night, an' I'm goin' stay an' see how that'll work
on 'im. But sun-up, min' you, I mus' get out o' yere."

Ozème had spent more comfortable nights than the
one passed in Aunt Tildy's bed, which she consider-
ately abandoned to him.

In the morning Sandy's fever was somewhat abated,
but had not taken a decided enough turn to justify
Ozème in quitting him before noon, unless he was
willing "to feel like a dog," as he told himself. He
appeared before Aunt Tildy stripped to the under-
shirt, and wearing his second-best pair of trousers.

"That's a nice pickle o' fish you got me in, ol'
woman. I guarantee, nex' time I go abroad, 'tain't
me that'll take any cut-off. W'ere's that cotton-basket
an' cotton-sack o' yo's?"

"I knowed it!" chanted Aunt Tildy—"I knowed
de Lord war gwine sen' somebody to holp me out. He
war n' gwine let de crap was'e atter he give Sandy an'
me de strenk to make hit. De Lord gwine shove you
'long de row, Mista Ozème. De Lord gwine give you
plenty mo' fingers an' han's to pick dat cotton nimble
an' clean."

"Neva you min' w'at the Lord's goin' to do; go

get me that cotton-sack. An' you put that poultice like I tol' you on you' han', an' set down there an' watch Sandy. It looks like you are 'bout as helpless as a' ol' cow tangled up in a potato-vine."

Ozème had not picked cotton for many years, and he took to it a little awkwardly at first; but by the time he had reached the end of the first row the old dexterity of youth had come back to his hands, which flew rapidly back and forth with the motion of a weaver's shuttle; and his ten fingers became really nimble in clutching the cotton from its dry shell. By noon he had gathered about fifty pounds. Sandy was not then quite so well as he had promised to be, and Ozème concluded to stay that day and one more night. If the boy were no better in the morning, he would go off in search of a doctor for him, and he himself would continue on down to Tante Sophie's; the Beltrans' was out of the question now.

Sandy hardly needed a doctor in the morning. Ozème's doctoring was beginning to tell favorably; but he would have considered it criminal indifference and negligence to go away and leave the boy to Aunt Tildy's awkward ministrations just at the critical moment when there was a turn for the better; so he stayed that day out, and picked his hundred and fifty pounds.

On the third day it looked like rain, and a heavy rain just then would mean a heavy loss to Aunt Tildy and Sandy, and Ozème again went to the field, this time urging Aunt Tildy with him to do what she might with her one good hand.

"Aunt Tildy," called out Ozème to the bent old woman moving ahead of him between the white rows of cotton, "if the Lord gets me safe out o' this ditch, 't ain't to-morro' I'll fall in anotha with my eyes open, I bet you."

"Keep along, Mista Ozème; don' grumble, don' stumble; de Lord's a-watchin' you. Look at yo' Aunt Tildy; she doin' mo' wid her one han' 'an you doin' wid yo' two, man. Keep right along, honey. Watch dat cotton how it fallin' in yo' Aunt Tildy's bag."

"I am watchin' you, ol' woman; you don' fool me. You got to work that han' o' yo's spryer than you doin', or I'll take the rawhide. You done fo'got w'at the rawhide tas'e like, I reckon"—a reminder which amused Aunt Tildy so powerfully that her big negro-laugh resounded over the whole cotton-patch, and even caused Sandy, who heard it, to turn in his bed.

The weather was still threatening on the succeeding day, and a sort of dogged determination or characteristic desire to see his undertakings carried to a satisfactory completion urged Ozème to continue his efforts to drag Aunt Tildy out of the mire into which circumstances seemed to have thrust her.

One night the rain did come, and began to beat softly on the roof of the old cabin. Sandy opened his eyes, which were no longer brilliant with the fever flame. "Granny," he whispered, "de rain! Des listen, granny; de rain a-comin', an' I ain' pick dat cotton yit. W'at time it is? Gi' me my pants—I got to go—"

"You lay whar you is, chile alive. Dat cotton put aside clean and dry. Me an' de Lord an' Mista Ozème done pick dat cotton."

Ozème drove away in the morning looking quite as spick and span as the day he left home in his blue suit and his light felt drawn a little over his eyes.

"You want to take care o' that boy," he instructed Aunt Tildy at parting, "an' get 'im on his feet. An', let me tell you, the nex' time I start out to broad, if you see me passin' in this yere cut-off, put on yo' specs an' look at me good, because it won't be me; it'll be my ghos', ol' woman."

Indeed, Ozème, for some reason or other, felt quite shamefaced as he drove back to the plantation. When he emerged from the lane which he had entered the week before, and turned into the river road, Lamérie, standing in the store door, shouted out:

"Hé, Ozème! you had good times yonda? I bet you danced holes in the sole of them new boots."

"Don't talk, Lamérie!" was Ozème's rather ambiguous reply, as he flourished the remainder of a whip over the old gray mare's sway-back, urging her to a gentle trot.

When he reached home, Bodé, one of Padue's boys, who was assisting him to unhitch, remarked:

"How come you didn' go yonda down de coas' like you said, Mista Ozème? Nobody didn' see you in Cloutierville, an' Mailitte say you neva cross' de twenty-fo'-mile ferry, an' nobody didn' see you no place."

Ozème returned, after his customary moment of reflection:

"You see, it's 'mos' always the same thing on Cane riva, my boy; a man gets tired o' that à la fin. This time I went back in the woods, 'way yonda in the Fédeau cut-off; kin' o' campin' an' roughin' like, you might say. I tell you, it was sport, Bodé."

A MATTER OF PREJUDICE

Madame Carambeau wanted it strictly understood that she was not to be disturbed by Gustave's birthday party. They carried her big rocking-chair from the back gallery, that looked out upon the garden where the children were going to play, around to the front gallery, which closely faced the green levee bank and the Mississippi coursing almost flush with the top of it.

The house—an old Spanish one, broad, low and completely encircled by a wide gallery—was far down in the French quarter of New Orleans. It stood upon a square of ground that was covered thick with a semi-tropical growth of plants and flowers. An impenetrable board fence, edged with a formidable row of iron spikes, shielded the garden from the prying glances of the occasional passer-by.

Madame Carambeau's widowed daughter, Madame Cécile Lalonde, lived with her. This annual party, given to her little son, Gustave, was the one defiant act of Madame Lalonde's existence. She persisted in it, to her own astonishment and the wonder of those who knew her and her mother.

For old Madame Carambeau was a woman of many prejudices—so many, in fact, that it would be difficult to name them all. She detested dogs, cats, organ-grinders, white servants and children's noises.

She despised Americans, Germans and all people of a
different faith from her own. Anything not French
had, in her opinion, little right to existence.

She had not spoken to her son Henri for ten years
because he had   married an American girl from
Prytania street. She would not permit green tea to be
introduced into her house, and those who could not
or would not drink coffee might drink tisane of *fleur
de Laurier* for all she cared.

Nevertheless, the children seemed to be having it
all their own way that day, and the organ-grinders
were let loose. Old madame, in her retired corner,
could hear the screams, the laughter and the music far
more distinctly than she liked. She rocked herself
noisily, and hummed "Partant pour la Syrie."

She was straight and slender. Her hair was white,
and she wore it in puffs on the temples. Her skin was
fair and her eyes blue and cold.

Suddenly she became aware that footsteps were
approaching, and threatening to invade her privacy
—not only footsteps, but screams! Then two little
children, one in hot pursuit of the other, darted
wildly around the corner near which she sat.

The child in advance, a pretty little girl, sprang
excitedly into Madame Carambeau's lap, and threw
her arms convulsively around the old lady's neck. Her
companion lightly struck her a "last tag," and ran
laughing gleefully away.

The most natural thing for the child to do then
would have been to wriggle down from madame's lap,
without a "thank you" or a "by your leave," after
the manner of small and thoughtless children. But she
did not do this. She stayed there, panting and fluttering, like a frightened bird.

Madame was greatly annoyed. She moved as if to put the child away from her, and scolded her sharply for being boisterous and rude. The little one, who did not understand French, was not disturbed by the reprimand, and stayed on in madame's lap. She rested her plump little cheek, that was hot and flushed, against the soft white linen of the old lady's gown.

Her cheek was very hot and very flushed. It was dry, too, and so were her hands. The child's breathing was quick and irregular. Madame was not long in detecting these signs of disturbance.

Though she was a creature of prejudice, she was nevertheless a skillful and accomplished nurse, and a connoisseur in all matters pertaining to health. She prided herself upon this talent, and never lost an opportunity of exercising it. She would have treated an organ-grinder with tender consideration if one had presented himself in the character of an invalid.

Madame's manner toward the little one changed immediately. Her arms and her lap were at once adjusted so as to become the most comfortable of resting places. She rocked very gently to and fro. She fanned the child softly with her palm leaf fan, and sang "Partant pour la Syrie" in a low and agreeable tone.

The child was perfectly content to lie still and prattle a little in that language which madame thought hideous. But the brown eyes were soon swimming in drowsiness, and the little body grew heavy with sleep in madame's clasp.

When the little girl slept Madame Carambeau arose, and treading carefully and deliberately, entered her room, that opened near at hand upon the gallery. The room was large, airy and inviting, with its cool matting upon the floor, and its heavy, old, polished mahogany furniture. Madame, with the child still in her arms, pulled a bell-cord; then she stood waiting, swaying gently back and forth. Presently an old black woman answered the summons. She wore gold hoops in her ears, and a bright bandanna knotted fantastically on her head.

"Louise, turn down the bed," commanded madame. "Place that small, soft pillow below the bolster. Here is a poor little unfortunate creature whom Providence must have driven into my arms." She laid the child carefully down.

"Ah, those Americans! Do they deserve to have children? Understanding as little as they do how to take care of them!" said madame, while Louise was mumbling an accompanying assent that would have been unintelligible to any one unacquainted with the negro patois.

"There, you see, Louise, she is burning up," remarked madame: "she is consumed. Unfasten the little bodice while I lift her. Ah, talk to me of such parents! So stupid as not to perceive a fever like that coming on, but they must dress their child up like a monkey to go play and dance to the music of organ-grinders.

"Haven't you better sense, Louise, than to take off a child's shoe as if you were removing the boot from the leg of a cavalry officer?" Madame would have required fairy fingers to minister to the sick. "Now go to Mamzelle Cécile, and tell her to send me one of those old, soft, thin nightgowns that Gustave wore two summers ago."

When the woman retired, madame busied herself with concocting a cooling pitcher of orange-flower water, and mixing a fresh supply of *eau sédative* with which agreeably to sponge the little invalid.

Madame Lalonde came herself with the old, soft nightgown. She was a pretty, blonde, plump little woman, with the deprecatory air of one whose will has become flaccid from want of use. She was mildly distressed at what her mother had done.

"But, mamma! But, mamma, the child's parents will be sending the carriage for her in a little while. Really, there was no use. Oh dear! oh dear!"

If the bedpost had spoken to Madame Carambeau, she would have paid more attention, for speech from such a source would have been at least surprising if not convincing. Madame Lalonde did not possess the faculty of either surprising or convincing her mother.

"Yes, the little one will be quite comfortable in this," said the old lady, taking the garment from her daughter's irresolute hands.

"But, mamma! What shall I say, what shall I do when they send? Oh, dear; oh, dear!"

"That is your business," replied madame, with lofty indifference. "My concern is solely with a sick child that happens to be under my roof. I think I know my duty at this time of life, Cécile."

As Madame Lalonde predicted, the carriage soon came, with a stiff English coachman driving it, and a red-cheeked Irish nurse-maid seated inside. Madame would not even permit the maid to see her little charge. She had an original theory that the Irish voice is distressing to the sick.

Madame Lalonde sent the girl away with a long letter of explanation that must have satisfied the parents; for the child was left undisturbed in Madame Carambeau's care. She was a sweet child, gentle and affectionate. And, though she cried and fretted a little throughout the night for her mother, she seemed, after all, to take kindly to madame's gentle nursing. It was not much of a fever that afflicted her, and after two days she was well enough to be sent back to her parents.

Madame, in all her varied experience with the sick, had never before nursed so objectionable a character as an American child. But the trouble was that after the little one went away, she could think of nothing really objectionable against her except the accident of her birth, which was, after all, her misfortune; and her ignorance of the French language, which was not her fault.

But the touch of the caressing baby arms; the pressure of the soft little body in the night; the tones of the voice, and the feeling of the hot lips when the child kissed her, believing herself to be with her mother, were impressions that had sunk through the crust of madame's prejudice and reached her heart.

She often walked the length of the gallery, looking out across the wide, majestic river. Sometimes she trod the mazes of her garden where the solitude was almost that of a tropical jungle. It was during such moments that the seed began to work in her soul—the seed planted by the innocent and undesigning hands of a little child.

The first shoot that it sent forth was Doubt. Madame plucked it away once or twice. But it sprouted again, and with it Mistrust and Dissatisfaction. Then from the heart of the seed, and amid the shoots of Doubt and Misgiving, came the flower of Truth. It was a very beautiful flower, and it bloomed on Christmas morning.

As Madame Carambeau and her daughter were about to enter her carriage on that Christmas morning, to be driven to church, the old lady stopped to give an order to her black coachman, François. François had been driving these ladies every Sunday morning to the French Cathedral for so many years—he had forgotten exactly how many, but ever since he had entered their service, when Madame Lalonde was a little girl. His astonishment may therefore be imagined when Madame Carambeau said to him:

"François, to-day you will drive us to one of the American churches."

"Plait-il, madame?" the negro stammered, doubting the evidence of his hearing.

"I say, you will drive us to one of the American churches. Any one of them," she added, with a sweep of her hand. "I suppose they are all alike," and she followed her daughter into the carriage.

Madame Lalonde's surprise and agitation were painful to see, and they deprived her of the ability to question, even if she had possessed the courage to do so.

François, left to his fancy, drove them to St. Patrick's Church on Camp street. Madame Lalonde looked and felt like the proverbial fish out of its element as they entered the edifice. Madame Carambeau, on the contrary, looked as if she had been attending St. Patrick's church all her life. She sat with unruffled calm through the long service and through a lengthy English sermon of which she did not understand a word.

When the mass was ended and they were about to enter the carriage again, Madame Carambeau turned, as she had done before, to the coachman.

"François," she said, coolly, "you will now drive us to the residence of my son, M. Henri Carambeau. No doubt Mamzelle Cécile can inform you where it is," she added, with a sharply penetrating glace that caused Madame Lalonde to wince.

Yes, her daughter Cécile knew, and so did François, for that matter. They drove out St. Charles avenue—very far out. It was like a strange city to old madame, who had not been in the American quarter since the town had taken on this new and splendid growth.

The morning was a delicious one, soft and mild; and the roses were all in bloom. They were not hidden behind spiked fences. Madame appeared not to notice them, or the beautiful and striking residences that lined the avenue along which they drove. She held a bottle of smelling-salts to her nostrils, as though she were passing through the most unsavory instead of the most beautiful quarter of New Orleans.

Henri's house was a very modern and very handsome one, standing a little distance away from the street. A well-kept lawn, studded with rare and charming plants, surrounded it. The ladies, dismounting, rang the bell, and stood out upon the banquette, waiting for the iron gate to be opened.

A white maid-servant admitted them. Madame did not seem to mind. She handed her a card with all proper ceremony, and followed with her daughter to the house.

Not once did she show a sign of weakness; not even when her son, Henri, came and took her in his arms and sobbed and wept upon her neck as only a warm-hearted Creole could. He was a big, good-looking, honest-faced man, with tender brown eyes like his dead father's and a firm mouth like his mother's.

Young Mrs. Carambeau came, too, her sweet, fresh face transfigured with happiness. She led by the hand her little daughter, the "American child" whom madame had nursed so tenderly a month before, never suspecting the little one to be other than an alien to her.

"What a lucky chance was that fever! What a happy accident!" gurgled Madame Lalonde.

"Cécile, it was no accident, I tell you; it was Providence," spoke madame, reprovingly, and no one contradicted her.

They all drove back together to eat Christmas dinner in the old house by the river. Madame held her little granddaughter upon her lap; her son Henri sat facing her, and beside her was her daughter-in-law.

Henri sat back in the carriage and could not speak. His soul was possessed by a pathetic joy that would not admit of speech. He was going back again to the home where he was born, after a banishment of ten long years.

He would hear again the water beat against the green levee-bank with a sound that was not quite like any other that he could remember. He would sit within the sweet and solemn shadow of the deep and overhanging roof; and roam through the wild, rich solitude of the old garden, where he had played his pranks of boyhood and dreamed his dreams of youth. He would listen to his mother's voice calling him, "mon fils," as it had always done before that day he had had to choose between mother and wife. No; he could not speak.

But his wife chatted much and pleasantly—in a French, however, that must have been trying to old madame to listen to.

"I am so sorry, ma mère," she said, "that our little one does not speak French. It is not my fault, I assure you," and she flushed and hesitated a little. "It—it was Henri who would not permit it."

"That is nothing," replied madame, amiably, drawing the child close to her. "Her grandmother will teach her French; and she will teach her grandmother English. You see, I have no prejudices. I am not like my son. Henri was always a stubborn boy. Heaven only knows how he came by such a character!"

AT CHÊNIÈRE CAMINADA

I

There was no clumsier looking fellow in church that Sunday morning than Antoine Bocaze—the one they called Tonie. But Tonie did not really care if he were clumsy or not. He felt that he could speak intelligibly to no woman save his mother; but since he had no desire to inflame the hearts of any of the island maidens, what difference did it make?

He knew there was no better fisherman on the Chênière Caminada than himself, if his face was too long and bronzed, his limbs too unmanageable and his eyes too earnest—almost too honest.

It was a midsummer day, with a lazy, scorching breeze blowing from the Gulf straight into the church windows. The ribbons on the young girls' hats fluttered like the wings of birds, and the old women clutched the flapping ends of the veils that covered their heads.

A few mosquitoes, floating through the blistering air, with their nipping and humming fretted the people to a certain degree of attention and consequent devotion. The measured tones of the priest at the altar rose and fell like a song: "Credo in unum Deum patrem omnipotentem" he chanted. And then the people all looked at one another, suddenly electrified.

Some one was playing upon the organ whose notes no one on the whole island was able to awaken; whose tones had not been heard during the many months since a passing stranger had one day listlessly dragged his fingers across its idle keys. A long, sweet strain of music floated down from the loft and filled the church.

It seemed to most of them—it seemed to Tonie standing there beside his old mother—that some heavenly being must have descended upon the Church of Our Lady of Lourdes and chosen this celestial way of communicating with its people.

But it was no creature from a different sphere; it was only a young lady from Grand Isle. A rather pretty young person with blue eyes and nut-brown hair, who wore a dotted lawn of fine texture and fashionable make, and a white Leghorn sailor-hat.

Tonie saw her standing outside of the church after mass, receiving the priest's voluble praises and thanks for her graceful service.

She had come over to mass from Grand Isle in Baptiste Beaudelet's lugger, with a couple of young men, and two ladies who kept a pension over there. Tonie knew these two ladies—the widow Lebrun and her old mother—but he did not attempt to speak with them; he would not have known what to say. He stood aside gazing at the group, as others were doing, his serious eyes fixed earnestly upon the fair organist.

Tonie was late at dinner that day. His mother must have waited an hour for him, sitting patiently with her coarse hands folded in her lap, in that little still room with its "brick-painted" floor, its gaping chimney and homely furnishings.

He told her that he had been walking—walking he hardly knew where, and he did not know why. He must have tramped from one end of the island to the other; but he brought her no bit of news or gossip. He did not know if the Cotures had stopped for dinner with the Avendettes; whether old Pierre François was worse, or better, or dead, or if lame Philibert was drinking again this morning. He knew nothing; yet he had crossed the village, and passed every one of its small houses that stood close together in a long, jagged line facing the sea; they were gray and battered by time and the rude buffets of the salt sea winds.

He knew nothing, though the Cotures had all bade him "good day" as they filed into Avendette's, where a steaming plate of crab gumbo was waiting for each. He had heard some woman screaming, and others saying it was because old Pierre François had just passed away. But he did not remember this, nor did he recall the fact that lame Philibert had staggered against him when he stood absently watching a "fiddler" sidling across the sun-baked sand. He could tell his mother nothing of all this; but he said he had noticed that the wind was fair and must have driven Baptiste's boat, like a flying bird, across the water.

Well, that was something to talk about, and old Ma'me Antoine, who was fat, leaned comfortably upon the table after she had helped Tonie to his courtbouillon, and remarked that she found Madame was getting old. Tonie thought that perhaps she was aging and her hair was getting whiter. He seemed glad to talk about her, and reminded his mother of old Madame's kindness and sympathy at the time his father and brothers had perished. It was when he was a little fellow, ten years before, during a squall in Barataria Bay.

Ma'me Antoine declared that she could never forget that sympathy, if she lived till Judgment Day; but all the same she was sorry to see that Madame Lebrun was also not so young or fresh as she used to be. Her chances of getting a husband were surely lessening every year; especially with the young girls around her, budding each spring like flowers to be plucked. The one who had played upon the organ was Mademoiselle Duvigné, Claire Duvigné, a great belle, the daughter of the Rampart street. Ma'me Antoine had found that out during the ten minutes she and others had stopped after mass to gossip with the priest.

"Claire Duvigné," muttered Tonie, not even making a pretense to taste his courtbouillon, but picking little bits from the half loaf of crusty brown bread that lay beside his plate. "Claire Duvigné; that is a pretty name. Don't you think so, mother? I can't think of anyone on the Chênière who has so pretty a one, nor at Grand Isle, either, for that matter. And you say she lives on Rampart street?"

It appeared to him a matter of great importance that he should have his mother repeat all that the priest had told her.

II

Early the following morning Tonie went out in search of lame Philibert, than whom there was no cleverer workman on the island when he could be caught sober.

Tonie had tried to work on his big lugger that lay

bottom upward under the shed, but it had seemed impossible. His mind, his hands, his tools refused to do their office, and in sudden desperation he desisted. He found Philibert and set him to work in his own place under the shed. Then he got into his small boat with the red lateen-sail and went over to Grand Isle.

There was no one at hand to warn Tonie that he was acting the part of a fool. He had, singularly, never felt those premonitory symptoms of love which afflict the greater portion of mankind before they reach the age which he had attained. He did not at first recognize this powerful impulse that had, without warning, possessed itself of his entire being. He obeyed it without a struggle, as naturally as he would have obeyed the dictates of hunger and thirst.

Tonie left his boat at the wharf and proceeded at once to Mme. Lebrun's pension, which consisted of a group of plain, stoutly built cottages that stood in mid island, about half a mile from the sea.

The day was bright and beautiful with soft, velvety gusts of wind blowing from the water. From a cluster of orange trees a flock of doves ascended, and Tonie stopped to listen to the beating of their wings and follow their flight toward the water oaks whither he himself was moving.

He walked with a dragging, uncertain step through the yellow, fragrant chamomile, his thoughts traveling before him. In his mind was always the vivid picture of the girl as it had stamped itself there yesterday, connected in some mystical way with that celestial music which had thrilled him and was vibrating yet in his soul.

But she did not look the same to-day. She was returning from the beach when Tonie first saw her,

leaning upon the arm of one of the men who had
accompanied her yesterday. She was dressed differ-
ently—in a dainty blue cotton gown. Her companion
held a big white sunshade over them both. They had
exchanged hats and were laughing with great aban-
donment.

Two young men walked behind them and were
trying to engage her attention. She glanced at Tonie,
who was leaning against a tree when the group
passed by; but of course she did not know him.
She was speaking English, a language which he hardly
understood.

There were other young people gathered under the
water oaks—girls who were, many of them, more
beautiful than Mlle. Duvigné; but for Tonie they
simply did not exist. His whole universe had suddenly
become converted into a glamorous background for
the person of Mlle. Duvigné, and the shadowy figures
of men who were about her.

Tonie went to Mme. Lebrun and told her he would
bring her oranges next day from the Chênière. She
was well pleased, and commissioned him to bring
her other things from the stores there, which she
could not procure at Grand Isle. She did not question
his presence, knowing that these summer days were
idle ones for the Chênière fishermen. Nor did she
seem surprised when he told her that his boat was
at the wharf, and would be there every day at her
service. She knew his frugal habits, and supposed
he wished to hire it, as others did. He intuitively
felt that this could be the only way.

And that is how it happened that Tonie spent so
little of his time at the Chênière Caminada that
summer. Old Ma'me Antoine grumbled enough about

it. She herself had been twice in her life to Grand Isle and once to Grand Terre, and each time had been more than glad to get back to the Chênière. And why Tonie should want to spend his days, and even his nights, away from home, was a thing she could not comprehend, especially as he would have to be away the whole winter; and meantime there was much work to be done at his own hearthside and in the company of his own mother. She did not know that Tonie had much, much more to do at Grand Isle than at the Chênière Caminada.

He had to see how Claire Duvigné sat upon the gallery in the big rocking chair that she kept in motion by the impetus of her slender, slippered foot; turning her head this way and that way to speak to the men who were always near her. He had to follow her lithe motions at tennis or croquet, that she often played with the children under the trees. Some days he wanted to see how she spread her bare, white arms, and walked out to meet the foam-crested waves. Even here there were men with her. And then at night, standing alone like a still shadow under the stars, did he not have to listen to her voice when she talked and laughed and sang? Did he not have to follow her slim figure whirling through the dance, in the arms of men who must have loved her and wanted her as he did. He did not dream that they could help it more than he could help it. But the days when she stepped into his boat, the one with the red lateen sail, and sat for hours within a few feet of him, were days that he would have given up for nothing else that he could think of.

III

There were always others in her company at such times, young people with jests and laughter on their lips. Only once she was alone.

She had foolishly brought a book with her, thinking she would want to read. But with the breath of the sea stinging her she could not read a line. She looked precisely as she had looked the day he first saw her, standing outside of the church at Chênière Caminada.

She laid the book down in her lap, and let her soft eyes sweep dreamily along the line of the horizon where the sky and water met. Then she looked straight at Tonie, and for the first time spoke directly to him.

She called him Tonie, as she had heard others do, and questioned him about his boat and his work. He trembled, and answered her vaguely and stupidly. She did not mind, but spoke to him anyhow, satisfied to talk herself when she found that he could not or would not. She spoke French, and talked about the Chênière Caminada, its people and its church. She talked of the day she had played upon the organ there, and complained of the instrument being woefully out of tune.

Tonie was perfectly at home in the familiar task of guiding his boat before the wind that bellied its taut, red sail. He did not seem clumsy and awkward as when he sat in church. The girl noticed that he appeared as strong as an ox.

As she looked at him and surprised one of his shifting glances, a glimmer of the truth began to dawn faintly upon her. She remembered how she had encountered him daily in her path, with his earnest, devouring eyes always seeking her out. She recalled—but there was no need to recall anything. There are women whose perception of passion is very keen; they are the women who most inspire it.

A feeling of complacency took possession of her with this conviction. There was some softness and sympathy mingled with it. She would have liked to lean over and pat his big, brown hand, and tell him she felt sorry and would have helped it if she could. With this belief he ceased to be an object of complete indifference in her eyes. She had thought, awhile before, of having him turn about and take her back home. But now it was really piquant to pose for an hour longer before a man—even a rough fisherman— to whom she felt herself to be an object of silent and consuming devotion. She could think of nothing more interesting to do on shore.

She was incapable of conceiving the full force and extent of his infatuation. She did not dream that under the rude, calm exterior before her a man's heart was beating clamorously, and his reason yielding to the savage instinct of his blood.

"I hear the Angelus ringing at Chênière, Tonie," she said. "I didn't know it was so late; let us go back to the island." There had been a long silence which her musical voice interrupted.

Tonie could now faintly hear the Angelus bell himself. A vision of the church came with it, the odor of incense and the sound of the organ. The girl before him was again the celestial being whom our Lady of Lourdes had once offered to his immortal vision.

It was growing dusk when they landed at the

pier, and frogs had begun to croak among the reeds in the pools. There were two of Mlle. Duvigné's usual attendants anxiously awaiting her return. But she chose to let Tonie assist her out of the boat. The touch of her hand fired his blood again.

She said to him very low and half-laughing, "I have no money tonight, Tonie; take this instead," pressing into his palm a delicate silver chain, which she had worn twined about her bare wrist. It was purely a spirit of coquetry that prompted the action, and a touch of the sentimentality which most women possess. She had read in some romance of a young girl doing something like that.

As she walked away between her two attendants she fancied Tonie pressing the chain to his lips. But he was standing quite still, and held it buried in his tightly-closed hand; wanting to hold as long as he might the warmth of the body that still penetrated the bauble when she thrust it into his hand.

He watched her retreating figure like a blotch against the fading sky. He was stirred by a terrible, an overmastering regret, that he had not clasped her in his arms when they were out there alone, and sprung with her into the sea. It was what he had vaguely meant to do when the sound of the Angelus had weakened and palsied his resolution. Now she was going from him, fading away into the mist with those figures on either side of her, leaving him alone. He resolved within himself that if ever again she were out there on the sea at his mercy, she would have to perish in his arms. He would go far, far out where the sound of no bell could reach him. There was some comfort for him in the thought.

But as it happened, Mlle. Duvigné never went out alone in the boat with Tonie again.

IV

It was one morning in January. Tonie had been collecting a bill from one of the fishmongers at the French Market, in New Orleans, and had turned his steps toward St. Philip street. The day was chilly; a keen wind was blowing. Tonie mechanically buttoned his rough, warm coat and crossed over into the sun.

There was perhaps not a more wretched-hearted being in the whole district, that morning, than he. For months the woman he so hopelessly loved had been lost to his sight. But all the more she dwelt in his thoughts, preying upon his mental and bodily forces until his unhappy condition became apparent to all who knew him. Before leaving his home for the winter fishing grounds he had opened his whole heart to his mother, and told her of the trouble that was killing him. She hardly expected that he would ever come back to her when he went away. She feared that he would not, for he had spoken wildly of the rest and peace that could only come to him with death.

That morning when Tonie had crossed St. Philip street he found himself accosted by Madame Lebrun and her mother. He had not noticed them approaching, and, moreover, their figures in winter garb appeared unfamiliar to him. He had never seen them elsewhere than at Grand Isle and the Chênière during the summer. They were glad to meet him, and shook his hand cordially. He stood as usual a little helplessly before them. A pulse in his throat was beating and almost choking him, so poignant were the recollections which their presence stirred up.

They were staying in the city this winter, they told him. They wanted to hear the opera as often as possible, and the island was really too dreary with everyone gone. Madame Lebrun had left her son there to keep order and superintend repairs, and so on.

"You are both well?" stammered Tonie.

"In perfect health, my dear Tonie," Madame Lebrun replied. She was wondering at his haggard eyes and thin, gaunt cheeks; but possessed too much tact to mention them.

"And—the young lady who used to go sailing— is she well?" he inquired lamely.

"You mean Mlle. Favette? She was married just after leaving Grand Isle."

"No; I mean the one you called Claire—Mamzelle Duvigné—is she well?"

Mother and daughter exclaimed together: "Impossible! You haven't heard? Why, Tonie," madame continued, "Mlle. Duvigné died three weeks ago. But that was something sad, I tell you!....Her family heartbroken...Simply from a cold caught by standing in thin slippers, waiting for her carriage after the opera....What a warning!"

The two were talking at once. Tonie kept looking from one to the other. He did not know what they were saying, after madame had told him, "Elle est morte."

As in a dream he finally heard that they said good-by to him, and sent their love to his mother.

He stood still in the middle of the banquette when they had left him, watching them go toward the market. He could not stir. Something had happened to him—he did not know what. He wondered if the news was killing him.

Some women passed by, laughing coarsely. He noticed how they laughed and tossed their heads. A mockingbird was singing in a cage which hung from a window above his head. He had not heard it before.

Just beneath the window was the entrance to a barroom. Tonie turned and plunged through its swinging doors. He asked the bartender for whisky. The man thought he was already drunk, but pushed the bottle toward him nevertheless. Tonie poured a great quantity of the fiery liquor into a glass and swallowed it at a draught. The rest of the day he spent among the fishermen and Barataria oystermen; and that night he slept soundly and peacefully until morning.

He did not know why it was so; he could not understand. But from that day he felt that he began to live again, to be once more a part of the moving world about him. He would ask himself over and over again why it was so, and stay bewildered before this truth that he could not answer or explain, and which he began to accept as a holy mystery.

One day in early spring Tonie sat with his mother upon a piece of drift-wood close to the sea.

He had returned that day to the Chênière Caminada. At first she thought he was like his former self again, for all his old strength and courage had returned. But she found that there was a new brightness in his face which had not been there before. It made her think of the Holy Ghost descending and bringing some kind of light to a man.

She knew that Mademoiselle Duvigné was dead, and all along had feared that this knowledge would be the death of Tonie. When she saw him come back to her like a new being, at once she dreaded that he did not know. All day the doubt had been fretting her, and she could bear the uncertainty no longer.

"You know, Tonie—that young lady whom you cared for—well, some one read it to me in the papers—she died last winter." She had tried to speak as cautiously as she could.

"Yes, I know she is dead. I am glad."

It was the first time he had said this in words, and it made his heart beat quicker.

Ma'me Antoine shuddered and drew aside from him. To her it was somehow like murder to say such a thing.

"What do you mean? Why are you glad?" she demanded, indignantly.

Tonie was sitting with his elbows on his knees. He wanted to answer his mother, but it would take time; he would have to think. He looked out across the water that glistened gem-like with the sun upon it, but there was nothing there to open his thought. He looked down into his open palm and began to pick at the callous flesh that was hard as a horse's hoof. Whilst he did this his ideas began to gather and take form.

"You see, while she lived I could never hope for anything," he began, slowly feeling his way. "Despair was the only thing for me. There were always men about her. She walked and sang and danced with them. I knew it all the time, even when I didn't see her. But I saw her often enough. I knew that some day one of them would please her and she would give herself to him—she would marry him. That thought haunted me like an evil spirit."

Tonie passed his hand across his forehead as if to sweep away anything of the horror that might have remained there.

"It kept me awake at night," he went on. "But

that was not so bad; the worst torture was to sleep, for then I would dream that it was all true.

"Oh, I could see her married to one of them—his wife—coming year after year to Grand Isle and bringing her little children with her! I can't tell you all that I saw—all that was driving me mad! But now"—and Tonie clasped his hands together and smiled as he looked again across the water—"she is where she belongs; there is no difference up there; the curé has often told us there is no difference between men. It is with the soul that we approach each other there. Then she will know who has loved her best. That is why I am so contented. Who knows what may happen up there?"

Ma'me Antoine could not answer. She only took her son's big, rough hand and pressed it against her.

"And now, ma mère," he exclaimed, cheerfully, rising, "I shall go light the fire for your bread; it is a long time since I have done anything for you," and he stooped and pressed a warm kiss on her withered old cheek.

With misty eyes she watched him walk away in the direction of the big brick oven that stood open-mouthed under the lemon trees.

A RESPECTABLE WOMAN

Mrs. Baroda was a little provoked to learn that her husband expected his friend, Gouvernail, up to spend a week or two on the plantation.

They had entertained a good deal during the winter; much of the time had also been passed in New Orleans in various forms of mild dissipation. She was looking forward to a period of unbroken rest, now, and undisturbed tête-a-tête with her husband, when he informed her that Gouvernail was coming up to stay a week or two.

This was a man she had heard much of but never seen. He had been her husband's college friend; was now a journalist, and in no sense a society man or "a man about town," which were, perhaps some of the reasons she had never met him. But she had unconsciously formed an image of him in her mind. She pictured him tall, slim, cynical; with eyeglasses, and his hands in his pockets; and she did not like him. Gouvernail was slim enough, but he wasn't very tall nor very cynical; neither did he wear eyeglasses nor carry his hands in his pockets. And she rather liked him when he first presented himself.

But why she liked him she could not explain satisfactorily to herself when she partly attempted to do so. She could discover in him none of those brilliant and promising traits which Gaston, her husband, had often assured her that he possessed. On the contrary, he sat rather mute and receptive before her chatty eagerness to make him feel at home and in face of Gaston's frank and wordy hospitality. His manner was as courteous toward her as the most exacting woman could require; but he made no direct appeal to her approval or even esteem.

Once settled at the plantation he seemed to like to sit upon the wide portico in the shade of one of the big Corinthian pillars, smoking his cigar lazily and listening attentively to Gaston's experience as a sugar planter.

"This is what I call living," he would utter with deep satisfaction, as the air that swept across the sugar field caressed him with its warm and scented velvety touch. It pleased him also to get on familiar terms with the big dogs that came about him, rubbing themselves sociably against his legs. He did not care to fish, and displayed no eagerness to go out and kill grosbecs when Gaston proposed doing so.

Gouvernail's personality puzzled Mrs. Baroda, but she liked him. Indeed, he was a lovable, inoffensive fellow. After a few days, when she could understand him no better than at first, she gave over being puzzled and remained piqued. In this mood she left her husband and her guest, for the most part, alone together. Then finding that Gouvernail took no manner of exception to her action, she imposed her society upon him, accompanying him in his idle strolls to the mill and walks along the batture. She persistently sought to penetrate the reserve in which he had unconsciously enveloped himself.

"When is he going—your friend?" she one day asked her husband. "For my part, he tires me frightfully."

"Not for a week yet, dear. I can't understand; he gives you no trouble."

"No. I should like him better if he did; if he were more like others, and I had to plan somewhat for his comfort and enjoyment."

Gaston took his wife's pretty face between his hands and looked tenderly and laughingly into her troubled eyes. They were making a bit of toilet sociably together in Mrs. Baroda's dressing room.

"You are full of surprises, ma belle," he said to her. "Even I can never count upon how you are going to act under given conditions." He kissed her and turned to fasten his cravat before the mirror.

"Here you are," he went on, "taking poor Gouvernail seriously and making a commotion over him, the last thing he would desire or expect."

"Commotion!" she hotly resented. "Nonsense! How can you say such a thing? Commotion, indeed! But, you know, you said he was clever."

"So he is. But the poor fellow is run down by overwork now. That's why I asked him here to take a rest."

"You used to say he was a man of ideas," she retorted, unconciliated. "I expected him to be interesting, at least. I'm going to the city in the morning to have my spring gowns fitted. Let me know when Mr. Gouvernail is gone; I shall be at my Aunt Octavie's."

That night she went and sat alone upon a bench that stood beneath a live oak tree at the edge of the gravel walk.

She had never known her thoughts or her intentions to be so confused. She could gather nothing from them but the feeling of a distinct necessity to quit her home in the morning.

Mrs. Baroda heard footsteps crunching the gravel; but could discern in the darkness only the approaching red point of a lighted cigar. She knew it was Gouvernail, for her husband did not smoke. She hoped to remain unnoticed, but her white gown revealed her to him. He threw away his cigar and seated himself upon the bench beside her, without a suspicion that she might object to his presence.

"Your husband told me to bring this to you, Mrs. Baroda," he said, handing her a filmy, white scarf with which she sometimes enveloped her head and shoulders. She accepted the scarf from him with a murmur of thanks, and let it lie in her lap.

He made some commonplace observation upon the baneful effect of the night air at that season. Then as his gaze reached out into the darkness, he murmured, half to himself:

> " 'Night of south winds—night of
> the large few stars!
> Still nodding night—' "

She made no reply to this apostrophe to the night, which indeed, was not addressed to her.

Gouvernail was in no sense a diffident man, for he was not a self-conscious one. His periods of reserve were not constitutional, but the result of moods. Sitting there beside Mrs. Baroda, his silence melted for the time.

He talked freely and intimately in a low, hesitating drawl that was not unpleasant to hear. He talked of the old college days when he and Gaston had been a good deal to each other; of the days of keen and blind ambitions and large intentions. Now there

was left with him, at least, a philosophic acquiescence to the existing order—only a desire to be
permitted to exist, with now and then a little whiff
of genuine life, such as he was breathing now.

Her mind only vaguely grasped what he was saying. Her physical being was for the moment pre-
dominant. She was not thinking of his words, only
drinking in the tones of his voice. She wanted to
reach out her hand in the darkness and touch him
with the sensitive tips of her fingers upon the face
or the lips. She wanted to draw close to him and
whisper against his cheek—she did not care what—
as she might have done if she had not been a respectable woman.

The stronger the impulse grew to bring herself
near him, the further, in fact, did she draw away
from him. As soon as she could do so without an
appearance of too great rudeness, she rose and
left him there alone.

Before she reached the house, Gouvernail had
lighted a fresh cigar and ended his apostrophe to
the night.

Mrs. Baroda was greatly tempted that night to
tell her husband—who was also her friend—of this
folly that had seized her. But she did not yield to
the temptation. Beside being a respectable woman
she was a very sensible one, and she knew there
are some battles in life which a human being must
fight alone.

When Gaston arose in the morning, his wife had
already departed. She had taken an early morning
train to the city. She did not return till Gouvernail
was gone from under her roof.

There was some talk of having him back during

the summer that followed. That is, Gaston greatly desired it, but the desire yielded to his wife's strenuous opposition.

However, before the year ended, she proposed, wholly from herself, to have Gouvernail visit them again. Her husband was surprised and delighted with the suggestion coming from her.

"I am glad, chère amie, to know that you have finally overcome your dislike for him; truly he did not deserve it."

"Oh," she told him, laughingly, after pressing a long, tender kiss upon his lips, "I have overcome everything! you will see. This time I shall be very nice to him."

REGRET

Mamzelle Aurélie possessed a good strong figure, ruddy cheeks, hair that was changing from brown to gray, and a determined eye. She wore a man's hat about the farm, and an old blue army overcoat when it was cold, and sometimes topboots.

Mamzelle Aurélie had never thought of marrying. She had never been in love. At the age of twenty she had received a proposal, which she had promptly declined, and at the age of fifty she had not yet lived to regret it.

So she was quite alone in the world, except for her dog Ponto, and the negroes who lived in her cabins and worked her crops, and the fowls, a few cows, a couple of mules, her gun (with which she shot chickenhawks), and her religion.

One morning Mamzelle Aurélie stood upon her gallery, contemplating, with arms akimbo, a small band of very small children who, to all intents and purposes, might have fallen from the clouds, so unexpected and bewildering was their coming, and so unwelcome. They were the children of her nearest neighbor, Odile, who was not such a near neighbor, after all.

The young woman had appeared but five minutes before, accompanied by these four children. In her arms she carried little Elodie; she dragged Ti Nomme by an unwilling hand; while Marcéline and Marcélette followed with irresolute steps.

Her face was red and disfigured from tears and excitement. She had been summoned to a neighboring parish by the dangerous illness of her mother; her husband was away in Texas—it seemed to her a million miles away; and Valsin was waiting with the mule-cart to drive her to the station.

"It's no question, Mamzelle Aurélie; you jus' got to keep those youngsters fo' me tell I come back. Dieu sait, I would n' botha you with 'em if it was any otha way to do! Make 'em mine you, Mamzelle Aurélie; don' spare 'em. Me, there, I'm half crazy between the chil'ren, an' Léon not home, an' maybe not even to fine po' maman alive encore!"— a harrowing possibility which drove Odile to take a final hasty and convulsive leave of her disconsolate family.

She left them crowded into the narrow strip of shade on the porch of the long, low house; the white sunlight was beating in on the white old boards; some chickens were scratching in the grass at the foot of the steps, and one had boldly mounted, and was stepping heavily, solemnly, and aimlessly across the gallery. There was a pleasant odor of pinks in the air, and the sound of negroes' laughter was coming across the flowering cotton-field.

Mamzelle Aurélie stood contemplating the children. She looked with a critical eye upon Marcéline, who had been left staggering beneath the weight of the chubby Elodie. She surveyed with the same calculating air Marcélette mingling her silent tears with the audible grief and rebellion of Ti Nomme. During those few contemplative moments she was collecting herself, determining upon a line of action which should be identical with a line of duty. She began by feeding them.

If Mamzelle Aurélie's responsibilities might have begun and ended there, they could easily have been dismissed; for her larder was amply provided against an emergency of this nature. But little children are not little pigs; they require and demand attentions which were wholly unexpected by Mamzelle Aurélie, and which she was ill prepared to give.

She was, indeed, very inapt in her management of Odile's children during the first few days. How could she know that Marcélette always wept when spoken to in a loud and commanding tone of voice? It was a peculiarity of Marcélette's. She became acquainted with Ti Nomme's passion for flowers only when he had plucked all the choicest gardenias and pinks for the apparent purpose of critically studying their botanical construction.

" 'Tain't enough to tell 'im, Mamzelle Aurélie," Marcéline instructed her; "you got to tie 'im in a chair. It's w'at maman all time do w'en he's bad: she tie 'im in a chair." The chair in which Mamzelle Aurélie tied Ti Nomme was roomy and comfortable, and he seized the opportunity to take a nap in it, the afternoon being warm.

At night, when she ordered them one and all to bed as she would have shooed the chickens into the hen-house, they stayed uncomprehending before her. What about the little white nightgowns that had to be taken from the pillow-slip in which they were brought over, and shaken by some strong hand till they snapped like ox-whips? What about the tub of water which had to be brought and set in the middle of the floor, in which the little tired, dusty, sunbrowned feet had every one to be washed sweet and clean? And it made Marcéline and Marcélette laugh merrily—

the idea that Mamzelle Aurélie should for a moment
have believed that Ti Nomme could fall asleep without
being told the story of *Croque-mitaine* or *Loup-garou*,
or both; or that Elodie could fall asleep at all without
being rocked and sung to.

"I tell you, Aunt Ruby," Mamzelle Aurélie informed
her cook in confidence; "me, I'd rather manage a
dozen plantation' than fo' chil'ren. It's terrassent!
Bonté! Don't talk to me about chil'ren!"

" 'Tain' ispected sich as you would know airy thing
'bout 'em, Mamzelle Aurélie. I see dat plainly yistiddy
w'en I spy dat li'le chile playin' wid yo' baskit o'
keys. You don' know dat makes chillun grow up
hard-headed, to play wid keys? Des like it make 'em
teeth hard to look in a lookin'-glass. Them's the
things you got to know in the raisin' an' manigement
o' chillun."

Mamzelle Aurélie certainly did not pretend or
aspire to such subtle and far-reaching knowledge on
the subject as Aunt Ruby possessed, who had "raised
five an' bared (buried) six" in her day. She was glad
enough to learn a few little mother-tricks to serve the
moment's need.

Ti Nomme's sticky fingers compelled her to
unearth white aprons that she had not worn for years,
and she had to accustom herself to his moist kisses—
the expressions of an affectionate and exuberant
nature. She got down her sewing-basket, which she
seldom used, from the top shelf of the armoire, and
placed it within the ready and easy reach which torn
slips and buttonless waists demanded. It took her
some days to become accustomed to the laughing, the
crying, the chattering that echoed through the house
and around it all day long. And it was not the first or

the second night that she could sleep comfortably with little Elodie's hot, plump body pressed close against her, and the little one's warm breath beating her cheek like the fanning of a bird's wing.

But at the end of two weeks Mamzelle Aurélie had grown quite used to these things, and she no longer complained.

It was also at the end of two weeks that Mamzelle Aurélie, one evening, looking away toward the crib where the cattle were being fed, saw Valsin's blue cart turning the bend of the road. Odile sat beside the mulatto, upright and alert. As they drew near, the young woman's beaming face indicated that her home-coming was a happy one.

But this coming, unannounced and unexpected, threw Mamzelle Aurélie into a flutter that was almost agitation. The children had to be gathered. Where was Ti Nomme? Yonder in the shed, putting an edge on his knife at the grindstone. And Marcéline and Marcélette? Cutting and fashioning doll-rags in the corner of the gallery. As for Elodie, she was safe enough in Mamzelle Aurélie's arms; and she had screamed with delight at sight of the familiar blue cart which was bringing her mother back to her.

The excitement was all over, and they were gone. How still it was when they were gone! Mamzelle Aurélie stood upon the gallery, looking and listening. She could no longer see the cart; the red sunset and the blue-gray twilight had together flung a purple mist across the fields and road that hid it from her view. She could no longer hear the wheezing and creaking of its wheels. But she could still faintly hear the shrill, glad voices of the children.

She turned into the house. There was much work

awaiting her, for the children had left a sad disorder behind them; but she did not at once set about the task of righting it. Mamzelle Aurélie seated herself beside the table. She gave one slow glance through the room, into which the evening shadows were creeping and deepening around her solitary figure. She let her head fall down upon her bended arm, and began to cry. Oh, but she cried! Not softly, as women often do. She cried like a man, with sobs that seemed to tear her very soul. She did not notice Ponto licking her hand.

ATHÉNAÏSE

Athénaïse went away in the morning to make a visit to her parents, ten miles back on rigolet de Bon Dieu. She did not return in the evening, and Cazeau, her husband fretted not a little. He did not worry much about Athénaïse, who, he suspected, was resting only too content in the bosom of her family; his chief solicitude was manifestly for the pony she had ridden. He felt sure those "lazy pigs," her brothers, were capable of neglecting it seriously. This misgiving Cazeau communicated to his servant, old Félicité, who waited upon him at supper.

His voice was low pitched, and even softer than Félicité's. He was tall, sinewy, swarthy, and altogether severe looking. His thick black hair waved, and it gleamed like the breast of a crow. The sweep of his mustache, which was not so black, outlined the broad contour of the mouth. Beneath the under lip grew a small tuft which he was much given to twisting, and which he permitted to grow, apparently for no other purpose. Cazeau's eyes were dark blue, narrow and overshadowed. His hands were coarse and stiff from close acquaintance with farming tools and implements, and he handled his fork and knife clumsily. But he was distinguished looking, and succeeded in commanding a good deal of respect, and even fear sometimes.

He ate his supper alone, by the light of a single coal-oil lamp that but faintly illuminated the big room, with its bare floor and huge rafters, and its heavy pieces of furniture that loomed dimly in the gloom of the apartment. Félicité, ministering to his wants, hovered about the table like a little, bent, restless shadow.

She served him with a dish of sunfish fried crisp and brown. There was nothing else set before him beside the bread and butter and the bottle of red wine which she locked carefully in the buffet after he had poured his second glass. She was occupied with her mistress's absence, and kept reverting to it after he had expressed his solicitude about the pony.

"Dat beat me! on'y marry two mont', an' got de head turn' a'ready to go 'broad. C'est pas Chrétien, ténez!"

Cazeau shrugged his shoulders for answer, after he had drained his glass and pushed aside his plate. Félicité's opinion of the unchristianlike behavior of his wife in leaving him thus alone after two months of marriage weighed little with him. He was used to solitude, and did not mind a day or a night or two of it. He had lived alone ten years, since his first wife died, and Félicité might have known better than to suppose that he cared. He told her she was a fool. It sounded like a compliment in his modulated, caressing voice. She grumbled to herself as she set about clearing the table, and Cazeau arose and walked outside on the gallery; his spur, which he had not removed upon entering the house, jangled at every step.

The night was beginning to deepen, and to gather black about the clusters of trees and shrubs that were grouped in the yard. In the beam of light from the open kitchen door a black boy stood feeding a brace of snarling, hungry dogs; further away, on the steps of a cabin, some one was playing the accordion; and in still another direction a little negro baby was crying lustily. Cazeau walked around to the front of the house, which was square, squat and one-story.

A belated wagon was driving in at the gate, and the impatient driver was swearing hoarsely at his jaded oxen. Félicité stepped out on the gallery, glass and polishing towel in hand, to investigate, and to wonder, too, who could be singing out on the river. It was a party of young people paddling around, waiting for the moon to rise, and they were singing Juanita, their voices coming tempered and melodious through the distance and the night.

Cazeau's horse was waiting, saddled, ready to be mounted, for Cazeau had many things to attend to before bedtime; so many things that there was not left to him a moment in which to think of Athénaïse. He felt her absence, though, like a dull, insistent pain.

However, before he slept that night he was visited by the thought of her, and by a vision of her fair young face with its dropping lips and sullen and averted eyes. The marriage had been a blunder; he had only to look into her eyes to feel that, to discover her growing aversion. But it was a thing not by any possibility to be undone. He was quite prepared to make the best of it, and expected no less than a like effort on her part. The less she revisited the rigolet, the better. He would find means to keep her at home hereafter.

These unpleasant reflections kept Cazeau awake far into the night, notwithstanding the craving of his whole body for rest and sleep. The moon was shining, and its pale effulgence reached dimly into the room, and with it a touch of the cool breath of the spring night. There was an unusual stillness abroad; no sound to be heard save the distant, tireless, plaintive note of the accordion.

II

Athénaïse did not return the following day, even though her husband sent her word to do so by her brother, Montéclin, who passed on his way to the village early in the morning.

On the third day Cazeau saddled his horse and went himself in search of her. She had sent no word, no message, explaining her absence, and he felt that he had good cause to be offended. It was rather awkward to have to leave his work, even though late in the afternoon,— Cazeau had always so much to do; but among the many urgent calls upon him, the task of bringing his wife back to a sense of her duty seemed to him for the moment paramount.

The Michés, Athénaïse's parents, lived on the old Gotrain place. It did not belong to them; they were "running" it for a merchant in Alexandria. The house was far too big for their use. One of the lower rooms served for the storing of wood and tools; the person "occupying" the place before Miché having pulled up the flooring in despair of being able to patch it. Upstairs, the rooms were so large, so bare, that they offered a constant temptation to lovers of the dance, whose importunities Madame Miché was accustomed to meet with amiable indulgence. A dance at Miché's and a plate of Madame Miché's gumbo filé at midnight were pleasure not to be neglected or despised, unless by such serious souls as Cazeau.

Long before Cazeau reached the house his approach

had been observed, for there was nothing to obstruct the view of the outer road; vegetation was not yet abundantly advanced, and there was but a patchy, straggling stand of cotton and corn in Miché's field.

Madame Miché, who had been seated on the gallery in a rocking-chair, stood up to greet him as he drew near. She was short and fat, and wore a black skirt and loose muslin sack fastened at the throat with a hair brooch. Her own hair, brown and glossy, showed but a few threads of silver. Her round pink face was cheery, and her eyes were bright and good humored. But she was plainly perturbed and ill at ease as Cazeau advanced.

Montéclin, who was there too, was not ill at ease, and made no attempt to disguise the dislike with which his brother-in-law inspired him. He was a slim, wiry fellow of twenty-five, short of stature like his mother, and resembling her in feature. He was in shirt-sleeves, half leaning, half sitting, on the insecure railing of the gallery, and fanning himself with his broad-rimmed felt hat.

"Cochon!" he muttered under his breath as Cazeau mounted the stairs, "sacré cochon!"

"Cochon" had sufficiently characterized the man who had once on a time declined to lend Montéclin money. But when this same man had had the presumption to propose marriage to his well-beloved sister, Athénaïse, and the honor to be accepted by her, Montéclin felt that a qualifying epithet was needed fully to express his estimate of Cazeau.

Miché and his oldest son were absent. They both esteemed Cazeau highly, and talked much of his qualities of head and heart, and thought much of his excellent standing with city merchants.

Athénaïse had shut herself up in her room. Cazeau had seen her rise and enter the house at perceiving him. He was a good deal mystified, but no one could have guessed it when he shook hands with Madame Miché. He had only nodded to Montéclin, with a muttered "Comment ça va?"

"Tiens! something tole me you were coming to-day!" exclaimed Madame Miché, with a little blustering appearance of being cordial and at ease, as she offered Cazeau a chair.

He ventured a short laugh as he seated himself.

"You know, nothing would do," she went on, with much gesture of her small, plump hands, "nothing would do but Athénaïse mus' stay las' night fo' a li'le dance. The boys wouldn' year to their sister leaving."

Cazeau shrugged his shoulders significantly, telling as plainly as words that he knew nothing about it.

"Comment! Montéclin didn' tell you we were going to keep Athénaïse?" Montéclin had evidently told nothing.

"An' how about the night befo'," questioned Cazeau, "an' las' night? It isn't possible you dance every night out yere on the Bon Dieu!"

Madame Miché laughed, with amiable appreciation of the sarcasm; and turning to her son, "Montéclin, my boy, go tell yo' sister that Monsieur Cazeau is yere."

Montéclin did not stir except to shift his position and settle himself more securely on the railing.

"Did you year me, Montéclin?"

"Oh yes, I yeard you plain enough," responded her son, "but you know as well as me it's no use to tell 'Thénaïse anything. You been talkin' to her yo'se'f since Monday, an' pa's preached himse'f hoa'se on the

subject, an' you even had uncle Achille down yere
yesterday to reason with her. W'en 'Thénaïse said she
wasn' goin' to set her foot back in Cazeau's house,
she meant it."

This speech, which Montéclin delivered with
thorough unconcern, threw his mother into a condition
of painful but dumb embarrassment. It brought two
fiery red spots to Cazeau's cheeks, and for the space
of a moment he looked wicked.

What Montéclin had spoken was quite true, though
his taste in the manner and choice of time and place
in saying it were not of the best. Athénaïse, upon the
first day of her arrival, had announced that she came
to stay, having no intention of returning under
Cazeau's roof. The announcement had scattered
consternation, as she knew it would. She had been
implored, scolded, entreated, stormed at, until she
felt herself like a dragging sail that all the winds of
heaven had beaten upon. Why in the name of God
had she married Cazeau? Her father had lashed her
with the question a dozen times. Why indeed? It was
difficult now for her to understand why, unless
because she supposed it was customary for girls to
marry when the right opportunity came. Cazeau, she
knew, would make life more comfortable for her; and
again, she had liked him, and had even been rather
flustered when he pressed her hands and kissed them,
and kissed her lips and cheeks and eyes, when she
accepted him.

Montéclin himself had taken her aside to talk the
thing over. The turn of affairs was delighting him.

"Come, now, 'Thénaïse, you mus' explain to me all
about it, so we can settle on a good cause, an' secu' a
separation fo' you. Has he been mistreating an'

abusing you, the sacré cochon?" They were alone together in her room, whither she had taken refuge from the angry domestic elements.

"You please to reserve yo' disgusting expressions, Montéclin. No, he has not abused me in any way that I can think."

"Does he drink? Come 'Thénaïse, think well over it. Does he ever get drunk?"

"Drunk! Oh, mercy, no,—Cazeau never gets drunk."

"I see; it's jus' simply you feel like me; you hate him."

"No, I don't hate him," she returned reflectively, adding with a sudden impulse, "It's jus' being married that I detes' an' despise. I hate being Mrs. Cazeau, an' would want to be Athénaïse Miché again. I can't stan' to live with a man, to have him always there, his coats an' pantaloons hanging in my room, his ugly bare feet—washing them in my tub, befo' my very eyes, ugh!" She shuddered with recollections, and resumed, with a sigh that was almost a sob: "Mon Dieu, mon Dieu! Sister Marie Angélique knew w'at she was saying; she knew me better than myse'f w'en she said God had sent me a vocation an' I was turning deaf ears. W'en I think of a blessed life in the convent, at peace! Oh, w'at was I dreaming of!" and then the tears came.

Montéclin felt disconcerted and greatly disappointed at having obtained evidence that would carry no weight with a court of justice. The day had not come when a young woman might ask the court's permission to return to her mamma on the sweeping ground of a constitutional disinclination for marriage. But if there was no way of untying this Gordian knot of marriage, there was surely a way of cutting it.

"Well, 'Thénaïse, I'm mightly durn sorry you got no better groun's 'an w'at you say. But you can count on me to stan' by you w'atever you do. God knows I don' blame you fo' not wantin' to live with Cazeau."

And now there was Cazeau himself, with the red spots flaming in his swarthy cheeks, looking and feeling as if he wanted to thrash Montéclin into some semblance of decency. He arose abruptly, and approaching the room which he had seen his wife enter, thrust open the door after a hasty preliminary knock. Athénaïse, who was standing erect at a far window, turned at his entrance.

She appeared neither angry nor frightened, but thoroughly unhappy, with an appeal in her soft dark eyes and a tremor on her lips that seemed to him expressions of unjust reproach, that wounded and maddened him at once. But whatever he might feel, Cazeau knew only one way to act toward a woman.

"Athénaïse, you are not ready?" he asked in his quiet tones. "It's getting late; we havn' any time to lose."

She knew that Montéclin had spoken out, and she had hoped for a wordy interview, a stormy scene, in which she might have held her own as she had held it for the past three days against her family, with Montéclin's aid. But she had no weapon with which to combat subtlety. Her husband's looks, his tones, his mere presence, brought to her a sudden sense of hopelessness, and instinctive realization of the futility of rebellion against a social and sacred institution.

Cazeau said nothing further, but stood waiting in the doorway. Madame Miché had walked to the far end of the gallery, and pretended to be occupied with having a chicken driven from her parterre. Montéclin stood by, exasperated, fuming, ready to burst out.

Athénaïse went and reached for her riding skirt that hung against the wall. She was rather tall, with a figure which, though not robust, seemed perfect in its fine proportions. "La fille de son père," she was often called, which was a great compliment to Miché. Her brown hair was brushed all fluffily back from her temples and low forehead, and about her features and expression lurked a softness, a prettiness, a dewiness, that were perhaps too childlike, that savored of immaturity.

She slipped the riding skirt, which was of black alpaca, over her head, and with impatient fingers hooked it at the waist over her pink linen-lawn. Then she fastened on her white sunbonnet and reached for her gloves on the mantel piece.

"If you don' wan' to go, you know w'at you got to do, 'Thénaïse," fumed Montéclin. "You don' set yo' feet back on Cane River, by God, unless you want to,—not w'ile I'm alive."

Cazeau looked at him as if he were a monkey whose antics fell short of being amusing.

Athénaïse still made no reply, said not a word. She walked rapidly past her husband, past her brother, bidding good-by to no one, not even to her mother. She descended the stairs, and without assistance from any one mounted the pony, which Cazeau had ordered to be saddled upon his arrival. In this way she obtained a fair start of her husband, whose departure was far more leisurely, and for the greater part of the way she managed to keep an appreciable gap between them. She rode almost madly at first, with the wind inflating her skirt balloon-like about her knees, and her sunbonnet falling back between her shoulders.

At no time did Cazeau make an effort to overtake her until traversing an old fallow meadow that was level and hard as a table. The sight of a great solitary oak tree, with its seemingly immutable outlines, that had been a landmark for ages—or was it the odor of elderberry stealing up from the gully to the south? or what was it that brought vividly back to Cazeau, by some association of ideas, a scene of many years ago? He had passed that old live-oak hundreds of times, but it was only now that the memory of one day came back to him. He was a very small boy that day, seated before his father on horseback. They were proceeding slowly, and Black Gabe was moving on before them at a little dogtrot. Black Gabe had run away, and had been discovered back in the Gotrain swamp. They had halted beneath this big oak to enable the negro to take breath; for Cazeau's father was a kind and considerate master, and every one had agreed at the time that Black Gabe was a fool, a great idiot indeed, for wanting to run away from him.

The whole impression was for some reason hideous, and to dispel it Cazeau spurred his horse to a swift gallop. Overtaking his wife, he rode the remainder of the way at her side in silence.

It was late when they reached home. Félicité was standing on the grassy edge of the road, in the moonlight, waiting for them.

Cazeau once more ate his supper alone, for Athénaïse went to her room, and there she was crying again.

III

Athénaïse was not one to accept the inevitable with patient resignation, a talent born in the souls of many women; neither was she the one to accept it with philosophical resignation, like her husband. Her sensibilities were alive and keen and responsive. She met the pleasureable things of life with frank, open appreciation, and against distasteful conditions she rebelled. Dissimulation was as foreign to her nature as guile to the breast of a babe, and her rebellious outbreaks, by no means rare, had hitherto been quite open and aboveboard. People often said that Athénaïse would know her own mind some day, which was equivalent to saying that she was at present unacquainted with it. If she ever came to such knowledge, it would be by no intellectual research, by no subtle analyses or tracing the motives of actions to their source. It would come to her as the song to the bird, the perfume and color to the flower.

Her parents had hoped—not without reason and justice—that marriage would bring the poise, the desirable pose, so glaringly lacking in Athénaïse's character. Marriage they knew to be a wonderful and powerful agent in the development and formation of a woman's character; they had seen its effect too often to doubt it.

"And if this marriage does nothing else," exclaimed Miché in an outburst of sudden exasperation, "it will rid us of Athénaïse, for I am at the end of my patience with her! You have never had the firmness to manage her"—he was speaking to his wife,—"I have not had the time, the leisure, to devote to her training; and what good we might have accomplished, that maudit Montéclin—Well, Cazeau is the one! It takes just such a steady hand to guide a disposition like Athénaïse's, a master hand, a strong will that compels obedience."

And now, when they had hoped for so much, here was Athénaïse, with gathered and fierce vehemence, beside which her former outbursts appeared mild, declaring that she would not, and she would not, and she would not continue to enact the role of wife to Cazeau. If she had had a reason! as Madame Miché lamented; but it could not be discovered that she had any sane one. He had never scolded, or called names, or deprived her of comforts, or been guilty of any of the many reprehensible acts commonly attributed to objectionable husbands. He did not slight nor neglect her. Indeed, Cazeau's chief offense seemed to be that he loved her, and Athénaïse was not the woman to be loved against her will. She called marriage a trap set for the feet of unwary and unsuspecting girls, and in round, unmeasured terms reproached her mother with treachery and deceit.

"I told you Cazeau was the man," chuckled Miché, when his wife had related the scene that had accompanied and influenced Athénaïse's departure.

Athénaïse again hoped, in the morning, that Cazeau would scold or make some sort of a scene, but he apparently did not dream of it. It was exasperating that he should take her acquiescence so for granted. It is true he had been up and over the fields and across the river and back long before she was out of bed, and he may have been thinking of something else, which was no excuse, which was even in some sense an aggravation. But he did say to her at breakfast, "That brother of yo's, that Montéclin, is unbearable."

"Montéclin? Par exemple!"

Athénaïse, seated opposite to her husband, was attired in a white morning wrapper. She wore a somewhat abused, long face, it is true—an expression of countenance familiar to some husbands,—but the expression was not sufficiently pronounced to mar the charm of her youthful freshness. She had little heart to eat, only playing with the food before her, and she felt a pang of resentment at her husband's healthy appetite.

"Yes, Montéclin," he reasserted. "He's developed into a firs'-class nuisance; an' you better tell him, Athénaïse,—unless you want me to tell him,—to confine his energies after this to matters that concern him. I have no use fo' him or fo' his interference in w'at regards you an' me alone."

This was said with unusual asperity. It was the little breach that Athénaïse had been watching for, and she charged rapidly: "It's strange, if you detes' Montéclin so heartily, that you would desire to marry his sister." She knew it was a silly thing to say, and was not surprised when he told her so. It gave her a little foothold for further attack, however. "I don't see, anyhow, w'at reason you had to marry me, w'en there were so many others," she complained, as if accusing him of persecution and injury. "There was Marianne running after you fo' the las' five years till it was disgraceful; an' any one of the Dortrand girls would have been glad to marry you. But no, nothing would do; you mus' come out on the rigolet fo' me." Her complaint was pathetic, and at the same time so amusing that Cazeau was forced to smile.

"I can't see w'at the Dortrand girls or Marianne have to do with it," he rejoined; adding, with no trace of amusement, "I married you because I loved you; because you were the woman I wanted to marry, an' the only one. I reckon I tole you that befo'. I thought—

of co'se I was a fool fo' taking things fo' granted—but I did think that I might make you happy in making things easier an' mo' comfortable fo' you. I expected— I was even that big a fool—I believed that yo' coming yere to me would be like the sun shining out of the clouds, an' that our days would be like w'at the story-books promise after the wedding. I was mistaken. But I can't imagine w'at induced you to marry me. W'atever it was, I reckon you foun' out you made a mistake, too. I don' see anything to do but make the best of a bad bargain, an' shake han's over it." He had arisen from the table, and, approaching, held out his hand to her. What he had said was commonplace enough, but it was significant, coming from Cazeau, who was not often so unreserved in expressing himself.

Athénaïse ignored the hand held out to her. She was resting her chin in her palm, and kept her eyes fixed moodily upon the table. He rested his hand, that she would not touch, upon her head of an instant, and walked away out of the room.

She heard him giving orders to workmen who had been waiting for him out on the gallery, and she heard him mount his horse and ride away. A hundred things would distract him and engage his attention during the day. She felt that he had perhaps put her and her grievance from his thoughts when he crossed the threshold; whilst she—

Old Félicité was standing there holding a shining tin pail, asking for flour and lard and eggs from the storeroom, and meal for the chicks.

Athénaïse seized the bunch of keys which hung from her belt and flung them at Félicité's feet.

"Tiens! tu vas les garder comme tu as jadis fait. Je

ne veux plus de ce train là, moi!"

The old woman stooped and picked up the keys from the floor. It was really all one to her that her mistress returned them to her keeping, and refused to take further account of the ménage.

IV

It seemed now to Athénaïse that Montéclin was the only friend left to her in the world. Her father and mother had turned from her in what appeared to be her hour of need. Her friends laughed at her, and refused to take seriously the hints which she threw out—feeling her way to discover if marriage were as distasteful to other women as to herself. Montéclin alone understood her. He alone had always been ready to act for her and with her, to comfort and solace her with his sympathy and his support. Her only hope for rescue from her hateful surroundings lay in Montéclin. Of herself she felt powerless to plan, to act, even to conceive a way out of this pitfall into which the whole world seemed to have conspired to push her.

She had a great desire to see her brother and wrote asking him to come to her. But it better suited Montéclin's spirit of adventure to appoint a meeting place at the turn of the lane, where Athénaïse might appear to be walking leisurely for health and recreation, and where he might seem to be riding along, bent on some errand of business or pleasure.

There had been a shower, a sudden downpour, short as it was sudden, that had laid the dust in the road. It had freshened the pointed leaves of the live oaks, and brightened up the big fields of cotton on either side of the lane till they seemed carpeted with green, glittering gems.

Athénaïse walked along the grassy edge of the road, lifting her crisp skirts with one hand, and with the other twirling a gay sunshade over her bare head. The scent of the fields after the rain was delicious. She inhaled long breaths of their freshness and perfume, that soothed and quieted her for the moment. There were birds splashing and spluttering in the pools, pluming themselves on the fence-rails, and sending out little sharp cries, twitters, and shrill rhapsodies of delight.

She saw Montéclin approaching from a great distance—almost as far away as the turn of the woods. But she could not feel sure it was he; it appeared too tall for Montéclin, but that was because he was riding a large horse. She waved her parasol to him; she was so glad to see him. She had never been so glad to see Montéclin before, not even the day when he had taken her out of the convent, against her parents' wishes, because she had expressed a desire to remain there no longer. He seemed to her, as he drew near, the embodiment of kindness, of bravery, of chivalry, even of wisdom, for she had never known Montéclin at a loss to extricate himself from a disagreeable situation.

He dismounted, and, leading his horse by the bridle, started to walk beside her, after he had kissed her affectionately and asked her what she was crying about. She protested that she was not crying, for she was laughing, though drying her eyes at the same time on her handkerchief, rolled in a soft mop for the purpose.

She took Montéclin's arm, and they strolled slowly down the lane; they could not seat themselves for a comfortable chat, as they would have liked, with the grass all sparkling and bristling wet.

Yes, she was quite as wretched as ever, she told him. The week which had gone by since she saw him had in no wise lightened the burden of her discontent. There had even been some additional provocations laid upon her, and she told Montéclin all about them,— about the keys, for instance, which in a fit of temper she had returned to Félicité's keeping; and she told how Cazeau had brought them back to her as if they were something she had accidentally lost, and he had recovered; and how he had said, in that aggravating tone of his, that it was not the custom on Cane river for the Negro servants to carry the keys, when there was a mistress at the head of the household.

But Athénaïse could not tell Montéclin anything to increase the disrespect which he already entertained for his brother-in-law; and it was then he unfolded to her a plan which he had conceived and worked out for her deliverance from this galling matrimonial yoke.

It was not a plan which met with instant favor, which she was at once ready to accept, for it involved secrecy and dissimulation, hateful alternatives, both of them. But she was filled with admiration for Montéclin's resources and wonderful talent for contrivance. She accepted the plan; not with the immediate determination to act upon it, rather with the intention to sleep and to dream upon it.

Three days later she wrote to Montéclin that she had abandoned herself to his counsel. Displeasing as it might be to her sense of honesty, it would yet be less trying than to live on with a soul full of bitterness and revolt, as she had done for the past two months.

V

When Cazeau awoke, one morning at his usual very

early hour, it was to find the place at his side vacant.
This did not surprise him until he discovered that
Athénaïse was not in the adjoining room, where he
had often found her sleeping in the morning on the
lounge. She had perhaps gone out for an early stroll,
he reflected, for her jacket and hat were not on the
rack where she had hung them the night before.
But there were other things absent,—a gown or two
from the armoire; and there was a great gap in the
piles of lingerie on the shelf; and her traveling-bag
was missing, and so were her bits of jewelry from the
toilet tray—and Athénaïse was gone!

But the absurdity of going during the night, as
if she had been a prisoner, and he the keeper of a
dungeon! So much secrecy and mystery, to go so-
journing out on the Bon Dieu? Well, the Miché's might
keep their daughter after this. For the companionship
of no woman on earth would he again undergo the
humiliating sensation of baseness that had overtaken him in passing the old oak-tree in the fallow
meadow.

But a terrible sense of loss overwhelmed Cazeau.
It was not new or sudden; he had felt it for weeks
growing upon him, and it seemed to culminate with
Athénaïse's flight from home. He knew that he
could again compel her return as he had done once
before,—compel her to return to the shelter of his
roof, compel her cold and unwilling submission to
his love and passionate transports; but the loss of
self-respect seemed to him too dear a price to pay
for a wife.

He could not comprehend why she had seemed to
prefer him above others; why she had attracted him
with eyes, with voice, with a hundred womanly

ways, and finally distracted him with love which she seemed, in her timid, maidenly fashion, to return. The great sense of loss came from the realization of having missed a chance for happiness,—a chance that would come his way again only through a miracle. He could not think of himself loving any other woman, and could not think of Athénaïse ever—even at some remote date—caring for him.

He wrote her a letter, in which he disclaimed any further intention of forcing his commands upon her. He did not desire her presence ever again in his home unless she came of her free will, uninfluenced by family or friends; unless she could be the companion he had hoped for in marrying her, and in some measure return affection and respect for the love which he continued and would always continue to feel for her. This letter he sent out to the rigolet by a messenger early in the day. But she was not out on the rigolet, and had not been there.

The family turned instinctively to Montéclin, and almost literally fell upon him for an explanation; he had been absent from home all night. There was much mystification in his answers, and a plain desire to mislead in his assurances of ignorance and innocence.

But with Cazeau there was no doubt or speculation when he accosted the young fellow. "Montéclin, w'at have you done with Athénaïse?" he questioned bluntly. They had met in the open road on horseback, just as Cazeau ascended the river bank before his house.

"W'at have you done to Athénaïse?" returned Montéclin for answer.

"I don't reckon you've considered yo' conduct by any light of decency an' propriety in encouraging yo' sister to such an action, but let me tell you—"

"Voyons! you can let me alone with yo' decency an' morality an' fiddlesticks. I know you mus' 'a' done Athénaïse pretty mean that she can't live with you; an' fo' my part, I'm mighty durn glad she had the spirit to quit you."

"I ain't in the humor to take any notice of yo' impertinence, Montéclin; but let me remine you that Athénaïse is nothing but a chile in character; besides that, she's my wife, an' I hole you responsible fo' her safety an' welfare. If any harm of any description happens to her, I'll strangle you, by God, like a rat, and fling you in Cane river, if I have to hang fo' it!" He had not lifted his voice. The only sign of anger was a savage gleam in his eyes.

"I reckon you better keep yo' big talk fo' the women, Cazeau," replied Montéclin, riding away.

But he went doubly armed after that, and intimated that the precaution was not needless, in view of the threats and menaces that were abroad touching his personal safety.

VI

Athénaïse reached her destination sound of skin and limb, but a good deal flustered, a little frightened, and altogether excited and interested by her unusual experiences.

Her destination was the house of Sylvie, on Dauphine Street, in New Orleans—a three-story gray brick, standing directly on the banquette, with three broad stone steps leading to the deep front entrance.

From the second-story balcony swung a small sign, conveying to passers-by the intelligence that within were "*chambres garnies.*"

It was one morning in the last week of April that Athénaïse presented herself at the Dauphine Street house. Sylvie was expecting her, and introduced her at once to her apartment, which was in the second story of the back ell, and accessible by an open, outside gallery. There was a yard below, paved with broad stone flagging; many fragrant flowering shrubs and plants grew in a bed along the side of the opposite wall, and others were distributed about in tubs and green boxes.

It was a plain but large enough room into which Athénaïse was ushered, with matting on the floor, green shades and Nottingham lace curtains at the windows that looked out on the gallery, and furnished with a cheap walnut suit. But everything looked exquisitely clean, and the whole place smelled of cleanliness.

Athénaïse at once fell into the rocking-chair, with the air of exhaustion and intense relief of one who has come to the end of her troubles. Sylvie, entering behind her, laid the big traveling-bag on the floor and deposited the jacket on the bed.

She was a portly quadroon of fifty or thereabout, clad in an ample *volante* of the old-fashioned purple calico so much affected by her class. She wore large golden hoop-earrings, and her hair was combed plainly, with every appearance of effort to smooth out the kinks. She had broad, coarse features, with a nose that turned up, exposing the wide nostrils, and that seemed to emphasize the loftiness and command of her bearing,—a dignity that in the presence of white people assumed a character of respectfulness, but never of obsequiousness. Sylvie believed firmly in maintaining the color-line, and would not suffer a white person, even a child, to call her "Madame Sylvie,"—a title which she exacted religiously, however, from those of her own race.

"I hope you be please' wid yo' room, madame," she observed amiably. "Dat's de same room w'at yo' brother, M'sieur Miché, all time like w'en he come to New Orlean'. He well, M'sieur Miché? I receive' his letter las' week, an' dat same day a gent'man want I give 'im dat room. I say, 'No, dat room already ingage'. 'Ev-body like dat room on 'count it so quite (quiet). M'sieur Gouvernail, dere in nax' room, you can't pay 'im! He been stay t'ree year' in dat room; but all fix' up fine wid his own furn'ture an' books, 'tel you can't see! I say to 'im plenty time', 'M'sieur Gouvernail, w'y you don't take dat t'ree-story front, now, long it's empty?' He tells me, 'Leave me 'lone, Sylvie; I know a good room w'en I fine it, me.' "

She had been moving slowly and majestically about the apartment, straightening and smoothing down bed and pillows, peering into ewer and basin, evidently casting an eye around to make sure that everything was as it should be.

"I sen' you some fresh water, Madame," she offered upon retiring from the room. "An' w'en you want an't'ing, you jus' go out on de gall'ry an' call Pousette: she year you plain,—she right down dere in de kitchen."

Athénaïse was really not so exhausted as she had every reason to be after that interminable and circuitous way by which Montéclin had seen fit to have her conveyed to the city.

Would she ever forget that dark and truly dangerous
midnight ride along the "coast" to the mouth of
Cane river! There Montéclin had parted with her,
after seeing her aboard the St. Louis and Shreveport
packet which he knew would pass there before dawn.
She had received instructions to disembark at the
mouth of Red river, and there transfer to the first
south-bound steamer for New Orleans, all of which
instructions she had followed implicitly, even to
making her way at once to Sylvie's upon her arrival in
the city. Montéclin had enjoined secrecy and much
caution; the clandestine nature of the affair gave it a
savor of adventure which was highly pleasing to him.
Eloping with his sister was only a little less engaging
than eloping with some one else's sister.

But Montéclin did not do the *grand seigneur* by
halves. He had paid Sylvie a whole month in advance
for Athénaïse's board and lodging. Part of the sum
he had been forced to borrow, it is true, but he was
not niggardly.

Athénaïse was to take her meals in the house,
which none of the other lodgers did; the one exception
being that Mr. Gouvernail was served with breakfast
on Sunday mornings.

Sylvie's clientèle came chiefly from the southern
parishes; for the most part, people spending but a few
days in the city. She prided herself upon the quality
and highly respectable character of her patrons, who
came and went unobtrusively.

The large parlor opening upon the front balcony
was seldom used. Her guests were permitted to
entertain in this sanctuary of elegance—but they
never did. She often rented it for the night to parties
of respectable and discreet gentlemen desiring to

enjoy a quiet game of cards outside the bosom of their families. The second-story hall also led by a long window out on the balcony. And Sylvie advised Athénaïse, when she grew weary of her back room, to go and sit on the front balcony, which was shady in the afternoon, and where she might find diversion in the sounds and sights of the street below.

Athénaïse refreshed herself with a bath, and was soon unpacking her few belongings, which she ranged neatly away in the bureau drawers and the armoire.

She had revolved certain plans in her mind during the past hour or so. Her present intention was to live on indefinitely in this big, cool clean back room on Dauphine street. She had thought seriously, for moments, of the convent, with all readiness to embrace the vows of poverty and chastity; but what about obedience? Later, she intended, in some roundabout way, to give her parents and her husband the assurance of her safety and welfare, reserving the right to remain unmolested and lost to them. To live on at the expense of Montéclin's generosity was wholly out of the question, and Athénaïse meant to look about for some suitable and agreeable employment.

The imperative thing to be done at present, however, was to go out in search of material for an inexpensive gown or two; for she found herself in the painful predicament of a young woman having almost literally nothing to wear. She decided upon pure white for one, and some sort of a sprigged muslin for the other.

VII

On Sunday morning, two days after Athénaïse's arrival in the city, she went in to breakfast somewhat later than usual, to find two covers laid at table instead of the one to which she was accustomed. She had been to mass, and did not remove her hat, but put her fan, parasol, and prayer-book aside. The dining-room was situated just beneath her own apartment, and, like all rooms of the house, was large and airy; the floor was covered with a glistening oil-cloth.

The small, round table, immaculately set, was drawn near the open window. There were some tall plants in boxes on the gallery outside; and Pousette, a little, old, intensely black woman, was splashing and dashing buckets of water on the flagging, and talking loud in her Creole patois to no one in particular.

A dish piled with delicate river shrimps and crushed ice was on the table; a caraffe of crystal-clear water, a few *hors d'oeuvres*, beside a small golden-brown crusty loaf of French bread at each plate. A half-bottle of wine and the morning paper were set at the place opposite Athénaïse.

She had almost completed her breakfast when Gouvernail came in and seated himself at table. He felt annoyed at finding his cherished privacy invaded. Sylvie was removing the remains of a mutton chop from before Athénaïse, and serving her with a cup of café au lait.

"M'sieur Gouvernail," offered Sylvie in her most insinuating and impressive manner, "you please leave me make you acquaint' wid Madame Cazeau. Dat's M'sieur Miché's sister; you meet 'im two t'ree time', you rec'lec', an' been one day to de race wid 'im. Madame Cazeau, you please leave me make you acquaint' wid M'sieur Gouvernail.''

Gouvernail expressed himself greatly pleased to meet the sister of Monsieur Miché, of whom he had not the slightest recollection. He inquired after Monsieur Miché's health, and politely offered Athénaïse a part of his newspaper—the part which contained the Woman's Page and the social gossip.

Athénaïse faintly remembered that Sylvie had spoken of a Monsieur Gouvernail occupying the room adjoining hers, living amid luxurious surroundings and a multitude of books. She had not thought of him further than to picture him a stout, middle-aged gentleman, with a bushy beard turning gray, wearing large gold-rimmed spectacles, and stooping somewhat from much bending over books and writing material. She had confused him in her mind with the likeness of some literary celebrity that she had run across in the advertising pages of a magazine.

Gouvernail's appearance was, in truth, in no sense striking. He looked older than thirty and younger than forty, was of medium height and weight, with a quiet, unobtrusive manner which seemed to ask that he be let alone. His hair was light brown, brushed carefully and parted in the middle. His mustache was brown, and so were his eyes, which had a mild, penetrating quality. He was neatly dressed in the fashion of the day; and his hands seemed to Athénaïse remarkably white and soft for a man's.

He had been buried in the contents of his newspaper, when he suddenly realized that some further little attention might be due to Miché's sister. He started to offer her a glass of wine, when he was surprised and relieved to find that she had quietly slipped away while he was absorbed in his own editorial on Corrupt Legislation.

Gouvernail finished his paper and smoked his cigar out on the gallery. He lounged about, gathered a rose for his buttonhole, and had his regular Sunday-morning confab with Pousette, to whom he paid a weekly stipend for brushing his shoes and clothing. He made a great pretense of haggling over the trans-action, only to enjoy her uneasiness and garrulous excitement.

He worked or read in his room for a few hours, and when he quitted the house, at three in the after-noon, it was to return no more till late at night. It was his almost invariable custom to spend Sunday evenings out in the American quarter, among a congenial set of men and women—*des esprits forts*, all of them, whose lives were irreproachable, yet whose opinions would startle even the traditional "sapeur," for whom "nothing is sacred." But for all his "advanced" opinions, Gouvernail was a liberal-minded fellow; a man or woman lost nothing of his respect by being married.

When he left the house in the afternoon, Athénaïse had already ensconced herself on the front balcony. He could see her through the jalousies when he passed on his way to the front entrance. She had not yet grown lonesome or homesick; the newness of her surroundings made them sufficiently entertaining. She found it diverting to sit there on the front bal-cony watching people pass by, even though there was no one to talk to. And then the comforting, comfortable sense of not being married!

She watched Gouvernail walk down the street, and could find no fault with his bearing. He could hear the sound of her rockers for some little dis-stance. He wondered what the "poor little thing" was doing in the city, and meant to ask Sylvie about her when he should happen to think of it.

VIII

The following morning, towards noon, when Gouvernail quitted his room, he was confronted by Athénaïse, exhibiting some confusion and trepidation at being forced to request a favor of him at so early a stage of their acquaintance. She stood in her doorway, and had evidently been sewing, as the thimble on her finger testified, as well as a long-threaded needle thrust in the bosom of her gown. She held a stamped but unaddressed letter in her hand.

And would Mr. Gouvernail be so kind as to address the letter to her brother, Mr. Montéclin Miché? She would hate to detain him with explanations this morning,—another time, perhaps,—but now she begged that he would give himself the trouble.

He assured her that it made no difference, that it was no trouble whatever; and he drew a fountain pen from his pocket and addressed the letter at her dictation, resting it on the inverted rim of his straw hat. She wondered a little at a man of his supposed erudition stumbing over the spelling of "Montéclin" and "Miché."

She demurred at overwhelming him with the additional trouble of posting it, but he succeeded in convincing her that so simple a task as the posting of a letter would not add an iota to the burden of the day. Moreover, he promised to carry it in his hand, and thus avoid any possible risk of forgetting it in his pocket.

After that, and after a second repetition of the favor, when she had told him that she had had a letter from Montéclin, and looked as if she wanted to tell him more, he felt that he knew her better. He felt that he knew her well enough to join her out on the balcony, one night, when he found her sitting there alone. He was not one who deliberately sought the society of women, but he was not wholly a bear. A little commiseration for Athénaïse's aloneness, perhaps some curiosity to know further what manner of woman she was, and the natural influence of her feminine charm were equal unconfessed factors in turning his steps towards the balcony when he discovered the shimmer of her white gown through the open hall window.

It was already quite late, but the day had been intensely hot, and neighboring balconies and doorways were occupied by chattering groups of humanity, loath to abandon the grateful freshness of the outer air. The voices about her served to reveal to Athénaïse the feeling of loneliness that was gradually coming over her. Notwithstanding certain dormant impulses, she craved human sympathy and companionship.

She shook hands impulsively with Gouvernail, and told him how glad she was to see him. He was not prepared for such an admission, but it pleased him immensely, detecting as he did that the expression was as sincere as it was outspoken. He drew a chair up within comfortable conversational distance of Athénaïse, though he had no intention of talking more than was barely necessary to encourage Madame—He had actually forgotten her name!

He leaned an elbow on the balcony rail, and

would have offered an opening remark about the
oppressive heat of the day, but Athénaïse did not
give him the opportunity. How glad she was to talk
to someone, and how she talked!

An hour later she had gone to her room, and
Gouvernail stayed smoking on the balcony. He
knew her quite well after that hour's talk. It was
not so much what she had said as what her half
saying had revealed to his quick intelligence. He
knew that she adored Montéclin, and he suspected
that she adored Cazeau without being herself aware
of it. He had gathered that she was self-willed, impulsive, innocent, ignorant, unsatisfied, dissatisfied;
for had she not complained that things seemed all
wrongly arranged in this world, and no one was
permitted to be happy in his own way? And he
told her he was sorry she had discovered that pri-
mordial fact of existence so early in life.

He commiserated her loneliness, and scanned
his bookshelves next morning for something to lend
her to read, rejecting everything that offered itself to
his view. Philosophy was out of the question, and so
was poetry; that is, such poetry as he possessed. He
had not sounded her literary tastes, and strongly
suspected she had none; that she would have rejected The Duchess as readily as Mrs. Humphrey
Ward. He compromised on a magazine.

It had entertained her passably, she admitted,
upon returning it. A New England story had puzzled
her, it was true, and a Creole tale had offended her,
but the pictures had pleased her greatly, especially
one which had reminded her so strongly of Montéclin after a hard day's ride that she was loath to
give it up. It was one of Remington's Cowboys,

and Gouvernail insisted upon her keeping it,—keeping the magazine.

He spoke to her daily after that, and was always eager to render her some service or to do something towards her entertainment.

One afternoon he took her out to the lake end. She had been there once, some years before, but in winter, so the trip was comparatively new and strange to her. The large expanse of water studded with pleasure-boats, the sight of children playing merrily along the grassy palisades, the music, all enchanted her. Gouvernail thought her the most beautiful woman he had ever seen. Even her gown—the sprigged muslin—appeared to him the most charming one imaginable. Nor could anything be more becoming than the arrangement of her brown hair under the white sailor hat, all rolled back in a soft puff from her radiant face. And she carried her parasol and lifted her skirts and used her fan in ways that seemed quite unique and peculiar to herself, and which he considered almost worthy of study and imitation.

They did not dine out there at the water's edge, as they might have done, but returned early to the city to avoid the crowd. Athénaïse wanted to go home, for she said Sylvie would have dinner prepared and would be expecting her. But it was not difficult to persuade her to dine instead in the quiet little restaurant that he knew and liked, with its sanded floor, its secluded atmosphere, its delicious menu, and its obsequious waiter wanting to know what he might have the honor of serving to "monsieur et madame." No wonder he made the mistake, with Gouvernail assuming such an air of proprietorship! But Athénaïse was very tired after it all; the sparkle went out of her face, and she hung draggingly on his arm in walking home.

He was reluctant to part from her when she bade him good-night at her door and thanked him for the agreeable evening. He had hoped she would sit outside until it was time for him to regain the newspaper office. He knew that she would undress and get into her peignoir and lie upon her bed; and what he wanted to do, what he would have given much to do, was to go and sit beside her, read to her something restful, soothe her, do her bidding, whatever it might be. Of course there was no use in thinking of that. But he was surprised at his growing desire to be serving her. She gave him an opportunity sooner than he looked for.

"Mr. Gouvernail," she called from her room, "will you be so kine as to call Pousette an' tell her she fo'-got to bring my ice-water?"

He was indignant at Pousette's negligence, and called severely to her over the banisters. He was sitting before his own door, smoking. He knew that Athénaïse had gone to bed, for her room was dark, and she had opened the slats of the door and windows. Her bed was near a window.

Pousette came flopping up with the ice water, and with a hundred excuses: "Mo pa oua vou à tab c'te lanuite, mo cri vou pé gagni deja la-bas; parole! Vou pas cri conté ca Madame Sylvie?" She had not seen Athénaïse at table, and thought she was gone. She swore to this, and hoped Madame Sylvie would not be informed of her remissness.

A little later Athénaïse lifted her voice again: "Mr. Gouvernail, did you remark that young man sitting on the opposite side from us, coming in, with a gray coat an' a blue ban' aroun' his hat?"

Of course Governail had not noticed any such

individual, but he assured Athénaïse that he had observed the young fellow particularly.

"Don't you think he looked something,—not very much, of co'se,—but don't you think he had a little faux-air of Montéclin?"

"I think he looked strikingly like Montéclin," asserted Gouvernail, with the one idea of prolonging the conversation. "I meant to call your attention to the resemblance, and something drove it out of my head."

"The same with me," returned Athénaïse. "Ah, my dear Montéclin! I wonder w'at he is doing now?"

"Did you receive any news, any letter from him today?" asked Gouvernail, determined that if the conversation ceased it should not be through lack of effort on his part to sustain it.

"Not today, but yesterday. He tells me that maman was so distracted with uneasiness that finally, to pacify her, he was fo'ced to confess that he knew w'ere I was, but that he was boun' by a vow of secrecy not to reveal it. But Cazeau has not noticed him or spoken to him since he threaten' to throw po' Montéclin in Cane river. You know Cazeau wrote me a letter the morning I lef', thinking I had gone to the rigolet. An' maman opened it, an' said it was full of the mos' noble sentiments, an' she wanted Montéclin to sen' it to me; but Montéclin refuse' poin' blank, so he wrote to me."

Gouvernail preferred to talk of Montéclin. He pictured Cazeau as unbearable, and did not like to think of him.

A little later Athénaïse called out, "Good night, Mr. Gouvernail."

"Good night," he returned reluctantly. And when he thought that she was sleeping, he got up and went

away to the midnight pandemonium of his newspaper office.

IX

Athénaïse could not have held out through the month
had it not been for Gouvernail. With the need of
caution and secrecy always uppermost in her mind,
she made no new acquaintances, and she did not
seek out persons already known to her; however,
she knew so few, it required little effort to keep
out of their way. As for Sylvie, almost every moment
of her time was occupied in looking after her house;
and, moreover, her deferential attitude towards her
lodgers forbade anything like the gossipy chats in
which Athénaïse might have condescended sometimes
to indulge with her landlady. The transient lodgers,
who came and went, she never had occasion to meet.
Hence she was entirely dependent upon Gouvernail
for company.

He appreciated the situation fully; and every moment that he could spare from his work he devoted to
her entertainment. She liked to be out of doors, and
they strolled together in the summer twilight through
the mazes of the old French quarter. They went again
to the lake end, and stayed for hours on the water;
returning so late that the streets through which they
passed were silent and deserted. On Sunday morning
he arose at an unconscionable hour to take her to
the French market, knowing that the sights and
sounds there would interest her. And he did not join
the intellectual coterie in the afternoon, as he usually
did, but placed himself all day at the disposition and
service of Athénaïse.

Notwithstanding all, his manner toward her was
tactful, and evinced intelligence and a deep knowledge of her character, surprising upon so brief an

acquaintance. For the time he was everything to her that she would have him; he replaced home and friends. Sometimes she wondered if he had ever loved a woman. She could not fancy him loving anyone passionately, rudely, offensively, as Cazeau loved her. Once she was so naïve as to ask him outright if he had ever been in love, and he assured her promptly that he had not. She thought it an admirable trait in his character, and esteemed him greatly therefor.

He found her crying one night, not openly or violently. She was leaning over the gallery rail, watching the toads that hopped about in the moonlight, down on the damp flagstones of the courtyard. There was an oppressively sweet odor rising from the cape jessamine. Pousette was down there, mumbling and quarreling with someone, and seeming to be having it all her own way,—as well she might, when her companion was only a black cat that had come in from a neighboring yard to keep her company.

Athénaïse did admit feeling heart-sick, body-sick, when he questioned her; she supposed it was nothing but homesick. A letter from Montéclin had stirred her all up. She longed for her mother, for Montéclin; she was sick for a sight of the cotton fields, the scent of the ploughed earth, for the dim, mysterious charm of the woods, and the old tumble-down home on the Bon Dieu.

As Gouvernail listened to her, a wave of pity and tenderness swept through him. He took her hands and pressed them against him. He wondered what would happen if he were to put his arms around her.

He was hardly prepared for what happened, but he stood it courageously. She twined her arms around his neck and wept outright on his shoulder; the hot tears scalding his cheek and neck, and her whole body shaken in his arms. The impulse was powerful to strain her to him; the temptation was fierce to seek her lips; but he did neither.

He understood a thousand times better than she herself understood it that he was acting as substitute for Montéclin. Bitter as the conviction was, he accepted it. He was patient; he could wait. He hoped some day to hold her with a lover's arms. That she was married made no particle of difference to Gouvernail. He could not conceive or dream of it making a difference. When the time came that she wanted him, — as he hoped and believed it would come, —he felt he would have a right to her. So long as she did not want him, he had no right to her, —no more than her husband had. It was very hard to feel her warm breath and tears upon his cheek, and her struggling bosom pressed against him and her soft arms clinging to him and his whole body and soul aching for her, and yet to make no sign.

He tried to think what Montéclin would have said and done, and to act accordingly. He stroked her hair, and held her in a gentle embrace, until the tears dried and the sobs ended. Before releasing herself she kissed him against the neck; she had to love somebody in her own way! Even that he endured like a stoic. But it was well he left her, to plunge into the thick of rapid, breathless, exacting work till nearly dawn.

Athénaïse was greatly soothed, and slept well. The touch of friendly hands and caressing arms had been very grateful. Henceforward she would not be lonely and unhappy, with Gouvernail there to comfort her.

X

The fourth week of Athénaïse's stay in the city was

drawing to a close. Keeping in view the intention which she had of finding some suitable and agreeable employment, she had made a few tentatives in that direction. But with the exception of two little girls who had promised to take piano lessons at a price that would be embarrassing to mention, these attempts had been fruitless. Moreover, the homesickness kept coming back, and Gouvernail was not always there to drive it away.

She spent much of her time weeding and pottering among the flowers down in the courtyard. She tried to take an interest in the black cat, and a mockingbird that hung in a cage outside the kitchen door, and a disreputable parrot that belonged to the cook next door, and swore hoarsely all day long in bad French.

Beside, she was not well; she was not herself, as she told Sylvie. The climate of New Orleans did not agree with her. Sylvie was distressed to learn this, as she felt in some measure responsible for the health and well being of Monsieur Miché's sister; and she made it her duty to inquire closely into the nature and character of Athénaïse's malaise.

Sylvie was very wise, and Athénaïse was very ignorant. The extent of her ignorance and the depth of her subsequent enlightenment were bewildering. She stayed a long, long time quite still, quite stunned, after her interview with Sylvie, except for the short, uneven breathing that ruffled her bosom. Her whole being was steeped in a wave of ecstasy. When she finally arose from the chair in which she had been seated, and looked at herself in the mirror, a face met hers which she seemed to see for the first time, so transfigured was it with wonder and rapture.

One mood quickly followed another, in this new turmoil of her senses, and the need of action became uppermost. Her mother must know at once, and her mother must tell Montéclin. And Cazeau must know. As she thought of him, the first purely sensuous tremor of her life swept over her. She half whispered his name, and the sound of it brought red blotches into her cheeks. She spoke it over and over, as if it were some new, sweet sound born out of darkness and confusion, and reaching her for the first time. She was impatient to be with him. Her whole passionate nature was aroused as if by a miracle.

She seated herself to write to her husband. The letter he would get in the morning, and she would be with him at night. What would he say? How would he act? She knew that he would forgive her, for had he not written a letter?—and a pang of resentment toward Montéclin shot through her. What did he mean by withholding that letter? How dared he not have sent it?

Athénaïse attired herself for the street, and went out to post the letter which she had penned with a single thought, a spontaneous impulse. It would have seemed incoherent to most people, but Cazeau would understand.

She walked along the street as if she had fallen heir to some magnificent inheritance. On her face was a look of pride and satisfaction that passers-by noticed and admired. She wanted to talk to some one, to tell some person; and she stopped at the corner and told the oyster-woman, who was Irish, and who God-blessed her, and wished prosperity to the race of Cazeaus for generations to come. She held the oyster-woman's fat, dirty little baby in her arms and scanned it curiously and observingly, as if a baby were a phenomenon that she encountered for the first time in life. She even kissed it!

Then what a relief it was to Athénaïse to walk the streets without dread of being seen and recognized by some chance acquaintance from Red River! No one could have said now that she did not know her own mind.

She went directly from the oyster-woman's to the office of Harding & Offdean, her husband's merchants; and it was with such an air of partnership, almost proprietorship, that she demanded a sum of money on her husband's account, they gave it to her as unhesitatingly as they would have handed it over to Cazeau himself. When Mr. Harding, who knew her, asked politely after her health, she turned so rosy and looked so conscious, he thought it a great pity for so pretty a woman to be such a little goose.

Athénaïse entered a dry-goods store and bought all manner of things—little presents for nearly everybody she knew. She bought whole bolts of sheerest, softest, downiest white stuff; and when the clerk, in trying to meet her wishes, asked if she intended it for infant's use, she could have sunk through the floor, and wondered how he might have suspected it.

As it was Montéclin who had taken her away from her husband, she wanted it to be Montéclin who should take her back to him. So she wrote him a very curt note,—in fact it was a postal card,—asking that he meet her at the train on the evening following. She felt convinced that after what had gone before, Cazeau would await her at their own home; and she preferred it so.

Then there was the agreeable excitement of getting ready to leave, of packing up her things. Pousette kept coming and going, coming and going; and each time that she quitted the room it was with something that Athénaïse had given her,—a handkerchief, a petticoat, a pair of stockings with two tiny holes at the toes, some broken prayer-beads, and finally a silver dollar.

Next it was Sylvie who came along bearing a gift of what she called "a set of pattern',"—things of complicated design which never could have been obtained in any newfangled bazaar or pattern store, that Sylvie had acquired of a foreign lady of distinction whom she had nursed years before at the St. Charles hotel. Athénaïse accepted and handled them with reverence, fully sensible of the great compliment and favor, and laid them religiously away in the trunk which she had lately acquired.

She was greatly fatigued after the day of unusual exertion, and went early to bed and to sleep. All day long she had not once thought of Gouvernail, and only did think of him when aroused for a brief instant by the sound of his footfalls on the gallery, as he passed in going to his room. He had hoped to find her up, waiting for him.

But the next morning he knew. Some one must have told him. There was no subject known to her which Sylvie hesitated to discuss in detail with any man of suitable years and discretion.

Athénaïse found Gouvernail waiting with a carriage to convey her to the railway station. A momentary pang visited her for having forgotten him so completely, when he said to her, "Sylvie tells me you are going away this morning."

He was kind, attentive, and amiable, as usual, but respected to the utmost the new dignity and reserve that her manner had developed since yesterday. She kept looking from the carriage window, silent, and embarrassed as Eve after losing her ignorance. He talked of the muddy streets and the murky morning, and of Montéclin. He hoped she would find everything comfortable and pleasant in the country, and trusted she would inform him whenever she came to visit the city again. He talked as if afraid or mistrustful of silence and himself.

At the station she handed him her purse, and he bought her ticket, secured for her a comfortable section, checked her trunk, and got all the bundles and things safely aboard the train. She felt very grateful. He pressed her hand warmly, lifted his hat, and left her. He was a man of intelligence, and took defeat gracefully; that was all. But as he made his way back to the carriage, he was thinking, "By heaven, it hurts, it hurts!"

XI

Athénaïse spent a day of supreme happiness and expectancy. The fair sight of the country unfolding itself before her was balm to her vision and to her soul. She was charmed with the rather unfamiliar, broad, clean sweep of the sugar plantations, with their monster sugar houses, their rows of neat cabins like little villages of a single street, and their impressive homes standing apart amid clusters of trees. There were sudden glimpses of a bayou curling between sunny, grassy banks, or creeping sluggishly out from a tangled growth of wood, and brush, and fern, and poison-vines, and palmettos. And passing through the long stretches of monotonous woodlands, she would close her eyes and taste in anticipation the moment of her meeting with Cazeau. She could think of nothing but him.

It was night when she reached her station. There was Montéclin, as she had expected, waiting for her with a two-seated buggy, to which he had hitched his own swift-footed, spirited pony. It was good, he felt, to have her back on any terms; and he had no fault to find since she came of her own choice. He more than suspected the cause of her coming; her eyes and her voice and her foolish little manner went far in revealing the secret that was brimming over in her heart. But after he had deposited her at her own gate, and as he continued his way toward the rigolet, he could not help feeling that the affair had taken a very disappointing, an ordinary, a most commonplace turn, after all. He left her in Cazeau's keeping.

Her husband lifted her out of the buggy, and neither said a word until they stood together within the shelter of the gallery. Even then they did not speak at first. But Athénaïse turned to him with an appealing gesture. As he clasped her in his arms, he felt the yielding of her whole body against him. He felt her lips for the first time respond to the passion of his own.

The country night was dark and warm and still, save for the distant notes of an accordion which some one was playing in a cabin away off. A little Negro baby was crying somewhere. As Athénaïse withdrew from her husband's embrace, the sound arrested her.

"Listen, Cazeau! How Juliette's baby is crying! Pauvre ti chou, I wonder w'at is the matter with it?"

A NIGHT IN ACADIE

There was nothing to do on the plantation so Telèsphore, having a few dollars in his pocket, thought he would go down and spend Sunday in the vicinity of Marksville.

There was really nothing more to do in the vicinity of Marksville than in the neighborhood of his own small farm; but Elvina would not be down there, nor Amaranthe, nor any of Ma'me Valtour's daughters to harass him with doubt, to torture him with indecision, to turn his very soul into a weather-cock for love's fair winds to play with.

Telèsphore at twenty-eight had long felt the need of a wife. His home without one was like an empty temple in which there is no altar, no offering. So keenly did he realize the necessity that a dozen times at least during the past year he had been on the point of proposing marriage to almost as many different young women of the neighborhood. Therein lay the difficulty, the trouble which Telèsphore experienced in making up his mind. Elvina's eyes were beautiful and had often tempted him to the verge of declaration. But her skin was over swarthy for a wife; and her movements were slow and heavy; he doubted she had Indian blood, and we all know what Indian blood is for treachery. Amaranthe presented in her person none of these obstacles to matrimony. If her eyes were not so handsome as Elvina's, her skin was fine, and being slender to a fault, she moved swiftly about her household affairs, or when she walked the country lanes in going to church or to the store. Telèsphore had once reached the point of believing that Amaranthe would make him an excellent wife. He had even started out one day with the intention of declaring himself, when, as the god of chance would have it, Ma'me Valtour espied him passing in the road and enticed him to enter and partake of coffee and "baignés." He would have been a man of stone to have resisted, or to have remained insensible to the charms and accomplishments of the Valtour girls. Finally there was Ganache's widow, seductive rather than handsome, with a good bit of property in her own right. While Telèsphore was considering his chances of happiness or even success with Ganache's widow, she married a younger man.

From these embarrassing conditions, Telèsphore sometimes felt himself forced to escape, to change his environment for a day or two and thereby gain a few new insights by shifting his point of view.

It was Saturday morning that he decided to spend Sunday in the vicinity of Marksville, and the same afternoon found him waiting at the country station for the south-bound train.

He was a robust young fellow with good, strong features and a somewhat determined expression—despite his vacillations in the choice of a wife. He was dressed rather carefully in navy-blue "store clothes" that fitted well because anything would have fitted Telèsphore. He had been freshly shaved and trimmed and carried an umbrella. He wore—a little tilted over one eye—a straw hat in preference to the conventional gray felt; for no other reason than that his uncle Telèsphore would have worn a felt, and a battered one at that. His whole conduct of life had been planned on lines in direct contradistinction to those of his uncle Telèsphore, whom he was thought in early youth to greatly resemble. The elder Telèsphore could not read nor write, therefore the younger had made it the object of his existence to acquire these accomplishments. The uncle pursued the avocations of hunting, fishing and moss-picking; employments which the nephew held in detestation. And as for carrying an umbrella, "Nonc" Telèsphore would have walked the length of the parish in a deluge before he would have so much as thought of one. In short, Telèsphore, by advisedly shaping his course in direct opposition to that of his uncle, managed to lead a rather orderly, industrious, and respectable existence.

It was a little warm for April but the car was not uncomfortably crowded and Telèsphore was fortunate enough to secure the last available window-seat on the shady side. He was not too familiar with railway travel, his expeditions being usually made on horse-back or in a buggy, and the short trip promised to interest him.

There was no one present whom he knew well enough to speak to: the district attorney, whom he knew by sight, a French priest from Natchitoches and a few faces that were familiar only because they were native.

But he did not greatly care to speak to anyone. There was a fair stand of cotton and corn in the fields and Telèsphore gathered satisfaction in silent contemplation of the crops, comparing them with his own.

It was toward the close of his journey that a young girl boarded the train. There had been girls getting on and off at intervals and it was perhaps because of the bustle attending her arrival that this one attracted Telèsphore's attention.

She called good-bye to her father from the platform and waved good-bye to him through the dusty, sunlit window pane after entering, for she was compelled to seat herself on the sunny side. She seemed inwardly excited and preoccupied save for the attention which she lavished upon a large parcel that she carried religiously and laid reverentially down upon the seat before her.

She was neither tall nor short, nor stout nor slender; nor was she beautiful, nor was she plain. She wore a figured lawn, cut a little low in the back, that exposed a round, soft nuque with a few little clinging circles of soft, brown hair. Her hat was of white straw, cocked up on the side with a bunch of pansies, and she wore gray lisle-thread gloves. The girl seemed very warm and kept mopping her face. She vainly sought her fan, then she fanned herself with her handkerchief, and finally made an attempt to open the window. She might as well have tried to move the banks of Red River.

Telèsphore had been unconsciously watching her the whole time and perceiving her strait he arose and went to her assistance. But the window could not be opened. When he had grown red in the face and wasted an amount of energy that would have driven the plow for a day, he offered her his seat on the shady side. She demurred—there would be no room for the bundle. He suggested that the bundle be left where it was and agreed to assist her in keeping an eye upon it. She accepted Telèsphore's place at the shady window and he seated himself beside her.

He wondered if she would speak to him. He feared she might have mistaken him for a Western drummer, in which event he knew that she would not; for the women of the country caution their daughters against speaking to strangers on the trains. But the girl was not one to mistake an Acadian farmer for a Western traveling man. She was not born in Avoyelles parish for nothing.

"I wouldn' want anything to happen to it," she said.

"It's all right w'ere it is," he assured her, following the direction of her glance, that was fastened upon the bundle.

"The las' time I came over to Foché's ball I got caught in the rain on my way up to my cousin's house, an' my dress! J' vous réponds! it was a sight. Li'le mo', I would miss the ball. As it was, the dress looked like I'd wo' it weeks without doin'-up."

"No fear of rain to-day," he reassured her, glancing out at the sky, "but you can have my umbrella if it does rain; you jus' as well take it as not."

"Oh, no! I wrap' the dress roun' in toile-cirée this time. You goin' to Foché's ball? Didn' I meet you once yonda on Bayou Derbanne? Looks like I know yo' face. You mus' come f'om Natchitoches pa'ish."

"My cousins, the Fédeau family, live yonda. Me, I live on my own place in Rapides since '92."

He wondered if she would follow up her inquiry relative to Foché's ball. If she did, he was ready with an answer, for he had decided to go to the ball. But her thoughts evidently wandered from the sub-

ject and were occupied with matters that did not
concern him, for she turned away and gazed silently
out of the window.

It was not a village; it was not even a hamlet at
which they descended. The station was set down
upon the edge of a cotton field. Near at hand was
the post office and store; there was a section house;
there were a few cabins at wide intervals, and one
in the distance the girl informed him was the home
of her cousin, Jules Trodon. There lay a good bit
of road before them and she did not hesitate to
accept Telèsphore's offer to bear her bundle on the
way.

She carried herself boldly and stepped out freely
and easily, like a negress. There was an absence of
reserve in her manner; yet there was no lack of wo-
manliness. She had the air of a young person accustomed to decide for herself and for those about
her.

"You said yo' name was Fédeau?" she asked,
looking squarely at Telèsphore. Her eyes were penetrating, but earnest and dark, and a little searching.
He noticed that they were handsome eyes; not so
large as Elvina's but finer in their expression. They
started to walk down the track before turning into
the lane leading to Trodon's house. The sun was
sinking and the air was fresh and invigorating by
contrast with the stifling atmosphere of the train.

"You said yo' name was Fédeau?" she asked.

"No," he returned. "My name is Telèsphore
Baquette."

"An' my name; it's Zaïda Trodon. It looks like you
ought to know me; I don' know w'y."

"It looks that way to me, somehow," he replied.

They were satisfied to recognize this feeling—almost conviction—of preacquaintance, without trying to penetrate its cause.

By the time they reached Trodon's house he knew that she lived over on Bayou de Glaize with her parents and a number of younger brothers and sisters. It was rather dull where they lived and she often came to lend a hand when her cousin's wife got tangled in domestic complications; or, as she was doing now, when Foché's Saturday ball promised to be unusually important and brilliant. There would be people there even from Marksville, she thought; there were often gentlemen from Alexandria. Telèsphore was as unreserved as she, and they appeared like old acquaintances when they reached Trodon's gate.

Trodon's wife was standing on the gallery with a baby in her arms, watching for Zaïda; and four little barefooted children were sitting in a row on the step, also waiting, but terrified and struck motionless and dumb at sight of a stranger. He opened the gate for the girl but stayed outside himself. Zaïda presented him formally to her cousin's wife, who insisted upon his entering.

"Ah, b'en, pour ça! you got to come in. It's any sense you goin' to walk yonda to Foché's! Ti Jules, run call yo' pa." As if Ti Jules could have run or walked even, or moved a muscle!

But Telèsphore was firm. He drew forth his silver watch and looked at it in a businesslike fashion. He always carried a watch; his uncle Telèsphore always told the time by the sun, or by instinct, like an animal. He was quite determined to walk on to Foché's a couple of miles away, where he expected to secure

supper and a lodging, as well as the pleasing distrac-
tion of the ball.

"Well, I reckon I see you all tonight," he uttered
in cheerful anticipation as he moved away.

"You'll see Zaïda; yes, an' Jules," called out Trodon's wife good-humoredly. "Me, I got no time to
fool with balls, J'vous réponds! with all them chil'ren."

"He's good-lookin'; yes," she exclaimed, when
Telèsphore was out of ear-shot. "An' dressed! it's
like a prince. I didn' know you knew any Baquettes,
you, Zaïda."

"It's strange you don' know 'em yo' se'f, cousine."
Well, there had been no question from Ma'me Trodon,
so why should there be an answer from Zaïda?

Telèsphore wondered as he walked why he had
not accepted the invitation to enter. He was not
regretting it; he was simply wondering what could
have induced him to decline. For it surely would have
been agreeable to sit there on the gallery waiting
while Zaïda prepared herself for the dance; to have
partaken of supper with the family and afterward
accompanied them to Foché's. The whole situation
was so novel, and had presented itself so unexpectedly that Telèsphore wished in reality to become acquainted with it, accustomed to it. He wanted to
view it from this side and that in comparison with
other, familiar situations. The girl had impressed
him—affected him in some way; but in some new,
unusual way, not as the others always had. He could
not recall details of her personality as he could
recall such details of Amaranthe or the Valtours,
or any of them. When Telèsphore tried to think of
her he could not think at all. He seemed to have
absorbed her in some way and his brain was not so

occupied with her as his senses were. At that moment he was looking forward to the ball; there was no doubt about that. Afterwards, he did not know what he would look forward to; he did not care; afterward made no difference. If he had expected the crash of doom to come after the dance at Foché's, he would only have smiled in his thankfulness that it was not to come before.

There was the same scene every Saturday at Foché's! A scene to have aroused the guardians of the peace in a locality where such commodities abound. And all on account of the mammoth pot of gumbo that bubbled, bubbled, bubbled out in the open air. Foché in shirt-sleeves, fat, red and enraged, swore and reviled, and stormed at old black Douté for her extravagance. He called her every kind of a name of every kind of animal that suggested itself to his lurid imagination. And every fresh invective that he fired at her she hurled it back at him while into the pot went the chickens and the pans-full of minced ham, and the fists-full of onion and sage and piment rouge and piment vert. If he wanted her to cook for pigs he had only to say so. She knew how to cook for pigs and she knew how to cook for people of les Avoyelles.

The gumbo smelled good, and Telèsphore would have liked a taste of it. Douté was dragging from the fire a stick of wood that Foché had officiously thrust beneath the simmering pot, and she muttered as she hurled it smouldering to one side:

"Vaux mieux y s'méle ces affaires, lui; si non!" But she was all courtesy as she dipped a steaming plate for Telèsphore, though she assured him it would not be fit for a Christian or a gentleman to taste till midnight.

Telèsphore having brushed, "spruced" and refreshed himself, strolled about, taking a view of the
surroundings. The house, big, bulky and weather-
beaten, consisted chiefly of galleries in every stage of
decrepitude and dilapidation. There were a few
chinaberry trees and a spreading live oak in the
yard. Along the edge of the fence, a good distance
away was a line of gnarled and distorted mulberry
trees; and it was there, out in the road, that the
people who came to the ball tied their ponies, their
wagons and carts.

Dusk was beginning to fall and Telèsphore, looking out across the prairie, could see them coming
from all directions. The little Creole ponies galloping in a line looked like hobby horses in the faint
distance; the mule-carts were like toy wagons.
Zaïda might be among those people approaching,
flying, crawling ahead of the darkness that was
creeping out of the far wood. He hoped so, but
he did not believe so; she would hardly have had
time to dress.

Foché was noisily lighting lamps, with the assistance of an inoffensive mulatto boy whom he intended in the morning to butcher, to cut into sections,
to pack and salt down in a barrel, like the Colfax
woman did to her old husband—a fitting destiny
for so stupid a pig as the mulatto boy. The negro
musicians had arrived: two fiddlers and an accordion
player, and they were drinking whiskey from a black
quart bottle which was passed socially from one to
the other. The musicians were really never at their
best till the quart bottle had been consumed.

The girls who came in wagons and on ponies from

a distance wore, for the most part, calico dresses and sun-bonnets. Their finery they brought along in pillow-slips or pinned up in sheets and towels. With these they at once retired to an upper room; later to appear be-ribboned and be-furbelowed; their faces masked with starch powder, but never a touch of rouge.

Most of the guests had assembled when Zaïda arrived—"dashed up" would better express her coming—in an open, two-seated buckboard, with her cousin Jules driving. He reined the pony suddenly and viciously before the time-eaten front steps, in order to produce an impression upon those who were gathered around. Most of the men had halted their vehicles outside and permitted their women folk to walk up from the mulberry trees.

But the real, the stunning effect was produced when Zaïda stepped upon the gallery and threw aside her light shawl in the full glare of half a dozen kerosene lamps. She was white from head to foot—literally, for her slippers even were white. No one would have believed, let alone suspected that they were a pair of old black ones which she had covered with pieces of her first communion sash. There is no describing her dress, it was fluffy, like a fresh powder-puff, and stood out. No wonder she had handled it so reverentially! Her white fan was covered with spangles that she herself had sewed all over it; and in her belt and in her brown hair were thrust small sprays of orange blossom.

Two men leaning against the railing uttered long whistles expressive equally of wonder and admiration.

"Tiens! t'es-pareille comme ain mariée, Zaïda;" cried out a lady with a baby in her arms. Some young women tittered and Zaïda fanned herself. The women's voices were almost without exception shrill and piercing, the men's, soft and low-pitched.

The girl turned to Telèsphore, as to an old and valued friend:

"Tiens! c'est vous?" He had hesitated at first to approach, but at this friendly sign of recognition he drew eagerly forward and held out his hand. The men looked at him suspiciously, inwardly resenting his stylish appearance, which they considered intrusive, offensive and demoralizing.

How Zaïda's eyes sparkled now! What very pretty teeth Zaïda had when she laughed, and what a mouth! Her lips were a revelation, a promise; something to carry away and remember in the night and grow hungry thinking of next day. Strictly speaking, they may not have been quite all that; but in any event, that is the way Telèsphore thought about them. He began to take account of her appearance: her nose, her eyes, her hair. And when she left him to go in and dance her first dance with cousin Jules, he leaned up against a post and thought of them: nose, eyes, hair, ears, lips and round, soft throat.

Later it was like Bedlam.

The musicians had warmed up and were scraping away indoors and calling the figures. Feet were pounding through the dance; dust was flying. The women's voices were piped high and mingled discordantly, like the confused, shrill clatter of waking birds, while the men laughed boisterously. But if some one had only thought of gagging Foché, there would have been less noise. His good humor permeated everywhere, like an atmosphere. He was louder than all the noise; he was more visible than the dust.

He called the young mulatto (destined for the knife) "my boy" and sent him flying hither and thither. He beamed upon Douté as he tasted the gumbo and congratulated her: "C'est-toi qui s'y connais, ma fille! 'cré tonnerre!"

Telèsphore danced with Zaïda and then he leaned out against the post; then he danced with Zaïda, and then he leaned against the post. The mothers of the other girls decided that he had the manners of a pig.

It was time to dance again with Zaïda and he went in search of her. He was carrying her shawl, which she had given him to hold.

"W'at time it is?" she asked him when he had found and secured her. They were under one of the kerosene lamps on the front gallery and he drew forth his silver watch. She seemed to be still laboring under some suppressed excitement that he had noticed before.

"It's fo'teen minutes pas' twelve," he told her exactly.

"I wish you'd fine out w'ere Jules is. Go look yonda in the card-room if he's there, an' come tell me." Jules had danced with all the prettiest girls. She knew it was his custom after accomplishing this agreeable feat, to retire to the card-room.

"You'll wait yere till I come back?" he asked.

"I'll wait yere; you go on." She waited but drew back a little into the shadow. Telèsphore lost no time.

"Yes, he's yonda playin' cards with Foché an' some others I don' know," he reported when he had discovered her in the shadow. There had been a spasm of alarm when he did not at once see her where he had left her under the lamp.

"Does he look—look like he's fixed yonda fo' good?"

"He's got his coat off. Looks like he's fixed pretty comf'table fo' the nex' hour or two."

"Gi' me my shawl."

"You cole?" offering to put it around her.

"No, I ain't cole." She drew the shawl about her shoulders and turned as if to leave him. But a sudden generous impulse seemed to move her, and she added:

"Come along yonda with me."

They descended the few rickety steps that led down to the yard. He followed rather than accompanied her across the beaten and trampled sward. Those who saw them thought they had gone out to take the air. The beams of light that slanted out from the house were fitful and uncertain, deepening the shadows. The embers under the empty gumbo-pot glared red in the darkness. There was a sound of quiet voices coming from under the trees.

Zaïda, closely accompanied by Telèsphore, went out where the vehicles and horses were fastened to the fence. She stepped carefully and held up her skirts as if dreading the least speck of dew or of dust.

"Unhitch Jules' ho'se an' buggy there an' turn 'em 'roun' this way, please." He did as instructed, first backing the pony, then leading it out to where she stood in the half-made road.

"You goin' home?" he asked her, "betta let me water the pony."

"Neva mine." She mounted and seating herself grasped the reins. "No, I ain't goin' home," she added. He, too, was holding the rein gathered in one hand across the pony's back.

"W'ere you goin'?" he demanded.

"Neva you mine w'ere I'm goin'."

"You ain't goin' anyw'ere this time o' night by yo'se'f?"

"W'at you reckon I'm 'fraid of?" she laughed. "Turn loose that ho'se," at the same time urging the animal forward. The little brute started away with a bound and Telèsphore, also with a bound, sprang into the buckboard and seated himself beside Zaïda.

"You ain't goin' anyw'ere this time o' night by yo'se'f." It was not a question now, but an assertion, and there was no denying it. There was even no disputing it, and Zaïda recognizing the fact drove on in silence.

There is no animal that moves so swiftly across a 'Cadian prairie as the little Creole pony. This one did not run nor trot; he seemed to reach out in galloping bounds. The buckboard creaked, bounced, jolted and swayed. Zaïda clutched her shawl while Telèsphore drew his straw hat further down over his right eye and offered to drive. But he did not know the road and she would not let him. They had soon reached the woods.

If there is any animal that can creep more slowly through a wooded road than the little Creole pony, that animal has not yet been discovered in Acadie. This particular animal seemed to be appalled by the darkness of the forest and filled with dejection. Hiss head drooped and he lifted his feet as if each hoof were weighted with a thousand pounds of lead. Any one unacquainted with the peculiarities of the breed would sometimes have fancied that he was standing still. But Zaïda and Telèsphore knew better. Zaïda uttered a deep sigh as she slackened her hold on the reins and Telèsphore, lifting his hat, let it swing from the back of his head.

"How you don' ask me w'ere I'm goin'?" she said finally. These were the first words she had spoken since refusing his offer to drive.

"Oh, it don' make any diff'ence w'ere you goin'."

"Then if it don' make any diff'ence w'ere I'm goin', I jus' as well tell you." She hesitated, however. He seemed to have no curiosity and did not urge her.

"I'm goin' to get married," she said.

He uttered some kind of an exclamation; it was nothing articulate—more like the tone of an animal that gets a sudden knife thrust. And now he felt how dark the forest was. An instant before it had seemed a sweet, black paradise; better than any heaven he had ever heard of.

"W'y can't you get married at home?" This was not the first thing that occurred to him to say, but this was the first thing he said.

"Ah, b'en oui! with perfec' mules fo' a father an' mother! it's good enough to talk."

"W'y couldn' he come an' get you? W'at kine of a scound'el is that to let you go through the woods at night by yo'se'f?"

"You betta wait till you know who you talkin' about. He didn' come an' get me because he knows I ain't 'fraid; an' because he's got too much pride to ride in Jules Trodon's buckboard afta he done been put out o' Jules Trodon's house."

"W'at's his name an' w'ere you goin' to fine 'im?"

"Yonda on the other side the woods up at ole Wat Gibson's—a kine of justice the peace or something. Anyhow he's goin' to marry us. An' afta we done married those têtes-de-mulets yonda on bayou de Glaize can say w'at they want."

"W'at's his name?"

"André Pascal."

The name meant nothing to Telèsphore. For all he knew, André Pascal might be one of the shining lights of Avoyelles; but he doubted it.

"You betta turn 'roun'," he said. It was an unselfish impulse that prompted the suggestion. It was the thought of this girl married to a man whom even Jules Trodon would not suffer to enter his house.

"I done give my word," she answered.

"W'at's the matta with 'im? W'y don't yo' father and mother want you to marry 'im?"

"W'y? Because it's always the same tune! W'en a man's down eve'ybody's got stones to throw at 'im. They say he's lazy. A man that will walk from St. Landry plumb to Rapides lookin' fo' work; an' they call that lazy. Then, somebody's been spreadin' yonda on the Bayou that he drinks. I don' b'lieve it. I neva saw 'im drinkin', me. Anyway, he won't drink afta he's married to me; he's too fon' of me fo' that. He say he'll blow out his brains if I don' marry 'im."

"I reckon you betta turn roun'."

"No, I done give my word." And they went creeping on through the woods in silence.

"W'at time is it?" she asked after an interval. He lit a match and looked at his watch.

"It's quarta to one. W'at time he say?"

"I tole 'im I'd come about one o'clock. I knew that was a good time to get away f'om the ball."

She would have hurried a little but the pony could not be induced to do so. He dragged himself, seemingly ready at any moment to give up the breath of life. But once out of the woods he made up for lost time. They were on the open prairie again, and he fairly ripped the air; some flying demon must have changed skins with him.

It was a few minutes of one o'clock when they drew up before Wat Gibson's house. It was not much more than a rude shelter, and in the dim starlight it seemed isolated, as if standing alone in the middle of the black, far-reaching prairie. As they halted at the gate a dog within set up a furious barking, and an old negro who had been smoking his pipe at that ghostly hour, advanced toward them from the shelter of the gallery. Telèsphore descended and helped his companion to alight.

"We want to see Mr. Gibson," spoke up Zaïda. The old fellow had already opened the gate. There was no light in the house.

"Marse Gibson, he yonda to ole Mr. Bodel's playin' kairds. But he neva' stay atter one o'clock. Come in, ma'am; come in, suh; walk right 'long in." He had drawn his own conclusions to explain their appearance. They stood upon the narrow porch waiting while he went inside to light the lamp.

Although the house was small, as it comprised but one room, that room was comparatively a large one. It looked to Telèsphore and Zaïda very large and gloomy when they entered it. The lamp was on a table that stood against the wall, and that held further a rusty looking ink bottle, a pen and an old blank book. A narrow bed was off in the corner. The brick chimney extended into the room and formed a ledge that served as mantel shelf. From the big, low-hanging rafters swung an assortment of fishing tackle, a gun, some discarded articles of clothing and a string of red peppers. The boards of the floor were broad, rough and loosely joined together.

Telèsphore and Zaïda seated themselves on opposite sides of the table and the Negro went out to the wood pile to gather chips and pieces of bois-gras with which to kindle a small fire.

It was a little chilly; he supposed the two would want coffee and he knew that Wat Gibson would ask for a cup the first thing on his arrival.

"I wonder w'at's keepin' 'im," muttered Zaïda impatiently. Telèsphore looked at his watch. He had been looking at it at intervals of one minute straight along.

"It's ten minutes pas' one," he said. He offered no further comment.

At twelve minutes past one Zaïda's restlessness again broke into speech.

"I can't imagine, me, w'at's become of André! He said he'd be yere sho' at one." The old Negro was kneeling before the fire that he had kindled, contemplating the cheerful blaze. He rolled his eyes toward Zaïda.

"You talkin' 'bout Mr. André Pascal? No need to look fo' him. Mr. André he b'en down to de P'int all day raisin' Cain."

"That's a lie," said Zaïda. Telèsphore said nothing.

"Tain't no lie, ma'am; he be'n sho' raisin' de ole Nick." She looked at him, too contemptuous to reply.

The Negro told no lie so far as his bald statement was concerned. He was simply mistaken in his estimate of André Pascal's ability to "raise Cain" during an entire afternoon and evening and still keep a rendezvous with a lady at one o'clock in the morning. For André was even then at hand, as the loud and menacing howl of the dog testified. The negro hastened out to admit him.

André did not enter at once; he stayed a while out-side abusing the dog and communicating to the negro his intention of coming out to shoot the animal after he had attended to more pressing business that was awaiting him within.

Zaïda arose, a little flurried and excited when he entered. Telèsphore remained seated.

Pascal was partially sober. There had evidently been an attempt at dressing for the occasion at some early part of the previous day but such evidences had almost wholly vanished. His linen was soiled and his whole appearance was that of a man who, by an effort, had aroused himself from a debauch. He was a little taller than Telèsphore, and more loosely put together. Most women would have called him a handsomer man. It was easy to imagine that when sober, he might betray by some subtle grace of speech or manner, evidences of gentle blood.

"W'y did you keep me waitin', André? w'en you knew—" she got no further, but backed up against the table and stared at him with earnest, startled eyes.

"Keep you waiting, Zaïda? my dear li'le Zaïda, how can you say such a thing! started up yere an hour ago an' that—w'ere that damned ole Gibson?" He had approached Zaïda with the evident intention of embracing her, but she seized his wrist and held him at arm's length away. In casting her eyes about for old Gibson his glance alighted upon Telèsphore.

The sight of the 'Cadian seemed to fill him with astonishment. He stood back and began to contem-plate the young fellow and lose himself in specu-lation and conjecture before him, as if before some unlabeled wax figure. He turned for information to Zaïda.

"Say, Zaïda, w'at you call this? W'at kine of damn fool you got sitting yere? Who let him in? W'at you reckon he's lookin' fo'? trouble?"

Telèsphore said nothing; he was awaiting his cue from Zaïda.

"André Pascal," she said, "you jus' as well take the do' an' go. You might stan' yere till the day o' judgment on yo' knees befo' me; an' blow out yo' brains if you a mine to. I ain't neva goin' to marry you."

"The hell you ain't!"

He had hardly more than uttered the words when he lay prone on his back. Telèsphore had knocked him down. The blow seemed to complete the process of sobering that had begun in him. He gathered himself together and rose to his feet; in doing so he reached back for his pistol. His hold was not yet steady, however, and the weapon slipped from his grasp and fell to the floor. Zaïda picked it up and laid it on the table behind her. She was going to see fair play.

The brute instinct that drives men at each other's throat was awake and stirring in these two. Each saw in the other a thing to be wiped out of his way—out of existence if need be. Passion and blind rage directed the blows which they dealt, and steeled the tension of muscles and clutch of fingers. They were not skillful blows, however.

The fire blazed cheerily; the kettle which the negro had placed upon the coals was steaming and singing. The man had gone in search of his master. Zaïda had placed the lamp out of harm's way on the high mantel ledge and she leaned back with her hands behind her upon the table.

She did not raise her voice or lift her finger to stay the combat that was acting before her. She was motionless, and white to the lips; only her eyes seemed to be alive and burning and blazing. At one moment she felt that André must have strangled Telèsphore; but she said nothing. The next instant she could hardly doubt that the blow from Telè- sphore's doubled fist could be less than a killing one; but she did nothing.

How the loose boards swayed and creaked be- neath the weight of the struggling men! the very old rafters seemed to groan; and she felt that the house shook.

The combat, if fierce, was short, and it ended out on the gallery whither they had staggered through the open door—or one had dragged the other—she could not tell. But she knew when it was over, for there was a long moment of utter stillness. Then she heard one of the men descend the steps and go away, for the gate slammed after him. The other went out to the cistern; the sound of the tin bucket splashing in the water reached her where she stood. He must have been endeavoring to remove traces of the encounter.

Presently Telèsphore entered the room. The ele- gance of his apparel had been somewhat marred; the men over at the 'Cadian ball would hardly have taken exception now to his appearance.

"W'ere is André?" the girl asked.

"He's gone," said Telèsphore.

She had never changed her position and now when she drew herself up her wrists ached and she rubbed them a little. She was no longer pale; the blood had come back into her cheeks and lips, staining them crimson. She held out her hand to him. He took it gratefully enough, but he did not know what to do with it; that is, he did not know what he might dare to do with it, so he let it drop gently away and went to the fire.

"I reckon we betta be goin', too," she said. He stooped and poured some of the bubbling water from the kettle upon the coffee which the Negro had set upon the hearth.

"I'll make a li'le coffee firs'," he proposed, "an' anyhow we betta wait till ole man w'at's-his-name comes back. It wouldn't look well to leave his house that way without some kine of excuse or explanation."

She made no reply, but seated herself submissively beside the table.

Her will, which had been overmastering and aggressive, seemed to have grown numb under the disturbing spell of the past few hours. An illusion had gone from her, and had carried her love with it. The absence of regret revealed this to her. She realized, but could not comprehend it, not knowing that the love had been part of the illusion. She was tired in body and spirit, and it was with a sense of restfulness that she sat all drooping and relaxed and watched Telèsphore make the coffee.

He made enough for them both and a cup for old Wat Gibson when he should come in, and also one for the negro. He supposed the cups, the sugar and spoons were in the safe over there in the corner, and that is where he found them.

When he finally said to Zaïda, "Come, I'm going to take you home now," and drew her shawl around her, pinning it under the chin, she was like a little child and followed whither he led in all confidence.

It was Telèsphore who drove on the way back, and he let the pony cut no capers, but held him to a steady and tempered gait. The girl was still quiet and silent; she was thinking tenderly—a little tearfully of those two old têtes-de-mulets yonder on Bayou de Glaize.

How they crept through the woods! and how dark it was and how still!

"W'at time it is?" whispered Zaïda. Alas! he could not tell her; his watch was broken. But almost for the first time in his life, Telèsphore did not care what time it was.

The Awakening

THE AWAKENING

I

A green and yellow parrot, which hung in a cage outside the door, kept repeating over and over: "*Allez vous-en! Allez vous-en! Sapristi!* That's all right!"

He could speak a little Spanish, and also a language which nobody understood, unless it was the mocking-bird that hung on the other side of the door, whistling his fluty notes out upon the breeze with maddening persistence.

Mr. Pontellier, unable to read his newspaper with any degree of comfort, arose with an expression and an exclamation of disgust. He walked down the gallery and across the narrow "bridges" which connected the Lebrun cottages one with the other. He had been seated before the door of the main house. The parrot and the mocking-bird were the property of Madame Lebrun, and they had the right to make all the noise they wished. Mr. Pontellier had the privilege of quitting their society when they ceased to be entertaining.

He stopped before the door of his own cottage, which was the fourth one from the main building and next to the last. Seating himself in a wicker rocker which was there, he once more applied himself to the task of reading the newspaper. The day was Sunday; the paper was a day old. The Sunday papers had not yet reached Grand Isle. He was already acquainted with the market reports, and he glanced restlessly over the editorials and bits of news which he had not had time to read before quitting New Orleans the day before.

Mr. Pontellier wore eye-glasses. He was a man of forty, of medium height and rather slender build; he stooped a little. His hair was brown and straight, parted on one side. His beard was neatly and closely trimmed.

Once in a while he withdrew his glance from the newspaper and looked about him. There was more noise than ever over at the house. The main building was called "the house," to distinguish it from the cottages. The chattering and whistling birds were still at it. Two young girls, the Farival twins, were playing a duet from "Zampa" upon the piano. Madame Lebrun was bustling in and out, giving orders in a high key to a yard-boy whenever she got inside the house, and directions in an equally high voice to a dining-room servant whenever she got outside. She was a fresh, pretty woman, clad always in white with elbow sleeves. Her starched skirts crinkled as she came and went. Farther down, before one of the cottages, a lady in black was walking demurely up and down, telling her beads. A good many persons of the *pension* had gone over to the *Chênière Caminada* in Beaudelet's lugger to hear mass. Some young people were out under the water oaks playing croquet. Mr. Pontellier's two children were there—sturdy little fellows of four and five. A quadroon nurse followed them about with a far-away, meditative air.

Mr. Pontellier finally lit a cigar and began to smoke, letting the paper drag idly from his hand. He fixed his gaze upon a white sunshade that was advancing at snail's pace from the beach. He could see it plainly between the gaunt trunks of the water oaks and across the stretch of yellow camomile. The gulf looked far away, melting hazily into the blue of the horizon. The sunshade continued to approach slowly. Beneath its pink-lined shelter were his wife, Mrs. Pontellier, and young Robert Lebrun. When they reached the cottage, the two seated themselves with some appearance of fatigue upon the upper step of the porch, facing each other, each leaning against a supporting post.

"What folly! to bathe at such an hour in such heat!" exclaimed Mr. Pontellier. He himself had taken a plunge at daylight. That was why the morning seemed long to him.

"You are burnt beyond recognition," he added, looking at his wife as one looks at a valuable piece of personal property which has suffered some damage. She held up her hands, strong, shapely hands, and surveyed them critically, drawing up her lawn sleeves above the wrists. Looking at them reminded her of her rings, which she had given to her husband before leaving for the beach. She silently reached out to him, and he, understanding, took the rings from his vest pocket and dropped them into her open palm. She slipped them upon her fingers; then clasping her knees, she looked across at Robert and began to laugh. The rings sparkled upon her fingers. He sent back an answering smile.

"What is it? asked Pontellier, looking lazily and amused from one to the other. It was some utter nonsense; some adventure out there in the water, and they both tried to relate it at once. It did not seem half so amusing when told. They realized this, and so did Mr. Pontellier. He yawned and stretched himself.

Then he got up, saying he had half a mind to go over to Klein's hotel and play a game of billiards.

"Come go along, Lebrun," he proposed to Robert. But Robert admitted quite frankly that he preferred to stay where he was and talk to Mrs. Pontellier.

"Well, send him about his business when he bores you, Edna," instructed her husband as he prepared to leave.

"Here, take the umbrella," she exclaimed, holding it out to him. He accepted the sunshade, and lifting it over his head descended the steps and walked away.

"Coming back to dinner?" his wife called after him. He halted a moment and shrugged his shoulders. He felt in his vest pocket; there was a ten-dollar bill there. He did not know; perhaps he would return for the early dinner and perhaps he would not. It all depended upon the company which he found over at Klein's and the size of "the game." He did not say this, but she understood it, and laughed, nodding good-by to him.

Both children wanted to follow their father when they saw him starting out. He kissed them and promised to bring them back bonbons and peanuts.

II

Mrs. Pontellier's eyes were quick and bright; they were a yellowish brown, about the color of her hair. She had a way of turning them swiftly upon an object and holding them there as if lost in some inward maze of contemplation or thought.

Her eyebrows were a shade darker than her hair. They were thick and almost horizontal, emphasizing the depth of her eyes. She was rather handsome than beautiful. Her face was captivating by reason of a certain frankness of expression and a contradictory subtle play of features. Her manner was engaging.

Robert rolled a cigarette. He smoked cigarettes because he could not afford cigars, he said. He had a cigar in his pocket which Mr. Pontellier had presented him with, and he was saving it for his after-dinner smoke.

This seemed quite proper and natural on his part. In coloring he was not unlike his companion. A clean-shaved face made the resemblance more pronounced than it would otherwise have been. There rested no shadow of care upon his open countenance. His eyes gathered in and reflected the light and languor of the summer day.

Mrs. Pontellier reached over for a palm-leaf fan that lay on the porch and began to fan herself, while Robert sent between his lips light puffs from his cigarette. They chatted incessantly: about the things around them; their amusing adventure out in the water—it had again assumed its entertaining aspect; about the wind, the trees, the people who had gone to the *Chênière;* about the children playing croquet under the oaks, and the Farival twins, who were now performing the overture to "The Poet and the Peasant."

Robert talked a good deal about himself. He was very young, and did not know any better. Mrs. Pontellier talked a little about herself for the same reason. Each was interested in what the other said. Robert spoke of his intention to go to Mexico in the autumn, where fortune awaited him. He was always intending to go to Mexico, but some way never got there. Meanwhile he held on to his modest position in a mercantile house in New Orleans, where an equal familiarity with English, French and Spanish gave him no small value as a clerk and correspondent.

He was spending his summer vacation, as he

always did, with his mother at Grand Isle. In former times, before Robert could remember, "the house" had been a summer luxury of the Lebruns. Now, flanked by its dozen or more cottages, which were always filled with exclusive visitors from the "*Quartier Francais*," it enabled Madame Lebrun to maintain the easy and comfortable existence which appeared to be her birthright.

Mrs. Pontellier talked about her father's Mississippi plantation and her girlhood home in the old Kentucky bluegrass country. She was an American woman, with a small infusion of French which seemed to have been lost in dilution. She read a letter from her sister, who was away in the East, and who had engaged herself to be married. Robert was interested, and wanted to know what manner of girls the sisters were, what the father was like, and how long the mother had been dead.

When Mrs. Pontellier folded the letter it was time for her to dress for the early dinner.

"I see Léonce isn't coming back," she said, with a glance in the direction whence her husband had disappeared. Robert supposed he was not, as there were a good many New Orleans club men over at Klein's.

When Mrs. Pontellier left him to enter her room, the young man descended the steps and strolled over toward the croquet players, where, during the half-hour before dinner, he amused himself with the little Pontellier children, who were very fond of him.

III

It was eleven o'clock that night when Mr. Pontellier returned from Klein's hotel. He was in an excellent humor, in high spirits, and very talkative. His entrance awoke his wife, who was in bed and fast asleep when he came in. He talked to her while he undressed, telling her anecdotes and bits of news and gossip that he had gathered during the day. From his trousers pockets he took a fistful of crumpled bank notes and a good deal of silver coin, which he piled on the bureau indiscriminately with keys, knife, handkerchief, and whatever else happened to be in his pockets. She was overcome with sleep, and answered him with little half utterances.

He thought it very discouraging that his wife, who was the sole object of his existence, evinced so little interest in things which concerned him, and valued so little his conversation.

Mr. Pontellier had forgotten the bonbons and peanuts for the boys. Notwithstanding he loved them very much, and went into the adjoining room where they slept to take a look at them and make sure that they were resting comfortably. The result of his investigation was far from satisfactory. He turned and shifted the youngsters about in bed. One of them began to kick and talk about a basket full of crabs.

Mr. Pontellier returned to his wife with the information that Raoul had a high fever and needed looking after. Then he lit a cigar and went and sat near the open door to smoke it.

Mrs. Pontellier was quite sure Raoul had no fever. He had gone to bed perfectly well, she said, and nothing had ailed him all day. Mr. Pontellier was too well acquainted with fever symptoms to be mistaken. He assured her the child was consuming at that moment in the next room.

He reproached his wife with her inattention, her habitual neglect of the children. If it was not a mother's place to look after children, whose on earth was it? He himself had his hands full with his brokerage business. He could not be in two places at once; making a living for his family on the street, and staying at home to see that no harm befell them. He talked in a monotonous, insistent way.

Mrs. Pontellier sprang out of bed and went into the next room. She soon came back and sat on the edge of the bed, leaning her head down on the pillow. She said nothing, and refused to answer her husband when he questioned her. When his cigar was smoked out he went to bed, and in half a minute he was fast asleep.

Mrs. Pontellier was by that time thoroughly awake. She began to cry a little, and wiped her eyes on the sleeve of her *peignoir*. Blowing out the candle, which her husband had left burning, she slipped her bare feet into a pair of satin *mules* at the foot of the bed and went out on the porch, where she sat down in the wicker chair and began to rock gently to and fro.

It was then past midnight. The cottages were all dark. A single faint light gleamed out from the hallway of the house. There was no sound abroad except the hooting of an old owl in the top of a water-oak, and the everlasting voice of the sea, that was not uplifted at that soft hour. It broke like a mournful lullaby upon the night.

The tears came so fast to Mrs. Pontellier's eyes that the damp sleeve of her *peignoir* no longer served to dry them. She was holding the back of her chair with one hand; her loose sleeve had slipped almost to the shoulder of her uplifted arm. Turning, she thrust her face, steaming and wet, into the bend of her arm, and she went on crying there, not caring any longer to dry her face, her eyes, her arms. She could not have told why she was crying. Such experiences as the foregoing were not uncommon in her married life. They seemed never before to have weighed much against the abundance of her husband's kindness and a uniform devotion which had come to be tacit and self-understood.

An indescribable oppression, which seemed to generate in some unfamiliar part of her consciousness, filled her whole being with a vague anguish. It was like a shadow, like a mist passing across her soul's summer day. It was strange and unfamiliar; it was a mood. She did not sit there inwardly upbraiding her husband, lamenting at Fate, which had directed her footsteps to the path which they had taken. She was just having a good cry all to herself. The mosquitoes made merry over her, biting her firm, round arms and nipping at her bare insteps.

The little stinging, buzzing imps succeeded in dispelling a mood which might have held her there in the darkness half a night longer.

The following morning Mr. Pontellier was up in good time to take the rockaway which was to convey him to the steamer at the wharf. He was returning to the city to his business, and they would not see him again at the Island till the coming Saturday. He had regained his composure, which seemed to have been somewhat impaired the night before. He was eager to be gone, as he looked forward to a lively week in Carondelet Street.

Mr. Pontellier gave his wife half of the money which he had brought away from Klein's hotel the evening before. She liked money as well as most women, and accepted it with no little satisfaction.

"It will buy a handsome wedding present for Sister Janet!" she exclaimed, smoothing out the bills as she counted them one by one.

"Oh! we'll treat Sister Janet better than that, my dear," he laughed, as he prepared to kiss her good-by.

The boys were tumbling about, clinging to his legs, imploring that numerous things be brought back to them. Mr. Pontellier was a great favorite, and ladies, men, children, even nurses, were always on hand to say good-by to him. His wife stood smiling and waving, the boys shouting, as he disappeared in the old rockaway down the sandy road.

A few days later a box arrived for Mrs. Pontellier from New Orleans. It was from her husband. It was filled with *friandises*, with luscious and toothsome bits—the finest of fruits, *patés*, a rare bottle or two, delicious syrups, and bonbons in abundance.

Mrs. Pontellier was always very generous with the contents of such a box; she was quite used to receiving them when away from home. The *patés* and fruit were brought to the dining-room; the bonbons were passed around. And the ladies, selecting with dainty and discriminating fingers and a little greedily, all declared that Mr. Pontellier was the best husband in the world. Mrs. Pontellier was forced to admit that she knew of none better.

IV

It would have been a difficult matter for Mr. Pontellier to define to his own satisfaction or any one else s‹ wherein his wife failed in her duty toward their children. It was something which he felt rather than perceived, and he never voiced the feeling without subsequent regret and ample atonement.

If one of the little Pontellier boys took a tumble whilst at play, he was not apt to rush crying to his mother's arms for comfort; he would more likely pick himself up, wipe the water out of his eyes and the sand out of his mouth, and go on playing. Tots as they were, they pulled together and stood their ground in childish battles with doubled fists and uplifted voices, which usually prevailed against the other mother-tots. The quadroon nurse was looked upon as a huge encumbrance, only good to button up waists and panties and to brush and part hair; since it seemed to be a law of society that hair must be parted and brushed.

In short, Mrs. Pontellier was not a mother-woman. The mother-women seemed to prevail that summer at Grand Isle. It was easy to know them, fluttering about with extended, protecting wings when any harm, real or imaginary, threatened their precious brood. They were women who idolized their children, worshiped their husbands, and esteemed it a holy privilege to efface themselves as individuals and grow wings as ministering angels.

Many of them were delicious in the rôle; one of them was the embodiment of every womanly grace and charm. If her husband did not adore

her, he was a brute, deserving of death by slow
torture. Her name was Adèle Ratignolle. There
are no words to describe her save the old ones that
have served so often to picture the bygone heroine of
romance and the fair lady of our dreams. There was
nothing subtle or hidden about her charms; her
beauty was all there, flaming and apparent: the
spun-gold hair that comb nor confining pin could
restrain; the blue eyes that were like nothing but
sapphires; two lips that pouted, that were so red one
could only think of cherries or some other delicious
crimson fruit in looking at them. She was growing a
little stout, but it did not seem to detract an iota
from the grace of every step, pose, gesture. One
would not have wanted her white neck a mite less full
or her beautiful arms more slender. Never were
hands more exquisite than hers, and it was a joy
to look at them when she threaded her needle or
adjusted her gold thimble to her taper middle finger
as she sewed away on the little night-drawers or
fashioned a bodice or a bib.

Madame Ratignolle was very fond of Mrs. Pontellier, and often she took her sewing and went over to
sit with her in the afternoons. She was sitting there
the afternoon of the day the box arrived from New
Orleans. She had possession of the rocker, and she
was busily engaged in sewing upon a diminutive pair
of night-drawers.

She had brought the pattern of the drawers for
Mrs. Pontellier to cut out—a marvel of construction, fashioned to enclose a baby's body so effec-
tually that only two small eyes might look out
from the garment, like an Eskimo's. They were
designed for winter wear, when treacherous drafts

came down chimneys and insidious currents of deadly cold found their way through key-holes.

Mrs. Pontellier's mind was quite at rest concerning the present material needs of her children, and she could not see the use of anticipating and making winter night garments the subject of her summer meditations. But she did not want to appear unamiable and uninterested, so she had brought forth newspapers, which she spread upon the floor of the gallery, and under Madame Ratignolle's directions she had cut a pattern of the impervious garment.

Robert was there, seated as he had been the Sunday before, and Mrs. Pontellier also occupied her former position on the upper step, leaning listlessly against the post. Beside her was a box of bonbons, which she held out at intervals to Madame Ratignolle.

That lady seemed at a loss to make a selection, but finally settled upon a stick of nougat, wondering if it were not too rich; whether it could possibly hurt her. Madame Ratignolle had been married seven years. About every two years she had a baby. At that time she had three babies, and was beginning to think of a fourth one. She was always talking about her "condition." Her "condition" was in no way apparent, and no one would have known a thing about it but for her persistence in making it the subject of conversation.

Robert started to reassure her, asserting that he had known a lady who had subsisted upon nougat during the entire—but seeing the color mount into Mrs. Pontellier's face he checked himself and changed the subject.

Mrs. Pontellier, though she had married a Creole, was

not thoroughly at home in the society of Creoles; never before had she been thrown so intimately among them. There were only Creoles that summer at Lebrun's. They all knew each other, and felt like one large family, among whom existed the most amicable relations. A characteristic which distinguished them and which impressed Mrs. Pontellier most forcibly was their entire absence of prudery. Their freedom of expression was at first incomprehensible to her, though she had no difficulty in reconciling it with a lofty chastity which in the Creole woman seems to be inborn and unmistakable.

Never would Edna Pontellier forget the shock with which she heard Madame Ratignolle relating to old Monsieur Farival the harrowing story of one of her *accouchements*, withholding no intimate detail. She was growing accustomed to like shocks, but she could not keep the mounting color back from her cheeks. Oftener than once her coming had interrupted the droll story with which Robert was entertaining some amused group of married women.

A book had gone the rounds of the *pension*. When it came her turn to read it, she did so with profound astonishment. She felt moved to read the book in secret and solitude, though none of the others had done so—to hide it from view at the sound of approaching footsteps. It was openly criticised and freely discussed at table. Mrs. Pontellier gave over being astonished, and concluded that wonders would never cease.

V

They formed a congenial group sitting there that summer afternoon—Madame Ratignolle sewing away, often stopping to relate a story or incident with much expressive gesture of her perfect hands; Robert and Mrs. Pontellier sitting idle, exchanging occasional words, glances or smiles which indicated a certain advanced stage of intimacy and *camaraderie*.

He had lived in her shadow during the past month. No one thought anything of it. Many had predicted that Robert would devote himself to Mrs. Pontellier when he arrived. Since the age of fifteen, which was eleven years before, Robert each summer at Grand Isle had constituted himself the devoted attendant of some fair dame or damsel. Sometimes it was a young girl, again a widow; but as often as not it was some interesting married woman.

For two consecutive seasons he lived in the sunlight of Mademoiselle Duvigné's presence. But she died between summers; then Robert posed as an inconsolable, prostrating himself at the feet of Madame Ratignolle for whatever crumbs of sympathy and comfort she might be pleased to vouchsafe.

Mrs. Pontellier liked to sit and gaze at her fair companion as she might look upon a faultless Madonna.

"Could any one fathom the cruelty beneath that fair exterior?" murmured Robert. "She knew that I adored her once, and she let me adore her. It was 'Robert, come; go; stand up; sit down; do this; do that; see if the baby sleeps; my thimble, please, that I left God knows where. Come and read Daudet to me while I sew.'"

"*Par exemple*! I never had to ask. You were always there under my feet, like a troublesome cat."

"You mean like an adoring dog. And just as soon as Ratignolle appeared on the scene, then it *was* like a dog. '*Passez! Adieu! Allez vous-en!*'"

"Perhaps I feared to make Alphonse jealous," she interjoined with excessive naïveté. That made them all laugh. The right hand jealous of the left! The heart jealous of the soul! But for that matter, the Creole husband is never jealous; with him the gangrene passion is one which has become dwarfed by disuse.

Meanwhile Robert, addressing Mrs. Pontellier, continued to tell of his one time hopeless passion for Madame Ratignolle; of sleepless nights, of consuming flames till the very sea sizzled when he took his daily plunge. While the lady at the needle kept up a little running, contemptuous comment:

"*Blagueur—farceur—gros bête, va!*"

He never assumed this serio-comic tone when alone with Mrs. Pontellier. She never knew precisely what to make of it; at that moment it was impossible for her to guess how much of it was jest and what proportion was earnest. It was understood that he had often spoken words of love to Madame Ratignolle, without any thought of being taken seriously. Mrs. Pontellier was glad he had not assumed a similar rôle toward herself. It would have been unacceptable and annoying.

Mrs. Pontellier had brought her sketching materials, which she sometimes dabbled with in an unprofessional way. She liked the dabbling. She felt in it satisfaction of a kind which no other employment afforded her.

She had long wished to try herself on Madame Ratignolle. Never had that lady seemed a more tempting subject than at that moment, seated there like some sensuous Madonna, with the gleam of the fading day enriching her splendid color.

Robert crossed over and seated himself upon the step below Mrs. Pontellier, that he might watch her work. She handled her brushes with a certain ease and freedom which came, not from long and close acquaintance with them, but from a natural aptitude. Robert followed her work with close attention, giving forth little ejaculatory expressions of appreciation in French, which he addressed to Madame Ratignolle.

"Mais ce n'est pas mal! Elle s'y connait, elle a de la force, oui."

During his oblivious attention he once quietly rested his head against Mrs. Pontellier's arm. As gently she repulsed him. Once again he repeated the offense. She could not but believe it to be thoughtlessness on his part, yet that was no reason she should submit to it. She did not remonstrate, except again to repulse him quietly but firmly. He offered no apology.

The picture completed bore no resemblance to Madame Ratignolle. She was greatly disappointed to find that it did not look like her. But it was a fair enough piece of work, and in many respects satisfying.

Mrs. Pontellier evidently did not think so. After surveying the sketch critically she drew a broad smudge of paint across its surface, and crumpled the paper between her hands.

The youngsters came tumbling up the steps,

the quadroon following at the respectful distance which they required her to observe. Mrs. Pontellier made them carry her paints and things into the house. She sought to detain them for a little talk and some pleasantry. But they were greatly in earnest. They had only come to investigate the contents of the bonbon box. They accepted without murmuring what she chose to give them, each holding out two chubby hands scoop-like, in the vain hope that they might be filled; and then away they went.

The sun was low in the west, and the breeze soft and languorous that came up from the south, charged with the seductive odor of the sea. Children, freshly befurbelowed, were gathering for their games under the oaks. Their voices were high and penetrating.

Madame Ratignolle folded her sewing, placing thimble, scissors and thread all neatly together in the roll, which she pinned securely. She complained of faintness. Mrs. Pontellier flew for the cologne water and a fan. She bathed Madame Ratignolle's face with cologne, while Robert plied the fan with unnecessary vigor.

The spell was soon over, and Mrs. Pontellier could not help wondering if there were not a little imagination responsible for its origin, for the rose tint had never faded from her friend's face.

She stood watching the fair woman walk down the long line of galleries with the grace and majesty which queens are sometimes supposed to possess. Her little ones ran to meet her. Two of them clung about her white skirts, the third she took from its nurse and with a thousand endearments bore it along in her own fond, encircling arms. Though,

as everbody well knew, the doctor had forbidden
her to lift so much as a pin!

"Are you going bathing?" asked Robert of Mrs.
Pontellier. It was not so much a question as a reminder.

"Oh, no," she answered, with a tone of indecision.
"I'm tired; I think not." Her glance wandered from
his face away toward the Gulf, whose sonorous
murmur reached her like a loving but imperative
entreaty.

"Oh, come!" he insisted. "You mustn't miss your
bath. Come on. The water must be delicious; it will
not hurt you. Come."

He reached up for her big, rough straw hat that
hung on a peg outside the door, and put it on her
head. They descended the steps, and walked away
together toward the beach. The sun was low in
the west and the breeze was soft and warm.

VI

Edna Pontellier could not have told why, wishing
to go to the beach with Robert, she should in the
first place have declined, and in the second place
have followed in obedience to one of the two contradictory impulses which impelled her.

A certain light was beginning to dawn dimly within her—the light which, showing the way, forbids it.

At that early period it served but to bewilder
her. It moved her to dreams, to thoughtfulness,
to the shadowy anguish which had overcome her
the midnight when she had abandoned herself to
tears.

In short, Mrs. Pontellier was beginning to realize
her position in the universe as a human being, and

to recognize her relations as an individual to the
world within and about her. This may seem like a
ponderous weight of wisdom to descend upon the
soul of a young woman of twenty-eight—perhaps
more wisdom than the Holy Ghost is usually pleased
to vouchsafe to any woman.

But the beginning of things, of a world especially, is necessarily vague, tangled, chaotic, and exceedingly disturbing. How few of us ever emerge from
such beginning! How many souls perish in its tumult!

The voice of the sea is seductive; never ceasing,
whispering, clamoring, murmuring, inviting the soul
to wander for a spell in abysses of solitude; to lose
itself in mazes of inward contemplation.

The voice of the sea speaks to the soul. The touch
of the sea is sensuous, enfolding the body in its soft,
close embrace.

VII

Mrs. Pontellier was not a woman given to confidences, a characteristic hitherto contrary to her nature. Even as a child she had lived her own small
life all within herself. At a very early period she had
apprehended instinctively the dual life—that outward existence which conforms, the inward life
which questions.

That summer at Grand Isle she began to loosen
a little the mantle of reserve that had always enveloped her. There may have been—there must have
been—influences, both subtle and apparent, working
in their several ways to induce her to do this; but the
most obvious was the influence of Adèle Ratignolle.
The excessive physical charm of the Creole had first

attracted her, for Edna had a sensuous susceptibility to beauty. Then the candor of the woman's whole existence, which every one might read, and which formed so striking a contrast to her own habitual reserve—this might have furnished a link. Who can tell what metals the gods use in forging the subtle bond which we call sympathy, which we might as well call love.

The two women went away one morning to the beach together, arm in arm, under the huge white sunshade. Edna had prevailed upon Madame Ratignolle to leave the children behind, though she could not induce her to relinquish a diminutive roll of needlework, which Adele begged to be allowed to slip into the depths of her pocket. In some unaccountable way they had escaped from Robert.

The walk to the beach was no inconsiderable one, consisting as it did of a long, sandy path, upon which a sporadic and tangled growth that bordered it on either side made frequent and unexpected inroads. There were acres of yellow camomile reaching out on either hand. Further away still, vegetable gardens abounded, with frequent small plantations of orange or lemon trees intervening. The dark green clusters glistened from afar in the sun.

The women were both of goodly height, Madame Ratignolle possessing the more feminine and matronly figure. The charm of Edna Pontellier's physique stole insensibly upon you. The lines of her body were long, clean and symmetrical; it was a body which occasionally fell into splendid poses; there was no suggestion of the trim, stereotyped fashion-plate about it. A casual and indiscriminating observer, in passing, might not cast a second glance

upon the figure. But with more feeling and discernment he would have recognized the noble beauty
of its modeling, and the graceful severity of poise
and movement, which made Edna Pontellier different from the crowd.

She wore a cool muslin that morning—white, with
a waving vertical line of brown running through
it; also a white linen collar and the big straw hat
which she had taken from the peg outside the door.
The hat rested any way on her yellow-brown hair,
that waved a little, was heavy, and clung close to
her head.

Madame Ratignolle, more careful of her complex-
ion, had twined a gauze veil about her head. She
wore dogskin gloves, with gauntlets that protected
her wrists. She was dressed in pure white, with a
fluffiness of ruffles that became her. The draperies
and fluttering things which she wore suited her
rich, luxuriant beauty as a greater severity of line
could not have done.

There were a number of bath-houses along the
beach, of rough but solid construction, built with
small, protecting galleries facing the water. Each
house consisted of two compartments, and each
family at Lebrun's possessed a compartment for
itself, fitted out with all the essential paraphernalia
of the bath and whatever other conveniences the
owners might desire. The two women had no intention of bathing; they had just strolled down to the
beach for a walk and to be alone and near the water.
The Pontellier and Ratignolle compartments adjoined one another under the same roof.

Mrs. Pontellier had brought down her key through
force of habit. Unlocking the door of her bath-room
she went inside, and soon emerged, bringing a rug,

which she spread upon the floor of the gallery, and
two huge hair pillows covered with crash, which she
placed against the front of the building.

The two seated themselves there in the shade
of the porch, side by side, with their backs against
the pillows and their feet extended. Madame Ratignolle removed her veil, wiped her face with a rather
delicate handkerchief, and fanned herself with the
fan which she always carried suspended somewhere
about her person by a long, narrow ribbon. Edna
removed her collar and opened her dress at the
throat. She took the fan from Madame Ratignolle
and began to fan both herself and her companion.
It was very warm, and for a while they did nothing
but exchange remarks about the heat, the sun, the
glare. But there was a breeze blowing, a choppy, stiff
wind that whipped the water into froth. It fluttered
the skirts of the two women and kept them for
a while engaged in adjusting, readjusting, tucking
in, securing hair-pins and hat-pins. A few persons
were sporting some distance away in the water. The
beach was very still of human sound at that hour.
The lady in black was reading her morning devotions
on the porch of a neighboring bath-house. Two
young lovers were exchanging their hearts' yearnings
beneath the children's tent, which they had found
unoccupied.

Edna Pontellier, casting her eyes about, had finally kept them at rest upon the sea. The day was
clear and carried the gaze out as far as the blue sky
went; there were a few white clouds suspended
idly over the horizon. A lateen sail was visible in
the direction of Cat Island, and others to the south
seemed almost motionless in the far distance.

"Of whom—of what are you thinking?" asked

Adèle of her companion, whose countenance she had been watching with a little amused attention, arrested by the absorbed expression which seemed to have seized and fixed every feature into a statuesque repose.

"Nothing," returned Mrs. Pontellier, with a start, adding at once: "How stupid! But it seems to me it is the reply we make instinctively to such a question. Let me see," she went on, throwing back her head and narrowing her fine eyes till they shone like two vivid points of light. "Let me see. I was not conscious of thinking of anything, but perhaps I can retrace my thoughts."

"Oh! never mind!" laughed Madame Ratignolle. "I am not quite so exacting. I will let you off this time. It is really too hot to think, especially to think about thinking."

"But for the fun of it," persisted Edna. "First of all, the sight of water stretching so far away, those motionless sails against the blue sky, made a delicious picture that I just wanted to sit and look at. The hot wind beating in my face made me think—without any connection that I can trace—of a summer day in Kentucky, of a meadow that seemed as big as the ocean to the very little girl walking through the grass, which was higher than her waist. She threw out her arms as if swimming when she walked, beating the tall grass as one strikes out in the water. Oh, I see the connection now!"

"Where were you going that day in Kentucky, walking through the grass?"

"I don't remember now. I was just walking diagonally across a big field. My sun-bonnet obstructed the view. I could see only the stretch of green before me, and I felt as if I must walk on forever, without coming to the end of it. I don't remember whether I was frightened or pleased. I must have been entertained.

"Likely as not it was Sunday," she laughed; "and I was running away from prayers, from the Presbyterian service, read in a spirit of gloom by my father that chills me yet to think of."

"And have you been running away from prayers ever since, *ma chére?*" asked Madame Ratignolle, amused.

"No! oh, no!" Edna hastened to say. "I was a little unthinking child in those days, just following a misleading impulse without question. On the contrary, during one period of my life religion took a firm hold upon me; after I was twelve and until—until—why, I suppose until now, though I never thought much about it—just driven along by habit. But do you know," she broke off, turning her quick eyes upon Madame Ratignolle and leaning forward a little so as to bring her face quite close to that of her companion, "sometimes I feel this summer as if I were walking through the green meadow again; idly, aimlessly, unthinking and unguided."

Madame Ratignolle laid her hand over that of Mrs. Pontellier, which was near her. Seeing that the hand was not withdrawn, she clasped it firmly and warmly. She even stroked it a little, fondly, with the other hand, murmuring in an undertone, *"Pauvre chérie."*

The action was at first a little confusing to Edna, but she soon lent herself readily to the Creole's gentle caress. She was not accustomed to an outward and spoken expression of affection, either in herself or in others. She and her younger sister, Janet, had quarreled a good deal through force of unfortunate habit. Her older sister, Margaret, was matronly and dignified, probably from having assumed matronly and housewifely responsibilities too early in life, their mother having died when they were quite young. Margaret was not effusive; she was practical. Edna had had an occasional girl friend, but whether accidentally or not, they seemed to have been all of one type—the self-contained. She never realized that the reserve of her own character had much, perhaps everything, to do with this. Her most intimate friend at school had been one of rather exceptional intellectual gifts, who wrote fine-sounding essays, which Edna admired and strove to imitate; and with her she talked and glowed over the English classics, and sometimes held religious and political controversies.

Edna often wondered at one propensity which sometimes had inwardly disturbed her without causing any outward show or manifestation on her part. At a very early age—perhaps it was when she traversed the ocean of waving grass—she remembered that she had been passionately enamored of a dignified and sad-eyed cavalry officer who visited her father in Kentucky. She could not leave his presence when he was there, nor remove her eyes from his face, which was something like Napoleon's, with a lock of black hair falling across the forehead. But the cavalry officer melted imperceptibly out of her existence.

At another time her affections were deeply engaged by a young gentleman who visited a lady on a neighboring plantation. It was after they went to Mississippi to live. The young man was engaged to be married to the young lady, and they sometimes called upon Margaret, driving over of afternoons in a buggy. Edna was a little miss, just merging into her teens; and the realization that she herself was nothing, nothing, nothing to the engaged young man was a bitter affliction to her. But he, too, went the way of dreams.

She was a grown young woman when she was overtaken by what she supposed to be the climax of her fate. It was when the face and figure of a great tragedian began to haunt her imagination and stir her senses. The persistence of the infatuation lent it an aspect of genuineness. The hopelessness of it colored it with the lofty tones of a great passion.

The picture of the tragedian stood enframed upon her desk. Any one may possess the portrait of a tragedian without exciting suspicion or comment. (This was a sinister reflection which she cherished.) In the presence of others she expressed admiration for his exalted gifts, as she handed the photograph around and dwelt upon the fidelity of the likeness. When alone she sometimes picked it up and kissed the cold glass passionately.

Her marriage to Léonce Pontellier was purely an accident, in this respect resembling many other marriages which masquerade as the decrees of Fate. It was in the midst of her secret great passion that she met him. He fell in love, as men are in the habit of doing, and pressed his suit with an earnestness and an ardor which left nothing to be desired. He pleased her; his absolute devotion flattered her. She fancied there was a sympathy of thought and taste between them, in which fancy she was mistaken. Add to this the violent opposition of her father and her sister Margaret to her marriage with a Catholic, and we need seek no further for the motives which led her to accept Monsieur Pontellier for her husband.

The acme of bliss, which would have been a marriage with the tragedian, was not for her in this world. As the devoted wife of a man who worshiped her, she felt she would take her place with a certain dignity in the world of reality, closing the portals forever behind her upon the realm of romance and dreams.

But it was not long before the tragedian had gone to join the cavalry officer and the engaged young man and a few others; and Edna found herself face to face with the realities. She grew fond of her husband, realizing with some unaccountable satisfaction that no trace of passion or excessive and fictitious warmth colored her affection, thereby threatening its dissolution.

She was fond of her children in an uneven, impulsive way. She would sometimes gather them passionately to her heart; she would sometimes forget them. The year before they had spent part of the summer with their grandmother Pontellier in Iberville. Feeling secure regarding their happiness and welfare, she did not miss them except with an occasional intense longing. Their absence was a sort of relief, though she did not admit this, even to herself. It seemed to free her of a responsibility which she had blindly assumed and for which Fate had not fitted her.

Edna did not reveal so much as all this to Madame Ratignolle that summer day when they sat with faces turned to the sea. But a good part of it escaped her. She had put her head down on Madame Ratignolle's shoulder. She was flushed and felt intoxicated with the sound of her own voice and the unaccustomed taste of candor. It muddled her like wine, or like a first breath of freedom.

There was the sound of approaching voices. It was Robert, surrounded by a troop of children, searching for them. The two little Pontelliers were with him, and he carried Madame Ratignolle's little girl in his arms. There were other children besides, and two nurse-maids followed, looking disagreeable and resigned.

The women at once rose and began to shake out their draperies and relax their muscles. Mrs. Pontellier threw the cushions and rug into the bath-house. The children all scampered off to the awning, and they stood there in a line, gazing upon the intruding lovers, still exchanging their vows and sighs. The lovers got up, with only a silent protest, and walked slowly away somewhere else.

The children possessed themselves of the tent, and Mrs. Pontellier went over to join them.

Madame Ratignolle begged Robert to accompany her to the house; she complained of cramp in her limbs and stiffness of the joints. She leaned draggingly upon his arm as they walked.

VIII

"Do me a favor, Robert," spoke the pretty woman at his side, almost as soon as she and Robert had started on their slow, homeward way. She looked up in his face, leaning on his arm beneath the encircling shadow of the umbrella which he had lifted.

"Granted; as many as you like," he returned, glancing down into her eyes that were full of thoughtfulness and some speculation.

"I only ask for one; let Mrs. Pontellier alone."

"*Tiens!*" he exclaimed, with a sudden, boyish laugh. "*Voila que Madame Ratignolles est jalouse!*"

"Nonsense! I'm in earnest; I mean what I say. Let Mrs. Pontellier alone."

"Why?" he asked; himself growing serious at his companion's solicitation.

"She is not one of us; she is not like us. She might make the unfortunate blunder of taking you seriously."

His face flushed with annoyance, and taking off his soft hat he began to beat it impatiently against his leg as he walked. "Why shouldn't she take me seriously?" he demanded sharply. "Am I a comedian, a clown, a jack-in-the-box? Why shouldn't she? You Creoles! I have no patience with you! Am I always to be regarded as a feature of an amusing programme? I hope Mrs. Pontellier does take me seriously. I hope she has discernment enough to find in me something besides the *blagueur*. If I thought there was any doubt—"

"Oh, enough, Robert!" she broke into his heated outburst. "You are not thinking of what you are saying. You speak with about as little reflection as we might expect from one of those children down there playing in the sand. If your attentions to any married women here were ever offered with any intention of being convincing, you would not be the gentleman we all know you to be, and you would be unfit to associate with the wives and daughters of the people who trust you."

Madame Ratignolle had spoken what she believed to be the law and the gospel. The young man shrugged his shoulders impatiently.

"Oh! well! That isn't it," slamming his hat down vehemently upon his head. "You ought to feel that such things are not flattering to say to a fellow."

"Should our whole intercourse consist of an exchange of compliments? *Ma foi!*"

"It isn't pleasant to have a woman tell you—" he went on, unheedingly, but breaking off suddenly: "Now if I were like Arobin—you remember Alcée Arobin and that story of the consul's wife at Biloxi?" And he related the story of Alcée Arobin and the consul's wife, and another about the tenor of the French Opera, who received letters which should never have been written, and still other stories, grave and gay, till Mrs. Pontellier and her possible propensity for taking young men seriously was apparently forgotten.

Madame Ratignolle, when they had regained her cottage, went in to take the hour's rest which she considered helpful. Before leaving her, Robert begged her pardon for the impatience—he called it rudeness—with which he had received her well-meant caution.

"You made one mistake, Adèle," he said, with a light smile; "there is no earthly possibility of Mrs. Pontellier ever taking me seriously. You should have warned me against taking myself seriously. Your advice might then have carried some weight and given me subject for some reflection. *Au revoir.* But you look tired," he added, solicitously. "Would you like a cup of bouillon? Shall I stir you a toddy? Let me mix you a toddy with a drop of Angostura."

She acceded to the suggestion of bouillon, which was grateful and acceptable. He went himself to the kitchen, which was a building apart from the cottages and lying to the rear of the house. And he himself brought her the golden-brown bouillon, in a dainty Sèvres cup, with a flaky cracker or two on the saucer.

She thrust a bare, white arm from the curtain which shielded her open door, and received the cup from his hands. She told him he was a *bon garçon*, and she meant it. Robert thanked her and turned away toward "the house."

The lovers were just entering the grounds of the *pension*. They were leaning toward each other as the water-oaks bent from the sea. There was not a particle of earth beneath their feet. Their heads might have been turned upside-down, so absolutely did they tread upon blue ether. The lady in black, creeping behind them, looked a trifle paler and more jaded than usual. There was no sign of Mrs. Pontellier and the children. Robert scanned the distance for any such apparition. They would doubtless remain away till the dinner hour. The young man ascended to his mother's room. It was situated at the top of the house, made up of odd angles and a queer, sloping ceiling. Two broad dormer windows looked out toward the Gulf, and as far across it as a man's eye might reach. The furnishings of the room were light, cool, and practical.

Madame Lebrun was busily engaged at the sewing-machine. A little black girl sat on the floor, and with her hands worked the treadle of the machine. The Creole woman does not take any chances which may be avoided of imperiling her health.

Robert went over and seated himself on the broad sill of one of the dormer windows. He took a book from his pocket and began energetically to read it, judging by the precision and frequency with which he turned the leaves. The sewing-machine made a resounding clatter in the room; it was of a ponderous, by-gone make. In the lulls, Robert and his mother exchanged bits of desultory conversation.

"Where is Mrs. Pontellier?"

"Down at the beach with the children."

"I promised to lend her the Goncourt. Don't forget to take it down when you go; it's there on the bookshelf over the small table." Clatter, clatter, clatter, bang! for the next five or eight minutes.

"Where is Victor going with the rockaway?"

"The rockaway? Victor?"

"Yes, down there in front. He seems to be getting ready to drive away somewhere."

"Call him." Clatter, clatter!

Robert uttered a shrill, piercing whistle which might have been heard back at the wharf.

"He won't look up."

Madame Lebrun flew to the window. She called "Victor!" She waved a handkerchief and called again. The young fellow below got into the vehicle and started the horse off at a gallop.

Madame Lebrun went back to the machine, crimson with annoyance. Victor was the younger son and brother—a *téte montée*, with a temper which invited violence and a will which no ax could break.

"Whenever you say the word I'm ready to thrash any amount of reason into him that he's able to hold."

"If your father had only lived!" Clatter, clatter, clatter, clatter, bang! It was a fixed belief with Madame Lebrun that the conduct of the universe and all things pertaining thereto would have been manifestly of a more intelligent and higher order had not Monsieur Lebrun been removed to other spheres during the early years of their married life.

"What do you hear from Montel?" Montel was a middle-aged gentleman whose vain ambition and desire for the past twenty years had been to fill the void which Monsieur Lebrun's taking off had left in the Lebrun household. Clatter, clatter, bang, clatter!

"I have a letter somewhere," looking in the machine drawer and finding the letter in the bottom of the work-basket. "He says to tell you he will be in Vera Cruz the beginning of next month"—clatter, clatter!—"and if you still have the intention of joining him"—bang! clatter, clatter, bang!

"Why didn't you tell me so before, mother? You know I wanted—" Clatter, clatter, clatter!

"Do you see Mrs. Pontellier starting back with the children? She will be in late to luncheon again. She never starts to get ready for luncheon till the last minute." Clatter, clatter! "Where are you going?"

"Where did you say the Goncourt was?"

IX

Every light in the hall was ablaze, every lamp turned as high as it could be without smoking the chimney or threatening explosion. The lamps were fixed at intervals against the wall, encircling the whole room. Some one had gathered orange and lemon branches, and with these fashioned graceful festoons between. The dark green of the branches stood out and glistened against the white muslin curtains which draped the windows, and which puffed, floated, and flapped at the capricious will of a stiff breeze that swept up from the Gulf.

It was Saturday night a few weeks after the intimate conversation held between Robert and Madame Ratignolle on their way from the beach. An unusual number of husbands, fathers, and friends had come down to stay over Sunday, and they were being suitably entertained by their families, with the material help of Madame Lebrun. The dining tables had all been removed to one end of the hall, and the chairs ranged about in rows and in clusters. Each little family group had had its say and exchanged its domestic gossip earlier in the evening. There was now an apparent disposition to relax, to widen the circle of confidences and give a more general tone to the conversation.

Many of the children had been permitted to sit up beyond their usual bedtime. A small band of them were lying on their stomachs on the floor looking at the colored sheets of the comic papers which Mr. Pontellier had brought down. The little Pontellier boys were permitting them to do so, and making their authority felt.

Music, dancing, and a recitation or two were the entertainments furnished, or rather, offered. But there was nothing systematic about the programme, no appearance of prearrangement nor even premeditation.

At an early hour in the evening the Farival twins were prevailed upon to play the piano. They were girls of fourteen, always clad in the Virgin's colors, blue and white, having been dedicated to the Blessed Virgin at their baptism. They played a duet from "Zampa," and at the earnest solicitation of every one present followed it with the overture to "The Poet and the Peasant."

"*Allez vous-en! Sapristi!*" shrieked the parrot outside the door. He was the only being present who possessed sufficient candor to admit that he was not listening to these gracious performances for the first time that summer. Old Monsieur Farival, grandfather of the twins, grew indignant over the interruption, and insisted upon having the bird removed and consigned to regions of darkness. Victor Lebrun objected; and his decrees were as immutable as those of Fate. The parrot fortunately offered no further interruption to the entertainment, the whole venom of his nature apparently having been cherished up and hurled against the twins in that one impetuous outburst.

Later a young brother and sister gave recitations, which every one present had heard many times at winter evening entertainments in the city.

A little girl performed a skirt dance in the center of the floor. The mother played her accompaniments and at the same time watched her daughter with greedy admiration and nervous apprehension. She need have had no apprehension. The child was mistress of the situation. She had been properly dressed for the occasion in black tulle and black silk tights. Her little neck and arms were bare, and her hair, artificially crimped, stood out like fluffy black plumes over her head. Her poses were full of grace, and her little black-shod toes twinkled as they shot out and upward with a rapidity and suddenness which were bewildering.

But there was no reason why every one should not dance. Madame Ratignolle could not, so it was

she who gaily consented to play for the others. She
played very well, keeping excellent waltz time and
infusing an expression into the strains which was
indeed inspiring. She was keeping up her music on
account of the children, she said, because she and
her husband both considered it a means of brightening the home and making it attractive.

Almost every one danced but the twins, who could
not be induced to separate during the brief period
when one or the other should be whirling around the
room in the arms of a man. They might have danced
together, but they did not think of it.

The children were sent to bed. Some went submissively; others with shrieks and protests as they
were dragged away. They had been permitted to
sit up till after the ice-cream, which naturally marked
the limit of human indulgence.

The ice-cream was passed around with cake—gold
and silver cake arranged on platters in alternate
slices; it had been made and frozen during the afternoon back of the kitchen by two black women,
under the supervision of Victor. It was pronounced
a great success—excellent if it had only contained
a little less vanilla or a little more sugar, if it had been
frozen a degree harder, and if the salt might have
been kept out of portions of it. Victor was proud of
his achievement, and went about recommending it
and urging every one to partake of it to excess.

After Mrs. Pontellier had danced twice with her
husband, once with Robert, and once with Monsieur
Ratignolle, who was thin and tall and swayed like a
reed in the wind when he danced, she went out
on the gallery and seated herself on the low window
sill, where she commanded a view of all that went

on in the hall and could look out toward the Gulf. There was a soft effulgence in the east. The moon was coming up, and its mystic shimmer was casting a million lights across the distant, restless water.

"Would you like to hear Mademoiselle Reisz play?" asked Robert, coming out on the porch where she was. Of course Edna would like to hear Mademoiselle Reisz play; but she feared it would be useless to entreat her.

"I'll ask her," he said. "I'll tell her that you want to hear her. She likes you. She will come." He turned and hurried away to one of the far cottages, where Mademoiselle Reisz was shuffling away. She was dragging a chair in and out of her room, and at intervals objecting to the crying of a baby, which a nurse in the adjoining cottage was endeavoring to put to sleep. She was a disagreeable little woman, no longer young, who had quarreled with almost every one, owing to a temper which was self-assertive and a disposition to trample upon the rights of others. Robert prevailed upon her without any too great difficulty.

She entered the hall with him during a lull in the dance. She made an awkward, imperious little bow as she went in. She was a homely woman, with a small weazened face and body and eyes that glowed. She had absolutely no taste in dress, and wore a batch of rusty black lace with a bunch of artificial violets pinned to the side of her hair.

"Ask Mrs. Pontellier what she would like to hear me play," she requested of Robert. She sat perfectly still before the piano, not touching the keys, while Robert carried her message to Edna at the window. A general air of surprise and genuine satisfaction fell upon every one as they saw the pianist enter. There was a settling down, and a prevailing air of expectancy everywhere. Edna was a trifle embarrassed at being thus signaled out for the imperious little woman's favor. She would not dare to choose, and begged that Mademoiselle Reisz would please herself in her selections.

Edna was what she herself called very fond of music. Musical strains, well rendered, had a way of evoking pictures in her mind. She sometimes liked to sit in the room of mornings when Madame Ratignolle played or practiced. One piece which that lady played Edna had entitled "Solitude." It was a short, plaintive, minor strain. The name of the piece was something else, but she called it "Solitude." When she heard it there came before her imagination the figure of a man standing beside a desolate rock on the seashore. He was naked. His attitude was one of hopeless resignation as he looked toward a distant bird winging its flight away from him.

Another piece called to her mind a dainty young woman clad in an Empire gown, taking mincing dancing steps as she came down a long avenue between tall hedges. Again, another reminded her of children at play, and still another of nothing on earth but a demure lady stroking a cat.

The very first chords which Mademoiselle Reisz struck upon the piano sent a keen tremor down Mrs. Pointellier's spinal column. It was not the first time she had heard an artist at the piano. Perhaps it was the first time she was ready, perhaps the first time her being was tempered to take an impress of the abiding truth.

She waited for the material pictures which she thought would gather and blaze before her imagination. She waited in vain. She saw no pictures of solitude, of hope, of longing, or of despair. But the very passions themselves were aroused within her soul, swaying it, lashing it, as the waves daily beat upon her splendid body. She trembled, she was choking, and the tears blinded her.

Mademoiselle had finished. She arose, and bowing her stiff, lofty bow, she went away, stopping for neither thanks nor applause. As she passed along the gallery she patted Edna upon the shoulder.

"Well, how did you like my music?" she asked. The young woman was unable to answer; she pressed the hand of the pianist convulsively. Mademoiselle Reisz perceived her agitation and even her tears. She patted her again upon the shoulder as she said:

"You are the only one worth playing for. Those others? Bah!" and she went shuffling and sidling on down the gallery toward her room.

But she was mistaken about "those others." Her playing had aroused a fever of enthusiasm. "What passion!" "What an artist!" "I have always said no one could play Chopin like Mademoiselle Reisz!" "That last prelude! Bon Dieu! It shakes a man!"

It was growing late, and there was a general disposition to disband. But some one, perhaps it was Robert, thought of a bath at that mystic hour and under that mystic moon.

X

At all events Robert proposed it, and there was

not a dissenting voice. There was not one but was ready to follow when he led the way. He did not lead the way, however, he directed the way; and he himself loitered behind with the lovers, who had betrayed a disposition to linger and hold themselves apart. He walked between them, whether with malicious or mischievous intent was not wholly clear, even to himself.

The Pointelliers and Ratignolles walked ahead; the women leaning upon the arms of their husbands. Edna could hear Robert's voice behind them, and could sometimes hear what he said. She wondered why he did not join them. It was unlike him not to. Of late he had sometimes held away from her for an entire day, redoubling his devotion upon the next and the next, as though to make up for hours that had been lost. She missed him the days when some pretext served to take him away from her, just as one misses the sun on a cloudy day without having thought much about the sun when it was shining.

The people walked in little groups toward the beach. They talked and laughed; some of them sang. There was a band playing down at Klein's hotel, and the strains reached them faintly, tempered by the distance. There were strange, rare odors abroad—a tangle of the sea smell and of weeds and damp, new-plowed earth, mingled with the heavy perfume of a field of white blossoms somewhere near. But the night sat lightly upon the sea and the land. There was no weight of darkness; there were no shadows. The white light of the moon had fallen upon the world like the mystery and the softness of sleep.

Most of them walked into the water as though into a native element. The sea was quiet now, and swelled lazily in broad billows that melted into one another and did not break except upon the beach in little foamy crests that coiled back like slow, white serpents.

Edna had attempted all summer to learn to swim. She had received instructions from both the men and women, in some instances from the children. Robert had pursued a system of lessons almost daily, and he was nearly at the point of discouragement in realizing the futility of his efforts. A certain ungovernable dread hung about her when in the water, unless there was a hand near by that might reach out and reassure her.

But that night she was like the little tottering, stumbling, clutching child, who of a sudden realizes its powers, and walks for the first time alone, boldly and with over-confidence. She could have shouted for joy. She did shout for joy, as with a sweeping stroke or two she lifted her body to the surface of the water.

A feeling of exultation overtook her, as if some power of significant import had been given her to control the working of her body and her soul. She grew daring and reckless, overestimating her strength. She wanted to swim far out, where no woman had swum before.

Her unlooked-for achievement was the subject of wonder, applause, and admiration. Each one congratulated himself that his special teachings had accomplished this desired end.

"How easy it is!" she thought. "It is nothing," she said aloud; "why did I not discover before that it was nothing. Think of the time I have lost splashing about like a baby!'' She would not join the groups in their sports and bouts, but intoxicated with her newly conquered power, she swam out alone.

She turned her face seaward to gather in an impression of space and solitude, which the vast expanse of water, meeting and melting with the moonlit sky, conveyed to her excited fancy. As she swam she seemed to be reaching out for the unlimited in which to lose herself.

Once she turned and looked toward the shore, toward the people she had left there. She had not gone any great distance—that is, what would have been a great distance for an experienced swimmer. But to her unaccustomed vision the stretch of water behind her assumed the aspect of a barrier which her unaided strength would never be able to overcome.

A quick vision of death smote her soul, and for a second of time appalled and enfeebled her senses. But by an effort she rallied her staggering faculties and managed to regain the land.

She made no mention of her encounter with death and her flash of terror, except to say to her husband, "I thought I should have perished out there alone."

"You were not so very far, my dear; I was watching you," he told her.

Edna went at once to the bathhouse, and she had put on her dry clothes and was ready to return home before the others had left the water. She started to walk away alone. They all called to her and shouted to her. She waved a dissenting hand, and went on, paying no further heed to their renewed cries which sought to detain her.

"Sometimes I am tempted to think that Mrs. Pontellier is capricious," said Madame Lebrun, who was amusing herself immensely and feared that Edna's abrupt departure might put an end to the pleasure.

"I know she is," assented Mr. Pontellier, "sometimes, not often."

Edna had not traversed a quarter of the distance on her way home before she was overtaken by Robert.

"Did you think I was afraid?" she asked him, without a shade of annoyance.

"No; I knew you weren't afraid."

"Then why did you come? Why didn't you stay out there with the others?"

"I never thought of it."

"Thought of what?"

"Of anything. What difference does it make?"

"I'm very tired," she uttered, complainingly.

"I know you are."

"You don't know anything about it. Why should you know? I never was so exhausted in my life. But it isn't unpleasant. A thousand emotions have swept through me to-night. I don't comprehend half of them. Don't mind what I'm saying; I am just thinking aloud. I wonder if I shall ever be stirred again as Mademoiselle Reisz's playing moved me to-night. I wonder if any night on earth will ever again be like this one. It is like a night in a dream. The people about me are like some uncanny, half-human beings. There must be spirits abroad to-night."

"There are," whispered Robert. "Didn't you know this was the twenty-eighth of August?"

"The twenty-eighth of August?"

"Yes. On the twenty-eighth of August, at the hour of midnight, and if the moon is shining—the moon must be shining—a spirit that has haunted these shores for ages rises up from the Gulf. With its own penetrating vision the spirit seeks some one mortal worthy to hold him company, worthy of being exalted for a few hours into realms of the semi-celestials. His search has always hitherto been fruitless, and he has sunk back, disheartened, into the sea. But tonight he found Mrs. Pontellier. Perhaps he will never wholly release her from the spell. Perhaps she will never again suffer a poor, unworthy earthling to walk in the shadow of her divine presence."

"Don't banter me," she said, wounded at what appeared to be his flippancy. He did not mind the entreaty, but the tone with its delicate note of pathos was like a reproach. He could not explain; he could not tell her that he had penetrated her mood and understood. He said nothing except to offer her his arm, for, by her own admission, she was exhausted. She had been walking alone with her arms hanging limp, letting her white skirts trail along the dewy path. She took his arm, but she did not lean upon it. She let her hand lie listlessly, as though her thoughts were elsewhere—somewhere in advance of her body, and she was striving to overtake them.

Robert assisted her into the hammock which swung from the post before her door out to the trunk of a tree.

"Will you stay out here and wait for Mr. Pontellier?" he asked.

"I'll stay out here. Goodnight."

"Shall I get you a pillow?"

"There's one here," she said, feeling about, for they were in the shadow.

"It must be soiled; the children have been tumbling it about."

"No matter." And having discovered the pillow, she adjusted it beneath her head. She extended herself in the hammock with a deep breath of relief. She was not a supercilious or an over-dainty woman. She was not much given to reclining in the hammock, and when she did so it was with no catlike suggestion of voluptuous ease, but with a beneficent repose which seemed to invade her whole body.

"Shall I stay with you till Mr. Pontellier comes?" asked Robert, seating himself on the outer edge of one of the steps and taking hold of the hammock rope which was fastened to the post.

"If you wish. Don't swing the hammock. Will you get my white shawl which I left on the window sill over at the house?"

"Are you chilly?"

"No; but I shall be presently."

"Presently?" he laughed. "Do you know what time it is? How long are you going to stay out here? '

"I don't know. Will you get the shawl?"

"Of course I will," he said, rising. He went over to the house, walking along the grass. She watched his figure pass in and out of the strips of moonlight. It was past midnight. It was very quiet.

When he returned with the shawl she took it and kept it in her hand. She did not put it around her.

"Did you say I should stay till Mr. Pontellier came back?"

"I said you might if you wished to."

He seated himself again and rolled a cigarette, which he smoked in silence. Neither did Mrs. Pontellier speak. No multitude of words could have been more significant than those moments of silence, or more pregnant with the first-felt throbbings of desire.

When the voices of the bathers were heard approaching, Robert said goodnight. She did not answer him. He thought she was asleep. Again she watched his figure pass in and out of the strips of moonlight as he walked away.

XI

"What are you doing out here, Edna? I thought I should find you in bed," said her husband, when he discovered her lying there. He had walked up with Madame Lebrun and left her at the house. His wife did not reply.

"Are you asleep?" he asked, bending down close to look at her.

"No." Her eyes gleamed bright and intense, with no sleepy shadows, as they looked into his.

"Do you know it is past one o'clock? Come on,' ' and he mounted the steps and went into their room.

"Edna!" called Mr. Pontellier from within, after a few moments had gone by.

"Don't wait for me," she answered. He thrust his head through the door.

"You will take cold out there," he said, irritably. "What folly is this? Why don't you come in?"

"It isn't cold; I have my shawl."

"The mosquitoes will devour you."

"There are no mosquitoes."

She heard him moving about the room; every sound indicating impatience and irritation. Another time she would have gone in at his request. She would, through habit, have yielded to his desire; not with any sense of submission or obedience to his compelling wishes, but unthinkingly, as we walk, move, sit, stand, go through the daily treadmill of the life which has been portioned out to us.

"Edna, dear, are you not coming in soon?" he asked again, this time fondly, with a note of entreaty.

"No; I am going to stay out here."

"This is more than folly," he blurted out. "I can't permit you to stay out there all night. You must come in the house instantly."

With a writhing motion she settled herself more securely in the hammock. She perceived that her will had blazed up, stubborn and resistant. She could not at that moment have done other than denied and resisted. She wondered if her husband had ever spoken to her like that before, and if she had submitted to his command. Of course she had; she remembered that she had. But she could not realize why or how she should have yielded, feeling as she then did.

"Léonce, go to bed," she said. "I mean to stay out here. I don't wish to go in, and I don't intend to. Don't speak to me like that again; I shall not answer you."

Mr. Pontellier had prepared for bed, but he slipped on an extra garment. He opened a bottle of wine, of which he kept a small and select supply in a buffet of his own. He drank a glass of the wine and went out on the gallery and offered a glass to his wife. She did not wish any. He drew up the rocker, hoisted his slippered feet on the rail, and proceeded to smoke a cigar. He smoked two cigars; then he went inside and drank another glass of wine. Mrs. Pontellier again declined to accept a glass when it was offered to her. Mr. Pontellier once more seated himself with elevated feet, and after a reasonable interval of time smoked some more cigars.

Edna began to feel like one who awakens gradually out of a dream, a delicious, grotesque, impossible dream, to feel again the realities pressing into her soul. The physical need for sleep began to overtake her; the exuberance which had sustained and exalted her spirit left her helpless and yielding to the conditions which crowded her in.

The stillest hour of the night had come, the hour before dawn, when the world seems to hold its breath. The moon hung low, and had turned from silver to copper in the sleeping sky. The old owl no longer hooted, and the water-oaks had ceased to moan as they bent their heads.

Edna arose, cramped from lying so long and still in the hammock. She tottered up the steps, clutching feebly at the post before passing into the house.

"Are you coming in, Léonce?" she asked, turning her face toward her husband.

"Yes, dear," he answered, with a glance following a misty puff of smoke. "Just as soon as I have finished my cigar."

XII

She slept but a few hours. They were troubled and feverish hours, disturbed with dreams that were intangible, that eluded her, leaving only an impression upon her half-awakened senses of something unattainable. She was up and dressed in the cool of the early morning. The air was invigorating and steadied somewhat her faculties. However, she was not seeking refreshment or help from any source, either external or from within. She was blindly following whatever impulse moved her, as if she had placed herself in alien hands for direction, and freed her soul of responsibility.

Most of the people at that early hour were still in bed and asleep. A few, who intended to go over to the *Chênière* for mass, were moving about. The lovers, who had laid their plans the night before, were already strolling toward the wharf. The lady in black, with her Sunday prayer-book, velvet and gold-clasped, and her Sunday silver beads, was following them at no great distance. Old Monsieur Farival was up, and was more than half inclined to do anything that suggested itself. He put on his big straw hat, and taking his umbrella from the stand in the hall, followed the lady in black, never overtaking her.

The little negro girl who worked Madame Lebrun's sewing machine was sweeping the galleries with long, absent-minded strokes of the broom. Edna sent her up into the house to awaken Robert.

"Tell him I am going to the *Chênière*. The boat is ready; tell him to hurry."

He had soon joined her. She had never sent for him before. She had never asked for him. She had never seemed to want him before. She did not appear conscious that she had done anything unusual in commanding his presence. He was apparently equally unconscious of anything extraordinary in the situation.

But his face was suffused with a quiet glow when he met her.

They went together back to the kitchen to drink coffee. There was no time to wait for any nicety of service. They stood outside the window and the cook passed them their coffee and a roll, which they drank and ate from the window sill. Edna said it tasted good. She had not thought of coffee nor of anything. He told her he had often noticed that she lacked forethought.

"Wasn't it enough to think of going to the *Chênière* and waking you up?" she laughed. "Do I have to think of everything?—as Léonce says when he's in a bad humor. I don't blame him; he'd never be in a bad humor if it weren't for me."

They took a short cut across the sands. At a distance they could see the curious procession moving toward the wharf—the lovers, shoulder to shoulder, creeping; the lady in black, gaining steadily upon them; old Monsieur Farival, losing ground inch by inch, and a young barefooted Spanish girl with a red kerchief on her head and a basket on her arm, bringing up the rear.

Robert knew the girl, and he talked to her a little in the boat. No one present understood what they said. Her name was Mariequita. She had a round, sly, piquant face and pretty black eyes. Her hands were small, and she kept them folded over the handle of her basket. Her feet were broad and coarse. She did not strive to hide them. Edna looked at her feet, and noticed the sand and slime between her brown toes.

Beaudelet grumbled because Mariequita was there, taking up so much room. In reality he was annoyed at having old Monsieur Farival, who considered himself the better sailor of the two. But he would not quarrel with so old a man as Monsieur Farival, so he quarreled with Mariequita. The girl was deprecatory at one moment, appealing to Robert. She was saucy the next, moving her head up and down, making "eyes" at Robert and making "mouths" at Beaudelet.

The lovers were all alone. They saw nothing, they heard nothing. The lady in black was counting her beads for the third time. Old Monsieur Farival talked incessantly of what he knew about handling a boat, and of what Beaudelet did not know on the same subject.

Edna liked it all. She looked Mariequita up and down, from her ugly brown toes to her pretty black eyes, and back again.

"Why does she look at me like that?" inquired the girl of Robert.

"Maybe she thinks you are pretty. Shall I ask her?"

"No. Is she your sweetheart?"

"She's a married lady, and has two children."

"Oh! well! Francisco ran away with Sylvano's wife, who had four children. They took all his money and one of the children and stole his boat."

"Shut up!"

"Does she understand?"

"Oh, hush!"

"Are those two married over there—leaning on each other?"

"Of course not," laughed Robert.

"Of course not," echoed Mariequita, with a serious, confirmatory bob of the head.

The sun was high up and beginning to bite. The

swift breeze seemed to Edna to bury the sting of it into the pores of her face and hands. Robert held his umbrella over her.

As they went cutting sidewise through the water, the sails bellied taut, with the wind filing and overflowing them. Old Monsieur Farival laughed sardonically at something as he looked at the sails, and Beaudelet swore at the old man under his breath.

Sailing across the bay to the *Chênière Caminada*, Edna felt as if she were being borne away from some anchorage which had held her fast, whose chains had been loosening—had snapped the night before when the mystic spirit was abroad, leaving her free to drift whithersoever she chose to set her sails. Robert spoke to her incessantly; he no longer noticed Mariequita. The girl had shrimps in her bamboo basket. They were covered with Spanish moss. She beat the moss down impatiently, and muttered to herself sullenly.

"Let us go to Grande Terre tomorrow?" said Robert in a low voice.

"What shall we do there?"

"Climb up the hill to the old fort and look at the little wriggling gold snakes, and watch the lizards sun themselves."

She gazed away toward Grande Terre and thought she would like to be alone there with Robert, in the sun, listening to the ocean's roar and watching the slimy lizards writhe in and out among the ruins of the old fort.

"And the next day or the next we can sail to the Bayou Brulow," he went on.

"What shall we do there?"

"Anything—cast bait for fish."

"No; we'll go back to Grande Terre. Let the fish alone."

"We'll go wherever you like," he said. "I'll have Tonie come over and help me patch and trim my boat. We shall not need Beaudelet nor any one. Are you afraid of the pirogue?"

"Oh, no."

"Then I'll take you some night in the pirogue when the moon shines. Maybe your Gulf spirit will whisper to you in which of these islands the treasures are hidden—direct you to the very spot, perhaps."

"And in a day we should be rich!" she laughed. "I'd give it all to you, the pirate gold and every bit of treasure we could dig up. I think you would know how to spend it. Pirate gold isn't a thing to be hoarded or utilized. It is something to squander and throw to the four winds, for the fun of seeing the golden specks fly."

"We'd share it, and scatter it together," he said. His face flushed.

They all went together up to the quaint little Gothic church of Our Lady of Lourdes, gleaming all brown and yellow with paint in the sun's glare.

Only Beaudelet remained behind, tinkering at his boat, and Mariequita walked away with her basket of shrimps, casting a look of childish ill-humor and reproach at Robert from the corner of her eye.

XIII

A feeling of oppression and drowsiness overcame Edna during the service. Her head began to ache, and the lights on the altar swayed before her eyes. Another time she might have made an effort to regain her composure; but her one thought was to quit the stifling atmosphere of church and reach the open air. She arose, climbing over Robert's feet with a muttered apology. Old Monsieur Farival, flurried, curious, stood up, but upon seeing that Robert had followed Mrs. Pontellier, he sank back into his seat. He whispered an anxious inquiry of the lady in black, who did not notice him or reply, but kept her eyes fastened upon the pages of her velvet prayer-book.

"I felt giddy and almost overcome," Edna said, lifting her hands instinctively to her head and pushing her straw hat up from her forehead. "I couldn't have stayed through the service." They were outside in the shadow of the church. Robert was full of solicitude.

"It was folly to have thought of going in the first place, let alone staying. Come over to Madame Antoine's; you can rest there." He took her arm and led her away, looking anxiously and continuously down into her face.

How still it was, with only the voice of the sea whispering through the reeds that grew in the salt-water pools! The long line of little gray, weather-beaten houses nestled peacefully among the orange trees. It must always have been God's day on that low, drowsy island, Edna thought. They stopped, leaning over a jagged fence made of sea-drift, to ask for water. A youth, a mild-faced Acadian, was drawing water from the cistern, which was nothing more than a rusty buoy, with an opening on one side, sunk in the ground. The water which the youth handed to them in a tin pail was not cold to taste, but it was cool to her heated face, and it greatly revived and refreshed her.

Madame Antoine's cot was at the far end of the village. She welcomed them with all the native hospitality, as she would have opened her door to let the sunlight in. She was fat, and walked heavily and clumsily across the floor. She could speak no English, but when Robert made her understand that the lady who accompanied him was ill and desired to rest, she was all eagerness to make Edna feel at home and to dispose of her comfortably.

The whole place was immaculately clean, and the big, four-posted bed, snow-white, invited one to repose. It stood in a small side room which looked out across a narrow grass plot toward the shed, where there was a disabled boat lying keel upward.

Madame Antoine had not gone to mass. Her son Tonie had, but she supposed he would soon be back, and she invited Robert to be seated and wait for him. But he went and sat outside the door and smoked. Madame Antoine busied herself in the large front room preparing dinner. She was boiling mullets over a few red coals in the huge fireplace.

Edna, left alone in the little side room, loosened her clothes, removing the greater part of them. She bathed her face, her neck and arms in the basin that stood between the windows. She took off her shoes and stockings and stretched herself in the very center of the high, white bed. How luxurious it felt to rest thus in a strange, quaint bed, with its sweet country odor of laurel lingering about the sheets and mattress! She stretched her strong limbs that ached a little. She ran her fingers through her loosened hair for a while. She looked at her round arms as she held them straight up and rubbed them one after the

other, observing closely, as if it were something she
saw for the first time, the fine, firm quality and
texture of her flesh. She clasped her hands easily
above her head, and it was thus she fell asleep.

She slept lightly at first, half awake and drowsily
attentive to the things about her. She could hear
Madame Antoine's heavy, scraping tread as she walked
back and forth on the sanded floor. Some chickens
were clucking outside the windows, scratching for
bits of gravel in the grass. Later she half heard the
voices of Robert and Tonie talking under the shed.
She did not stir. Even her eyelids rested numb and
heavily over her sleepy eyes. The voices went on—
Tonie's slow, Acadian drawl, Robert's quick, soft,
smooth French. She understood French imperfectly
unless directly addressed, and the voices were only
part of the other drowsy, muffled sounds lulling
her senses.

When Edna awoke it was with the conviction that
she had slept long and soundly. The voices were
hushed under the shed. Madame Antoine's step was
no longer to be heard in the adjoining room. Even
the chickens had gone elsewhere to scratch and
cluck. The mosquito bar was drawn over her; the
old woman had come in while she slept and let down
the bar. Edna arose quietly from the bed, and looking between the curtains of the window, she saw
by the slanting rays of the sun that the afternoon
was far advanced. Robert was out there under the
shed, reclining in the shade against the sloping keel
of the overturned boat. He was reading from a book.
Tonie was no longer with him. She wondered what
had become of the rest of the party. She peeped
out at him two or three times as she stood wash-

ing herself in the little basin between the windows.

Madame Antoine had laid some coarse, clean towels upon a chair, and had placed a box of *poudre de riz* within easy reach. Edna dabbed the powder upon her nose and cheeks as she looked at herself closely in the little distorted mirror which hung on the wall above the basin. Her eyes were bright and wide awake and her face glowed.

When she had completed her toilet she walked into the adjoining room. She was very hungry. No one was there. But there was a cloth spread upon the table that stood against the wall, and a cover was laid for one, with a crusty brown loaf and a bottle of wine beside the plate. Edna bit a piece from the brown loaf, tearing it with her strong, white teeth. She poured some of the wine into the glass and drank it down. Then she went softly out of doors, and plucking an orange from the low-hanging bough of a tree, threw it at Robert, who did not know she was awake and up.

An illumination broke over his whole face when he saw her and joined her under the orange tree.

"How many years have I slept?" she inquired. "The whole island seems changed. A new race of beings must have sprung up, leaving only you and me as past relics. How many ages ago did Madame Antoine and Tonie die? and when did our people from Grand Isle disappear from the earth?"

He familiarly adjusted a ruffle upon her shoulder.

"You have slept precisely one hundred years. I was left here to guard your slumbers; and for one hundred years I have been under the shed reading a book. The only evil I couldn't prevent was to keep a broiled fowl from drying up."

"If it has turned to stone, still will I eat it," said Edna, moving with him into the house. "But really, what has become of Monsieur Farival and the others?"

"Gone hours ago. When they found that you were sleeping they thought it best not to awake you. Any way, I wouldn't have let them. What was I here for?"

"I wonder if Léonce will be uneasy!" she speculated, as she seated herself at table.

"Of course not; he knows you are with me," Robert replied, as he busied himself among sundry pans and covered dishes which had been left standing on the hearth.

"Where are Madame Antoine and her son?" asked Edna.

"Gone to Vespers, and to visit some friends, I believe. I am to take you back in Tonie's boat whenever you are ready to go."

He stirred the smoldering ashes till the broiled fowl began to sizzle afresh. He served her with no mean repast, dripping the coffee anew and sharing it with her. Madame Antoine had cooked little else than the mullets, but while Edna slept Robert had foraged the island. He was childishly gratified to discover her appetite, and to see the relish with which she ate the food which he had procured for her.

"Shall we go right away?" she asked, after draining her glass and brushing together the crumbs of the crusty loaf.

"The sun isn't as low as it will be in two hours," he answered.

"The sun will be gone in two hours."

"Well, let it go; who cares!"

They waited a good while under the orange trees, till Madame Antoine came back, panting, waddling, with a thousand apologies to explain her absence. Tonie did not dare to return. He was shy, and would not willingly face any woman except his mother.

It was very pleasant to stay there under the orange trees, while the sun dipped lower and lower, turning the western sky to flaming copper and gold. The shadows lengthened and crept out like stealthy, grotesque monsters across the grass.

Edna and Robert both sat upon the ground—that is, he lay upon the ground beside her, occasionally picking at the hem of her muslin gown.

Madame Antoine seated her fat body, broad and squat, upon a bench beside the door. She had been talking all the afternoon, and had wound herself up to the story-telling pitch.

And what stories she told them! But twice in her life she had left the *Chênière Caminada*, and then for the briefest span. All her years she had squatted and waddled there upon the island, gathering legends of the Baratarians and the sea. The night came on, with the moon to lighten it. Edna could hear the whispering voices of dead men and the click of muffled gold.

When she and Robert stepped into Tonie's boat, with the red lateen sail, misty spirit forms were prowling in the shadows and among the reeds, and upon the water were phantom ships, speeding to cover.

XIV

The youngest boy, Etienne, had been very naughty,

Madame Ratignolle said, as she delivered him into
the hands of his mother. He had been unwilling to go
to bed and had made a scene; whereupon she had
taken charge of him and pacified him as well as
she could. Raoul had been in bed and asleep for two
hours.

The youngster was in his long white nightgown,
that kept tripping him up as Madame Ratignolle led
him along by the hand. With the other chubby fist
he rubbed his eyes, which were heavy with sleep
and ill humor. Edna took him in her arms, and
seating herself in the rocker, began to coddle and
caress him, calling him all manner of tender names,
soothing him to sleep.

It was not more than nine o'clock. No one had yet
gone to bed but the children.

Léonce had been very uneasy at first, Madame
Ratignolle said, and had wanted to start at once for
the *Chênière*. But Monsieur Farival had assured him
that his wife was only overcome with sleep and
fatigue, that Tonie would bring her safely back later
in the day; and he had thus been dissuaded from
crossing the bay. He had gone over to Klein's, looking
up some cotton broker whom he wished to see in
regard to securities, exchanges, stocks, bonds, or
something of the sort, Madame Ratignolle did not
remember what. He said he would not remain away
late. She herself was suffering from heat and oppression, she said. She carried a bottle of salts and a large
fan. She would not consent to remain with Edna, for
Monsieur Ratignolle was alone, and he detested
above all things to be left alone.

When Etienne had fallen asleep Edna bore him into
the back room, and Robert went and lifted the mos-

quito bar that she might lay the child comfortably in his bed. The quadroon had vanished. When they emerged from the cottage Robert bade Edna good-night.

"Do you know we have been together the while livelong day, Robert—since early this morning?" she said at parting.

"All but the hundred years when you were sleeping. Good-night."

He pressed her hand and went away in the direction of the beach. He did not join any of the others, but walked alone toward the Gulf.

Edna stayed outside, awaiting her husband's return. She had no desire to sleep or to retire; nor did she feel like going over to sit with the Ratignolles, or to join Madame Lebrun and a group whose animated voices reached her as they sat in conversation before the house. She let her mind wander back over her stay at Grand Isle, and she tried to discover wherein this summer had been different from any and every other summer of her life. She could only realize that she herself—her present self—was in some way different from the other self. That she was seeing with different eyes and making the acquaintance of new conditions in herself that colored and changed her environment, she did not yet suspect.

She wondered why Robert had gone away and left her. It did not occur to her to think he might have grown tired of being with her the livelong day. She was not tired, and she felt that he was not. She regretted that he had gone. It was so much more natural to have him stay, when he was not absolutely required to leave her.

As Edna waited for her husband she sang low a
little song that Robert had sung as they crossed the
bay. It began with "Ah! *Si tu savais*," and every verse
ended with "*si tu savais*."

Robert's voice was not pretentious. It was musical
and true. The voice, the notes, the whole refrain
haunted her memory.

XV

When Edna entered the dining-room one evening a
little late, as was her habit, an unusually animated
conversation seemed to be going on. Several persons
were talking at once, and Victor's voice was predomi-
nating, even over that of his mother. Edna had
returned late from her bath, had dressed in some
haste, and her face was flushed. Her head, set off by
her dainty white gown, suggested a rich, rare blossom.
She took her seat at table between old Monsieur
Farival and Madame Ratignolle.

As she seated herself and was about to begin to
eat her soup, which had been served when she entered
the room, several persons informed her simultaneously that Robert was going to Mexico. She laid her
spoon down and looked about her bewildered. He
had been with her, reading to her all the morning,
and had never even mentioned such a place as Mexico.
She had not seen him during the afternoon; she had
heard some one say he was at the house, upstairs
with his mother. This she had thought nothing of,
though she was surprised when he did not join her
later in the afternoon, when she went down to the
beach.

She looked across at him, where he sat beside

Madame Lebrun, who presided. Edna's face was a blank picture of bewilderment, which she never thought of disguising. He lifted his eyebrows with the pretext of a smile as he returned her glance. He looked embarrassed and uneasy.

"When is he going?" she asked of everybody in general, as if Robert were not there to answer for himself.

"Tonight!" "This very evening!" "Did you ever!" "What possesses him!" were some of the replies she gathered, uttered simultaneously in French and English.

"Impossible!" she exclaimed. "How can a person start off from Grand Isle to Mexico at a moment's notice, as if he were going over to Klein's or to the wharf or down to the beach?"

"I said all along I was going to Mexico; I've been saying so for years!" cried Robert, in an excited and irritable tone, with the air of a man defending himself against a swarm of stinging insects.

Madame Lebrun knocked on the table with her knife handle.

"Please let Robert explain why he is going, and why he is going tonight," she called out. "Really, this table is getting to be more and more like Bedlam every day, with everybody talking at once. Sometimes—I hope God will forgive me—but positively, sometimes I wish Victor would lose the power of speech."

Victor laughed sardonically as he thanked his mother for her holy wish, of which he failed to see the benefit to anybody, except that it might afford her a more ample opportunity and license to talk herself.

Monsieur Farival thought that Victor should have been taken out in mid-ocean in his earliest youth and drowned. Victor thought there would be more logic in thus disposing of old people with an established claim for making themselves universally obnoxious. Madame Lebrun grew a trifle hysterical; Robert called his brother some sharp, hard names.

"There's nothing much to explain, mother," he said, though he explained, nevertheless—looking chiefly at Edna—that he could only meet the gentleman whom he intended to join at Vera Cruz by taking such and such a steamer, which left New Orleans on such a day; that Beaudelet was going out with his lugger-load of vegetables that night, which gave him an opportunity of reaching the city and making his vessel in time.

"But when did you make up your mind to all this?" demanded Monsieur Farival.

"This afternoon," returned Robert, with a shade of annoyance.

"At what time this afternoon?" persisted the old gentleman, with nagging determination, as if he were cross-questioning a criminal in a court of justice.

"At four o'clock this afternoon, Monsieur Farival," Robert replied, in a high voice and with a lofty air, which reminded Edna of some gentleman on the stage.

She had forced herself to eat most of her soup, and now she was picking the flaky bits of a *court bouillon* with her fork.

The lovers were profiting by the general conversation on Mexico to speak in whispers of matters which they rightly considered were interesting to no one but themselves. The lady in black had once received a pair of prayer-beads of curious workmanship from Mexico, with very special indulgence attached to them, but she had never been able to ascertain whether the indulgence extended outside the Mexican border. Father Fochel of the Cathedral had attempted to explain it; but he had not done so to her satisfaction. And she begged that Robert would interest himself, and discover, if possible, whether she was entitled to the indulgence accompanying the remarkably curious Mexican prayer-beads.

Madame Ratignolle hoped that Robert would exercise extreme caution in dealing with the Mexicans, who, she considered, were a treacherous people, unscrupulous and revengeful. She trusted she did them no injustice in thus condemning them as a race. She had known personally but one Mexican, who made and sold excellent tamales, and whom she would have trusted implicitly, so soft-spoken was he. One day he was arrested for stabbing his wife. She never knew whether he had been hanged or not.

Victor had grown hilarious, and was attempting to tell an anecdote about a Mexican girl who served chocolate one winter in a restaurant in Dauphine Street. No one would listen to him but old Monsieur Farival, who went into convulsions over the droll story.

Edna wondered if they had all gone mad, to be talking and clamoring at that rate. She herself could think of nothing to say about Mexico or the Mexicans.

"At what time do you leave?" she asked Robert.

"At ten," he told her. "Beaudelet wants to wait for the moon."

"Are you all ready to go?"

"Quite ready. I shall only take a handbag, and shall pack my trunk in the city."

He turned to answer some question put to him by his mother, and Edna, having finished her black coffee, left the table.

She went directly to her room. The little cottage was close and stuffy after leaving the outer air. But she did not mind; there appeared to be a hundred different things demanding her attention indoors.

She began to set the toilet stand to rights, grumbling at the negligence of the quadroon, who was in the adjoining room putting the children to bed. She gathered together stray garments that were hanging on the backs of chairs, and put each where it belonged in closet or bureau drawer. She changed her gown for a more comfortable and commodious wrapper. She rearranged her hair, combing and brushing it with unusual energy. Then she went in and assisted the quadroon in getting the boys to bed.

They were very playful and inclined to talk—to do anything but lie quiet and go to sleep. Edna sent the quadroon away to her supper and told her she need not return. Then she sat and told the children a story. Instead of soothing it excited them, and added to their wakefulness. She left them in heated argument, speculating about the conclusion of the tale which their mother promised to finish the following night.

The little black girl came in to say that Madame Lebrun would like to have Mrs. Pontellier go and sit with them over at the house till Mr. Robert went away. Edna returned answer that she had already undressed, that she did not feel quite well, but perhaps she would go over to the house later. She started to dress again, and got as far advanced as to remove her *peignoir*. But changing her mind once more she resumed the *peignoir*, and went outside and sat down before her door. She was over - heated and irritable, and fanned herself energetically for a while. Madame Ratignolle came down to dis- cover what was the matter.

"All that noise and confusion at the table must have upset me," replied Edna, "and moreover, I hate shocks and surprises. The idea of Robert starting off in such a ridiculously sudden and dramatic way! As if it were a matter of life and death! Never saying a word about it all morning when he was with me."

"Yes," agreed Madame Ratignolle. "I think it was showing us all—you especially—very little considera- tion. It wouldn't have surprised me in any of the others; those Lebruns are all given to heroics. But I must say I should never have expected such a thing from Robert. Are you not coming down? Come on, dear; it doesn't look friendly."

"No," said Edna, a little sullenly. "I can't go to the trouble of dressing again; I don't feel like it."

"You needn't dress; you look all right; fasten a belt around your waist. Just look at me!"

"No," persisted Edna; "but you go on. Madame Lebrun might be offended if we both stayed away."

Madame Ratignolle kissed Edna goodnight, and went away, being in truth rather desirous of join- ing in the general and animated conversation which was still in progress concerning Mexico and the Mexicans.

Somewhat later Robert came up, carrying his handbag.

"Aren't you feeling well?" he asked.

"Oh, well enough. Are you going right away?"

He lit a match and looked at his watch. "In twenty minutes," he said. The sudden and brief flare of the match emphasized the darkness for a while. He sat down upon a stool which the children had left out on the porch.

"Get a chair," said Edna.

"This will do," he replied. He put on his soft hat and nervously took it off again, and wiping his face with his handkerchief, complained of the heat.

"Take the fan," said Edna, offering it to him.

"Oh, no! Thank you. It does no good; you have to stop fanning sometime, and feel all the more uncomfortable afterward."

"That's one of the ridiculous things which men always say. I have never known one to speak otherwise of fanning. How long will you be gone?"

"Forever, perhaps. I don't know. It depends upon a good many things."

"Well, in case it shouldn't be forever, how long will it be?"

"I don't know."

"This seems to me perfectly preposterous and uncalled for. I don't like it. I don't understand your motive for silence and mystery, never saying a word to me about it this morning." He remained silent, not offering to defend himself. He only said, after a moment:

"Don't part from me in an ill-humor. I never knew you to be out of patience with me before.

"I don't want to part in any ill-humor," she

said. "But can't you understand? I've grown used to seeing you, to having you with me all the time, and your action seems unfriendly, even unkind. You don't even offer an excuse for it. Why, I was planning to be together, thinking of how pleasant it would be to see you in the city next winter."

"So was I," he blurted. "Perhaps that's the—" He stood up suddenly and held out his hand. "Good-by, my dear Mrs. Pontellier; good-by. You won't—I hope you won't completely forget me." She clung to his hand, striving to detain him.

"Write to me when you get there, won't you, Robert?" she entreated.

"I will, thank you. Good-by."

How unlike Robert! The merest acquaintance would have said something more emphatic than "I will, thank you; good-by," to such a request.

He had evidently already taken leave of the people over at the house, for he descended the steps and went to join Beaudelet, who was out there with an oar across his shoulder waiting for Robert. They walked away in the darkness. She could only hear Beaudelet's voice; Robert had apparently not even spoken a word of greeting to his companion.

Edna bit her handkerchief convulsively, striving to hold back and to hide, even from herself as she would have hidden from another, the emotion which was troubling—tearing—her. Her eyes were brimming with tears.

For the first time she recognized anew the symptoms of infatuation which she had felt incipiently as a child, as a girl in her earliest teens, and later as a young woman. The recognition did not lessen the reality, the poignancy of the revelation by any suggestion or promise of instability. The past was nothing to her; offered no lesson which she was willing to heed. The future was a mystery which she never attempted to penetrate. The present alone was significant, was hers, to torture her as it was doing then with the biting conviction that she had lost that which she had held, that she had been denied that which her impassioned, newly awakened being demanded.

XVI

"Do you miss your friend greatly?" asked Mademoiselle Reisz one morning as she came creeping up behind Edna, who had just left her cottage on her way to the beach. She spent much of her time in the water since she had acquired finally the art of swimming. As their stay at Grand Isle drew near its close, she felt that she could not give too much time to a diversion which afforded her the only pleasurable moments that she knew. When Mademoiselle Reisz came and touched her upon the shoulder and spoke to her, the woman seemed to echo the thought which was ever in Edna's mind; or, better, the feeling which constantly possessed her.

Robert's going had some way taken the brightness, the color, the meaning out of everything. The conditions of her life were in no way changed, but her whole existence was dulled, like a faded garment which seems to be no longer worth wearing. She sought him everywhere—in others whom she induced to talk about him. She went up in the mornings to Madame Lebrun's room, braving the clatter of the old sewing-machine. She sat there and chatted at intervals as Robert had done. She gazed around the room at the pictures and photographs hanging upon

the wall, and discovered in some corner an old family
album, which she examined with the keenest interest,
appealing to Madame Lebrun for enlightenment
concerning the many figures and faces which she
discovered between its pages.

There was a picture of Madame Lebrun with Robert
as a baby, seated in her lap, a round-faced infant
with a fist in his mouth. The eyes alone in the baby
suggested the man. And that was he also in kilts,
at the age of five, wearing long curls and holding
a whip in his hand. It made Edna laugh, and she
laughed, too, at the portrait in his first long trousers;
while another interested her, taken when he left
for college, looking thin, long-faced, with eyes full
of fire, ambition and great intentions. But there
was no recent picture, none which suggested the
Robert who had gone away five days ago, leaving a
void and wildnerness behind him.

"Oh, Robert stopped having his pictures taken
when he had to pay for them himself! He found wiser
use for his money, he says," explained Madame
Lebrun. She had a letter from him, written before
he left New Orleans. Edna wished to see the letter,
and Madame Lebrun told her to look for it either
on the table or the dresser, or perhaps it was on
the mantlepiece.

The letter was on the bookshelf. It possessed the
greatest interest and attraction for Edna; the envelope,
its size and shape, the post-mark, the handwriting.
She examined every detail of the outside before
opening it. There were only a few lines, setting
forth that he would leave the city that afternoon,
that he had packed his trunk in good shape, that
he was well, and sent her his love and begged to be

affectionately remembered to all. There was no special message to Edna except a postscript saying that if Mrs. Pontellier desired to finish the book which he had been reading to her, his mother would find it in his room, among other books there on the table. Edna experienced a pang of jealousy because he had written to his mother rather than to her.

Every one seemed to take for granted that she missed him. Even her husband, when he came down the Saturday following Robert's departure, expressed regret that he had gone.

"How do you get on without him, Edna?" he asked.

"It's very dull without him," she admitted. Mr. Pontellier had seen Robert in the city, and Edna asked him a dozen questions or more. Where had they met? On Carondelet Street, in the morning. They had gone "in" and had a drink and a cigar together. What had they talked about? Chiefly about his prospects in Mexico, which Mr. Pontellier thought were promising. How did he look? How did he seem—grave, or gay, or how? Quite cheerful, and wholly taken up with the idea of his trip, which Mr. Pontellier found altogether natural in a young fellow about to seek fortune and adventure in a strange, queer country.

Edna tapped her foot impatiently, and wondered why the children persisted in playing in the sun when they might be under the trees. She went down and led them out of the sun, scolding the quadroon for not being more attentive.

It did not strike her as in the least grotesque that she should be making of Robert the object of conversation and leading her husband to speak of him.

The sentiment which she entertained for Robert in no way resembled that which she felt for her husband, or had ever felt, or ever expected to feel. She had all her life long been accustomed to harbor thoughts and emotions which never voiced themselves. They had never taken the form of struggles. They belonged to her and were her own, and she entertained the conviction that she had a right to them and that they concerned no one but herself. Edna had once told Madame Ratignolle that she would never sacrifice herself for her children, or for any one. Then had followed a rather heated argument; the two women did not appear to understand each other or to be talking the same language. Edna tried to appease her friend, to explain.

"I would give up the unessential; I would give my money, I would give my life for my children; but I wouldn't give myself. I can't make it more clear; it's only something which I am beginning to comprehend, which is revealing itself to me."

"I don't know what you would call the essential, or what you mean by the unessential," said Madame Ratignolle, cheerfully, "but a woman who would give her life for her children could do no more than that—your Bible tells you so. I'm sure I couldn't do more than that."

"Oh, yes you could!" laughed Edna.

She was not surprised at Mademoiselle Reisz's question the morning that lady, following her to the beach, tapped her on the shoulder and asked if she did not greatly miss her young friend.

"Oh, good morning, Mademoiselle; is it you? Why, of course I miss Robert. Are you going down to bathe?"

"Why should I go down to bathe at the very end of the season when I haven't been in the surf all summer," replied the woman, disagreeably.

"I beg your pardon," offered Edna, in some embarrassment, for she should have remembered that Mademoiselle Reisz's avoidance of the water had furnished a theme for much pleasantry. Some among them thought it was on account of her false hair, or the dread of getting the violets wet, while others attributed it to the natural aversion for water sometimes believed to accompany the artistic temperament. Mademoiselle offered Edna some chocolates in a paper bag, which she took from her pocket, by way of showing that she bore no ill feeling. She habitually ate chocolates for their sustaining quality; they contained much nutriment in small compass, she said. They saved her from starvation, as Madame Lebrun's table was utterly impossible, and no one save so impertinent a woman as Madame Lebrun could think of offering such food to people and requiring them to pay for it.

"She must feel very lonely without her son," said Edna, desiring to change the subject. "Her favorite son, too. It must have been quite hard to let him go."

Mademoiselle laughed maliciously.

"Her favorite son! Oh, dear! Who could have been imposing such a tale upon you? Aline Lebrun lives for Victor, and for Victor alone. She has spoiled him into the worthless creature he is. She worships him and the ground he walks on. Robert is very well in a way, to give up all the money he can earn to the family, and keep the barest pittance for himself. Favorite son, indeed! I miss the poor fellow myself, my dear. I liked to see him and to hear him

about the place—the only Lebrun who is worth
a pinch of salt. He comes to see me often in the city.
I like to play to him. That Victor! hanging would
be too good for him. It's a wonder Robert hasn't
beaten him to death long ago."

"I thought he had great patience with his brother,"
offered Edna, glad to be talking about Robert, no
matter what was said.

"Oh! he thrashed him well enough a year or two
ago," said Mademoiselle. "It was about a Spanish
girl, whom Victor considered that he had some sort
of claim upon. He met Robert one day talking
to the girl, or walking with her, or bathing with her,
or carrying her basket—I don't remember what—and
he became so insulting and abusive that Robert gave
him a thrashing on the spot that has kept him comparatively in order for a good while. It's about
time he was getting another."

"Was her name Mariequita?" asked Edna.

"Mariequita—yes, that was it; Mariequita. I had
forgotten. Oh, she's a sly one, and a bad one, that
Mariequita!"

Edna looked down at Mademoiselle Reisz and
wondered how she could have listened to her venom
so long. For some reason she felt depressed, almost
unhappy. She had not intended to go into the water;
but she donned her bathing suit, and left Mademoiselle
alone, seated under the shade of the children's tent.
The water was growing cooler as the season advanced.
Edna plunged and swam about with an abandon that
thrilled and invigorated her. She remained a long
time in the water, half hoping that Mademoiselle
Reisz would not wait for her.

But Mademoiselle waited. She was very amiable

during the walk back, and raved much over Edna's appearance in her bathing suit. She talked about music. She hoped that Edna would go to see her in the city, and wrote her address with the stub of a pencil on a piece of card which she found in her pocket.

"When do you leave?" asked Edna.

"Next Monday; and you?"

"The following week," answered Edna, adding, "It has been a pleasant summer, hasn't it, Mademoiselle?"

"Well," agreed Mademoiselle Reisz, with a shrug, "rather pleasant, if it hadn't been for the mosquitoes and the Farival twins."

XVII

The Pontelliers possessed a very charming home on Esplanade Street in New Orleans. It was a large, double cottage, with a broad front veranda, whose round, fluted columns supported the sloping roof. The house was painted a dazzling white; the outside shutters, or jalousies, were green. In the yard, which was kept scrupulously neat, were flowers and plants of every description which flourishes in South Louisiana. Within doors the appointments were perfect after the conventional type. The softest carpets and rugs covered the floors; rich and tasteful draperies hung at doors and windows. There were paintings, selected with judgment and discrimination, upon the walls. The cut glass, the silver, the heavy damask which daily appeared upon the table were the envy of many women whose husbands were less generous than Mr. Pontellier.

Mr. Pontellier was very fond of walking about

his house examining its various appointments and details, to see that nothing was amiss. He greatly valued his possessions, chiefly because they were his, and derived genuine pleasure from contemplating a painting, a statuette, a rare lace curtain—no matter what—after he had bought it and placed it among his household gods.

On Tuesday afternoons—Tuesday being Mrs. Pontellier's reception day—there was a constant stream of callers—women who came in carriages or in the street cars, or walked when the air was soft and distance permitted. A light-colored mulatto boy, in dress coat and bearing a diminutive silver tray for the reception of cards, admitted them. A maid, in white fluted cap, offered the callers liqueur, coffee, or chocolate, as they might desire. Mrs. Pontellier, attired in a handsome reception gown, remained in the drawing room the entire afternoon receiving her visitors. Men sometimes called in the evening with their wives.

This had been the programme which Mrs. Pontellier had religiously followed since her marriage, six years before. Certain evenings during the week she and her husband attended the opera or sometimes the play.

Mr. Pontellier left his home in the mornings between nine and ten o'clock, and rarely returned before half-past six or seven in the evening—dinner being served at half-past seven.

He and his wife seated themselves at table one Tuesday evening, a few weeks after their return from Grand Isle. They were alone together. The boys were being put to bed; the patter of their bare, escaping feet could be heard occasionally, as well as the pursuing voice of the quadroon, lifted in mild protest and entreaty. Mrs. Pontellier did not wear her usual Tuesday reception gown; she was in ordinary house dress. Mr. Pontellier, who was observant about such things, noticed it, as he served the soup and handed it to the boy in waiting.

"Tired out, Edna? Whom did you have? Many callers?" he asked. He tasted his soup and began to season it with pepper, salt, vinegar, mustard—everything within reach.

"There were a good many," replied Edna, who was eating her soup with evident satisfaction. "I found their cards when I got home; I was out."

"Out!" exclaimed her husband, with something like genuine consternation in his voice as he laid down the vinegar cruet and looked at her through his glasses. "Why, what could have taken you out on Tuesday? What did you have to do?"

"Nothing. I simply felt like going out, and I went out."

"Well, I hope you left some suitable excuse," said her husband, somewhat appeased, as he added a dash of cayenne pepper to the soup.

"No, I left no excuse. I told Joe to say I was out, that was all."

"Why, my dear, I should think you'd understand by this time that people don't do such things; we've got to observe *les convenances* if we ever expect to get on and keep up with the procession. If you felt that you had to leave home this afternoon, you should have left some suitable explanation for your absence.

"This soup is really impossible; it's strange that woman hasn't learned yet to make a decent soup. Any free lunch stand in town serves a better one. Was Mrs. Belthrop here?"

"Bring the tray with the cards, Joe. I don't remember who was here."

The boy retired and returned after a moment, bringing the tiny silver tray, which was covered with ladies' visiting cards. He handed it to Mrs. Pontellier.

"Give it to Mr. Pontellier," she said.

Joe offered the tray to Mr. Pontellier, and removed the soup.

Mr. Pontellier scanned the names of his wife's callers, reading some of them aloud, with comments as he read.

" 'The Misses Delasidas.' I worked a big deal in futures for their father this morning; nice girls; it's time they were getting married. 'Mrs. Belthrop.' I tell you what it is, Edna; you can't afford to snub Mrs. Belthrop. Why, Belthrop could buy and sell us ten times over. His business is worth a good, round sum to me. You'd better write her a note. 'Mrs. James Highcamp.' Hugh! the less you have to do with Mrs. Highcamp, the better. 'Madame Laforcé.' Came all the way from Carrolton, too, poor old soul. 'Miss Wiggs,' 'Mrs. Eleanor Boltons.' " He pushed the cards aside.

"Mercy!" exclaimed Edna, who had been fuming. "Why are you taking the thing so seriously and making such a fuss over it?"

"I'm not making any fuss over it. But it's just such seeming trifles that we've got to take seriously; such things count."

The fish was scorched. Mr. Pontellier would not touch it. Edna said she did not mind a little scorched taste. The roast was in some way not to his fancy, and he did not like the manner in which the vegetables were served.

"It seems to me," he said, "we spend money enough in this house to procure at least one meal a day which a man could eat and retain his self-respect."

"You used to think the cook was a treasure," returned Edna, indifferently.

"Perhaps she was when she first came; but cooks are only human. They need looking after, like any other class of persons that you employ. Suppose I didn't look after the clerks in my office, just let them run things their own way; they'd soon make a nice mess of me and my business."

"Where are you going?" asked Edna, seeing that her husband arose from table without having eaten a morsel except a taste of the highly-seasoned soup.

"I'm going to get my dinner at the club. Good night." He went into the hall, took his hat and stick from the stand, and left the house.

She was somewhat familiar with such scenes. They had often made her very unhappy. On a few previous occasions she had been completely deprived of any desire to finish her dinner. Sometimes she had gone into the kitchen to administer a tardy rebuke to the cook. Once she went to her room and studied the cookbook during an entire evening, finally writing out a menu for the week, which left her harassed with a feeling that, after all, she had accomplished no good that was worth the name.

But that evening Edna finished her dinner alone, with forced deliberation. Her face was flushed and her eyes flamed with some inward fire that lighted them. After finishing her dinner she went to her room, having instructed the boy to tell any other callers that she was indisposed.

It was a large, beautiful room, rich and picturesque in the soft, dim light which the maid had turned low. She went and stood at an open window and looked out upon the deep tangle of the garden below. All the mystery and witchery of the night seemed to have gathered there amid the perfumes and the dusky and tortuous outlines of flowers and foliage. She was seeking herself and finding herself in just such sweet, half-darkness which met her moods. But the voices were not soothing that came to her from the darkness and the sky above and the stars. They jeered and sounded mournful notes without promise, devoid even of hope. She turned back into the room and began to walk to and fro down its whole length, without stopping, without resting. She carried in her hands a thin handkerchief, which she tore into ribbons, rolled into a ball, and flung from her. Once she stopped, and taking off her wedding ring, flung it upon the carpet. When she saw it lying there, she stamped her heel upon it, striving to crush it. But her small boot heel did not make an indenture, not a mark upon the little glittering circlet.

In a sweeping passion she seized a glass vase from the table and flung it upon the tiles of the hearth. She wanted to destroy something. The crash and clatter were what she wanted to hear.

A maid, alarmed at the din of breaking glass, entered the room to discover what was the matter.

"A vase fell upon the hearth," said Edna. "Never mind; leave it till morning."

"Oh! you might get some of the glass in your feet,

ma'am," insisted the young woman, picking up bits of the broken vase that scattered upon the carpet. "And here's your ring, ma'am, under the chair."

Edna held out her hand, and taking the ring, slipped it upon her finger.

XVIII

The following morning Mr. Pontellier, upon leaving for his office, asked Edna if she would not meet him in town in order to look at some new fixtures for the library.

"I hardly think we need new fixtures, Léonce. Don't let us get anything new; you are too extravagant. I don't believe you ever think of saving or putting by."

"The way to become rich is to make money, my dear Edna, not to save it," he said. He regretted that she did not feel inclined to go with him and select new fixtures. He kissed her good-by, and told her she was not looking well and must take care of herself. She was unusually pale and very quiet.

She stood on the front veranda as he quitted the house, and absently picked a few sprays of jessamine that grew upon a trellis near by. She inhaled the odor of the blossoms and thrust them into the bosom of her white morning gown. The boys were dragging along the banquette a small "express wagon," which they had filled with blocks and sticks. The quadroon was following them with little quick steps, having assumed a fictitious animation and alacrity for the occasion. A fruit vender was crying his wares in the street.

Edna looked straight before her with a self-absorbed expression upon her face. She felt no interest in anything about her. The street, the children, the fruit vender, the flowers growing there under her eyes, were all part and parcel of an alien world which had suddenly become antagonistic.

She went back into the house. She had thought of speaking to the cook concerning her blunders of the previous night; but Mr. Pontellier had saved her that disagreeable mission, for which she was so poorly fitted. Mr. Pontellier's arguments were usually convincing with those whom he employed. He left home feeling quite sure that he and Edna would sit down that evening, and possibly a few subsequent evenings, to a dinner deserving of the name.

Edna spent an hour or two in looking over some of her old sketches. She could see their shortcomings and defects, which were glaring in her eyes. She tried to work a little, but found she was not in the humor. Finally she gathered together a few of the sketches—those which she considered the least discreditable; and she carried them with her when, a little later, she dressed and left the house. She looked handsome and distinguished in her street gown. The tan of the seashore had left her face, and her forehead was smooth, white, and polished beneath her heavy, yellow-brown hair. There were a few freckles on her face, and a small, dark mole near the under lip and one on the temple, half-hidden in her hair.

As Edna walked along the street she was thinking of Robert. She was still under the spell of her infatuation. She had tried to forget him, realizing the inutility of remembering. But the thought of him was like an obsession, ever pressing itself upon her.

It was not that she dwelt upon details of their acquaintance, or recalled in any special or peculiar
way his personality; it was his being, his existence,
which dominated her thought, fading sometimes
as if it would melt into the mist of the forgotten,
reviving again with an intensity which filled her
with an incomprehensible longing.

Edna was on her way to Madame Ratignolle's.
Their intimacy, begun at Grand Isle, had not declined, and they had seen each other with some
frequency since their return to the city. The Ratignolles lived at no great distance from Edna's home,
on the corner of a side street, where Monsieur Ratignolle owned and conducted a drug store which enjoyed
a steady and prosperous trade. His father had been in
the business before him, and Monsieur Ratignolle
stood well in the community and bore an enviable
reputation for integrity and clearheadedness. His family lived in commodious apartments over the store, having an entrance on the side within the *porte cochère*.
There was something which Edna thought very French,
very foreign, about their whole manner of living. In
the large and pleasant salon which extended across
the width of the house, the Ratignolles entertained
their friends once a fortnight with a *soirée musicale*,
sometimes diversified by card-playing. There was a
friend who played upon the 'cello. One brought his
flute and another his violin, while there were some
who sang and a number who performed upon the
piano with various degrees of taste and agility. The
Ratignolles' *soirées musicales* were widely known,
and it was considered a privilege to be invited to
them.

Edna found her friend engaged in assorting the
clothes which had returned that morning from

the laundry. She at once abandoned her occupation upon seeing Edna, who had been ushered without ceremony into her presence.

"Cité can do it as well as I; it is really her business," she explained to Edna, who apologized for interrupting her. And she summoned a young black woman, whom she instructed, in French, to be very careful in checking off the list which she handed her. She told her to notice particularly if a fine linen handkerchief of Monsieur Ratignolle's, which was missing last week, had been returned; and to be sure to set to one side such pieces as required mending and darning.

Then placing an arm around Edna's waist, she led her to the front of the house, to the salon, where it was cool and sweet with the odor of great roses that stood upon the hearth in jars.

Madame Ratignolle looked more beautiful than ever there at home, in a negligé which left her arms almost wholly bare and exposed the rich, melting curves of her white throat.

"Perhaps I shall be able to paint your picture some day," said Edna with a smile when they were seated. She produced the roll of sketches and started to unfold them. "I believe I ought to work again. I feel as if I wanted to be doing something. What do you think of them? Do you think it worth while to take it up again and study some more? I might study for a while with Laidpore."

She knew that Madame Ratignolle's opinion in such a matter would be next to valueless, that she herself had not alone decided, but determined; but she sought the words of praise and encouragement that would help her to put heart into her venture.

"Your talent is immense, dear!"

"Nonsense!" protested Edna, well pleased.

"Immense, I tell you," persisted Madame Ratignolle, surveying the sketches one by one, at close range, then holding them at arm's length, narrowing her eyes, and dropping her head on one side. "Surely, this Bavarian peasant is worthy of framing; and this basket of apples! never have I seen anything more lifelike. One might almost be tempted to reach out a hand and take one."

Edna could not control a feeling which bordered upon complacency at her friend's praise, even realizing, as she did, its true worth. She retained a few of the sketches, and gave all the rest to Madame Ratignolle, who appreciated the gift far beyond its value and proudly exhibited the pictures to her husband when he came up from the store a little later for his midday dinner.

Mr. Ratignolle was one of those men who are called the salt of the earth. His cheerfulness was unbounded, and it was matched by his goodness of heart, his broad charity, and common sense. He and his wife spoke English with an accent which was only discernible through its un-English emphasis and a certain carefulness and deliberation. Edna's husband spoke English with no accent whatever. The Ratignolles understood each other perfectly. If ever the fusion of two human beings into one has been accomplished on this sphere it was surely in their union.

As Edna seated herself at table with them she thought, "Better a dinner of herbs," though it did not take her long to discover that was no dinner of herbs, but a delicious repast, simple, choice, and in every way satisfying.

Monsieur Ratignolle was delighted to see her, though he found her looking not so well as at Grand Isle, and he advised a tonic. He talked a good deal on various topics, a little politics, some city news and neighborhood gossip. He spoke with an animation and earnestness that gave an exaggerated importance to every syllable he uttered. His wife was keenly interested in everything he said, laying down her fork the better to listen, chiming in, taking the words out of his mouth.

Edna felt depressed rather than soothed after leaving them. The little glimpse of domestic harmony which had been offered her, gave her no regret, no longing. It was not a condition of life which fitted her, and she could see in it but an appalling and hopeless ennui. She was moved by a kind of commiseration for Madame Ratignolle—a pity for that colorless existence which never uplifted its possessor beyond the region of blind contentment, in which no moment of anguish ever visited her soul, in which she would never have the taste of life's delirium. Edna vaguely wondered what she meant by "life's delirium." It had crossed her thought like some unsought, extraneous impression.

XIX

Edna could not help but think that it was very foolish, very childish, to have stamped upon her wedding ring and smashed the crystal vase upon the tiles. She was visited by no more outbursts, moving her to such futile expedients. She began to do as she liked and to feel as she liked. She completely abandoned her Tuesdays at home, and did not return the visits of those who had called upon her. She made no ineffectual efforts to conduct her household *en bonne ménagère*, going and coming as it suited her fancy, and, so far as she was able, lending herself to any passing caprice.

Mr. Pontellier had been a rather courteous husband so long as he met a certain tacit submissiveness in his wife. But her new and unexpected line of conduct completely bewildered him. It shocked him. Then her absolute disregard for her duties as a wife angered him. When Mr. Pontellier became rude, Edna grew insolent. She had resolved never to take another step backward.

"It seems to me the utmost folly for a woman at the head of a household, and the mother of children, to spend in an atelier days which would be better employed contriving for the comfort of her family."

"I feel like painting," answered Edna. "Perhaps I shan't always feel like it."

"Then in God's name paint! but don't let the family go to the devil. There's Madame Ratignolle; because she keeps up her music, she doesn't let everything else go to chaos. And she's more of a musician than you are a painter."

"She isn't a musician, and I'm not a painter. It isn't on account of painting that I let things go."

"On account of what, then?"

"Oh! I don't know. Let me alone; you bother me."

It sometimes entered Mr. Pontellier's mind to wonder if his wife were not growing a little unbalanced mentally. He could see plainly that she was not herself. That is, he could not see that she was becoming herself and daily casting aside that fictitious self which we assume like a garment with which to appear before the world.

Her husband let her alone as she requested, and went away to his office. Edna went up to her atelier—a bright room in the top of the house. She was working with great energy and interest, without accomplishing anything, however, which satisfied her even in the smallest degree. For a time she had the whole household enrolled in the service of art. The boys posed for her. They thought it amusing at first, but the occupation soon lost its attractiveness when they discovered that it was not a game arranged especially for their entertainment. The quadroon sat for hours before Edna's palette, patient as a savage, while the housemaid took charge of the children, and the drawing-room went undusted. But the housemaid, too, served her term as model when Edna perceived that the young woman's back and shoulders were molded on classic lines, and that her hair, loosened from its confining cap, became an inspiration. While Edna worked she sometimes sang low the little air, "*Ah! sit tu savais!*"

It moved her with recollections. She could hear again the ripple of the water, the flapping sail. She could see the glint of the moon upon the bay, and could feel the soft, gusty beating of the hot south wind. A subtle current of desire passed through her body, weakening her hold upon the brushes and making her eyes burn.

There were days when she was very happy without knowing why. She was happy to be alive and breathing, when her whole being seemed to be one with

the sunlight, the color, the odors, the luxuriant
warmth of some perfect Southern day. She liked
then to wander alone into strange and unfamiliar
places. She discovered many a sunny, sleepy corner,
fashioned to dream in. And she found it good to
dream and to be alone and unmolested.

There were days when she was unhappy, she did
not know why—when it did not seem worth while to
be glad or sorry, to be alive or dead, when life
appeared to her like a grotesque pandemonium
and humanity like worms struggling blindly toward
inevitable annihilation. She could not work on such
a day, nor weave fancies to stir her pulses and warm
her blood.

XX

It was during such a mood that Edna hunted up
Mademoiselle Reisz. She had not forgotten the
rather disagreeable impression left upon her by
their last interview; but she nevertheless felt a desire
to see her—above all, to listen while she played upon
the piano. Quite early in the afternoon she started
upon her quest for the pianist. Unfortunately she had
mislaid or lost Mademoiselle Reisz's card, and looking
up her address in the city directory, she found
that the woman lived on Bienville Street, some
distance away. The directory which fell into her
hands was a year or more old, however, and upon
reaching the number indicated, Edna discovered
that the house was occupied by a respectable family
of mulattoes who had *chambres garnies* to let. They
had been living there for six months, and knew
absolutely nothing of a Mademoiselle Reisz. In

fact, they knew nothing of any of their neighbors; their lodgers were all people of the highest distinction, they assured Edna. She did not linger to discuss class distinctions with Madame Pouponne, but hastened to a neighboring grocery store, feeling sure that Mademoiselle would have left her address with the proprietor.

He knew Mademoiselle Reisz a good deal better than he wanted to know her, he informed his questioner. In truth, he did not want to know her at all, or anything concerning her—the most disagreeable and unpopular woman who ever lived in Bienville Street. He thanked heaven she had left the neighborhood, and was equally thankful that he did not know where she had gone.

Edna's desire to see Mademoiselle Reisz had increased tenfold since these unlooked-for obstacles had arisen to thwart it. She was wondering who could give her the information she sought, when it suddenly occurred to her that Madame Lebrun would be the one most likely to do so. She knew it was useless to ask Madame Ratignolle, who was on the most distant terms with the musician, and preferred to know nothing concerning her. She had once been almost as emphatic in expressing herself upon the subject as the corner grocer.

Edna knew that Madame Lebrun had returned to the city, for it was the middle of November. And she also knew where the Lebruns lived, on Chartres Street.

Their home from the outside looked like a prison, with iron bars before the door and lower windows. The iron bars were a relic of the old *régime*, and no one had ever thought of dislodging them. At the side was a high fence enclosing the garden. A gate or door opening upon the street was locked. Edna rang the bell at this side garden gate, and stood upon the banquette, waiting to be admitted.

It was Victor who opened the gate for her. A black woman, wiping her hands upon her apron, was close at his heels. Before she saw them Edna could hear them in altercation, the woman—plainly an anomaly— claiming the right to be allowed to perform her duties, one of which was to answer the bell.

Victor was surprised and delighted to see Mrs. Pontellier, and he made no attempt to conceal either his astonishment or his delight. He was a dark-browed, good-looking youngster of nineteen, greatly resembling his mother, but with ten times her impetuosity. He instructed the black woman to go at once and inform Madame Lebrun that Mrs. Pontellier desired to see her. The woman grumbled a refusal to do part of her duty when she had not been permitted to do it all, and started back to her interrupted task of weeding the garden. Whereupon Victor administered a rebuke in the form of a volley of abuse, which, owing to its rapidity and incoherence, was all but incomprehensible to Edna. Whatever it was, the rebuke was convincing, for the woman dropped her hoe and went mumbling into the house.

Edna did not wish to enter. It was very pleasant there on the side porch, where there were chairs, a wicker lounge, and a small table. She seated herself, for she was tired from her long tramp; and she began to rock gently and smooth out the folds of her silk parasol. Victor drew up his chair beside her. He at once explained that the black woman's offensive conduct was all due to imperfect training, as he was not there to take her in hand. He had only come up from the island the morning before, and expected to return next day. He stayed all winter at the island; he lived there, and kept the place in order and got things ready for the summer visitors.

But a man needed occasional relaxation, he informed Mrs. Pontellier, and every now and again he drummed up a pretext to bring him to the city. My! but he had had a time of it the evening before! He wouldn't want his mother to know, and he began to talk in a whisper. He was scintillant with recollections. Of course, he couldn't think of telling Mrs. Pontellier all about it, she being a woman and not comprehending such things. But it all began with a girl peeping and smiling at him through the shutters as he passed by. Oh! but she was a beauty! Certainly he smiled back, and went up and talked to her. Mrs. Pontellier did not know him if she supposed he was one to let an opportunity like that escape him. Despite herself, the youngster amused her. She must have betrayed in her look some degree of interest or entertainment. The boy grew more daring, and Mrs. Pontellier might have found herself, in a little while, listening to a highly colored story but for the timely appearance of Madame Lebrun.

That lady was still clad in white, according to her custom of the summer. Her eyes beamed an effusive welcome. Would not Mrs. Pontellier go inside? Would she partake of some refreshment? Why had she not been there before? How was that dear Mr. Pontellier and how were those sweet children? Had Mrs. Pontellier ever known such a warm November?

Victor went and reclined on the wicker lounge behind his mother's chair, where he commanded a view of Edna's face. He had taken her parasol from her hands while he spoke to her, and he now lifted it and twirled it above him as he lay on his back. When Madame Lebrun complained that it was *so* dull coming back to the city; that she saw *so* few people now; that even Victor, when he came up from the island for a day or two, had *so* much to occupy him and engage his time; then it was that the youth went into contortions on the lounge and winked mischievously at Edna. She somehow felt like a confederate in crime, and tried to look severe and disapproving.

There had been but two letters from Robert, with little in them, they told her. Victor said it was really not worth while to go inside for the letters, when his mother entreated him to go in search of them. He remembered the contents, which in truth he rattled off very glibly when put to the test.

One letter was written from Vera Cruz and the other from the City of Mexico. He had met Montel, who was doing everything toward his advancement. So far, the financial situation was no improvement over the one he had left in New Orleans, but of course the prospects were vastly better. He wrote of the City of Mexico, the buildings, the people and their habits, the conditions of life which he found there. He sent his love to the family. He inclosed a check to his mother, and hoped she would affectionately remember him to all his friends. That was about the substance of the two letters. Edna felt that if there had been a message for her, she would have received it. The despondent frame of mind in which she had left home began again to overtake her, and she remembered that she wished to find Mademoiselle Reisz.

Madame Lebrun knew where Mademoiselle Reisz lived. She gave Edna the address, regretting that she would not consent to stay and spend the remainder of the afternoon, and pay a visit to Mademoiselle Reisz some other day. The afternoon was already well advanced.

Victor escorted her out upon the banquette, lifted her parasol, and held it over her while he walked to the car with her. He entreated her to bear in mind that the disclosures of the afternoon were strictly confidential. She laughed and bantered him a little, remembering too late that she should have been dignified and reserved.

"How handsome Mrs. Pontellier looked!" said Madame Lebrun to her son.

"Ravishing!" he admitted. "The city atmosphere has improved her. Some way she doesn't seem like the same woman."

XXI

Some people contended that the reason Mademoiselle Reisz always chose apartments up under the roof was to discourage the approach of beggars, peddlars and callers. There were plenty of windows in her little front room. They were for the most part dingy, but as they were nearly always open it did not make so much difference. They often admitted into the room a good deal of smoke and soot; but at the same time all the light and air that there was came through them. From her windows could be seen the crescent of the river, the masts of ships and the big chimneys of the Mississippi steamers. A magnificent piano crowded the apartment. In the next room she slept, and in the third and last she harbored a gasoline stove on which she cooked her meals when disinclined to descend to the neighboring restaurant. It was there also that she ate, keeping her belongings in a rare old buffet, dingy and battered from a hundred years of use.

When Edna knocked at Mademoiselle Reisz's front room door and entered, she discovered that person standing beside the window, engaged in mending or patching an old prunella gaiter. The little musician laughed all over when she saw Edna. Her laugh consisted of a contortion of the face and all the muscles of the body. She seemed strikingly homely, standing there in the afternoon light. She still wore the shabby lace and the artificial bunch of violets on the side of her head.

"So you remembered me at last," said Mademoiselle. "I had said to myself, 'Ah, bah! she will never come.'"

"Did you want me to come?" asked Edna with a smile.

"I had not thought much about it," answered Mademoiselle. The two had seated themselves on a little bumpy sofa which stood against the wall. "I am glad, however, that you came. I have the water boiling back there, and was just about to make some coffee. You will drink a cup with me. And how is *la belle dame?* Always handsome! always healthy! always contented!" She took Edna's hand between her strong wiry fingers, holding it loosely without warmth, and executing a sort of double theme upon the back and palm.

"Yes," she went on; "I sometimes thought: 'She will never come. She promised as those women in society always do, without meaning it. She will not come. For I really don't believe you like me, Mrs. Pontellier.'"

"I don't know whether I like you or not," replied Edna, gazing down at the little woman with a quizzical look.

The candor of Mrs. Pontellier's admission greatly pleased Mademoiselle Reisz. She expressed her gratification by repairing forthwith to the region of the gasoline stove and rewarding her guest with the promised cup of coffee. The coffee and the biscuit accompanying it proved very acceptable to Edna, who had declined refreshment at Madame Lebrun's and was now beginning to feel hungry. Mademoiselle set the tray which she brought in upon a small table near at hand, and seated herself once again on the lumpy sofa.

"I have had a letter from your friend," she remarked, as she poured a little cream into Edna's cup and handed it to her.

"My friend?"

"Yes, your friend Robert. He wrote to me from the City of Mexico."

"Wrote to *you?*" repeated Edna in amazement, stirring her coffee absently.

Yes, to me. Why not? Don't stir all the warmth out of your coffee; drink it. Though the letter might as well have been sent to you; it was nothing but Mrs. Pontellier from beginning to end."

"Let me see it," requested the young woman, entreatingly.

"No; a letter concerns no one but the person who writes it and the one to whom it is written."

"Haven't you just said it concerned me from beginning to end?"

"It was written about you, not to you. 'Have you seen Mrs. Pontellier? How is she looking?' he asks. 'As Mrs. Pontellier says,' or 'as Mrs. Pontellier once said.' 'If Mrs. Pontellier should call upon you, play for her that Impromptu of Chopin's, my favorite. I heard it here a day or two ago, but not as you play it. I should like to know how it affects her,' and so on, as if he supposed we were constantly in each other's society."

"Let me see the letter."

"Oh, no."

"Have you answered it?"

"No."

"Let me see the letter."

"No, and again, no."

"Then play the Impromptu for me."

"It is growing late; what time do you have to be home?"

"Time doesn't concern me. Your question seems a little rude. Play the Impromptu."

"But you have told me nothing of yourself. What are you doing?"

"Painting!" laughed Edna. "I am becoming an artist. Think of it!"

"Ah! an artist! You have pretensions, Madame."

"Why pretensions? Do you think I could not become an artist?"

"I do not know you well enough to say. I do not know your talent or your temperament. To be an artist includes much; one must possess many gifts —absolute gifts—which have not been acquired by one's own effort. And, moreover, to succeed, the artist must possess the courageous soul."

"What do you mean by the courageous soul?"

"Courageous, *ma foi!* The brave soul. The soul that dares and defies."

"Show me the letter and play for me the Impromptu. You see that I have persistence. Does that quality count for anything in art?"

"It counts with a foolish old woman whom you have captivated," replied Mademoiselle, with her wriggling laugh.

The letter was right there at hand in the drawer of the little table upon which Edna had just placed her coffee cup. Mademoiselle opened the drawer and drew forth the letter, the topmost one. She placed it in Edna's hands, and without further comment arose and went to the piano.

Mademoiselle played a soft interlude. It was an improvisation. She sat low at the instrument, and the lines of her body settled into ungraceful curves and angles that gave it an appearance of deformity. Gradually and imperceptibly the interlude melted into the soft opening minor chords of the Chopin Impromptu.

Edna did not know when the Impromptu began or ended. She sat in the sofa corner reading Robert's letter by the fading light. Mademoiselle had glided from the Chopin into the quivering love-notes of Isolde's song, and back again to the Impromptu with its soulful and poignant longing.

The shadows deepened in the little room. The music grew strange and fantastic—turbulent, insistent, plaintive and soft with entreaty. The shadows grew deeper. The music filled the room. It floated out upon the night, over the housetops, the crescent of the river, losing itself in the silence of the upper air.

Edna was sobbing, just as she had wept one midnight at Grand Isle when strange, new voices awoke in her. She arose in some agitation to take her departure. "May I come again, Mademoiselle?" she asked at the threshold.

"Come whenever you feel like it. Be careful; the stairs and landings are dark; don't stumble."

Mademoiselle reentered and lit a candle. Robert's letter was on the floor. She stooped and picked it up. It was crumpled and damp with tears. Mademoiselle smoothed the letter out, restored it to the envelope, and replaced it in the table drawer.

XXII

One morning on his way into town Mr. Pontellier stopped at the house of his old friend and family physician, Doctor Mandelet. The Doctor was a semi-retired physician, resting, as the saying is, upon his laurels. He bore a reputation for wisdom rather than skill—leaving the active practice of medicine to his assistants and younger contemporaries—and was much sought for in matters of consultation. A few families, united to him by bonds of friendship, he still attended when they required the services of a physician. The Pontelliers were among these.

Mr. Pontellier found the Doctor reading at the open window of his study. His house stood rather far back from the street, in the center of a delightful garden, so that it was quiet and peaceful at the old gentleman's study window. He was a great reader. He stared up disapprovingly over his eyeglasses as Mr. Pontellier entered, wondering who had the temerity to disturb him at that hour of the morning.

"Ah, Pontellier! Not sick, I hope. Come and have a seat. What news do you bring this morning?" He was quite portly, with a profusion of gray hair, and small blue eyes which age had robbed of much of their brightness but none of their penetration.

"Oh! I'm never sick, Doctor. You know that I come of tough fiber—of that old Creole race of Pontelliers that dry up and finally blow away. I came to consult—no, not precisely to consult—to talk to you about Edna. I don't know what ails her."

"Madame Pontellier not well?" marveled the Doctor. "Why, I saw her—I think it was a week ago—walking along Canal Street, the picture of health, it seemed to me."

"Yes, yes; she seems quite well," said Mr. Pontellier, leaning forward and whirling his stick between his two hands; "but she doesn't act well. She's odd, she's not like herself. I can't make her out, and I thought perhaps you'd help me."

"How does she act?" inquired the doctor.

"Well, it isn't easy to explain," said Mr. Pontellier, throwing himself back in his chair. "She lets the housekeeping go to the dickens."

"Well, well; women are not all alike, my dear Pontellier. We've got to consider—"

"I know that; I told you I couldn't explain. Her whole attitude—toward me and everybody and everything—has changed. You know I have a quick temper, but I don't want to quarrel or be rude to a woman, especially my wife; yet I'm driven to it, and feel like ten thousand devils after I've made a fool of myself. She's making it devilishly uncomfortable for me," he went on nervously. "She's got some sort of notion in her head concerning the eternal rights of women; and—you understand—we meet in the morning at the breakfast table."

The old gentleman lifted his shaggy eyebrows,

protruded his thick nether lip, and tapped the arms of his chair with his cushioned fingertips.

"What have you been doing to her, Pontellier?"

"Doing! *Parbleu!*"

"Has she," asked the Doctor, with a smile, "has she been associating of late with a circle of pseudo-intellectual women—superspiritual superior beings? My wife has been telling me about them."

"That's the trouble," broke in Mr. Pontellier, "she hasn't been associating with any one. She has abandoned her Tuesdays at home, has thrown over all her acquaintances, and goes tramping about by herself, moping in the street cars, getting in after dark. I tell you she's peculiar. I don't like it; I feel a little worried over it."

This was a new aspect for the Doctor. "Nothing hereditary?" he asked, seriously. "Nothing peculiar about her family antecedents, is there?"

"Oh, no, indeed! She comes of sound old Presbyterian Kentucky stock. The old gentleman, her father, I have heard, used to atone for his weekday sins with his Sunday devotions. I know for a fact, that his race horses literally ran away with the prettiest bit of Kentucky farming land I ever laid eyes upon. Margaret—you know Margaret—she has all the Presbyterianism undiluted. And the youngest is something of a vixen. By the way, she gets married in a couple of weeks from now."

"Send your wife up to the wedding," exclaimed the Doctor, foreseeing a happy solution. "Let her stay among her own people for a while; it will do her good."

"That's what I want her to do. She won't go to the marriage. She says a wedding is one of the most lamentable spectacles on earth. Nice thing for a woman to say to her husband!" exclaimed Mr. Pontellier, fuming anew at the recollection.

"Pontellier," said the Doctor, after a moment's reflection, "let your wife alone for a while. Don't bother her, and don't let her bother you. Woman, my dear friend, is a very peculiar and delicate organism—a sensitive and highly organized woman, such as I know Mrs. Pontellier to be, is especially peculiar. It would require an inspired psychologist to deal successfully with them. And when ordinary fellows like you and me attempt to cope with their idiosyncrasies the result is bungling. Most women are moody and whimsical. This is some passing whim of your wife, due to some cause or causes which you and I needn't try to fathom. But it will pass happily over, especially if you let her alone. Send her around to see me."

"Oh! I couldn't do that; there'd be no reason for it," objected Mr. Pontellier.

"Then I'll go around and see her," said the Doctor. "I'll drop in to dinner some evening *en bon ami*."

"Do! by all means," urged Mr. Pontellier. "What evening will you come? Say Thursday. Will you come Thursday?" he asked, rising to take his leave.

"Very well; Thursday. My wife may possibly have some engagement for me Thursday. In case she has, I shall let you know. Otherwise, you may expect me."

Mr. Pontellier turned before leaving to say:

"I am going to New York on business very soon. I have a big scheme on hand, and want to be on the field proper to pull the ropes and handle the ribbons. We'll let you in on the inside if you say so, Doctor," he laughed.

"No, I thank you, my dear sir," returned the Doctor. "'I leave such ventures to you younger men with the fever of life still in your blood."

"What I wanted to say," continued Mr. Pontellier, with his hands on the knob; "I may have to be absent a good while. Would you advise me to take Edna along?"

"By all means, if she wishes to go. If not, leave her here. Don't contradict her. The mood will pass, I assure you. It may take a month, two, three —possibly longer, but it will pass; have patience."

"Well, good-by, *à jeudi,*" said Mr. Pontellier, as he let himself out.

The Doctor would have liked during the course of conversation to ask, "Is there any man in the case?" but he knew his Creole too well to make such a blunder as that.

He did not resume his book immediately, but sat for a while meditatively looking out into the garden.

XXIII

Edna's father was in the city, and had been with them several days. She was not very warmly or deeply attached to him, but they had certain tastes in common, and when together they were companionable. His coming was in the nature of a welcome disturbance; it seemed to furnish a new direction for her emotions.

He had come to purchase a wedding gift for his daughter, Janet, and an outfit for himself in which he might make a creditable appearance at her marriage. Mr. Pontellier had selected the bridal gift, as every one immediately connected with him always deferred to his taste in such matters. And his suggestions on the question of dress—which too often assumes the nature of a problem—were of inestimable value to his father-in-law. But for the past few days the old gentleman had been upon Edna's hands, and in his society she was becoming acquainted with a new set of sensations. He had been a colonel in the Confederate army, and still maintained, with the title, the military bearing which had always accompanied it. His hair and mustache were white and silky, emphasizing the rugged bronze of his face. He was tall and thin, and wore his coats padded, which gave a fictitious breadth and depth to his shoulders and chest. Edna and her father looked very distinguished together, and excited a good deal of notice during their perambulations. Upon his arrival she began by introducing him to her atelier and making a sketch of him. He took the whole matter very seriously. If her talent had been tenfold greater than it was, it would not have surprised him, convinced as he was that he had bequeathed to all of his daughters the germs of a masterful capability, which only depended upon their own efforts to be directed toward successful achievement.

Before her pencil he sat rigid and unflinching, as he had faced the cannon's mouth in days gone by. He resented the intrusion of the children, who gaped with wondering eyes at him, sitting so stiff up there in their mother's bright atelier. When they drew near he motioned them away with an expressive action of the foot, loath to disturb the fixed lines of his countenance, his arms, or his rigid shoulders.

Edna, anxious to entertain him, invited Mademoiselle Reisz to meet him, having promised him a treat in her piano playing; but Mademoiselle declined the invitation. So together they attended a *soirée musicale* at the Ratignolle's. Monsieur and Madame Ratignolle made much of the Colonel, installing him as the guest of honor and engaging him at once to dine with them the following Sunday, or any day which he might select. Madame coquetted with him in the most captivating and naïve manner, with eyes, gestures, and a profusion of compliments, till the Colonel's old head felt thirty years younger on his padded shoulders. Edna marveled, not comprehending. She herself was almost devoid of coquetry.

There were one or two men whom she observed at the *soirée musicale*; but she would never have felt moved to any kittenish display to attract their notice—to any feline or feminine wiles to express herself toward them. Their personality attracted her in an agreeable way. Her fancy selected them, and she was glad when a lull in the music gave them an opportunity to meet her and talk with her. Often on the street the glance of strange eyes had lingered in her memory, and sometimes had disturbed her.

Mr. Pontellier did not attend these *soirées musicales*. He considered them *bourgeois*, and found more diversion at the club. To Madame Ratignolle he said the music dispensed at her *soirées* was too "heavy," too far beyond his untrained comprehension. His excuse flattered her. But she disapproved of Mr. Pontellier's club, and she was frank enough to tell Edna so.

"It's a pity Mr. Pontellier doesn't stay home more in the evenings. I think you would be more—well, if you don't mind me saying it—more united, if he did."

"Oh! dear no!" said Edna, with a blank look in her eyes. "What should I do if he stayed home? We wouldn't have anything to say to each other."

She had not much of anything to say to her father, for that matter; but he did not antagonize her. She discovered that he interested her, though she realized that he might not interest her long; and for the first time in her life she felt as if she were thoroughly acquainted with him. He kept her busy serving him and ministering to his wants. It amused her to do so. She would not permit a servant or one of the children to do anything for him which she might do herself. Her husband noticed, and thought it was the expression of a deep filial attachment which he had never suspected.

The Colonel drank numerous "toddies" during the course of the day, which left him, however, imperturbed. He was an expert at concocting strong drinks. He had even invented some, to which he had given fantastic names, and for whose manufacture he required diverse ingredients that it devolved upon Edna to procure for him.

When Doctor Mandelet dined with the Pontelliers on Thursday he could discern in Mrs. Pontellier no trace of that morbid condition which her husband had reported to him. She was excited and in a manner radiant. She and her father had been to the race course, and their thoughts when they seated themselves at table were still occupied with the events of the afternoon, and their talk was still of the track. The Doctor had not kept pace with turf affairs. He had certain recollections of racing in what he called "the good old times" when the Lecompte stables flourished, and he drew upon this fund of memories so that he might not be left out and seem wholly devoid of the modern spirit. But he failed to impose upon the Colonel, and was even far from impressing him with this trumped-up knowledge of bygone days. Edna had staked her father on his last venture, with the most gratifying results to both of them. Besides, they had met some very charming people, according to the Colonel's impressions. Mrs. Mortimer Merriman and Mrs. James Highcamp, who were there with Alcée Arobin, had joined them and had enlivened the hours in a fashion that warmed him to think of.

Mr. Pontellier himself had no particular leaning toward horse racing, and was even rather inclined to discourage it as a pastime, especially when he considered the fate of that bluegrass farm in Kentucky. He endeavored, in a general way, to express a particular disapproval, and only succeeded in arousing the ire and opposition of his father-in-law. A pretty dispute followed, in which Edna warmly espoused her father's cause and the Doctor remained neutral.

He observed his hostess attentively from under his shaggy brows, and noted a subtle change which had transformed her from the listless woman he had known into a being who, for the moment, seemed palpitant with the forces of life. Her speech was warm and energetic. There was no repression in her glance or gesture. She reminded him of some beautiful, sleek animal waking up in the sun.

The dinner was excellent. The claret was warm and the champagne was cold, and under their beneficent influence the threatened unpleasantness melted and vanished with the fumes of the wine.

Mr. Pontellier warmed up and grew reminiscent. He

told some amusing plantation experiences, recollections of old Iberville and his youth, when he hunted
'possum in company with some friendly darky;
thrashed the pecan trees, shot the grosbec, and
roamed the woods and fields in mischievous idleness.

The Colonel, with little sense of humor and of the
fitness of things, related a somber episode of those
dark and bitter days, in which he had acted a con-
spicuous part and always formed a central figure.
Nor was the doctor happier in his selection, when
he told the old, ever new and curious story of the
waning of a woman's love, seeking strange, new
channels, only to return to its legitimate source
after days of fierce unrest. It was one of the many
little human documents which had been unfolded
to him during his long career as a physician. The
story did not seem especially to impress Edna. She
had one of her own to tell, of a woman who paddled
away with her lover one night in a pirogue and never
came back. They were lost amid the Baratarian
Islands, and no one ever heard of them or found
trace of them from that day to this. It was a pure
invention. She said that Madame Antoine had related
it to her. That, also, was an invention. Perhaps it
was a dream she had had. But every glowing word
seemed real to those who listened. They could feel
the hot breath of the Southern night; they could
hear the long sweep of the pirogue through the
glistening moonlit water, the beating of birds' wings,
rising startled from among the reeds in the salt-water
pools; they could see the faces of the lovers, pale,
close together, rapt in oblivious forgetfulness, drift-
ing into the unknown.

The champagne was cold, and its subtle fumes

played fantastic tricks with Edna's memory that night.

Outside, away from the glow of the fire and the soft lamplight, the night was chill and murky. The doctor doubled his old-fashioned cloak across his breast as he strode home through the darkness. He knew his fellow creatures better than most men, knew that inner life which so seldom unfolds itself to unanointed eyes. He was sorry he had accepted Pontellier's invitation. He was growing old, and beginning to need rest and an imperturbed spirit. He did not want the secrets of other lives thrust upon him.

"I hope it isn't Arobin," he muttered to himself as he walked. "I hope to heaven it isn't Alcée Arobin."

XXIV

Edna and her father had a warm, and almost violent dispute upon the subject of her refusal to attend her sister's wedding. Mr. Pontellier declined to interfere, to interpose either his influence or his authority. He was following Doctor Mandelet's advice, and letting her do as she liked. The Colonel reproached his daughter for her lack of filial kindness and respect, her want of sisterly affection and womanly consideration. His arguments were labored and unconvincing. He doubted if Janet would accept any excuse—forgetting that Edna had offered none. He doubted if Janet would ever speak to her again, and he was sure Margaret would not.

Edna was glad to be rid of her father when he finally took himself off with his wedding garments and his bridal gifts, with his padded shoulders, his

Bible reading, his "toddies" and ponderous oaths.

Mr. Pontellier followed him closely. He meant to stop at the wedding on his way to New York and endeavor by every means which money and love could devise to atone somewhat for Edna's incomprehensible action.

"You are too lenient, too lenient by far, Léonce," asserted the Colonel. "Authority, coercion are what is needed. Put your foot down good and hard; the only way to manage a wife. Take my word for it."

The Colonel was perhaps unaware that he had coerced his own wife into her grave. Mr. Pontellier had a vague suspicion of it which he thought it needless to mention at that late day.

Edna was not so consciously gratified at her husband's leaving home as she had been over the departure of her father. As the day approached when he was to leave her for a comparatively long stay, she grew melting and affectionate, remembering his many acts of consideration and his repeated expressions of an ardent attachment. She was solicitous about his health and his welfare. She bustled around, looking after his clothing, thinking about heavy underwear, quite as Madame Ratignolle would have done under similar circumstances. She cried when he went away, calling him her dear, good friend, and she was quite certain she would grow lonely before very long and go to join him in New York.

But after all, a radiant peace settled upon her when she at last found herself alone. Even the children were gone. Old Madame Pontellier had come herself and carried them off to Iberville with their quadroon. The old madame did not venture to say she was afraid they would be neglected during Léonce's absence; she hardly ventured to think so. She was hungry for them —even a little fierce in her attachment. She did not want them to be wholly "children of the pavement," she always said when begging to have them for a space. She wished them to know the country, with its streams, its fields, its woods, its freedom, so delicious to the young. She wished them to taste something of the life their father had lived and known and loved when he, too, was a little child.

When Edna was at last alone, she breathed a big, genuine sigh of relief. A feeling that was unfamiliar but very delicious came over her. She walked all through the house, from one room to another, as if inspecting it for the first time. She tried the various chairs and lounges, as if she had never sat and reclined upon them before. And she perambulated around the outside of the house, investigating, looking to see if windows and shutters were secure and in order. The flowers were like new acquaintances; she approached them in a familiar spirit, and made herself at home among them. The garden walks were damp, and Edna called to the maid to bring out her rubber sandals. And there she stayed, and stooped, digging around the plants, trimming, picking dead, dry leaves. The children's little dog came out, interfering, getting in her way. She scolded him, laughed at him, played with him. The garden smelled so good and looked so pretty in the afternoon sunlight. Edna plucked all the bright flowers she could find, and went into the house with them, she and the little dog.

Even the kitchen assumed a sudden interesting character which she had never before perceived. She went in to give directions to the cook, to say that the butcher would have to bring much less meat, that they would require only half their usual quantity of bread, of milk and groceries. She told the cook that she herself would be greatly occupied during Mr. Pontellier's absence, and she begged her to take all thought and responsibility of the larder upon her own shoulders.

That night Edna dined alone. The candelabra, with a few candles in the center of the table, gave all the light she needed. Outside the circle of light in which she sat, the large dining-room looked solemn and shadowy. The cook, placed upon her mettle, served a delicious repast—a luscious tenderloin broiled à point. The wine tasted good; the marron glacé seemed to be just what she wanted. It was so pleasant, too, to dine in a comfortable peignoir.

She thought a little sentimentally about Léonce and the children, and wondered what they were doing. As she gave a dainty scrap or two to the doggie, she talked intimately to him about Etienne and Raoul. He was beside himself with astonishment and delight over these companionable advances, and showed his appreciation by his little quick, snappy barks and a lively agitation.

Then Edna sat in the library after dinner and read Emerson until she grew sleepy. She realized that she had neglected her reading, and determined to start anew upon a course of improving studies, now that her time was completely her own to do with as she liked.

After a refreshing bath, Edna went to bed. And as she snuggled comfortably beneath the eiderdown a sense of restfulness invaded her, such as she had not known before.

XXV

When the weather was dark and cloudy Edna could not work. She needed the sun to mellow and temper her mood to the sticking point. She had reached a stage when she seemed to be no longer feeling her way, working, when in the humor, with sureness and ease. And being devoid of ambition, and striving not toward accomplishment, she drew satisfaction from the work in itself.

On rainy or melancholy days Edna went out and sought the society of the friends she had made at Grand Isle. Or else she stayed indoors and nursed a mood with which she was becoming too familiar for her own comfort and peace of mind. It was not despair, but it seemed to her as if life were passing by, leaving its promise broken and unfulfilled. Yet there were other days when she listened, was led on and deceived by fresh promises which her youth held out to her.

She went again to the races, and again. Alcée Arobin and Mrs. Highcamp called for her one bright afternoon in Arobin's drag. Mrs. Highcamp was a worldly but unaffected, intelligent, slim, tall blonde woman in the forties, with an indifferent manner and blue eyes that stared. She had a daughter who served her as a pretext for cultivating the society of young men of fashion. Alcée Arobin was one of them. He was a familiar figure at the race course, the opera, the fashionable clubs. There was a perpetual smile in his eyes, which seldom failed to awaken a corresponding cheerfulness in any one who looked into them and listened to his good-humored voice. His manner was quiet, and at times a little insolent. He possessed a good figure, a pleasing face, not overburdened with depth of thought or feeling; and his dress was that of the conventional man of fashion.

He admired Edna extravagantly, after meeting her at the races with her father. He had met her before on other occasions, but she had seemed to him unapproachable until that day. It was at his instigation that Mrs. Highcamp called to ask her to go with them to the Jockey Club to witness the turf event of the season.

There were possibly a few track men out there who knew the race horse as well as Edna, but there was certainly none who knew it better. She sat between her two companions as one having authority to speak. She laughed at Arobin's pretensions, and deplored Mrs. Highcamp's ignorance. The race horse was a friend and intimate associate of her childhood. The atmosphere of the stables and the breath of the blue grass paddock revived in her memory and lingered in her nostrils. She did not perceive that she was talking like her father as the sleek geldings ambled in review before them. She played for very high stakes, and fortune favored her. The fever of the game flamed in her cheeks and eyes, and it got into her blood and into her brain like an intoxicant. People turned their heads to look at her, and more than one lent an attentive ear to her utterances, hoping thereby to secure the elusive but ever-desired "tip." Arobin caught the contagion of excitement which drew him to Edna like a magnet. Mrs. Highcamp remained, as usual, unmoved, with her indifferent stare and uplifted eyebrows.

Edna stayed and dined with Mrs. Highcamp upon being urged to do so. Arobin also remained and sent away his drag.

The dinner was quiet and uninteresting, save for the cheerful efforts of Arobin to enliven things. Mrs. Highcamp deplored the absence of her daughter from the races, and tried to convey to her what she had missed by going to the "Dante reading" instead of joining them. The girl held a geranium leaf up to her nose and said nothing, but looked knowing and noncommittal. Mr. Highcamp was a plain, bald-headed man, who only talked under compulsion. He was unresponsive. Mrs. Highcamp was full of delicate courtesy and consideration toward her husband. She addressed most of her conversation to him at table. They sat in the library after dinner and read the evening papers together under the drop-light, while the younger people went into the drawing-room near by and talked. Miss Highcamp played some selections from Grieg upon the piano. She seemed to have apprehended all of the composer's coldness and none of his poetry. While Edna listened she could not help wondering if she had lost her taste for music.

When the time came for her to go home, Mr. Highcamp grunted a lame offer to escort her, looking down at his slippered feet with tactless concern. It was Arobin who took her home. The car ride was long, and it was late when they reached Esplanade Street. Arobin asked permission to enter for a second to light his cigarette—his match safe was empty. He filled his match safe, but did not light his cigarette until he left her, after she had expressed her willingness to go to the races with him again.

Edna was neither tired nor sleepy. She was hungry again, for the Highcamp dinner, though of excellent quality, had lacked abundance. She rummaged in the larder and brought forth a slice of "Gruyère" and some crackers. She opened a bottle of beer which she found in the icebox. Edna felt extremely restless and excited. She vacantly hummed a fantastic tune as she poked at the wood embers on the hearth and munched a cracker.

She wanted something to happen—something, anything; she did not know what. She regretted that she had not made Arobin stay a half hour to talk over the horses with her. She counted the money she had won. But there was nothing else to do, so she went to bed, and tossed there for hours in a sort of monotonous agitation.

In the middle of the night she remembered that she had forgotten to write her regular letter to her husband; and she decided to do so next day and tell him about her afternoon at the Jockey Club. She lay wide awake composing a letter which was nothing like the one which she wrote next day. When the maid awoke her in the morning Edna was dreaming of Mr. Highcamp playing the piano at the entrance of a music store on Canal Street, while his wife was saying to Alcée Arobin, as they boarded an Esplanade Street car:

"What a pity that so much talent has been neglected! but I must go."

When, a few days later, Alcée Arobin again called for Edna in his drag, Mrs. Highcamp was not with him. He said they would pick her up. But as that lady had not been apprised of his intention of picking her up, she was not at home. The daughter was just leaving the house to attend the meeting of a branch Folk Lore Society, and regretted that she could not accompany them. Arobin appeared nonplused, and asked Edna if there were any one else she cared to ask.

She did not deem it worth while to go in search of any of the fashionable acquaintances from whom she had withdrawn herself. She thought of Madame Ratignolle, but knew that her fair friend did not leave the house, except to take a languid walk around the block with her husband after nightfall. Mademoiselle Reisz would have laughed at such a request from Edna. Madame Lebrun might have enjoyed the outing, but for some reason Edna did not want her. So they went alone, she and Arobin.

The afternoon was intensely interesting to her. The excitement came back upon her like a remittent fever. Her talk grew familiar and confidential. It was no labor to become intimate with Arobin. His manner invited easy confidence. The preliminary stage of becoming acquainted was one which he always endeavored to ignore when a pretty and engaging woman was concerned.

He stayed and dined with Edna. He stayed and sat beside the wood fire. They laughed and talked; and before it was time to go he was telling her how different life might have been if he had known her years before. With ingenuous frankness he spoke of what a wicked, ill-disciplined boy he had been, and impulsively drew up his cuff to exhibit upon his wrist the scar from a saber cut which he had received in a duel outside of Paris when he was nineteen. She touched his hand as she scanned the red cicatrice on the inside of his white wrist. A quick impulse that was somewhat spasmodic impelled her fingers to close in a sort of clutch upon his hand. He felt the pressure of her pointed nails in the flesh of his palm.

She arose hastily and walked toward the mantel. "The sight of a wound or scar always agitates and sickens me," she said. "I shouldn't have looked at it."

"I beg your pardon," he entreated, following her; "it never occurred to me that it might be repulsive."

He stood close to her, and the effrontery in his eyes repelled the old, vanishing self in her, yet drew all her awakening sensuousness. He saw enough in her face to impel him to take her hand and hold it while he said his lingering good night.

"Will you go to the races again?" he asked.

"No," she said. "I've had enough of the races. I don't want to lose all the money I've won, and I've got to work when the weather is bright, instead of—"

"Yes; work; to be sure. You promised to show me your work. What morning may I come up to your atelier? Tomorrow?"

"No!"

"Day after?"

"No, no."

"Oh, please don't refuse me! I know something of such things. I might help you with a stray suggestion or two."

"No. Good night. Why don't you go after you have said good night? I don't like you," she went on in a high, excited pitch, attempting to draw away her hand. She felt that her words lacked dignity and sincerity, and she knew that he felt it.

"I'm sorry you don't like me. I'm sorry I offended you. How have I offended you? What have I done? Can't you forgive me?" And he bent and pressed his lips upon her hand as if he wished never more to withdraw them.

"Mr. Arobin," she complained, "I'm greatly upset by the excitement of the afternoon; I'm not myself. My manner must have misled you in some way. I wish you to go, please." She spoke in a monotonous, dull tone. He took his hat from the table, and stood with eyes turned from her, looking into the dying fire. For a moment or two he kept an impressive silence.

"Your manner has not misled me, Mrs. Pontellier," he said finally. "My own emotions have done that. I couldn't help it. When I'm near you, how could I help it? Don't think anything of it, don't bother, please. You see, I go when you command me. If you wish me to stay away, I shall do so. If you let me come back, I—oh! you will let me come back?"

He cast one appealing glance at her, to which she made no response. Alcée Arobin's manner was so genuine that it often deceived even himself.

Edna did not care or think whether it were genuine or not. When she was alone she looked mechanically at the back of her hand which he had kissed so warmly. Then she leaned her head down on the mantelpiece. She felt somewhat like a woman who in a moment of passion is betrayed into an act of infidelity, and realizes the significance of the act without being wholly awakened from its glamour. The thought was passing vaguely through her mind, "What would he think?"

She did not mean her husband; she was thinking of Robert Lebrun. Her husband seemed to her now like a person whom she had married without love as an excuse.

She lit a candle and went up to her room. Alcée Arobin was absolutely nothing to her. Yet his presence, his manners, the warmth of his glances, and above all the touch of his lips upon her hand had acted like a narcotic upon her.

She slept a languorous sleep, interwoven with vanishing dreams.

XXVI

Alcée Arobin wrote Edna an elaborate note of apology, palpitant with sincerity. It embarrassed her, for in a cooler, quieter moment it appeared to her absurd that she should have taken his action so seriously, so dramatically. She felt sure that the significance of the whole occurrence had lain in her own self-consciousness. If she ignored his note it would give undue importance to a trivial affair. If she replied to it in a serious spirit it would still leave in his mind the impression that she had in a susceptible moment yielded to his influence. After all, it was no great matter to have one's hand kissed. She was provoked at his having written the apology. She answered in as light and bantering a spirit as she fancied it deserved, and said she would be glad to have him look in upon her at work whenever he felt the inclination and his business gave him the opportunity.

He responded at once by presenting himself at her home with all his disarming naïveté. And then there was scarcely a day which followed that she did not see him or was not reminded of him. He was prolific in pretexts. His attitude became one of good-humored subservience and tacit adoration. He was ready at all times to submit to her moods, which were as often kind as they were cold. She grew accustomed to him. They became intimate and friendly by imperceptible degrees, and then by leaps. He sometimes talked in a way that astonished her at first and brought the crimson into her face; in a way that pleased her at last, appealing to the animalism that stirred impatiently within her.

There was nothing which so quieted the turmoil of Edna's senses as a visit to Mademoiselle Reisz. It was then, in the presence of that personality which was offensive to her, that the woman, by her divine art, seemed to reach Edna's spirit and set it free.

It was misty, with heavy, lowering atmosphere, one afternoon, when Edna climbed the stairs to the pianist's apartments under the roof. Her clothes were dripping with moisture. She felt chilled and pinched as she entered the room. Mademoiselle was poking at a rusty stove that smoked a little and warmed the room indifferently. She was endeavoring to heat a pot of chocolate on the stove. The room looked cheerless and dingy to Edna as she entered. A bust of Beethoven, covered with a hood of dust, scowled at her from the mantelpiece.

"Ah! here comes the sunlight!" exclaimed Mademoiselle, rising from her knees before the stove. "Now it will be warm and bright enough; I can let the fire alone."

She closed the stove door with a bang, and approaching, assisted in removing Edna's dripping mackintosh.

"You are cold; you look miserable. The chocolate will soon be hot. But would you rather have a taste of brandy? I have scarcely touched the bottle which you brought me for my cold." A piece of red flannel was wrapped around Mademoiselle's throat; a stiff neck compelled her to hold her head on one side.

"I will take some brandy," said Edna, shivering as she removed her gloves and overshoes. She drank the liquor from the glass as a man would have done. Then flinging herself upon the uncomfortable sofa she said, "Mademoiselle, I am going to move away from my house on Esplanade Street."

"Ah!" ejaculated the musician, neither surprised nor especially interested. Nothing ever seemed to astonish her very much. She was endeavoring to adjust the bunch of violets which had become loose from its fastening in her hair. Edna drew her down upon the sofa, and taking a pin from her own hair, secured the shabby artificial flowers in their accustomed place.

"Aren't you astonished?"

"Passably. Where are you going? to New York? to Iberville? to your father in Mississippi? where?"

"Just two steps away," laughed Edna, "in a little four-room house around the corner. It looks so cozy, so inviting and restful, whenever I pass by; and it's for rent. I'm tired looking after that big house. It never seemed like mine, anyway—like home. It's too much trouble. I have to keep too many servants. I am tired bothering with them."

"That is not your true reason, *ma belle*. There is no use in telling me lies. I don't know your reason, but you have not told me the truth." Edna did not protest or endeavor to justify herself.

"The house, the money that provides for it, are not mine. Isn't that enough reason?"

"They are your husband's," returned Mademoiselle, with a shrug and a malicious elevation of the eyebrows.

"Oh! I see there is no deceiving you. Then let me tell you: It is a caprice. I have a little money of my own from my mother's estate, which my father sends me by driblets. I won a large sum this winter on the races, and I am beginning to sell my sketches. Laidpore is more and more pleased with my work; he says it grows in force and individuality. I cannot judge of that myself, but I feel that I have gained in ease and confidence. However, as I said, I have sold a good many through Laidpore. I can live in the tiny house for little or nothing, with one servant. Old Celestine, who works occasionally for me, says she will come stay with me and do my work. I know I shall like it, like the feeling of freedom and independence."

"What does your husband say?"

"I have not told him yet. I only thought of it this morning. He will think I am demented, no doubt. Perhaps you think so."

Mademoiselle shook her head slowly. "Your reason is not yet clear to me," she said.

Neither was it quite clear to Edna herself; but it unfolded itself as she sat for a while in silence. Instinct had prompted her to put away her husband's bounty in casting off her allegiance. She did not know how it would be when he returned. There would have to be an understanding, an explanation. Conditions would some way adjust themselves, she felt; but whatever came, she had resolved never again to belong to another than herself.

"I shall give a grand dinner before I leave the old house!" Edna exclaimed. "You will have to come to it, Mademoiselle. I will give you everything that you like to eat and to drink. We shall sing and laugh and be merry for once." And she uttered a sigh that came from the very depths of her being.

If Mademoiselle happened to have received a letter from Robert during the interval of Edna's visits, she would give her the letter unsolicited. And she would seat herself at the piano and play as her humor prompted her while the young woman read the letter.

The little stove was roaring; it was red-hot, and the chocolate in the tin sizzled and sputtered. Edna went forward and opened the stove door, and Mademoiselle rising, took a letter from under the bust of Beethoven and handed it to Edna.

"Another! so soon!" she exclaimed, her eyes filled with delight. "Tell me, Mademoiselle, does he know that I see his letters?"

"Never in the world! He would be angry and would never write to me again if he thought so. Does he write to you? Never a line. Does he send you a message? Never a word. It is because he loves you, poor fool, and is trying to forget you, since you are not free to listen to him or to belong to him."

"Why do you show me his letters, then?"

"Haven't you begged for them? Can I refuse you anything? Oh! you cannot deceive me," and Mademoiselle approached her beloved instrument and began to play. Edna did not at once read the letter. She sat holding it in her hand, while the music penetrated her whole being like an effulgence, warming and brightening the dark places of her soul. It prepared her for joy and exultation.

"Oh!" she exclaimed, letting the letter fall to the floor. "Why did you not tell me?" She went and grasped Mademoiselle's hands up from the keys. "Oh! unkind! malicious! Why did you not tell me?"

"That he was coming back? No great news, *ma foi*. I wonder he did not come long ago."

"But when, when?" cried Edna, impatiently. "He does not say when."

"He says 'very soon.' You know as much about it as I do; it is all in the letter."

"But why? Why is he coming? Oh, if I thought—" and she snatched the letter from the floor and turned the pages this way and that way, looking for the reason, which was left untold.

"If I were young and in love with a man," said Mademoiselle, turning on the stool and pressing her wiry hands between her knees as she looked down at Edna, who sat on the floor holding the letter, "it seems to me he would have to be some *grand esprit*, a man with lofty aims and ability to reach them; one who stood high enough to attract the notice of his fellow-men. It seems to me if I were young and in love I should never deem a man of ordinary caliber worthy of my devotion."

"Now it is you who are telling lies and seeking to deceive me, Mademoiselle; or else you have never been in love, and know nothing about it. Why," went on Edna, clasping her knees and looking up into Mademoiselle's twisted face, "do you suppose a woman knows why she loves? Does she select? Does she say to herself: 'Go to! Here is a distinguished statesman with presidential possibilities; I shall proceed to fall in love with him.' Or, 'I shall set my heart upon this musician, whose fame is on every tongue?' Or, 'This financier, who controls the world's money markets?'"

"You are purposely misunderstanding me, *ma reine*. Are you in love with Robert?"

"Yes," said Edna. It was the first time she had admitted it, and a glow overspread her face, blotching it with red spots.

"Why?" asked her companion. "Why do you love him when you ought not to?"

Edna, with a motion or two, dragged herself on her knees before Mademoiselle Reisz, who took the glowing face between her two hands.

"Why? Because his hair is brown and grows away from his temples; because he opens and shuts his eyes, and his nose is a little out of drawing, because he has two lips and a square chin, and a little finger which he can't straighten from having played baseball too energetically in his youth. Because—"

"Because you do, in short," laughed Mademoiselle. "What will you do when he comes back?" she asked.

"Do? Nothing, except feel glad and happy to be alive."

She was already glad and happy to be alive at the mere thought of his return. The murky, lowering sky, which had depressed her a few hours before, seemed bracing and invigorating as she splashed through the streets on her way home.

She stopped at a confectioner's and ordered a huge box of bonbons for the children in Iberville. She slipped a card in the box, on which she scribbled a tender message and sent an abundance of kisses.

Before dinner in the evening Edna wrote a charming letter to her husband, telling him of her intention to move for a while into the little house around the block, and to give a farewell dinner before leaving, regretting that he was not there to share it, to help her out with the menu and assist her in entertaining the guests. Her letter was brilliant and brimming with cheerfulness.

XXVII

"What is the matter with you?" asked Arobin that evening. "I never found you in such a happy mood." Edna was tired by that time, and was reclining on the lounge before the fire.

"Don't you know the weather prophet has told us we shall see the sun pretty soon?"

"Well, that ought to be reason enough," he acquiesced. "You wouldn't give me another if I sat here all night imploring you." He sat close to her on a low tabouret, and as he spoke his fingers lightly touched the hair that fell a little over her forehead. She liked the touch of his fingers through her hair, and closed her eyes sensitively.

"One of these days," she said, "I'm going to pull myself together for a while and think—try to determine what character of a woman I am, for, candidly, I don't know. By all the codes which I am acquainted with, I am a devilishly wicked specimen of the sex. But some way I can't convince myself that I am. I must think about it."

"Don't. What's the use? Why should you bother thinking about it when I can tell you what manner of woman you are." His fingers strayed occasionally down to her warm, smooth cheeks and firm chin, which was growing a little full and double.

"Oh, yes! You will tell me that I am adorable, everything that is captivating. Spare yourself the effort."

"No, I shan't tell you anything of the sort, though I shouldn't be lying if I did."

"Do you know Mademoiselle Reisz?" she asked irrelevantly.

"The pianist? I know her by sight. I've heard her play."

"She says queer things sometimes in a bantering way that you don't notice at the time and you find yourself thinking about afterward."

"For instance?"

"Well, for instance, when I left her today, she put her arms around me and felt my shoulder blades, to see if my wings were strong, she said. 'The bird that would soar above the level plain of tradition and prejudice must have strong wings. It is a sad spectacle to see the weaklings bruised, exhausted, fluttering back to earth.'"

"Whither would you soar?"

"I'm not thinking of any extraordinary flights. I only half comprehend her."

"I've heard she's partially demented," said Arobin.

"She seems to me wonderfully sane," Edna replied.

"I'm told she's extremely disagreeable and unpleasant. Why have you introduced her at a moment when I desired to talk of you?"

"Oh! talk of me if you like," cried Edna, clasping her hands beneath her head; "but let me think of something else while you do."

"I'm jealous of your thoughts tonight. They're

making you a little kinder than usual, but some way I feel as if they were wandering, as if they were not here with me." She only looked at him and smiled. His eyes were very near. He leaned upon the lounge with an arm extended across her, while the other hand still rested upon her hair. They continued silently to look into each other's eyes. When he leaned forward and kissed her, she clasped his head, holding his lips to hers.

It was the first kiss of her life to which her nature had really responded. It was a flaming torch that kindled desire.

XXVIII

Edna cried a little that night after Arobin left her. It was only one phase of the multitudinous emotions which had assailed her. There was with her an overwhelming feeling of irresponsibility. There was the shock of the unexpected and the unaccustomed. There was her husband's reproach looking at her from the external things around her which he had provided for her external existence. There was Robert's reproach making itself felt by a quicker, fiercer, more overpowering love, which had awakened within her toward him. Above all, there was understanding. She felt as if a mist had been lifted from her eyes, enabling her to look upon and comprehend the significance of life, that monster made up of beauty and brutality. But among the conflicting sensations which assailed her, there was neither shame nor remorse. There was a dull pang of regret because it was not the kiss of love which had inflamed her, because it was not love which had held this cup of life to her lips.

XXIX

Without even waiting for an answer from her
husband regarding his opinion or wishes in the matter, Edna hastened her preparations for quitting
her home on Esplanade Street and moving into the
little house around the block. A feverish anxiety
attended her every action in that direction. There
was no moment of deliberation, no interval of repose
between the thought and its fulfillment. Early upon
the morning following those hours passed in Arobin's
society, Edna set about securing her new abode and
hurrying her arrangements for occupying it. Within
the precincts of her home she felt like one who has
entered and lingered within the portals of some
forbidden temple in which a thousand muffled
voices bade her begone.

Whatever was her own in the house, everything
which she had acquired aside from her husband's
bounty, she caused to be transported to the other
house, supplying simple and meager deficiencies
from her own resources.

Arobin found her with rolled sleeves, working
in company with the house-maid when he looked
in during the afternoon. She was splendid and robust,
and had never appeared handsomer than in the old
blue gown, with a red silk handkerchief knotted at
random around her head to protect her hair from the
dust. She was mounted upon a high step-ladder,
unhooking a picture from the wall when he entered.
He had found the front door open, and had
followed his ring by walking in unceremoniously.

"Come down!" he said. "Do you want to kill yourself?" She greeted him with affected carelessness, and appeared absorbed in her occupation.

If he had expected to find her languishing, reproachful, or indulging in sentimental tears, he must have been greatly surprised.

He was no doubt prepared for any emergency, ready for any one of the foregoing attitudes, just as he bent himself easily and naturally to the situation which confronted him.

"Please come down," he insisted, holding the ladder and looking up at her.

"No," she answered; "Ellen is afraid to mount the ladder. Joe is working over at the 'pigeon house'— that's the name Ellen gives it, because it's so small and looks like a pigeon house—and some one has to do this."

Arobin pulled off his coat, and expressed himself ready and willing to tempt fate in her place. Ellen brought him one of her dust-caps, and went into contortions of mirth, which she found it impossible to control, when she saw him put it on before the mirror as grotesquely as he could. Edna herself could not refrain from smiling when she fastened it at his request. So it was he who in turn mounted the ladder, unhooking pictures and curtains, and dislodging ornaments as Edna directed. When he had finished he took off his dust-cap and went out to wash his hands.

Edna was sitting on the tabouret, idly brushing the tips of a feather duster along the carpet when he came in again.

"Is there anything more you will let me do?" he asked.

"That is all," she answered. "Ellen can manage the rest." She kept the young woman occupied in the drawing-room, unwilling to be left alone with Arobin.

"What about the dinner?" he asked; "the grand event, the *coup d'état?*"

"It will be a day after to-morrow. Why do you call it the '*coup d'état?*' Oh! it will be very fine; all my best of everything—crystal, silver and gold, Sèvres, flowers, music, and champagne to swim in. I'll let Léonce pay the bills. I wonder what he'll say when he sees the bills."

"And you ask me why I call it a *coup d'état?*" Arobin had put on his coat, and he stood before her and asked if his cravat was plumb. She told him it was, looking no higher than the tip of his collar.

"When do you go to the 'pigeon house?'—with all due acknowledgment to Ellen."

"Day after tomorrow, after the dinner. I shall sleep there."

"Ellen, will you very kindly get me a glass of water?" asked Arobin. "The dust in the curtains, if you will pardon me for hinting such a thing, has parched my throat to a crisp."

"While Ellen gets the water," said Edna, rising, "I will say good-by and let you go. I must get rid of this grime, and I have a million things to do and think of."

"When shall I see you?" asked Arobin, seeking to detain her, the maid having left the room.

"At the dinner, of course. You are invited."

"Not before?—not tonight or tomorrow morning or tomorrow noon or night? or the day after morning or noon? Can't you see yourself, without my telling you, what an eternity it is?"

He had followed her into the hall and to the foot of the stairway, looking up at her as she mounted with her face half turned to him.

"Not an instant sooner," she said. But she laughed and looked at him with eyes that at once gave him courage to wait and made it torture to wait.

XXX

Though Edna had spoken of the dinner as a very grand affair, it was in truth a very small affair and very select, in so much as the guests invited were few and were selected with discrimination. She had counted upon an even dozen seating themselves at her round mahogany board, forgetting for the moment that Madame Ratignolle was to the last degree *souffrante* and unpresentable, and not forseeing that Madame Lebrun would send a thousand regrets at the last moment. So there were only ten, after all, which made a cozy, comfortable number.

There were Mr. and Mrs. Merriman, a pretty, vivacious little woman in the thirties; her husband, a jovial fellow, something of a shallow-pate, who laughed a good deal at other people's witticisms, and had thereby made himself extremely popular. Mrs. Highcamp had accompanied them. Of course, there was Alcée Arobin, and Mademoiselle Reisz had consented to come. Edna had sent her a fresh bunch of violets with black lace trimmings for her hair. Monsieur Ratignolle brought himself and his wife's excuses. Victor Lebrun, who happened to be in the city, bent upon relaxation, had accepted with alacrity. There was a Miss Mayblunt, no longer in her teens, who looked at the world through lorgnettes and with the keenest interest. It was thought and said that she was intellectual; it was suspected of her that she wrote under a *nom de guerre.* She had come with a gentleman by the name of Gouvernail, connected with one of the daily papers, of whom nothing special could be said, except that he was observant and seemed quiet and inoffensive. Edna herself made the tenth, and at half-past eight they seated themselves at table, Arobin and Monsieur Ratignolle on either side of their hostess.

Mrs. Highcamp sat between Arobin and Victor Lebrun. Then came Mrs. Merriman, Mr. Gouvernail, Miss Mayblunt, Mr. Merriman, and Mademoiselle Reisz next to Monsieur Ratignolle.

There was something extremely gorgeous about the appearance of the table, an effect of splendor conveyed by a cover of pale yellow satin under strips of lace-work. There were wax candles in massive brass candelabra, burning softly under yellow silk shades; full, fragrant roses, yellow and red, abounded. There were silver and gold, as she had said there would be, and crystal which glittered like the gems which the women wore.

The ordinary stiff dining chairs had been discarded for the occasion and replaced by the most commodious and luxurious which could be collected throughout the house. Mademoiselle Reisz, being exceedingly diminutive, was elevated upon cushions, as small children are sometimes hoisted at table upon bulky volumes.

"Something new, Edna?" exclaimed Miss Mayblunt, with lorgnette directed toward a magnificent

cluster of diamonds that sparkled, that almost sputtered, in Edna's hair, just over the center of her
forehead.

"Quite new, 'brand' new, in fact, a present from
my husband. It arrived this morning from New York.
I may as well admit that this is my birthday, and that
I am twenty-nine. In good time I expect you to drink
my health. Meanwhile, I shall ask you to begin with
this cocktail, composed—would you say 'composed?' "
with an appeal to Miss Mayblunt—"composed by my
father in honor of Sister Janet's wedding."

Before each guest stood a tiny glass that looked
and sparkled like a garnet gem.

"Then, all things considered," spoke Arobin,
"it might not be amiss to start out by drinking
the Colonel's health in the cocktail which he composed, on the birthday of the most charming of
women—the daughter whom he invented."

Mr. Merriman's laugh at this sally was such a
genuine outburst and so contagious that it started the
dinner with an agreeable swing that never slackened.

Miss Mayblunt begged to be allowed to keep
her cocktail untouched before her, just to look
at. The color was marvelous! She could compare
it to nothing she had ever seen, and the garnet
lights which it emitted were unspeakably rare. She
pronounced the Colonel an artist, and stuck to it.

Monsieur Ratignolle was prepared to take things
seriously: the *mets*, the *entre-mets*, the service, the
decorations, even the people. He looked up from
his pompono and inquired of Arobin if he were
related to the gentleman of that name who formed
one of the firm of Laitner and Arobin, lawyers.
The young man admitted that Laitner was a warm

personal friend, who permitted Arobin's name to decorate the firm's letterheads and to appear upon a shingle that graced Perdido Street.

"There are so many inquisitive people and institutions abounding," said Arobin, "that one is really forced as a matter of convenience these days to assume the virtue of an occupation if he has it not."

Monsieur Ratignolle stared a little, and turned to ask Mademoiselle Reisz if she considered the symphony concerts up to the standard which had been set the previous winter. Mademoiselle Reisz answered Monsieur Ratignolle in French, which Edna thought a little rude, under the circumstances, but characteristic. Mademoiselle had only disagreeable things to say of the symphony concerts, and insulting remarks to make of all the musicians of New Orleans, singly and collectively. All her interest seemed to be centered upon the delicacies placed before her.

Mr. Merriman said that Mr. Arobin's remark about inquisitive people reminded him of a man from Waco the other day at the St. Charles Hotel—but as Mr. Merriman's stories were always lame and lacking point, his wife seldom permitted him to complete them. She interrupted him to ask if he remembered the name of the author whose book she had bought the week before to send to a friend in Geneva. She was talking "books" with Mr. Gouvernail and trying to draw from him his opinion upon current literary topics. Her husband told the story of the Waco man privately to Miss Mayblunt, who pretended to be greatly amused and to think it extremely clever.

Mrs. Highcamp hung with languid but unaffected interest upon the warm and impetuous volubility of her left-hand neighbor, Victor Lebrun. Her attention was never for a moment withdrawn from him after seating herself at table; and when he turned to Mrs. Merriman, who was prettier and more vivacious than Mrs. Highcamp, she waited with easy indifference for an opportunity to reclaim his attention. There was the occasional sound of music, of mandolins, sufficiently removed to be an agreeable accompaniment rather than an interruption to the conversation. Outside the soft, monotonous splash of a fountain could be heard; the sound penetrated into the room with the heavy odor of jessamine that came through the open windows.

The golden shimmer of Edna's satin gown spread in rich folds on either side of her. There was a soft fall of lace encircling her shoulders. It was the color of her skin, without the glow, the myriad living tints that one may sometimes discover in vibrant flesh. There was something in her attitude, in her whole appearance when she leaned her head against the high-backed chair and spread her arms, which suggested the regal woman, the one who rules, who looks on, who stands alone.

But as she sat there amid her guests, she felt the old ennui overtaking her, the hopelessness which so often assailed her, which came upon her like an obsession, like something extraneous, independent of volition. It was something which announced itself; a chill breath that seemed to issue from some vast cavern wherein discords wailed. There came over her the acute longing which always summoned into her spiritual vision the presence of the beloved one, overpowering her at once with a sense of the unattainable.

The moments glided on, while a feeling of good fellowship passed around the circle like a mystic cord, holding and binding these people together with jest and laughter. Monsieur Ratignolle was the first to break the pleasant charm. At ten o'clock he excused himself. Madame Ratignolle was waiting for him at home. She was *bien souffrante*, and she was filled with vague dread, which only her husband's presence could allay.

Mademoiselle Reisz arose with Monsieur Ratignolle, who offered to escort her to the car. She had eaten well; she had tasted the good, rich wines, and they must have turned her head, for she bowed pleasantly to all as she withdrew from table. She kissed Edna upon the shoulder, and whispered: *"Bonne nuit, ma reine; soyez sage."* She had been a little bewildered upon rising, or rather, descending from her cushions, and Monsieur Ratignolle gallantly took her arm and led her away.

Mrs. Highcamp was weaving a garland of roses, yellow and red. When she had finished the garland, she laid it lightly upon Victor's black curls. He was reclining far back in the luxurious chair, holding a glass of champagne to the light.

As if a magician's wand had touched him, the garland of roses transformed him into a vision of Oriental beauty. His cheeks were the color of crushed grapes, and his dusky eyes glowed with a languishing fire.

"Sapristi!" exclaimed Arobin.

But Mrs. Highcamp had one more touch to add to the picture. She took from the back of her chair a white silken scarf, with which she had covered her shoulders in the early part of the evening. She draped it across the boy in graceful folds, and in a way to conceal his black, conventional evening dress. He did not seem to mind what she did to him, only smiled, showing a faint gleam of white teeth, while he continued to gaze with narrowing eyes at the light through his glass of champagne.

"Oh! to be able to paint in color rather than in words!" exclaimed Miss Mayblunt, losing herself in a rhapsodic dream as she looked at him.

" 'There was a graven image of Desire
Painted with red blood on a ground of gold.' "

murmured Gouvernail, under his breath.

The effect of the wine upon Victor was, to change his accustomed volubility into silence. He seemed to have abandoned himself to a reverie, and to be seeing pleasing visions in the amber bead.

"Sing," entreated Mrs. Highcamp. "Won't you sing to us?"

"Let him alone," said Arobin.

"He's posing," offered Mr. Merriman; "let him have it out."

"I believe he's paralyzed," laughed Mrs. Merriman. And leaning over the youth's chair, she took the glass from his hand and held it to his lips. He sipped the wine slowly, and when he had drained the glass she laid it upon the table and wiped his lips with her little filmy handkerchief.

"Yes, I'll sing for you," he said, turning in his chair toward Mrs. Highcamp. He clasped his hands behind his head, and looking up at the ceiling began to him a little, trying his voice like a musician tuning an instrument. Then, looking at Edna, he began to sing:

"Ah! si tu savais!"

"Stop!" she cried, "don't sing that. I don't want you to sing it," and she laid her glass so impetuously and blindly upon the table as to shatter it against a caraffe. The wine spilled over Arobin's legs and some of it trickled down upon Mrs. Highcamp's black gauze gown. Victor had lost all idea of courtesy, or else he thought his hostess was not in earnest, for he laughed and went on:

"Ah! si tu savais
Ce que tes yeux me disent"—

"Oh! you mustn't! you mustn't," exclaimed Edna, and pushing back her chair she got up, and going behind him placed her hand over his mouth. He kissed the soft palm that pressed upon his lips.

"No, no, I won't, Mrs. Pontellier. I didn't know you meant it," looking up at her with caressing eyes. The touch of his lips was like a pleasing sting to her hand. She lifted the garland of roses from his head and flung it across the room.

"Come, Victor; you've posed long enough. Give Mrs. Highcamp her scarf."

Mrs. Highcamp undraped the scarf from about him with her own hands. Miss Mayblunt and Mr. Gouvernail suddenly conceived the notion that it was time to say good night. And Mr. and Mrs. Merriman wondered how it could be so late.

Before parting from Victor, Mrs. Highcamp invited him to call upon her daughter, who she knew would be charmed to meet him and talk French and sing French songs with him. Victor expressed his desire and intention to call upon Miss Highcamp at the first opportunity which presented itself. He asked if Arobin were going his way. Arobin was not.

The mandolin players had long since stolen away. A profound stillness had fallen upon the broad, beautiful street. The voices of Edna's disbanding guests jarred like a discordant note upon the quiet harmony of the night.

XXXI

"Well?" questioned Arobin, who had remained with Edna after the others had departed.

"Well," she reiterated, and stood up, stretching her arms, and feeling the need to relax her muscles after having been so long seated.

"What next?" he asked.

"The servants are all gone. They left when the musicians did. I have dismissed them. The house has to be closed and locked, and I shall trot around to the pigeon house, and shall send Celestine over in the morning to straighten things up."

He looked around, and began to turn out some of the lights.

"What about upstairs?" he inquired.

"I think it is all right; but there may be a window or two unlatched. We had better look; you might take a candle and see. And bring me my wrap and hat on the foot of the bed in the middle room."

He went up with the light, and Edna began closing

doors and windows. She hated to shut in the smoke
and the fumes of the wine. Arobin found her cape
and hat, which he brought down and helped her to
put on.

When everything was secured and the lights put
out, they left through the front door, Arobin locking
it and taking the key, which he carried for Edna. He
helped her down the steps.

"Will you have a spray of jessamine?" he asked,
breaking off a few blossoms as he passed.

"No; I don't want anything."

She seemed disheartened, and had nothing to say.
She took his arm, which he offered her, holding
up the weight of her satin train with the other hand.
She looked down, noticing the black line of his leg
moving in and out so close to her against the yellow
shimmer of her gown. There was the whistle of a
railway train somewhere in the distance, and the
midnight bells were ringing. They met no one in their
short walk.

The "pigeon-house" stood behind a locked gate,
and a shallow *parterre* that had been somewhat
neglected. There was a small front porch, upon which
a long window and the front door opened. The door
opened directly into the parlor; there was no side
entry. Back in the yard was a room for servants,
in which old Celestine had been ensconced.

Edna had left a lamp burning low upon the table.
She had succeeded in making the room look habit-
able and homelike. There were some books on the
table and a lounge near at hand. On the floor was
a fresh matting, covered with a rug or two; and
on the walls hung a few tasteful pictures. But the
room was filled with flowers. These were a surprise

to her. Arobin had sent them, and had had Celestine distribute them during Edna's absence. Her bedroom was adjoining, and across a small passage were the dining room and kitchen.

Edna seated herself with every appearance of discomfort.

"Are you tired?" he asked.

"Yes, and chilled, and miserable. I feel as if I had been wound up to a certain pitch—too tight—and something inside of me had snapped." She rested her head against the table upon her bare arm.

"You want to rest," he said, "and to be quiet. I'll go; I'll leave you and let you rest."

"Yes," she replied.

He stood up beside her and smoothed her hair with his soft, magnetic hand. His touch conveyed to her a certain physical comfort. She could have fallen quietly asleep there if he had continued to pass his hand over her hair. He brushed the hair upward from the nape of her neck.

"I hope you will feel better and happier in the morning," he said. "You have tried to do too much in the past few days. The dinner was the last straw; you might have dispensed with it."

"Yes," she admitted; "it was stupid."

"No, it was delightful; but it has worn you out." His hand had strayed to her beautiful shoulders, and he could feel the response of her flesh to his touch. He seated himself beside her and kissed her lightly upon the shoulder.

"I thought you were going away," she said, in an uneven voice.

"I am, after I have said good night."

"Good night," she murmured.

He did not answer, except to continue to caress her. He did not say good night until she had become supple to his gentle, seductive entreaties.

XXXII

When Mr. Pontellier learned of his wife's intention to abandon her home and take up her residence elsewhere, he immediately wrote her a letter of unqualified disapproval and remonstrance. She had given reasons which he was unwilling to acknowledge as adequate. He hoped she had not acted upon her rash impulse; and he begged her to consider first, foremost, and above all else, what people would say. He was not dreaming of scandal when he uttered this warning; that was a thing which would never have entered into his mind to consider in connection with his wife's name or his own. He was simply thinking of his financial integrity. It might get noised about that the Pontelliers had met with reverses, and were forced to conduct their *ménage* on a humbler scale than heretofore. It might do incalculable mischief to his business prospects.

But remembering Edna's whimsical turn of mind of late, and foreseeing that she had immediately acted upon her impetuous determination, he grasped the situation with his usual promptness and handled it with his well-known business tact and cleverness.

The same mail which brought to Edna his letter of disapproval carried instructions—the most minute instructions—to a well-known architect concerning the remodeling of his home, changes which he had long contemplated, and which he desired carried forward during his temporary absence.

Expert and reliable packers and movers were
engaged to convey the furniture, carpets, pictures
—everything movable, in short—to places of security.
And in an incredibly short time the Pontellier house
was turned over to the artisans. There was to be an
addition—a small snuggery; there was to be frescoing,
and hardwood flooring was to be put into such rooms
as had not yet been subjected to this improvement.

Furthermore, in one of the daily papers appeared
a brief notice to the effect that Mr. and Mrs. Pontellier were contemplating a summer sojourn abroad,
and that their handsome residence on Esplanade
Street was undergoing sumptuous alterations, and
would not be ready for occupancy until their return. Mr. Pontellier had saved appearances!

Edna admired the skill of his maneuver, and
avoided any occasion to balk his intentions. When
the situation as set forth by Mr. Pontellier was
accepted and taken for granted, she was apparently
satisfied that it should be so.

The pigeon-house pleased her. It at once assumed
the intimate character of a home, while she herself
invested it with a charm which it reflected like a
warm glow. There was with her a feeling of having
descended in the social scale, with a corresponding
sense of having risen to the spiritual. Every step
which she took toward relieving herself from obligations added to her strength and expansion as an
individual. She began to look with her own eyes;
to see and to apprehend the deeper undercurrents
of life. No longer was she content to "feed upon
opinion" when her own soul had invited her.

After a little while, a few days, in fact, Edna went
up and spent a week with her children in Iberville.

They were delicious February days, with all the summer's promise hovering in the air.

How glad she was to see the children! She wept for very pleasure when she felt their little arms clasping her; their hard, ruddy cheeks pressed against her own glowing cheeks. She looked into their faces with hungry eyes that could not be satisfied with looking. And what stories they had to tell their mother! About the pigs, the cows, the mules! About riding to the mill behind Gluglu, fishing back in the lake with their Uncle Jasper, picking pecans with Lidie's little black brood, and hauling chips in their express wagon. It was a thousand times more fun to haul real chips for old lame Susie's real fire than to drag painted blocks along the banquette on Esplanade Street!

She went with them herself to see the pigs and the cows, to look at the darkies laying the cane, to thrash the pecan trees, and catch fish in the back lake. She lived with them a whole week long, giving them all of herself, and gathering and filling herself with their young existence. They listened, breathless, when she told them the house in Esplanade Street was crowded with workmen, hammering, nailing, sawing, and filling the place with clatter. They wanted to know where their bed was, what had been done with their rocking horse; and where did Joe sleep, and where had Ellen gone, and the cook? But, above all, they were fired with a desire to see the little house around the block. Was there any place to play? Were there any boys next door? Raoul, with pessimistic foreboding, was convinced that there were only girls next door. Where would they sleep, and where would papa sleep? She told them the fairies would fix it all right.

The old Madame was charmed with Edna's visit, and showered all manner of delicate attentions upon her. She was delighted to know that the Esplanade Street house was in a dismantled condition. It gave her the promise and pretext to keep the children indefinitely.

It was with a wrench and a pang that Edna left her children. She carried away with her the sound of their voices and the touch of their cheeks. All along the journey homeward their presence lingered with her like the memory of a delicious song. But by the time she had regained the city the song no longer echoed in her soul. She was again alone.

XXXIII

It happened sometimes when Edna went to see Mademoiselle Reisz that the little musician was absent, giving a lesson or making some small necessary household purchase. The key was always left in a secret hiding-place in the entry, which Edna knew. If Mademoiselle happened to be away, Edna would usually enter and wait for her return.

When she knocked at Mademoiselle Reisz's door one afternoon there was no response; so unlocking the door, as usual, she entered and found the apartment deserted, as she had expected. Her day had been quite filled up, and it was for a rest, for a refuge, and to talk about Robert, that she sought out her friend.

She had worked at her canvas--a young Italian character study—all the morning, completing the work without the model, but there had been many interruptions, some incident to her modest housekeeping, and others of a social nature.

Madame Ratignolle had dragged herself over, avoiding the too public thoroughfares, she said. She complained that Edna had neglected her much of late. Besides, she was consumed with curiosity to see the little house and the manner in which it was conducted. She wanted to hear all about the dinner party; Monsieur Ratignolle had left *so* early. What had happened after he left? The champagne and grapes which Edna sent over were *too* delicious. She had so little appetite; they had refreshed and toned her stomach. Where on earth was she going to put Mr. Pontellier in that little house, and the boys? And then she made Edna promise to go to her when her hour of trial overtook her.

"At any time—any time of the day or night, dear," Edna assured her.

Before leaving Madame Ratignolle said:

"In some way you seem to me like a child, Edna. You seem to act without a certain amount of reflection which is necessary in this life. That is the reason I want to say you mustn't mind if I advise you to be a little careful while you are living here alone. Why don't you have some one come and stay with you? Wouldn't Mademoiselle Reisz come?"

"No; she wouldn't wish to come, and I shouldn't want her always with me."

"Well, the reason—you know how evil-minded the world is—some one was talking of Alcée Arobin visiting you. Of course, it wouldn't matter if Mr. Arobin had not such a dreadful reputation. Monsieur Ratignolle was telling me that his attentions alone are considered enough to ruin a woman's name."

"Does he boast of his successes?" asked Edna, indifferently, squinting at her picture.

"No, I think not. I believe he is a decent fellow as far as that goes. But his character is so well known among the men. I shan't be able to come back and see you; it was very, very imprudent today."

"Mind the step!" cried Edna.

"Don't neglect me," entreated Madame Ratignolle; "and don't mind what I said about Arobin, or having some one to stay with you."

"Of course not," Edna laughed. "You may say anything you like to me." They kissed each other good-by. Madame Ratignolle had not far to go, and Edna stood on the porch a while watching her walk down the street.

Then in the afternoon Mrs. Marriman and Mrs. Highcamp had made their "party call." Edna felt that they might have dispensed with the formality. They had also come to invite her to play *vingt-et-un* one evening at Mrs. Merriman's. She was asked to go early, to dinner, and Mr. Merriman or Mr. Arobin would take her home. Edna accepted in a half-hearted way. She sometimes felt very tired of Mrs. Highcamp and Mrs. Merriman.

Late in the afternoon she sought refuge with Mademoiselle Reisz, and stayed there alone, waiting for her, feeling a kind of repose invade her with the very atmosphere of the shabby, unpretentious little room.

Edna sat at the window, which looked out over the housetops and across the river. The window frame was filled with pots of flowers, and she sat and picked the dry leaves from a rose geranium. The day was warm, and the breeze which blew from the river was very pleasant. She removed her hat and laid it on the piano. She went on picking the leaves and digging around the plants with her hat pin. Once she thought she heard Mademoiselle Reisz approaching. But it was a young black girl, who came in, bringing a small bundle of laundry, which she deposited in the adjoining room, and went away.

Edna seated herself at the piano, and softly picked out with one hand the bars of a piece of music which lay open before her. A half hour went by. There was the occasional sound of people going and coming in the lower hall. She was growing interested in her occupation of picking out the aria, when there was a second rap at the door. She vaguely wondered what these people did when they found Mademoiselle's door locked.

"Come in," she called, turning her face toward the door. And this time it was Robert Lebrun who presented himself. She attempted to rise; she could not have done so without betraying the agitation which mastered her at sight of him, so she fell back upon the stool, only exclaiming, "Why, Robert!"

He came and clasped her hand, seemingly without knowing what he was saying or doing.

"Mrs. Pontellier! How do you happen—oh! how well you look! Is Mademoiselle Reisz not here? I never expected to see you."

"When did you come back?" asked Edna in an unsteady voice, wiping her face with her handkerchief. She seemed ill at ease on the piano stool, and he begged her to take the chair by the window. She did so, mechanically, while he seated himself on the stool.

"I returned day before yesterday," he answered, while he leaned his arm on the keys, bringing forth a crash of discordant sound.

"Day before yesterday!" she repeated, aloud; and went on thinking to herself, "day before yesterday," in a sort of an uncomprehending way. She had pictured him seeking her at the very first hour, and he had lived under the same sky since day before yesterday, while only by accident had he stumbled upon her. Mademoiselle must have lied when she said, "Poor fool, he loves you."

"Day before yesterday," she repeated, breaking off a spray of Mademoiselle's geranium; "then if you had not met me here today you wouldn't—when —that is, didn't you mean to come and see me?"

"Of course, I should have gone to see you. There have been so many things—" he turned the leaves of Mademoiselle's music nervously. "I started in at once yesterday with the old firm. After all there is as much chance for me here as there was there—that is, I might find it profitable some day. The Mexicans were not very congenial."

So he had come back because the Mexicans were not congenial; because business was as profitable here as there; because of any reason, and not because he cared to be near her. She remembered the day she sat on the floor, turning the pages of his letter, seeking the reason which was left untold.

She had not noticed how he looked—only feeling his presence; but she turned deliberately and observed him. After all, he had been absent but a few months, and was not changed. His hair—the color of hers— waved back from his temples in the same way as before. His skin was not more burned than it had been at Grand Isle. She found in his eyes, when he looked at her for one silent moment, the same tender caress, with an added warmth and entreaty which had not been there before—the same glance which had penetrated to the sleeping places of her soul and awakened them.

A hundred times Edna had pictured Robert's return, and imagined their first meeting. It was usually at her home, whither he had sought her out at once. She always fancied him expressing or betraying in some way his love for her. And here, the reality was that they sat ten feet apart, she at the window, crushing geranium leaves in her hand and smelling them, he twirling around on the piano stool, saying:

"I was very much surprised to hear of Mr. Pontellier's absence; it's a wonder Mademoiselle Reisz did not tell me; and your moving—mother told me yesterday. I should think you would have gone to New York with him, or to Iberville with the children, rather than be bothered here with housekeeping. And you are going abroad, too, I hear. We shan't have you at Grand Isle next summer; it won't seem—do you see much of Mademoiselle Reisz? She often spoke of you in the few letters she wrote."

"Do you remember that you promised to write to me when you went away?" A flush overspread his whole face.

"I couldn't believe that my letters would be of any interest to you."

"That is an excuse; it isn't the truth." Edna reached for her hat on the piano. She adjusted it, sticking the hat pin through the heavy coil of hair with some deliberation.

"Are you not going to wait for Mademoiselle Reisz?" asked Robert.

"No; I have found when she is absent this long, she is liable not to come back till late." She drew on her gloves, and Robert picked up his hat.

"Won't you wait for her?" asked Edna.

"Not if you think she will not be back till late," adding, as if suddenly aware of some discourtesy in his speech, "and I should miss the pleasure of walking home with you." Edna locked the door and put the key back in its hiding place.

They went together, picking their way across muddy streets and sidewalks encumbered with the cheap display of small tradesmen. Part of the distance they rode in the car, and after disembarking, passed the Pontellier mansion, which looked broken and half torn asunder. Robert had never known the house, and looked at it with interest.

"I never knew you in your home," he remarked.

"I am glad you did not."

"Why?" She did not answer. They went on around the corner, and it seemed as if her dreams were coming true after all, when he followed her into the little house.

"You must stay and dine with me, Robert. You see I am all alone, and it is so long since I have seen you. There is so much I want to ask you."

She took off her hat and gloves. He stood irresolute, making some excuse about his mother who expected him; he even muttered something about an engagement. She struck a match and lit the lamp on the table; it was growing dusk. When he saw her face in the lamp-light, looking pained, with all the soft lines gone out of it, he threw his hat aside and seated himself.

"Oh! you know I want to stay if you will let me!" he exclaimed. All the softness came back. She laughed, and went and put her hand on his shoulder.

"This is the first moment you have seemed like the old Robert. I'll go tell Celestine." She hurried away to tell Celestine to set an extra place. She even sent her off in search of some added delicacy which she had not thought of for herself. And she recommended great care in dripping the coffee and having the omelet done to a proper turn.

When she reentered, Robert was turning over magazines, sketches, and things that lay upon the table in great disorder. He picked up a photograph, and exclaimed:

"Alcée Arobin! What on earth is his picture doing here?"

"I tried to make a sketch of his head one day," answered Edna, "and he thought the photograph might help me. It was at the other house. I thought it had been left there. I must have packed it up with my drawing materials."

"I should think you would give it back to him if you have finished with it."

"Oh! I have a great many such photographs. I never think of returning them. They don't amount to anything." Robert kept on looking at the picture.

"It seems to me—do you think his head worth drawing? Is he a friend of Mr. Pontellier's? You never said you knew him."

"He isn't a friend of Mr. Pontellier's; he's a friend of mine. I always knew him—that is, it is only of late that I know him pretty well. But I'd rather talk about you, and know what you have been seeing and doing and feeling out there in Mexico." Robert threw aside the picture.

"I've been seeing the waves and the white beach of Grand Isle, the quiet, grassy street of the *Chênière*, the old fort at Grande Terre. I've been working like a machine, and feeling like a lost soul. There was nothing interesting."

She leaned her head upon her hand to shade her eyes from the light.

"And what have you been seeing and doing and feeling all these days?" he asked.

"I've been seeing the waves and the white beach of Grand Isle, the quiet, grassy street of the *Chênière Caminada*, the old sunny fort at Grande Terre. I've been working with a little more comprehension than a machine, and still feeling like a lost soul. There was nothing interesting."

"Mrs. Pontellier, you are cruel," he said, with feeling, closing his eyes and resting his head back in his chair. They remained in silence till old Celestine announced dinner.

XXXIV

The dining-room was very small. Edna's round mahogany would have almost filled it. As it was there was but a step or two from the little table to the kitchen, to the mantel, the small buffet, and the side door that opened out on the narrow brick-paved yard.

A certain degree of ceremony settled upon them with the announcement of dinner. There was no return to personalities. Robert related incidents of his sojourn in Mexico, and Edna talked of events likely to interest him, which had occurred during his absence. The dinner was of ordinary quality, except for the few delicacies which she had sent out to purchase. Old Celestine, with a bandana *tignon* twisted about her head, hobbled in and out, taking a personal interest in everything; and she lingered occasionally to talk patois with Robert, whom she had known as a boy.

He went out to a neighboring cigar stand to purchase cigarette papers, and when he came back he found that Celestine had served the black coffee in the parlor.

"Perhaps I shouldn't have come back," he said. "When you are tired of me, tell me to go."

"You never tire me. You must have forgotten the hours and hours at Grand Isle in which we grew accustomed to each other and used to being together."

"I have forgotten nothing at Grand Isle," he said, not looking at her, but rolling a cigarette. His tobacco pouch, which he laid upon the table, was a fantastic embroidered silk affair, evidently the handiwork of a woman.

"You used to carry your tobacco in a rubber pouch," said Edna, picking up the pouch and examining the needlework.

"Yes; it was lost."

"Where did you buy this one? In Mexico?"

"It was given to me by a Vera Cruz girl; they are very generous," he replied, striking a match and lighting his cigarette.

"They are very handsome, I suppose, those Mexican women; very picturesque, with their black eyes and their lace scarfs."

"Some are; others are hideous. Just as you find women everywhere."

"What was she like—the one who gave you the pouch? You must have known her very well."

"She was very ordinary. She wasn't of the slightest importance. I knew her well enough."

"Did you visit at her house? Was it interesting? I should like to know and hear about the people you met, and the impressions they made on you."

"There are some people who leave impressions not so lasting as the imprint of an oar upon the water."

"Was she such a one?"

"It would be ungenerous for me to admit that she was of that order and kind." He thrust the pouch back in his pocket, as if to put away the subject with the trifle which had brought it up.

Arobin dropped in with a message from Mrs. Merriman, to say that the card party was postponed on account of the illness of one of her children.

"How do you do, Arobin?" said Robert, rising from the obscurity.

"Oh! Lebrun. To be sure! I heard yesterday you were back. How did they treat you down in Mexique?"

"Fairly well."

"But not well enough to keep you there. Stunning girls, though, in Mexico. I thought I should never get away from Vera Cruz when I was down there a couple of years ago."

"Did they embroider slippers and tobacco pouches and hatbands and things for you?" asked Edna.

"Oh! my! no! I didn't get so deep in their regard. I fear they made more impression on me tban I made on them."

"You were less fortunate than Robert. Has he been imparting tender confidences?"

"I've been imposing myself long enough," said Robert, rising, and shaking hands with Edna. "Please convey my regards to Mr. Pontellier when you write."

He shook hands with Arobin and went away.

"Fine fellow, that Lebrun," said Arobin when Robert had gone. "I never heard you speak of him."

"I knew him last summer at Grand Isle," she replied. "Here is that photograph of yours. Don't you want it?"

"What do I want with it? Throw it away." She threw it back on the table.

"I'm not going to Mrs. Merriman's," she said. "If you see her, tell her so. But perhaps I had better write. I think I shall write now, and say that I am sorry her child is sick, and tell her not to count on me."

"It would be a good scheme," acquiesced Arobin. "I don't blame you; stupid lot!"

Edna opened the blotter, and having procured paper and pen, began to write the note. Arobin lit a cigar and read the evening paper, which he had in his pocket.

"What is the date?" she asked. He told her.

"Will you mail this for me when you go out?"

"Certainly." He read to her little bits out of the newspaper, while she straightened things on the table.

"What do you want to do?" he asked, throwing aside the paper. "Do you want to go out for a walk or a drive or anything? It would be a fine night to drive."

"No; I don't want to do anything but just be quiet. You go away and amuse yourself. Don't stay."

"I'll go away if I must; but I shan't amuse myself. You know that I only live when I am near you."

He stood up to bid her good night.

"Is that one of the things you al ays say to women?"

"I have said it before, but I don't think I ever came so near meaning it," he answered with a smile. There were no warm lights in her eyes; only a dreamy, absent look.

"Good night. I adore you. Sleep well," he said, and he kissed her hand and went away.

She stayed alone in a kind of reverie—a sort of stupor. Step by step she lived over every instant of the time she had been with Robert after he had entered Mademoiselle Reisz's door. She recalled his words, his looks. How few and meager they had been for her hungry heart! A vision—a transcendently seductive vision of a Mexican girl arose before her. She writhed with a jealous pang. She wondered when he would come back. He had not said he would come back. She had been with him, had heard his voice and touched his hand. But some way he had seemed nearer to her off there in Mexico.

XXXV

The morning was full of sunlight and hope. Edna could see before her no denial—only the promise of excessive joy. She lay in bed awake, with bright eyes full of speculation. "He loves you, poor fool." If she could but get that conviction firmly fixed in her mind, what mattered about the rest? She felt she had been childish and unwise the night before in giving herself over to despondency. She recapitulated the motives which no doubt explained Robert's reserve. They were not insurmountable; they would not hold if he really loved her; they could not hold against her own passion, which he must come to realize in time. She pictured him going to his business that morning. She even saw how he was dressed, how he walked down one street, and turned the corner of another, saw him bending over his desk, talking to people who entered the office, going to his lunch, and perhaps watching for her on the street. He would come to her in the afternoon or evening, sit and roll his cigarette, talk a little, and go away as he had done the night before. But how delicious it would be to have him there with her! She would have no regrets, nor seek to penetrate his reserve if he still chose to wear it.

Edna ate her breakfast only half dressed. The maid brought her a delicious printed scrawl from Raoul, expressing his love, asking her to send him some bonbons, and telling her they had found that morning ten tiny white pigs all lying in a row beside Lidie's big white pig.

A letter also came from her husband, saying he hoped to be back early in March, and then they would get ready for that journey abroad which he had promised her so long, which he felt now fully able to afford; he felt able to travel as people should, without any thought of small economies—thanks to his recent speculations in Wall Street.

Much to her surprise she received a note from Arobin, written at midnight from the club. It was to say good morning to her, to hope that she had slept well, to assure her of his devotion, which he trusted she in some faintest manner returned.

All these letters were pleasing to her. She answered the children in a cheerful frame of mind, promising them bonbons, and congratulating them upon their happy find of the little pigs.

She answered her husband with friendly evasiveness,—not with any fixed design to mislead him, only because all sense of reality had gone out of her life; she had abandoned herself to Fate, and awaited the consequences with indifference.

To Arobin's note she made no reply. She put it under Celestine's stove lid.

Edna worked several hours with much spirit. She saw no one but a picture dealer, who asked her if it were true that she was going abroad to study in Paris.

She said possibly she might, and he negotiated with her for some Parisian studies to reach him in time for the holiday trade in December.

Robert did not come that day. She was keenly disappointed. He did not come the following day, nor the next. Each morning she awoke with hope, and each night she was a prey to despondency. She was tempted to seek him out. But far from yielding to the impulse, she avoided any occasion which might throw her in his way. She did not go to Mademoiselle Reisz's nor pass by Madame Lebrun's, as she might have done if he had still been in Mexico.

When Arobin, one night, urged her to drive with him, she went—out to the lake, on the Shell Road. His horses were full of mettle, and even a little unmanageable. She liked the rapid gait at which they spun along, and the quick, sharp sound of the horses'

hoofs on the hard road. They did not stop anywhere
to eat or to drink. Arobin was not needlessly imprudent. But they ate and they drank when they
regained Edna's little dining room—which was comparatively early in the evening.

It was late when he left her. It was getting to be
more than a passing whim with Arobin to see her and
be with her. He had detected the latent sensuality,
which unfolded under his delicate sense of her
nature's requirements like a torpid, torrid, sensitive
blossom.

There was no despondency when she fell asleep
that night, nor was there hope when she awoke in the
morning.

XXXVI

There was a garden out in the suburbs, a small,
leafy corner, with a few green tables under the
orange trees. An old cat slept all day on the stone
step in the sun, and an old *mulatresse* slept her
idle hours away in her chair at the open window,
till some one happened to knock on one of the green
tables. She had milk and cream cheese to sell, and
bread and butter. There was no one who could make
such excellent coffee or fry a chicken so golden
brown as she.

The place was too modest to attract the attention
of people of fashion, and so quiet as to have escaped
the notice of those in search of pleasure and dissipation. Edna had discovered it accidentally one
day when the high board gate stood ajar. She caught
sight of a little green table, blotched with the checkered
sunlight that filtered through the quivering leaves

overhead. Within she had found the slumbering *mulatresse*, the drowsy cat, and a glass of milk which reminded her of the milk she had tasted in Iberville.

She often stopped there during her perambulations; sometimes taking a book with her, and sitting an hour or two under the trees when she found the place deserted. Once or twice she took a quiet dinner there alone, having instructed Celestine beforehand to prepare no dinner at home. It was the last place in the city where she would have expected to meet any one she knew.

Still she was not astonished when, as she was partaking of a modest dinner late in the afternoon, looking into an open book, stroking the cat, which had made friends with her—she was not greatly astonished to see Robert come in at the tall garden gate.

"I am destined to see you only by accident," she said, shoving the cat off the chair beside her. He was surprised, ill at ease, almost embarrassed at meeting her thus so unexpectedly.

"Do you come here often?" he asked.

"I almost live here," she said.

"I used to drop in very often for a cup of Catiche's good coffee. This is the first time since I came back."

"She'll bring you a plate, and you will share my dinner. There's always enough for two—even three." Edna had intended to be indifferent and as reserved as he when she met him; she had reached the determination by a laborious train of reasoning, incident to one of her despondent moods. But her resolve melted when she saw him before her, seated there beside her in the little garden, as if a designing Providence had led him into her path.

"Why have you kept away from me, Robert?" she asked, closing the book that lay open upon the table.

"Why are you so personal, Mrs. Pontellier? Why do you force me to idiotic subterfuges?" he exclaimed with sudden warmth. "I suppose there's no use telling you I've been very busy, or that I've been sick, or that I've been to see you and not found you at home. Please let me off with any one of these excuses."

"You are the embodiment of selfishness," she said. "You save yourself something—I don't know what—but there is some selfish motive, and in sparing yourself you never consider for a moment what I think, or how I feel your neglect and indifference. I suppose this is what you would call unwomanly; but I have got into a habit of expressing myself. It doesn't matter to me, and you may think me unwomanly if you like."

"No; I only think you cruel, as I said the other day. Maybe not intentionally cruel; but you seem to be forcing me into disclosures which can result in nothing; as if you would have me bare a wound for the pleasure of looking at it, without the intention or power of healing it."

"I'm spoiling your dinner, Robert; never mind what I say. You haven't eaten a morsel."

"I only came in for a cup of coffee." His sensitive face was all disfigured with excitement.

"Isn't this a delightful place?" she remarked. "I am so glad it has never actually been discovered. It is so quiet, so sweet, here. Do you notice there is scarcely a sound to be heard? It's so out of the way; and a good walk from the car. However, I don't mind walking. I always feel so sorry for women

who don't like to walk; they miss so much—so many
rare little glimpses of life; and we women learn so
little of life on the whole.

"Catiche's coffee is always hot. I don't know how
she manages it, here in the open air. Celestine's coffee
gets cold bringing it from the kitchen to the dining
room. Three lumps! How can you drink it so sweet?
Take some of the cress with your chop; it's so biting
and crisp. Then there's the advantage of being able to
smoke with your coffee out here. Now, in the city—
aren't you going to smoke?"

"After a while," he said, laying a cigar on the
table.

"Who gave it to you?" she laughed.

"I bought it. I suppose I'm getting reckless; I
bought a whole box." She was determined not
to be personal again and make him uncomfortable.

The cat made friends with him, and climbed into
his lap when he smoked his cigar. He stroked her silky
fur, and talked a little about her. He looked at Edna's
book, which he had read; and he told her the end,
to save her the trouble of wading through it, he said.

Again he accompanied her back to her home; and
it was after dusk when they reached the little
"pigeon-house." She did not ask him to remain,
which he was grateful for, as it permitted him to
stay without the discomfort of blundering through
an excuse which he had no intention of considering.
He helped her to light the lamp; then she went into
her room to take off her hat and to bathe her face
and hands.

When she came back Robert was not examining
the pictures and magazines as before; he sat off
in the shadow, leaning his head back on the chair

as if in a reverie. Edna lingered a moment beside the table, arranging the books there. Then she went across the room to where he sat. She bent over the arm of his chair and called his name.

"Robert," she said, "are you asleep?"

"No," he answered, looking up at her.

She leaned over and kissed him—a soft, cool, delicate kiss, whose voluptuous sting penetrated his whole being—then she moved away from him. He followed, and took her in his arms, just holding her close to him. She put her hand up to his face and pressed his cheek against her own. The action was full of love and tenderness. He sought her lips again. Then he drew her down upon the sofa beside him and held her hand in both of his.

"Now you know," he said, "now you know what I have been fighting against since last summer at Grand Isle, what drove me away and drove me back again."

"Why have you been fighting against it?" she asked. Her face glowed with soft lights.

"Why? Because you were not free; you were Léonce Pontellier's wife. I couldn't help loving you if you were ten times his wife, but so long as I went away from you and kept away I could help telling you so." She put her free hand up to his shoulder, and then against his cheek, rubbing it softly. He kissed her again. His face was warm and flushed.

"There in Mexico I was thinking of you all the time, and longing for you."

"But not writing to me," she interrupted.

"Something put into my head that you cared for me, and I lost my senses. I forgot everything but a wild dream of your some way becoming my wife."

"Your wife!"

"Religion, loyalty, everything would give way if only you cared."

"Then you must have forgotten that I was Léonce Pontellier's wife."

"Oh! I was demented, dreaming of wild, impossible things, recalling men who had set their wives free, we have heard of such things."

"Yes, we have heard of such things."

"I came back full of vague, mad intentions. And when I got here—"

"When you got here you never came near me!" She was still caressing his cheek.

"I realized what a cur I was to dream of such a thing, even if you had been willing."

She took his face between her hands and looked into it as if she would never withdraw her eyes more. She kissed him on the forehead, the eyes, the cheeks, and the lips.

"You have been a very, very foolish boy, wasting your time dreaming of impossible things when you speak of Mr. Pontellier setting me free! I am no longer one of Mr. Pontellier's possessions to dispose of or not. I give myself where I choose. If he were to say, 'Here, Robert, take her and be happy, she is yours,' I should laugh at you both."

His face grew a little white. "What do you mean?" he asked.

There was a knock at the door. Old Celestine came in to say that Madame Ratignolle's servant had come around the back way with a message that Madame had been taken sick and begged Mrs. Pontellier to go to her immediately.

"Yes, yes," said Edna, rising; "I promised. Tell her yes—to wait for me. I'll go back with her."

"Let me walk over with you," offered Robert.

"No," she said; "I will go with the servant." She went into her room to put on her hat, and when she came in again she sat once more upon the sofa beside him. He had not stirred. She put her arms about his neck.

"Good-by, my sweet Robert. Tell me good-by." He kissed her with a degree of passion which had not before entered into his caress, and strained her to him.

"I love you," she whispered, "only you, no one but you. It was you who awoke me last summer out of a life-long, stupid dream. Oh! you have made me so unhappy with your indifference. Oh! I have suffered, suffered! Now you are here we shall love each other, my Robert. We shall be everything to each other. Nothing else in the world is of any consequence. I must go to my friend; but you will wait for me? No matter how late; you will wait for me, Robert?"

"Don't go, don't go! Oh! Edna, stay with me," he pleaded. "Why should you go? Stay with me, stay with me."

"I shall come back as soon as I can; I shall find you here." She buried her face in his neck, and said good-by again. Her seductive voice, together with his great love for her, had enthralled his senses, had deprived him of every impulse but the longing to hold her and keep her.

XXXVII

Edna looked in at the drug store. Monsieur Ratignolle was putting up a mixture himself, very carefully, dropping a red liquid into a tiny glass. He was grateful to Edna for having come, her presence would be a comfort to his wife. Madame Ratignolle's sister, who had always been with her at such trying times, had not been able to come up from the plantation, and Adèle had been inconsolable until Mrs. Pontellier so kindly promised to come to her. The nurse had been with them at night for the past week, as she lived a great distance away. And Dr. Mandelet had been coming and going all the afternoon. They were then looking for him any moment.

Edna hastened upstairs by a private stairway that led from the rear of the store to the apartments above. The children were all sleeping in a back room. Madame Ratignolle was in the salon, whither she had strayed in her suffering impatience. She sat on the sofa, clad in an ample white *peignoir*, holding a handkerchief tight in her hand with a nervous clutch. Her face was drawn and pinched, her sweet blue eyes haggard and unnatural. All her beautiful hair had been drawn back and plaited. It lay in a long braid on the sofa pillow, coiled like a golden serpent. The nurse, a comfortable looking *Griffe* woman in white apron and cap, was urging her to return to her bedroom.

"There is no use, there is no use," she said at once to Edna. "We must get rid of Mandelet; he is getting too old and careless. He said he would be here at half-past seven; now it must be eight. See what time it is, Joséphine."

The woman was possessed of a cheerful nature, and refused to take any situation too seriously, especially a situation with which she was so familiar. She urged Madame to have courage and patience. But Madame only set her teeth hard into her under lip, and Edna saw the sweat gather in beads on her white forehead. After a moment or two she uttered a profound sigh and wiped her face with the handkerchief rolled in a ball. She appeared exhausted. The nurse gave her a fresh handkerchief, sprinkled with cologne water.

"This is too much!" she cried. "Mandelet ought to be killed! Where is Alphonse? Is it possible I am to be abandoned like this—neglected by every one?"

"Neglected, indeed!" exclaimed the nurse. Wasn't she there? And here was Mrs. Pontellier leaving, no doubt, a pleasant evening at home to devote to her? And wasn't Monsieur Ratignolle coming that very instant through the hall? And Joséphine was quite sure she had heard Doctor Mandelet's coupé. Yes, there it was, down at the door.

Adèle consented to go back to her room. She sat on the edge of a little low couch next to her bed.

Doctor Mandelet paid no attention to Madame Ratignolle's upbraidings. He was accustomed to them at such times, and was too well convinced of her loyalty to doubt it.

He was glad to see Edna, and wanted her to go with him into the salon and entertain him. But Madame Ratignolle would not consent that Edna should leave her for an instant. Between agonizing moments, she chatted a little, and said it took her mind off her sufferings.

Edna began to feel uneasy. She was seized with a vague dread. Her own like experiences seemed far away, unreal, and only half remembered. She recalled faintly an ecstasy of pain, the heavy odor of chloroform, a stupor which had deadened sensation, and an awakening to find a little new life to which she had given being, added to the great unnumbered multitude of souls that come and go.

She began to wish she had not come; her presence was not necessary. She might have invented a pretext for staying away; she might even invent a pretext now for going. But Edna did not go. With an inward agony, with a flaming, outspoken revolt against the ways of Nature, she witnessed the scene's torture.

She was still stunned and speechless with emotion when later she leaned over her friend to kiss her and softly say good-by. Adèle, pressing her cheek, whispered in an exhausted voice: "Think of the children, Edna. Oh think of the children! Remember them!"

XXXVIII

Edna still felt dazed when she got outside in the open air. The Doctor's coupé had returned for him and stood before the *porte cochère*. She did not wish to enter the coupé, and told Doctor Mandelet she would walk; she was not afraid, and would go alone. He directed his carriage to meet him at Mrs. Pontellier's, and he started to walk home with her.

Up—away up, over the narrow street between the tall houses, the stars were blazing. The air was mild and caressing, but cool with the breath of spring and the night.

They walked slowly, the Doctor with a heavy, measured tread and his hands behind him: Edna, in absent-minded way, as she had walked one night at Grand Isle, as if her thoughts had gone ahead of her and she was striving to overtake them.

"You shouldn't have been there, Mrs. Pontellier," he said. "That was no place for you. Adèle is full of whims at such times. There were a dozen women she might have had with her, unimpressionable women. I felt that it was cruel, cruel. You shouldn't have gone."

"Oh, well!" she answered, indifferently. "I don't know that it matters after all. One has to think of the children some time or other, the sooner the better."

"When is Léonce coming back?"

"Quite soon. Some time in March."

"And you are going abroad?"

"Perhaps—no, I am not going. I'm not going to be forced into doing things. I don't want to go abroad. I want to be let alone. Nobody had any right—except children, perhaps—and even then, it seems to me—or it did seem—" She felt that her speech was voicing the incoherency of her thoughts, and stopped abruptly.

"The trouble is," sighed the Doctor, grasping her meaning intuitively, "that youth is given up to illusions. It seems to be a provision of Nature, a decoy to secure mothers for the race. And Nature takes no account of moral consequences, of arbitary conditions which were create, and which we feel obliged to maintain at any cost."

"Yes," she said. "The years that are gone seem like dreams—if one might go on sleeping and dreaming—but to wake up and find—oh! well! perhaps it is better to wake up after all, even to suffer, rather than to remain a dupe to illusions all one's life."

"It seems to me, my dear child," said the Doctor at parting, holding her hand, "you seem to me to be in trouble. I am not going to ask for your confidence. I will only say that if ever you feel moved to give it to me, perhaps I might help you. I know I would understand, and I tell you there are not many who would—not many, my dear."

"Some way I don't feel moved to speak of things that trouble me. Don't think I am ungrateful or that I don't appreciate your sympathy. There are periods of despondency and suffering which take possession of me. But I don't want anything but my own way. That is wanting a good deal, of course, when you have to trample upon the lives, the hearts, the prejudices of others—but no matter—still, I shouldn't want to trample upon the little lives. Oh! I don't know what I'm saying, Doctor. Good night. Don't blame me for anything."

"Yes, I will blame you if you don't come and see me soon. We will talk of things you never have dreamt of talking about before. It will do us both good. I don't want you to blame yourself, whatever comes. Good night, my child."

She let herself in at the gate, but instead of entering she sat upon the step of the porch. The night was quiet and soothing. All the tearing emotion of the last few hours seemed to fall away from her like a somber, uncomfortable garment, which she had but to loosen to be rid of. She went back to that hour before Adèle had sent for her; and her senses kindled afresh in thinking of Robert's words, the pressure of his arms, and the feeling of his lips upon her own. She could picture at that moment no greater bliss on earth than possession of the beloved one. His expression of love had already given him to her in part. When she thought that he was there at hand, waiting for her, she grew numb with the intoxication of expectancy. It was so late; he would be asleep perhaps. She would awaken him with a kiss. She hoped he would be asleep that she might arouse him with her caresses.

Still, she remembered Adèle's voice whispering, "Think of the children; think of them." She meant to think of them; that determination had driven into her soul like a death wound—but not to-night. To-morrow would be time to think of everything.

Robert was not waiting for her in the little parlor. He was nowhere at hand. The house was empty. But he had scrawled on a piece of paper that lay in the lamplight:

"I love you. Good-by—because I love you."

Edna grew faint when she read the words. She went and sat on the sofa. Then she stretched herself out there, never uttering a sound. She did not sleep. She did not go to bed. The lamp sputtered and went out. She was still awake in the morning, when Celestine unlocked the kitchen door and came in to light the fire.

XXXIX

Victor, with hammer and nails and scraps of scantling, was patching a corner of one of the galleries. Mariequita sat near by, dangling her legs, watching him work, and handing him nails from the tool box. The sun was beating down upon them. The girl had covered her head with her apron folded into a square pad. They had been talking for an hour or more. She was never tired of hearing Victor describe the dinner at Mrs. Pontellier's. He exaggerated every detail, making it appear a veritable Lucillean feast. The flowers were in tubs, he said. The champagne was quaffed from huge golden goblets. Venus rising from the foam could have presented no more entrancing a spectacle than Mrs. Pontellier, blazing with beauty and diamonds at the head of the board, while the other women were all of them youthful houris, possessed of incomparable charms.

She got it into her head that Victor was in love with Mrs. Pontellier, and he gave her evasive answers, framed so as to confirm her belief. She grew sullen and cried a little, threatening to go off and leave him to his fine ladies. There were a dozen men crazy about her at the *Chênière*, and since it was the fashion to be in love with married people, why, she could run away any time she liked to New Orleans with Célina's husband.

Célina's husband was a fool, a coward, and a pig, and to prove it to her, Victor intended to hammer his head into a jelly the next time he encountered him. This assurance was very consoling to Marie-quita. She dried her eyes, and grew cheerful at the prospect.

They were still talking of the dinner and the allurements of city life when Mrs. Pontellier herself slipped around the corner of the house. The two youngsters stayed dumb with amazement before what they considered to be an apparition. But it was really she in flesh and blood, looking tired and a little travel-stained.

"I walked up from the wharf," she said, "and heard the hammering. I supposed it was you, mending

the porch. It's a good thing. I was always tripping
over those loose planks last summer. How dreary
and deserted everything looks!"

It took Victor some little time to comprehend
that she had come in Beaudelet's lugger, that she
had come alone, and for no purpose but to rest.

"There's nothing fixed up yet, you see. I'll give
you my room; it's the only place."

"Any corner will do," she assured him.

"And if you can stand Philomel's cooking," he
went on, "though I might try to get her mother
while you are here. Do you think she would come?"
turning to Mariequita.

Mariequita thought that perhaps Philomel's mother
might come for a few days, and money enough.

Beholding Mrs. Pontellier make her appearance,
the girl had at once suspected a lovers' rendezvous.
But Victor's astonishment was so genuine, and Mrs.
Pontellier's indifference so apparent, that the disturbing notion did not lodge long in her brain. She contemplated with the greatest interest this woman
who gave the most sumptuous dinners in America,
and who had all the men in New Orleans at her feet.

"What time will you have dinner?" asked Edna.
"I'm very hungry; but don't get anything extra."

"I'll have it ready in little or no time," he said,
bustling and packing away his tools. "You may go
to my room to brush up and rest yourself. Mariequita will show you."

"Thank you," said Edna. "But, do you know, I
have a notion to go down to the beach and take a
good wash and even a little swim, before dinner?"

"The water is too cold!" they both exclaimed.
"Don't think of it."

"Well, I might go down and try—dip my toes in. Why, it seems to me the sun is hot enough to have warmed the very depths of the ocean. Could you get me a couple of towels? I'd better go right away, so as to be back in time. It would be a little too chilly if I waited till this afternoon."

Mariequita ran over to Victor's room, and returned with some towels, which she gave to Edna.

"I hope you have fish for dinner," said Edna, as she started to walk away, "but don't do anything extra if you haven't."

"Run and find Philomel's mother," Victor instructed the girl. "I'll go to the kitchen and see what I can do. By Giminy! Women have no consideration! She might have sent me word."

Edna walked on down to the beach rather mechanically, not noticing anything special except that the sun was hot. She was not dwelling upon any particular train of thought. She had done all the thinking which was necessary after Robert went away, when she lay awake upon the sofa till morning.

She had said over and over to herself: "Today it is Arobin; tomorrow it will be some one else. It makes no difference to me, it doesn't matter about Léonce Pontellier—but Raoul and Étienne!" She understood now clearly what she had meant long ago when she said to Adèle Ratignolle that she would give up the unessential, but she would never sacrifice herself for her children.

Despondency had come upon her there in the wakeful night, and had never lifted. There was no one thing in the world that she desired. There was no human being whom she wanted near her except Robert; and she even realized that the day would come when he, too, and the thought of him would melt out of her existence, leaving her alone. The children appeared before her like antagonists who had overcome her, who had overpowered and sought to drag her into the soul's slavery for the rest of her days. But she knew a way to elude them. She was not thinking of these things when she walked down to the beach.

The water of the Gulf stretched out before her, gleaming with the million lights of the sun. The voice of the sea is seductive, never ceasing, whispering, clamoring, murmuring, inviting the soul to wander in abysses of solitude. All along the white beach, up and down, there was no living thing in sight. A bird with a broken wing was beating the air above, reeling, fluttering, circling disabled down, down to the water.

Edna had found her old bathing suit still hanging, faded, upon its accustomed peg.

She put it on, leaving her clothing in the bathhouse. But when she was there beside the sea, absolutely alone, she cast the unpleasant, pricking garments from her, and for the first time in her life she stood naked in the open air, at the mercy of the sun, the breeze that beat upon her, and the waves that invited her.

How strange and awful it seemed to stand naked under the sky! how delicious! She felt like some newborn creature, opening its eyes in a familiar world that it had never known.

The foamy wavelets curled up to her white feet, and coiled like serpents about her ankles. She walked out. The water was chill, but she walked on. The water was deep, but she lifted her white body and reached out with a long, sweeping stroke. The touch of the sea is sensuous, enfolding the body in its soft, close embrace.

She went on and on. She remembered the night she swam far out, and recalled the terror that seized her at the fear of being unable to regain the shore. She did not look back now, but went on and on, thinking of the bluegrass meadow that she had traversed when a little child, believing that it had no beginning and no end.

Her arms and legs were growing tired.

She thought of Léonce and the children. They were a part of her life. But they need not have thought that they could possess her, body and soul. How Mademoiselle Reisz would have laughed, perhaps sneered, if she knew! "And you call yourself an artist! What pretensions, Madame! The artist must possess the courageous soul that dares and defies."

Exhaustion was pressing upon and overpowering her.

"Good-by—because, I love you." He did not know; he did not understand. He would never understand. Perhaps Doctor Mandelet would have understood if she had seen him—but it was too late; the shore was far behind her, and her strength was gone.

She looked into the distance, and the old terror flamed up for an instant, then sank again. Edna heard her father's voice and her sister Margaret's. She heard the barking of an old dog that was chained to the sycamore tree. The spurs of the cavalry officer clanged as he walked across the porch. There was the hum of bees, and the musky odor of pinks filled the air.

An Alphabetical Glossary
of French Words and Phrases
used in *The Awakening*.

à jeudi, until Thursday.

à point, cooked medium rare.

Acadian, French-speaking descendents of the French Canadians expelled by the British from Canada in 1755. Also called "Cajuns."

accouchement, lying in, process of giving birth.

adieu, goodbye.

allez vous-en, go away.

atelier, studio

au revoir, goodbye.

blageur—farceur—gros bete, va!, joker, clown, silly, stop it!

bon Dieu, good Lord.

bon garcon, good boy.

bonne nuit, ma reine; soyez sage, good night, my queen; be good.

bourgeois, middle-class, ordinary.

camaraderie, good friendship.

chambres garnies, furnished rooms.

Creole, a person descended from the original French or Spanish settlers of the Louisiana Territory.

coup d' état, overthrow of a government

en bon ami, as a good friend.

en bonne ménagère, as a good housekeeper.

court bouillon, fish broth.

friandise, gourmet delicacy.

grand esprit, noble soul.

Griffe, woman of mixed black and mulatto, or mulatto and native American ancestry.

Gruyère, a hard Swiss cheese.

la belle dame, the beautiful lady.

ma foi, my goodness, my word (exclamation).

ma reine, my queen.

mais ce n'est pas mal! Elle s'y connait, elle a de la force, oui!, that's not bad! She knows what she's doing, she has talent!

marron glacé, candied chestnuts.

ménage, household.

mulatresse, woman of mixed black-white ancestry.

nom de guerre, pseudonym.

parbleu, by God.

par example, for goodness sake.

parterre, yard.

passez, go on! (slang).

paté, a spicy spread of mixed meats.

patois, a dialect of mixed languages.

peignoir, lounging robe.

pension, family-type hotel.

pirogue, canoe.

poudre de riz, white face powder, made from rice.

porte cochère, entrance to a house protected by an overhang so carriages can desposit passengers out of the weather.

quadroon, person of one-quarter black ancestry.

Quartier Francais, the French Quarter, oldest section of New Orleans and residence of most of the Creoles.

sapristi, for God's sake.

si tu savais, if you only knew.

soirèe musicale, evening of musical entertainment.

souffrante, uncomfortably ill.

tiens . . . Voila que Madame Ratignolle est jalouse!,
Well! Can it be that Madame Ratignolle is jealous!
(expressed in very colloquial form).

tignon, close fitting head wrap.

vingt-et-un, twenty-one, a card game like baccarat.